BARNSTORMING

Jonathan Carroll

Published in the United States 2019.

ISBN 978-1-7328701-0-9

Cover concept by Jonathan Carroll
Cover art by Gerald Hamdani and his freelance team Shyft Book Solutions

Book design by Nancy Viall Shoemaker, West Barnstable Press
www.westbarnstablepress.com

Barnstorming

Barn-storm

(v, intr.) To travel around an area appearing in exhibition sports events, especially baseball games.

Dedicated to
my beautiful mother
Jacqueline Leola Carroll

CHAPTER ONE

DARK DAYS

It was a typical muggy evening in Central Florida in the summer of 1929. The air was hot. The skies were clear – full of moonlight. But the night wasn't quiet. Field hands were excited: the fruits of their labor were about to pay off. The strawberry crop was ready to be picked.

The interesting thing about strawberry harvests is that they're done at night. Picking strawberries during the cool of the night yields a better crop than under the heat of the sun. There's less bruising of the fruit and the berries just seem to taste sweeter.

On this particular evening in Winter Park, all you could see when you looked out across the fields were lanterns, moving around like fireflies, glowing and dancing in the darkness.

The workers were singing Negro spirituals as generations had before them. But these songs were not signals to runaway slaves on their journeys to freedom as in the past. Tonight the spirituals were being sung by the pickers to keep each other company – to feel a connection with each other while working in the fields with their lanterns and the moonlight guiding them in the harvest.

Night harvests were good-paying money as far as coloreds were concerned. It was hard work – truly for the young and the very fit. Harvesting in the dark made the work more difficult. Not many older folk were out there; it was mostly women doing the picking, young men doing the hauling, and some poor whites who were looked at as no better than the coloreds.

For no particularly good reason, the Klan decided it was time to show the local coloreds just who was in charge, and the strawberry harvest was the perfect target. Without warning, out of the dark, men in masks and hoods came from all directions. Some were riding horses, some were driving pick-ups, and some were on foot. In seconds they filled the field and started beating coloreds with bats and chains and butts of hand guns and shotguns.

When it was over, fields were on fire from broken lanterns. There were injured colored men all over – many close to death. There was no telling in the dark who was there and who got away. The fields looked like a war zone.

At the crack of dawn the next morning, Columbus Jones, who was the Mayor of Eatonville, a neighboring town to Winter Park, saw a car barreling up the road. He and his wife Hoyt came out to the porch, curious as to why anyone would be visiting at this hour. Eatonville was a unique town, not just in the South, but anywhere in the United States. It was the first and only all-Negro run incorporated town in the country. Columbus and his wife were colored. This, plus the fact they owned and ran the best general store for miles, made Eatonville a very unusual place indeed.

They were on the porch when they saw County Sheriff Jonny Turner pull up. Jonny had known the Jones family his entire life from coming to their general store; he had a sincere liking for them. He thought well of them because they were hard-working, kept to themselves, and were raising a fine hard-working family. He knew their place well. Columbus and Hoyt had always been friendly with Jonny and his family when Jonny was a kid. Jonny's family came to the Jones's general store because it was just the best in the area. Jonny had heard plenty of criticism from whites because he went there, but he knew that was just because they were bothered by the fact that colored people ran an establishment better than their own kind did.

"Mr. Mayor," Sheriff Turner began. He always called Columbus 'Mr. Mayor' as a sign of respect. "Do you mind if I come in to talk to y'all?"

"Come on in, Mr. Jonny," Columbus answered, stepping aside for the sheriff to enter. "I hope my boys ain't in no kind of trouble. You know how teenagers can be sometimes. They're good, hard-working boys, Mr. Jonny, you know that. In fact they've been out working in the fields all night."

"I surely do know how hard it can be Mr. Mayor," the sheriff said, with a forced smile avoiding Columbus's eyes.

"Somethin' the matter, Sheriff?" Columbus asked. "You look a little, well, more than a little, concerned. Have the boys gotten themselves into some kind of trouble? I was only joshin'; those boys know better than to . . ."

"It ain't what they done." The sheriff stopped Columbus from finishing his sentence. "The boys, they didn't do a thing wrong, Mr. Mayor," he continued, his voice cracking at the end of the sentence.

Hoyt spoke up. "Mr. Jonny, what in the world is going on here? Now, you're startin' to give me a scare. Just come out with it, already, please."

"There's no easy way for me to say this. There was a lynchin' in Winter Park. That damn Klan decided to raid the strawberry fields last night. A couple of locals have already been caught." The sheriff continued, his voice wavering, "They told me that your boys were too uppity because your family has a few dollars – because y'all have more than a lot of whites in these parts." Hoyt let out a strangled cry and fell to her knees, holding on to Columbus's leg. He held her tight. "They said they believed they needed to teach y'all a lesson, Mr. Mayor," his voice still wavering, trying to keep his composure, "I am just so sorry. I don't even know what else to say." The sheriff looked to the ground so as not to catch Columbus's eyes and break down himself.

Columbus grabbed for a chair and fell into it. "They were just boys, just boys, just boys." he kept repeating in a low tearful voice. "They hadn't even lived their lives yet. They hadn't seen anything of the world and its possibilities. They . . ."

"Feels like nothing's changed sometimes," the sheriff said when Columbus's words fell away. "They say everybody has a voice in now'a days, but that ain't true, it just ain't," the sheriff said with an angry tone. "There's still whites hunting Negroes like animals, stringin' them up when they think they've stepped out of line. It's a damned shame."

"It's an outrage," Columbus said, his voice deep and full of fire. "My boys are gone, Mr. Jonny," tears rolling down his face. "My two boys are gone, forever, 'cause they had the guts to want to be more than just brown skin in the South. My boys are good boys – smart boys with a future. How do I tell their sister that her brothers have been murdered for no good reason except for being the wrong color in central Florida? Huh?!" Hoyt, who was still on her knees at Columbus's feet, was crying unconsolably, yet trying to console her husband. Their boys were everything to them.

"I wish there was something I could do or say, Mr. Mayor," Jonny said, shaking his head.

With his words barely audible, Columbus said, "You know what I wish? I wish we didn't need words to tell people their babies were dead. I wish that words like 'Klan' and 'lynch' and 'nigger' didn't exist. I wish that people toting Bibles around under their arms believed the words written in them. I wish a lot of things right now, Mr. Jonny, but what I don't wish is that we can find the right words to say when a mother's children have been killed, when a father's off-spring have been stolen from him, 'cause there ain't no right words."

Hoyt sat softly crying. Columbus stared out in the backyard where the boys had been building a chicken coop. The sheriff stared at a family photo that hung on the living room wall with Columbus, Hoyt and the three children – taken in better times. He felt his ribs squeezing tight around all his insides and his lungs draw up. He had a son of his own who was just five. He wondered if there would still be white men lynching Negroes when his son turned sixteen. It made him hurt.

"You go on, now, Mr. Jonny," Columbus said softly, still staring out the window. "I thank you for coming out and telling us yourself. I need to wake Leola and tell her, but I think I will let her dream a bit longer in a world where her brothers are still here. Please find all the people that did this to my boys, my Daniel and Zachary, not that it will make a difference."

CHAPTER TWO

THE DARE OF '46

On the seventh floor of the Boston Ritz-Carlton, a young man with family money and wanderlust lies sleeping, glad to be any place that's not his hometown of Houston, Texas. He is Davis Sterling and his name is a perfect match to his physical appearance. Even as he snores through a deep sleep, Davis is a good-looking man. Beside him is an equally attractive young woman – her makeup almost perfect from the night before. The sun drenches the room with pale, yellow light, bouncing off the cool marble surfaces of the hotel room and highlighting the curves of her body as she sleeps on her side. The room is quiet, except for the hum of the overhead fans, until a loud banging on the door disrupts the quiet and wakes the sleeping pair. Davis springs forward, like a lion startled from his mid-day nap. The woman rolls away from the sound. Davis pulls his trousers on and rubs his eyes as he makes for the door.

Who in the hell? Davis thinks as he takes unsure steps toward the noise. He walks like a sailor trying to get his land legs again, his feet pounding down hard on the tile beneath them.

"Who is it?" Davis rasps from behind the closed door. His vocal cords, strained from snoring, make his voice sound as if it were scraping past gravel to escape.

"The bellhop, sir," a man's voice calls back, quick and clear. "I have a very important telegram for a Mr. Davis Sterling."

Davis opens the door a crack and takes the telegram, nodding thanks to the bellhop before he closes the door. But not before the bellhop gets a glance at the beautiful woman in bed. She is still asleep. Davis sees only the curve of her shoulder and the small of her back exposed by the satin sheet. He flashes a quick smile then returns to the envelope. It's from his father. His smile fades. Without reading another word, he throws the telegram on the entry table and hurries over to the bed.

"Sylvia, it's time to go," he says as he gathers the rest of his clothes from the floor and frantically dresses. She groans wearily. "Come on, now, up and at 'em," he adds.

"It's Katherine by the way," the woman corrects him with a frown. "What's going on?" she asks as she turns to face him, blinking away the sunlight.

"It's an emergency. You have to get going and quick. Here's your dress," he says, thrusting a small wad of crumpled black material at the groggy woman. "You look great. No need to freshen up."

"Is something wrong, Davis?" she asks. "Wha–what's going on here?"

"Nothing wrong – just gotta go," he replies brusquely, rushing her along.

Before her dress is even zipped, Davis is handing her shoes to her and helping her up from the bed and to the door. The woman stumbles, trying to slip her shoes on as she goes. Her head is spinning from his strange behavior – and last night's champagne.

"Will I see you again?" she asks as Davis coaxes her along to the door.

"We'll see," Davis replies without looking at her.

"Your number? Can I get–"

"I'll just see you around, okay?" He cuts her off. "I'll meet you after work, maybe." He pushes her into the hall and shuts the door.

Katherine is standing in the hallway outside the door in a daze when Davis swings the door open again. She starts to smile and her lips part to say something until Davis hands her an apron and a silver name tag. Smiling quickly, he slams the door closed again. She stands stunned, then turns to leave, still wearing her uniform from the night before. She reaches in her purse to find her lipstick and comes up with a coat check stub from last night's work. She studies the ticket for a moment : *D. Sterling, 752*, then crumples it and jams it back into her purse.

"What a charmer," she grumbles as she waits for the elevator.

Back in the hotel room, Davis cleans himself up, shaving and combing his hair as he finishes dressing. He straightens his silk vest and tie and adjusts his silver cufflinks before returning to the telegram. As his eyes glide across the words, his brow begins to knit. His jaw juts out as he clenches his teeth through the last part of the message.

Davis returns the telegram to the entry table and picks up the telephone.

"This is Davis Sterling in Room 752. I'm going to need a taxi to the airport – right away."

_____

"Here we are, Mr. Sterling," the chauffeur announces as he pulls the Cadillac Series 75 Fleetwood limousine alongside the curb in front of a towering building on Erie Street in Houston.

"Thank you, Simon," Davis says as he gets out of the car and makes for the giant glass doors at the front of the building. In the lobby he walks across an elaborate marble mosaic with the name _The Houston Star_. Davis nods his head and chirps "hello" to various people as they pass. He moves from the lobby to the bullpen and then across the press floor to get to the elevator, where an older colored man in a red coat and tan trousers stands waiting.

"We were not expecting to see you here, young Mr. Sterling. How were your travels abroad?" the elevator man asks, closing the elevator doors.

"Same as always, Jeffrey, love 'em and leave 'em, and never leave a forwarding address," Davis replies with a grin. They share a chuckle about this, but Davis has developed quite a reputation so Jeffrey knows he's not joking.

"Well, you know that one day one of them is going to grab that heart of yours and she ain't gonna let it go," Jeffrey says after their laugh. "Then, what you gonna do?"

"Well, if it was up to Mama, she would already have one of those blue bell weights around my neck and we all know that ain't happening any time soon," Davis replies, nudging Jeffrey with an elbow and flashing a sly grin.

Jeffrey winks in response and answers, "Yessir, I do. Yessir."

The elevator stops at the top floor and, as the doors open, Jeffrey warns the young man, "Now you step lightly this time, young Mr. Davis, he seems to be a bit more ornery than usual today."

"You're a good man, Jeffrey. I appreciate you. You know that," Davis says back to the older man as he hands him two dollars.

"Thank you, sir, and yes, I do. We need more people like you in the world, young Mr. Davis, if you don't mind me saying so, more people like you, for sure."

Davis stops for a moment; his expression turns serious. Locking eyes with Jeffrey, he said, "I always wonder about that, Jeffrey, but I understand what you mean. Just don't let these folks get you down, you hear?"

"No, no, sir, I never do," replied Jeffrey, "I never do. But you have yourself a good day and remember what I told you, hear?"

Davis walks up to the secretary's desk where a woman in her late twenties with dark brunette locks sits. Her eyes dart from her typewriter to the hand-written memo on her left and back again. When she sees Davis out of the corner of her eye, she stops and greets him with a bit of a smitten smile. She tells him to go right in.

"He has been waiting for you," she says as she cuts her eyes toward the office.

Underneath his breath Davis sighs, "I know he has."

Davis takes a big breath and firmly opens the office door. Behind the massive oak desk is a larger-than-life man dressed as smartly as Davis. He radiates authority. He doesn't even look up when Davis enters. He is too busy yelling into the phone about missed deadlines. The older man's face is ruddy with agitation; his forehead is a perpetual wrinkle and the corners of his mouth look as if weights are attached to each end. Davis stands quietly in the doorway, feeling like a schoolboy called to the principal's office. He waits for the agitated man to acknowledge him. The man finally waves him in. Davis walks carefully to a chair placed in front of the desk and takes a seat.

"Your mama has not heard from you in a month, Davis!" the man loudly growls as he slams down the receiver of the phone. Davis stays silent, his eyes trained on the placard that sits just a few feet from his face: Hunter Sterling, President/Owner. "You know she has the whole place turned upside down over your sistah's wedding and her worries add to my headaches and I don't like headaches!" the man bellows, getting in Davis's personal space.

"Look, Daddy, I know I should call more, but," Davis starts to make an excuse, but his father interrupts him.

"What are you thinking, son? What are you doing? *Nothing*. That is what you are doing. Nothing!" Davis leans forward and begins to open his mouth to respond, but his father cuts him off.

"All you do is spend money, traveling all over the place, no direction, no drive, no goals, no ambition! You know what I was doing at your age? I was writing my ass off, makin' a name for myself so I could start my own newspaper some day. And do you know why you get to screw off all the time like you do, son?" the father asks. Davis recognizes this as a rhetorical question and stays silent. "Because your father didn't waste his time globe-trottin'. Instead he was he-ah, building the *Houston Star* from the ground up, son! And what in the hell are you doin'? Do tell!"

"I thought –"

"Did I say it was time for you to speak?" Hunter barks. "Well, this is all gonna change, I guarantee you that. Since you won't make any career decisions, I have made one for you. You are going to make something of yourself at this here paper, son, come hell or high water. Now, because I am a fair and just man, I will allow you to choose where you are goin' to start using that fancy degree of yours. But, by God, you are goin' to use it, if it kills me and you, too."

Davis sits motionless, stunned by this outburst. His father has always allowed him to do whatever he wanted to do without question. In fact, it was his father's idea to "go see the world" for what it had to offer. His father's only stipulation was that, in the end, Davis had to make sure to always come home. *So, here I am once again, home in Houston, Texas, the land that time forgot,* Davis thought to himself. *And there is my father, just waiting for the day to tell me I have to stay put for good. Here of all places.*

Davis is both shocked and infuriated at what his father has to say – and not just because it means his playboy good-times are ending. He always thought his father was different, more open minded than his stuffy, conservative buddies, who were training their sons to follow in their footsteps like all the other gun-toting, tobacco-chewing good ol' boys who had more pride than common sense or intellect. Davis believed that his father had set aside that deep South mentality, remembering several talks with him about trying to raise Houston above just another backwater Southern town. As he listens to his father's rant, Davis wonders if he really knows Hunter Sterling at all. Once the shock of that thought wears off, Davis begins to dread that his father might be more like those other good ol' boys than he thought.

Hunter continues to blast out at Davis, spittle gathering at the corners of his deep frown. "Son, I am giving you two days to come back here with some answers – for a change. You can take that as an order or as a challenge. Hell, take it as a dare – but you are going to do something with your life. People are starting to talk, and I can't have that. You know we have too many important irons in the fire to have my directionless playboy son shoot them all to hell. Now, get outta here."

As Davis walks away and closes the office door, he hears his father's bellowing voice behind him, warning him, "Two days, Davis. And I mean it, boy!"

CHAPTER THREE

A BREAKTHROUGH

Davis finds himself driving along Alabama Street toward the Montrose and his oft-abandoned Wilshire Village apartment. Once home, he swings the front door open and drops his suitcase onto the polished oak floor in the entry. His sleek furniture and dead house plants await him. Davis is still fuming over his father's tongue-lashing. Revisiting the conversation he just had with his father, Davis collapses on the couch and stares forward, squinting his icy blue eyes and biting into his bottom lip, a tell-tale sign that he is working through a conundrum. The expression of anxiety gives way to a look of realization as he springs off the couch. He grabs his telephone and dials the number of Elvinia Kincade.

Elvinia Kincade was Davis's journalism professor at Washington and Lee University. The school boasted one of the best journalism programs in the country. As much as he hated to admit it, he went there because of his father. And, as hardheaded as he can be, he knows that his father has always been right about one thing: journalism is Davis's God-given talent. Professor Kincade always saw the potential in her young student. Initially taken by his good looks, she soon found that this Texas boy had something special. The young professor had then, and still has to this day, a deep respect for Davis's ability to find a good story. She knew from the beginning that he had a lot more in him than the small-minded bigots she had met from the South. He saw things they didn't. She liked this about Davis; he was one of her favorites.

From the first day of class, Davis was as enchanted with his professor as she was him. Elvinia is a British woman of Irish descent, a 'tell it like it is' kind of woman who always lets the chips fall where they may. She came to the States in the late 1930s for an education and to keep out of harm's way during the burgeoning war. In her early forties, Professor Kincade was the youngest professor in the department when Davis showed up. Her youth gave her an edge – one that she still possesses. Davis remarked once that her sharp wit matches her fiery red hair.

Davis decides to call her. She's one of the few people in the world who really understands him.

Elvinia has seen a lot and been through even more. Beyond the student-professor bond that they share, Davis in many ways considers her his confidante. He knows she is transparent and blunt. Perhaps because she is a Brit, Elvinia has never wasted time glossing over the truth. Growing up in the South among oil tycoons, businessmen, Texas politicians, and debutantes, Davis is drawn to her candor and transparency. There is no politicking with Elvinia and he likes that.

After Davis's graduation from Washington and Lee, Elvinia encouraged him to take up his father's offer to bankroll his travels in the advancement of his writing skills. However, she wasn't thinking of his travels in the same way that Hunter Sterling was. Hunter's advice was to "go sow your oats in some other countries where no one in our family's social circle will see." Elvinia told Davis to see the world so he could "open his eyes to all of its possibilities." She felt he should break out from the narrow-mindedness that had surrounded him every time he went home to Houston.

The professor and student remained close long after Davis's graduation. As he hopped from continent to continent, Davis consistently wrote letters to her. He explained his travels and the new things he had learned. He shared insights that he had developed after meeting a Hindu woman in New Delhi or a Buddhist woman in Beijing. Through his letters, she could see that his mind was opening up beyond the prejudices otherwise known as "tradition" back in Houston. She always knew that, as the journalist that he was, he would, someday, look deeper and develop insights into the world beyond Houston. His travels would help him discover truths beyond the backwards traditions and oppressive ideologies that had surrounded him. Elvinia also knew that this was something Davis needed to discover on his own. She knew that the only true counterpunch against a lifetime of homegrown regressive politics of Davis's childhood would be the wisdom gained by life experience and by asking hard questions of others and of himself.

"Hello? Elvinia? Davis here. Do you have a minute?"

"Davis! How has my favorite world traveler been? I've come to expect to hear from you only through epistolary. To what do I owe the pleasure of an actual phone call? You aren't in jail, are you?" She laughs a little into the receiver. "Because you know I've no bail money."

"I wish it were so simple as bail money," Davis replies, countering her levity with his gloom.

Elvinia took note of Davis's surprising low spirits. "I rarely hear you so disconcerted, Davis. What's going on? The world isn't chipping away at its most promising idealist, is it?"

Davis always appreciated his former professor's ability to keep things light and he especially appreciated it tonight. "It's my father," he admits. "He has challenged me to make something of myself professionally."

"Well, that's something that can certainly be expected from someone who's been bankrolling you. I've actually been waiting for this call for some time."

"Really? I wasn't. After all, he's the one who suggested I travel in the first place. I thought it was part of his plan," Davis replies.

"But he wouldn't be a true newspaper tycoon if he didn't start itching for his own son to make something of himself, would he?"

Davis lets out a quick chuckle. He knows what Elvinia thinks of his father's paper and the quality of journalism that the *Houston Star* produces. Rich, fat, white men reporting news that rich, fat, white men want to read, she always says.

"I suppose not," Davis replies.

"As I see it, Davis, there's but one choice you have and that's to do what you truly love to do in your heart of hearts."

"I should follow my heart?" Davis asks, a bit confused by the unexpected advice from such a hard-hitting journalist. "What does that even mean, Elvinia?"

"Listen to me, Davis," as she launched into her familiar lecturer's voice. Davis slouches back and settles in for an earful. "Rather than going on despising a passion your father shares with others, you need to find your own path – your own truth. Since graduation, you have essentially enjoyed handing power over to your father. While you thought you were thumbing your nose at him from every corner of the world, you have in fact led yourself astray and given him the power to dictate your life. Stop running from what you do best. Yes, you and your father share a love for the same craft; but that doesn't mean that you can't find a niche in journalism to call your own. You don't have to approach it in the same fashion as he does. Ultimately, your refusing to be a journalist isn't just hurting your father. It's hurting you too. Is any of this registering?"

Davis sits and mulls over for a moment what she has said before responding, "I think so."

"Your challenge will be nothing less and nothing more than to be yourself and write the kinds of stories from a place where you can take pride in the byline. But do remember, Davis; like many people before you, these challenges will come with consequences.

"You want to write front page stories for a newspaper that lives in a decidedly small town? Be warned, the first time you commit yourself to writing what you feel is right and honest (instead of falling in line with what others would like to see), be prepared to hear a lot from those around you. You'll learn a lot about yourself. Journalists don't change the world by making the status quo feel safe and comfy in all its traditional beliefs. Journalists write what they see and type from the heart. In time – but not too much time – you will have some difficult decisions to make."

"So, if I hear you correctly, you're telling me that it's time to put up or shut up, and most of all, to grow up."

"I have always admired how very succinct you are, Davis Sterling," she replies. "That is exactly what I am saying."

Elvinia feels in her heart that this is a turning point for Davis. Knowing him the way she does, she is convinced that not only will he step up to the challenge, but he will also surpass it, even if this decision brings more than a few surprises along the way.

"I'll stay close by as always, my young idealist. I don't want to miss a millisecond," Elvinia says before she hangs up the phone.

As soon as he hangs up, Davis goes over to his desk and sits down. In front of him is a bronze Remington typewriter, a gift from his father. To the left of the typewriter are a notepad and pens. He opens a side drawer and pulls out a sheet of typing paper. He rolls the paper into place and begins tapping away. His fingers finally stop dancing over the keys. They hover over the typewriter as he reads what he has written.

I will use my journalistic know-how to write about what I love – sports. Particularly baseball, Davis thinks to himself.

Davis has always had a real passion for sports. He has excelled in several sports over the years, but baseball is his real love. With Elvinia's words to guide him, he knows what he is going to do, but first, he has to get his father's approval. He knows that it will be no easy task to convince

Hunter, a journalistic snob, that writing a sports column is journalism. Davis also knows his father well enough to understand that he will back off if Davis tells him that this is his passion. His father has told him that he could do anything at the *Houston Star*, and if nothing else, his father is a man of his word. Davis fully realizes what his decision will look like to his parents' circle of friends; they'll think it's asinine.

Hell, this could invite retaliation against the family newspaper, Davis thinks as he stares at the sheet of paper stuck in his Remington. He realizes he doesn't care; he can't care. His father needs a tough lesson and Davis will teach it to him, "come hell or high water." Despite how angry he is at his father tonight, Davis knows that if he takes this idea to him as something he really wants to do with his life, his father will back off. He'll respect Davis's choice and, besides, it'll be fun to see how Hunter presents "my son the sports writer" to the inner circle at the newspaper and the good ol' boys' network in Houston. Most important, Davis knows that he has to be a good sports writer to make it all work.

Here is where Davis has one of his best ideas: he'll start by talking with Jeffrey, the *Star's* elevator operator. Jeffrey had talked with him several times about baseball and the Negro Leagues. Davis realizes he has already found his first trusted source.

The next day Davis gets to the office early so he has time to speak with Jeffrey before the morning crowd arrives.

"Good morning, young Mr. Sterling," Jeffrey says as a gloved hand extends from his long arm to hold the elevator door open. "You had a good first evening home, I hope."

"A strange one, Jeffrey," Davis tells him as he steps into the elevator. "I'm still trying to figure out if it was good or bad."

"Well, I'll stay positive and hope for good," Jeffrey says, nodding his head.

"Say, Jeffrey," Davis says. "Do you have any plans for lunch?"

"Plans, sir? Well, no. I just eat down in our break room. Sometimes I take a walk. Haven't really thought of it yet, to tell you the truth. Do you need me for an errand?"

"I'd like to have lunch with you, in the park across the street, if that suits you," Davis replies.

Jeffrey's eyes cut toward Davis as he studies him to see if he is joking or if he's lost his mind. "It's a whites-only park, young Mr. Davis. I don't think you and I should be seen together there."

"Nonsense, Jeffrey, that's exactly where we're going," Davis replies. "Let me know what you want for lunch. I'll grab it before we head out."

When Davis glances up, it's a quarter to noon. He makes a run to the sandwich shop downstairs to pick up two tuna salads on rye and goes to meet Jeffrey at the elevator.

"I'd say it's lunch time, Jeffrey," Davis says as he approaches an obviously anxious elevator man. "Shall we?"

"I hope you know what you're doing, Mr. Davis."

So off they go to the whites-only park across the street. The only black people they pass are servants, tending to white children. Everyone, black and white, look at the pair as they settle down at a picnic table and Davis hands Jeffrey a sandwich. Smiles spread over the black caretakers' faces as they watch a white man give a black man lunch. The white folks, on the other hand, balk at such a sight. Some are uncomfortable; others are annoyed. Davis can see that Jeffrey isn't the least bit comfortable himself.

"Young Mr. Davis, I am not sure this is the best place for lunch," he says, his voice lowered to almost a whisper. "Black men are not even allowed to walk through here."

"Don't you worry about that, Jeffrey, if any one of them has a problem, they can talk to me. Don't you worry about that, you hear? We are going to do this more often, as a matter of fact. Every hard workin' man, white or black, deserves to have a lunch break, in my opinion, and I am going to see to that personally here at the paper," Davis announces loudly so all in earshot can hear him clearly.

Jeffrey's arthritic fingers fumble with the wrapping of his sandwich. Davis sees this and takes the sandwich from him. As he unwraps it, he smiles and says, "I don't know why they have to make these so darn hard to get into. Must be some good sandwiches, wrapped up so tight." As Davis places the open wax paper on Jeffrey's lap, a number of white people pass. Two grumble something about an abomination; the others glare as if their eyes might curse both men for such an outrage.

"Do you have a problem?" Davis asks one of the grumblers. "Haven't you seen two gentlemen having lunch together before?" The grumblers and glarers alike scurry when Davis addresses them. "I guess you really had nothing to say after all," he calls out to them.

"I always knew since you were a little boy…" Jeffrey looks Davis in the eye and grabs his hand. "that you were one of the good ones, you sure are."

Davis is taken aback by Jeffrey's comment. His heart feels like a boulder beneath his ribs. It is so heavy, but so full. *Why has it taken me this long to take this man out for lunch?* Davis wonders as he looks at Jeffrey. "I appreciate that, Jeffrey, I really do," Davis says. "Now let's talk some baseball."

As they nibble on their tuna fish sandwiches, the two men start talking shop. "I know you read the Negro sports pages every day and I wanted to ask a few questions, since the only person I know that knows baseball more than me is you," Davis starts.

"What do you want to talk about?" Jeffrey asks. Davis points back at Jeffrey's newspaper. "Your paper there says that they are considering a Negro for the National League."

"Yes sir," Jeffrey replies proudly, his eyes on the image of a black man in a baseball uniform. "Mr. Jackie Robinson from the *Kansas City Monarchs.*"

"Now you and I have talked a lot of Negro baseball, Jeffrey, but I have never heard you mention this Jackie Robinson before," Davis teases.

"Well, he a very good player, sir, very good. But I suspect that ain't the only reason they are looking at him in particular."

"Go on," Davis urges Jeffrey as he leans in toward him like a child listening to a storyteller.

"You see, a lot of Negroes would be considered, well, not right to play with whites, and I suspect that he is the right color black they want, if you know what I mean."

"I see." Davis nods. He feels a hot rock burn in his stomach as he considers what Jeffrey is saying.

"To be honest with you, young Mr. Davis, it is going to have to be a special kind of Negro to do what they are considering, very special. Someone who is strong enough to do what they need."

"I'm not sure I know what you mean, Jeffrey," Davis says. "It's every baseball player's dream to play in the National Leagues."

Jeffrey falls into a reverent silence for a brief moment and then continues. "Pardon me for sayin' this, but not all Negroes feel that way, and this particular Negro is going to have to have the strength of a thousand Negroes. He look at a white man wrong, he argues with a call, he even steps into the 'whites only' shower, and he is a dead man. And no Negro will ever be considered worthy again, no matter how great a player."

Davis ponders this. "I guess I never thought about it that way."

"Why would you?" Jeffrey asks innocently. "You'll never have to."

"Well, trust me, no way, no how, is the National League going to let a Negro play," Davis says. "No offense, Jeffrey, but it just ain't gonna happen. No way, no how." Davis's words get a bit louder and a bit faster now as he talks. He starts swinging his arms in the air to emphasize his points. "I mean, think about it. If for no other reason, whites will never want to be shown up by the talent these Negro ball players have. They will never let themselves be shown up like that, am I right, Jeffrey?"

As the last word slips from Davis's tongue, he feels his skin burn from embarrassment as he realizes he might be offending Jeffrey with his persistent opinions.

"I'm sorry, Jeffrey," he says in a much softer tone. "It wasn't my intention to bring you out here to insult you. I am very sorry. Please, forgive me. I can get carried away."

"Oh, no, I am not offended, young Mr. Davis," Jeffrey replies without hesitation. "You are not the first white man to say that and you won't be the last. But now there are Negro ball players blowing white league hitting records out of the water and even if it don't count in the books, that doesn't mean it isn't happenin'. Yes sir, it's happenin' for sure, and as a baseball man, you know it's true." Jeffrey puts down his sandwich and leans toward Davis. "But you know, sir, that this isn't even the craziest Negro baseball news out here these days, believe you me."

Davis leans in, too, eating up every word Jeffrey is telling him. "What do you mean? Have you been holding out on me, Jeffrey, my friend?"

"I been hearing of a Negro barnstorming team manager who is thinking about doing the reverse," Jeffrey explains. Davis can see the satisfaction Jeffrey feels in sharing this tidbit, in his friend's beaming face.

"The reverse? What the hell are you talkin' about, Jeffrey?" Davis exclaims. "I think the sun and fresh air are getting to your head. Are you telling me that a Negro team is trying to recruit a white player?"

Jeffrey nods quietly.

"Oh, that's a good one, Jeffrey, that sure is a good one."

"Yes sir, that is exactly what I'm saying," Jeffrey shoots back. "They are a championship barnstorming team from Central Florida. The manager is here already and he's sayin' that he's lookin' for a good pitcher and he has talked some young white boy into trying out. Now mind you, I don't know when or where, but I do know that this is the word out there. And you know that I would never repeat anything to you that I didn't hear from a good source."

Davis can't believe what he is hearing. "Well, I know you wouldn't, but do you know what kind of hell would break loose if that happened here in Texas? Now I don't know what goes on in Florida, but that just would not happen here. No white man is that crazy, and I am shocked that a Negro manager would even consider it."

Davis leans back a minute, looking up at the *Houston Star* building next to the park. He glances back at Jeffrey, grabs the old man's shoulders, and smiles. "Jeffrey, you have just helped me make up my mind for sure about what I am going to say to my father. I've never been more sure than I am right now after talking with you. Now I have some diggin' to do, and I am going to need you to find out as much as you can about this Negro team manager. Can you do that for me?"

"Sir, for a fine lunch with you in this park today, I will get all the information you want."

The two men finish their lunch sitting across from one another in the whites-only park. Against all odds, they haven't a care in the world. After they've polished off their sandwiches, the two men walk back into the *Star* building together.

"You mind takin' 'er up to my dad's office, Mr. Jeffrey?" Davis asks as they enter the elevator.

"You got it," Jeffrey replies as he closes the elevator doors. "Thank you, again, young Mr. Davis," he says as they wait for the doors to open again.

"No, thank you, Jeffrey. You've helped me today more than you'll ever know," Davis replies as he steps out of the elevator.

Hunter is surprised to see his son, but still prepared. He barks, "Well, son, what's the plan? Please tell me you have a plan and that I don't have to decide this for you."

With a knowing smile on his face, Davis announces, "Yes, sir, I have decided what I am going to do. But I have a few things I want out of this deal."

"Well, hot damn!" Hunter shouts as he pounds his palms down on his desk. "What is it you want? Secretary? Corner office? What is it?"

"I have decided to focus on the *Star's* sports column," Davis tells him. "And before you say anything, our sports column is almost nonexistent and it needs real work. I love sports, and as you know, I am a good writer."

Hunter's face starts to redden and his jaw bulges like a bulldog's. "Son, you know that sports is not real journalism! You are killing me here. I own the newspaper and my only son wants to report on sports?"

"Daddy, you said make a decision and I have." Davis's demeanor is cool and collected. "The column needs lots of polish and I have the skill and knowledge to do it. I will make my way up from there."

Hunter starts to blow his top again, but something stops him. He sees something in his son he hasn't in some time; he sees the fire of ambition burning in his eyes and realizes that his son might be on to something. He hates the idea of sports writing – detests it. But he knows his son will never grow if he keeps him in his shadow. So he takes a deep breath and says, "Okay, son. I want to say for the record, right here and now, I think this is insane. But I told you to make a plan and you did, so I am going to honor my word and step back. The baby bird is out of the nest now, boy. You better get to flappin' them *sports writer* wings of yours."

"Noted," Davis replies. "But here's the deal, Daddy. No matter what, you have to let me do my job and leave me alone to do real journalism no matter where it takes me. No interference from you at all. Do we have a deal?"

"Those britches have gotten pretty big, son," Hunter says with a chuckle. "I'll tell you what, if you want to call sports real journalism, I may not agree, but a deal's a deal. Remember though, if you fall on your face, I am not going to be there to bail you out."

"Good then, we have a deal. I will start on Monday morning." Davis hides his smile until he sees Jeffrey in the elevator. He gives him a quick wink. Jeffrey nods a satisfied smile in return.

CHAPTER FOUR

MEET THE JONES FAMILY

Because this small town of Eatonville was the home to many freed slaves, it was also the target for lynching and race riots by bitter Southerners who couldn't let go of a bygone era. The Negro community had an ally from the beginning, however, in another small town called Maitland. Maitland was, and still is, a white community, but not the kind of white community you might expect to find in the Jim Crow South. In fact, the residents of Maitland often protected their neighbors from bigots and rioters. In dire times, the people of Maitland opened their homes to their Negro brothers and sisters when Confederate hangers-on went on a rampage. It was through one of these generous Maitland families that the family of Columbus's wife, Hoyt Jones, came to settle in Eatonville.

Hoyt Jones's family had been a part of the fabric of Eatonville since before its creation. Hoyt's mother Delilah had been a slave and had bought her own freedom. She had originally settled in Maitland as a mammy for a few very prominent white families. This was during the Jim Crow days, when mammies were usually only servants to the families they worked for, but not in Delilah's case. Delilah acted as the right hand of Miss Camp. The Camps were one of the most prominent families in Maitland. Delilah ran the Camps' household and raised the Camp children. Where most families might consider a mammy a house servant, the Camps treated Delilah with the utmost respect, which most white people could not understand. The Camps weren't like most white people back then, and Maitland was not like most white Southern towns.

Delilah had raised two sets of Camp children. She lived in Maitland with the Camps for their first three children. But by the time the second set came along (Mrs. Camp birthed two more children later in life), Delilah commuted from Eatonville, where she now had a home. Every day, she was there helping to raise the children – before sunrise until well after sunset. While Maitland itself was a peaceful town, compassionate about the plight of freed slaves, the Camps still worried about the safety of Delilah and her family. After all, not every town in central Florida had residents so forward-thinking as the citizens of Maitland. To ensure that Delilah and her family stayed safe, the well-to-do Camps arranged a safety net for all of the citizens of Eatonville. They put Delilah in charge of matching up every Eatonville citizen with a white family in Maitland. If any racial unrest made its way to Eatonville, the townspeople could flock to Maitland to their assigned white families, where they would be safe until things blew over. Young Hoyt grew up watching her mother handle these important matters. Working alongside whites gave her a different view than most Negro children had at that time. Even though Negroes were relegated to laborious jobs, they had a chance, by doing their jobs well, to reach places other Negroes could dream about.

Hoyt was not the only one who grew up seeing life from a different angle. Columbus, also originally from Maitland, knew Hoyt's family all his life. He, too, had an impressive family history tied to Eatonville. Some of Mr. Jones's family members were on the Founders' Committee of the town. His great uncles, grandfathers and the like, helped to form its government and infrastructure. Columbus's uncle was also the sheriff when he was a child, although Eatonville never had a jail to speak of. The sheriff was so ornery that no one dared cross him. So there was no need for a jail cell in Eatonville, but if the need ever arose, Maitland's jail was just fine to hold the occasional troublemaker. After Columbus's uncle stepped down, the town figured it was time to build a jail since they didn't have Sheriff Jones' reputation to keep people in order. The story goes that a man who had moved into Eatonville (citizens were always clear about the fact he was not originally from Eatonville, thus saving the reputation of the town) stole all the cement blocks meant for the jail and sold them to a white man in Maitland. The Eatonville jail was never finished, but the perpetrator was caught and taken to, of course, the Maitland jail house.

So both Columbus and Hoyt grew up with free-thinkers, people who weren't afraid of taking risks and putting themselves out there to see where it might take them. Perhaps that is what drew the two of them together in the first place. Once they were married, they decided to keep on blazing the paths their families had begun by starting a milk delivery service for Negroes, something that had never been done before. Hoyt made delicious homemade breads and baked goods, which she sold, along with honey. Eatonville had three churches, two schoolhouses, and a library, but nothing that resembled a general store, so the Jones's milk and bread service took off. The whites in Maitland were just as excited as the people of Eatonville. Hoyt's baked goods and blossom honey had a reputation in both towns. The business became so big that they decided they'd open the very first black-owned general store right there in Eatonville. With clientele who were both Negro and white, the store became quite prosperous over time.

Columbus and Hoyt went on to have two sons, Daniel and Zachary, and a daughter, Leola, who was named after her great grandmother. Hoyt gave her daughter that name because it meant loyal and faithful lion. She knew from the day Leola took her first screeching breath that she was going to be strong. Hoyt herself was half Cherokee; she was proud of her Indian blood. She strongly believed that both her Negro and Cherokee blood made her and her children resilient.

"We know how to survive," she'd always tell her sons and daughter. "It's in us to be able to overcome whatever hardships come our way. Our people survived more than we could ever know. And because of them, we were born strong."

As well as their general store fared, Hoyt and Columbus were constantly thinking of ways to do a little better financially so they could make a better life for their children. They understood that, although they were doing quite well, the fact that they were Negroes made it harder for them, especially in the South. More than anything, they wanted their children to receive an education, something neither of them had the opportunity to have. Regardless of what it took, they were determined that their children's lives would be different – better.

To bring attention to the general store, Columbus had created a Negro baseball team. Up until then, Negro men in town had played baseball only in church leagues after services on Sundays. But, Negro teams were catching on in the area. Jones thought that putting his own team together would get more people into Eatonville and into the store – people from outside of Eatonville and Maitland. Businesses all around were beginning to sponsor these teams. The original intent of the teams was to keep Negro men happy and quiet; men from around the rural areas who worked the railroads or in the fields joined. The sport caught on and became more than a little pastime to keep hard workers working hard. All sorts of people began getting involved, and Columbus wanted to get in on it from the beginning.

Around the time Columbus started considering organizing a local baseball team, he also started thinking about the ways he might help to move Eatonville into the future.

"There's just one way to do it, Hoyt, and it's my becoming mayor of this town," he told his wife as they cleaned up the general store one night, getting ready to close.

"Well, what's stopping you, Daddy?" Hoyt asked as she winked at her husband. She leaned on her broom for a moment and said, "Most of this town knows and likes you. Almost everyone in Eatonville shops here and they know you're a good man – a man of your word."

"If I could really get a team goin' like I want, that could also bring some attention to my political life," he thought aloud as he wiped down a counter.

Hoyt knew her husband well enough to know that his mind was made up. She supported 100 percent both the idea of his baseball team and his running for mayor, because they were great ideas.

"But so you know, this team is all yours. I have enough to do running the store," Hoyt told him. "I'll never stray from your side, but I don't have the time in the day to put myself into some baseball team." And so it was that Columbus organized Eatonville's first Negro baseball team, the *Eatonville Catfish*. With the help of his best childhood friend, Isaac Manns, one hell of a ball player himself in his day who knew all there was to know about the sport, Columbus pulled off something quite extraordinary for a town of only 350 people.

"Why the *Catfish*?" Hoyt asked when the two told her the name.

"Well, because when we were boys, that was what we loved to do most," Isaac told her. "Sneak off along the river and spend the whole day cat fishing."

"And we made no excuses about it," Columbus added with a grin.

Because Isaac was like family, Columbus had him run things whenever he wasn't around. Isaac was there for them when they faced the loss of their dear boys that horrible night during strawberry harvest.

Columbus paid him to run the day-to-day operations, while Columbus made all the important decisions. This was agreed to on both sides, since, for the most part, playing ball is what Isaac was truly interested in, anyway.

Not long after the *Catfish* played their first season, Columbus was elected the tenth mayor of Eatonville; all the while he and Hoyt worked hard to keep the general store growing while Leola went off to college, studying to become a business adviser for the store and other business ventures. Even with so much already on their plate, Columbus and Isaac managed to make the *Eatonville Catfish* the best Negro baseball team around. In the meantime, little Leola became a force to reckon with. She returned from college bold and sharp as they come, unafraid to take risks when needed – a product of both her parents, for sure!

"Isaac, we need to have ourselves a meeting," Columbus tells his friend and partner after a late practice one sticky July evening.

"I know that tone," Isaac replies, eyeing his friend. "Must be something big. I hope it's good big, not bad big."

"I think the *Catfish* have done all they can do in Florida, Isaac," he says, never one to beat around the bush. "With segregationists gettin' all riled up and the Klan makin' so much noise and worse, I'd just as soon move the team somewhere new."

"Somewhere new?" Isaac parrots back.

"Yes, sir. Some place where our *Catfish* can compete at a higher level. Somewhere that we don't have to worry about . . . you know, the safety of our boys. Somewhere with a larger Negro population so I can put our team up aginst some of the bigger barnstorming teams; maybe even some professional Negro teams.

"I know this is no small thing I'm asking here, Isaac, but the really serious teams aren't in Florida and they ain't comin' here any time soon."

"You have any idea where this new place might be?" Isaac asks with an eyebrow raised. He's skeptical, but interested. He knows Columbus has never steered him in the wrong direction, so he is listening closely.

"Looks like to me that the high level teams are out in Texas, or traveling through that area anyway. I know this team has what it takes, and I want to prove it, Isaac. The store is doing well. I can afford to send them. I just need you to be behind me on this, because you know I'm not makin' a move without your blessing."

"Texas?" Isaac gasps a little. "I don't know. Is Texas any better than Florida?"

"It is for baseball," he replies quickly. "This is our shot, Isaac. I wouldn't send you if I didn't think so."

With a little more convincing, Columbus talks Isaac into it.

"I'll send you ahead to scout out the best place for the team to be once they get into town," Columbus chirps. "This is gonna be big for us, Isaac. Just wait. And I wouldn't have anyone else by my side to do it."

———

"You're not looking so good, Daddy," Hoyt says to her husband as they sit down for dinner. "Your color is off. Do you feel well?"

"I've just been tired, I suppose, with all the excitement of everything," he replies, bringing a handkerchief to dab the dampness from his head.

"Well, you're sweating, dear," she says, coming up out of her chair. Columbus puts a hand up to stop her.

"It's fine. I probably just need some . . ."

"Columbus?" Hoyt blurts as her husband collapses onto the kitchen floor. "Columbus!"

———

"Well, I do hate to be the bearer of bad news," the doctor says as he holds a stethoscope to Columbus's bare chest, "but traveling to Texas, even for a short time, could be the last trip you ever take."

"I just need some rest, is all," Columbus insists. "I'm just a bit worn out from doing so much lately."

"Listen, Columbus," the doctor says, training his eyes on the exhausted figure before him. "I mean this when I say it – if you want to live to see that team become great, you'll stay right here in Eatonville and let Isaac take care of them out there in Texas."

Leola overhears the conversation and waits until the doctor has left the room to talk to her father. She knows how important the team is to him and she also knows that she could go out to Texas to take his place. This would both help her father and give her an excuse to get out of Eatonville, where women are expected to get married, have babies, and take care of the house while their husbands go out and live their lives and make their own careers. She has known since she was just a girl that she wanted more than what Eatonville could ever offer her. She realizes that this is her chance to break away from the town.

"Daddy, I want to talk with you about something and I don't want you to get all upset about it."

"What is it, lady bug?" Columbus responds, weakly. Leola pauses and studies her father for a moment. She has always seen him as strong and robust. He looks so small and frail now.

"I know that the doctors are telling you that you can't join Uncle Isaac in Texas and that you have been fretting over it. I think I have a solution to the problem. Well, to a few problems," she says, stumbling over her words a bit.

Columbus's interest is piqued, because he knows his daughter well and can see she has a plan and is aiming to convince him of something. He's observed this several times before, like when she's wanted to change something in the store. He could always see it coming a mile away, but this time he hasn't a clue what she has in mind.

"Go ahead, Leola," he sighs and pats her on the hand. "You know I'm always interested in what you have to say. You are your daddy's daughter and always thinking. What's on your mind, lady bug?"

"I'm thinking that since you can't go to Texas right now, you could send me to help Uncle Isaac with the business end of things until you can get there.

"Now, I know what you are going to say: I am a woman, baseball is a man's domain, and a woman has never done anything like this. I have a rebuttal for every one of those thoughts, but to be honest, who helps you do all the team business now?" She doesn't wait long enough for her father to get a word in. "Me! Who takes care of the books? I do! Besides you and Uncle Isaac, who knows the ins and outs of this league and the *Catfish*? Me, once again! Daddy, you know I cannot stay in this town and just have babies. That's just not me, and you didn't raise me like that. There is so much out there and I am missing it all here in Eatonville. Please give me a chance, even just for a little while. If I don't do a good job, you can bring me home."

When Leola finally stops speaking, Columbus doesn't say a word. He sits back and thinks as he looks at his daughter. Her eyes shine with passion. She purses her lips together tightly, the way she always does when she is set on something.

"Do you have any idea what you are asking?" Columbus finally says.

"You are asking me to allow my only daughter to go to Texas and run a baseball team! This is unheard of! No woman runs a baseball team!"

"Well, Daddy, I take care of most of the team business now – and I *am* a woman," she retorts, placing her palms firmly on the tabletop as she speaks.

Before Columbus can respond, Hoyt walks into the room. She pretends not to hear the conversation as she stays within earshot, pretending to tidy up.

Leola continues, "I am not sure what other teams do, but don't you think that women are behind most of the businesses in the world? Daddy, you know they are. I know this is a small town, but it is not that small. You know as well as I do, that there is a strong woman behind every accomplished man."

As Hoyt dusts the same shelf she has already dusted three times now, she smiles at her daughter and gives her a small nod. Leola would never bring her into the conversation out of respect for her father, but she is glad her mother is close by and supports her in this.

"Leola, you are part of the backbone of all we do in this family," her father admits. "You're just asking me for a lot and I am going to have to give some serious thought to this." What he really means is, he needs some time to think of some good reasons why this is a bad idea, besides the obvious.

"Okay, Daddy," Leola acquiesces. "Please do give it some serious thought. This is the right thing to do until you get better and can head to Texas. I know what I am doing, and I know you understand that."

Columbus knows his daughter is more than capable of running the baseball team. But he also knows that black women in Texas do not fare well, and this black woman happens to be his baby, his only daughter, and now his only child.

After Leola leaves the room, Hoyt stops dusting and sets her eyes on her husband. The corners of her mouth are downturned and her eyes are cool and unblinking. She has something to say, but she is not going to start the conversation, so Columbus does.

"This room has never been so organized, Mother," he says to break the silence with a smirk. "I know you are bursting at the seams to say something, so go on and say it."

Hoyt looks at him a bit longer and finally says, "Now, I was not going to bring it up, so I am glad you did. I have to say it has been a very long time since I have been so disappointed in you, Father."

Columbus is a bit taken aback, but not surprised. Hoyt is always one to speak her mind and why should this time be any different?

"Now, Father, you know that Leola knows that team in and out. She runs the business of this store and the operations of everything we do, so, for the life of me, I cannot figure out why you would not let her do this. Isaac is a smart man, but he cannot run the team and the business. The doctor has already told you that it's not the time for you to go, so why not?"

Columbus looks at her and blurts, "This is a man's work."

"Now, look here! Do you mean that men pretend to work, while the women do all the hard work in the background?" Hoyt shoots back. Columbus sinks back in his chair knowing he is in real trouble now.

Hoyt calms down a bit and continues, "It is not my dream to see my baby go off to some God-forsaken spot in Texas," she says, with some caution and tenderness in her voice. "I would much rather see her with a nice strong, hard-working man making us some grandbabies and never leaving us or this town. But that is not how we raised her and you know that. We gave all our children independence, education, and a voice. And you know as well as I, there is a price we have to pay for giving them that. You can't just pull the rug from up under her, now that her time has come."

"This is not woman's work," Columbus spits back.

"Well, twenty years ago we could have never owned this store or have educated our children either. Times have changed and they are going to keep on changing, whether we want them to or not."

Columbus looks away now to try to escape the conversation. She has him backed in a corner and he knows it. "Father, look at me. Would you be saying this if this was one of our boys approaching you to do this?"

Columbus shifts uncomfortably in his chair at the question and diverts his eyes again.

"Would you?" Hoyt demands. "We have paid too high a price not to let her go and see what the world has to offer her. And, if you are only acting this way because she is a woman, then we are going to have a much bigger problem. And that is all I am going to say on the subject. Now you go ahead and do your thinking, and let's see how this day is going to end, sir."

Columbus knows Hoyt is right about everything, but Leola is his baby girl. There is the harsh reality of black men's sports, but in all honesty, he is also terrified he'll lose his baby girl to the world. As ferociously as Hoyt fights for her daughter, she feels the same fear in her heart. She wants Leola to live the life she deserves, but Hoyt cannot help but feel a deep ache when she thinks of Leola off in Texas.

Hoyt walks out to her daughter's favorite place, a place Leola goes to when she has thinking to do, the orchard by the beehives. As Hoyt approaches, she can see the hurt in Leola's soft, brown eyes.

"Baby, don't look so sad," Hoyt tells her. "But I do have to ask, are you sure this is what you want?"

"Mama, I am sad because I don't want you and Daddy to think that I want to leave you. What I need is not here and I have known that a long time. I don't want to end up like some of these other girls, barefoot and pregnant with no real future to look forward to. You and Daddy have opened up the world to me and now I want to experience it for myself. There are so many places to go and things to see and this is the ticket out of here. You have to know that."

Hoyt, who is dying inside hearing these things, knows them all to be true.

"Leola, I don't want you to ever believe that we think that it is just because you want to leave us. We knew this time would come. We just didn't think it would be so hard on us. Don't worry about your daddy. I think he will come around, and I want you to see the things you want to see – have all those experiences you want to have. Those are things I never had the opportunity to do. To be honest, I have always been happy right here, taking care of you, your brothers, and your father . . . and all of this."

"But things are . . ."

"I know things are changing," Hoyt interrupts. "That is why we worked so hard to educate you, so you would be ready for those changes. And now here we are. I am excited for you. Don't you worry about us; we are going to be just fine here, okay?"

Hoyt knows just how to make Leola feel justified in wanting more, which is rare for a Southern mother. But Hoyt is not just any Southern mother. She comes from a family of innovators – people who think outside of the box – and she knows that Leola has that in her, too.

"Give your daddy some time. He will see his way clear."

"How do you know?" Leola asks.

Hoyt just smiles and says, "Now, this is something you are just not going to know until you are a wife first, and then a mother, so you are just going to have to trust your mama on this one. He will. Honey, let's get some stuff done around here. Everyone's sleeping on the job today."

At dinner the tension hangs thick in the air. Hoyt looks over to Columbus who's avoiding her gaze. Her face is hard in places where it is usually soft. Columbus can feel the hardness without looking up. Again he breaks the silence.

"Leola, I have been giving your proposal a lot of thought. You are right. You are the backbone of the team and you should go on ahead and help them until I get there."

"Thank you, Daddy!" Leola nearly shouts. "You are doing the right thing here," she adds, keeping her voice as even as she can.

Leola is excited but also anxious when the weight of what she has taken on suddenly falls down on her. Her daddy loves that team and would never want to see anything bad happen to it. And now it is up to her to be sure it doesn't.

"Now understand, this is just until I get out there. Plus you need to be ready to come home and help your mother once I am feeling better, is that understood?"

"Of course," Leola answers, fighting back her smile. "I am not going to let anyone down."

"Baby, it was never a thought in my mind," Columbus tells her. "Now we are going to have to come up with a solid plan for the team and come up with the best way to approach Texas on the whole."

"Don't worry, Daddy," she assures him. "I've already got some ideas. I'll share them with you once I get them all worked out."

She gets up from the table and Hoyt says, "He did not mean right this minute, child."

"Mama, I have to strike while the iron is hot. I have so many things to do. Oh, by the way, Daddy, what about Uncle Isaac?"

"Don't worry about your uncle. I will let him know what is going on. You just focus on the things you need to do and I will take care of that."

As Leola leaves the room, Hoyt looks at Columbus again, this time with a smile.

"What are you smiling at?" Columbus asks. Without answering she gets up and kisses him on the head.

"This was the right thing, Father. This was the right thing," she tells him as she gathers the dishes from the table.

Leola, simultaneously terrified and thrilled, has come to a few realities – and very quickly. She knows that, no matter how smart she is, she is going to need someone to help her do this. She can think of only one person: her childhood partner-in-crime and best friend, Clarence. The problem is, when Clarence went north, he vowed to never come back to the South. She really needs him; so her final step is to hatch a plan about how to get him to come back down and help her.

CHAPTER FIVE

LEOLA TAKES OVER THE CATFISH

It's been two months since Isaac and the team settled in Texas and they are right on the schedule he and Columbus had worked out. The *Catfish* have a roster of 18 steady players with games lined up through the season, one game every week. They are using an old school bus to get the team from place to place. The team is also practicing with nearby teams every day in a field that Isaac found. Every barnstorming team needs a place to call home, even if the place is in need of some serious elbow grease.

Isaac hangs back one evening after practice, proud of all he's accomplished in such a short amount of time. He takes a look around the field that he has weeded and chalked with his own hands. He has built makeshift bleachers and painted them to look like new. He realizes that he has to get going because he and Columbus have a phone call in half an hour.

"Uncle Isaac! I'm so glad to hear from you," Leola says into the phone when she hears Isaac's voice. "Mama is making a pork roast, your favorite. We wish you were here. How are things going in Texas?"

"Honey Blossom, it's always so nice to hear your sweet voice," Isaac answers. "Texas is big, let me tell you. But it's nothing your daddy's team can't handle, and we're doing fine. How are you doing, college girl?"

"Uncle Isaac, I swear you've always had more nicknames for me than any young lady can handle. Why, sometimes I think you believe I'm a whole town full of girls, or flowers, or little animals in a petting zoo. I'm fine. It's great to be back home with Mama and Daddy. When am I going to see you?"

Isaac never gets tired of talking with Leola. She has her father's business smarts and charm, along with her mother's grace and kindness. As far as Isaac is concerned, she is the most beautiful woman in town. "Why my little Lady Lamb, I'm actually calling today to invite your daddy to come here and see what his *Catfish* look like."

"Have you gotten them in shape then?"

"I'll tell you this, my little Petunia Flower, they are on their way to adding the Texas State Championship to your daddy's trophy room. You ought to tag along, Sugar Plum, and see what old Uncle Isaac has done with the team."

Leola catches herself, remembering that she has to wait for her father to break the news to Isaac about her coming to Texas. "You know, I'd love that, Uncle Isaac, but someone has to stay here and run the store while you and Daddy are playing Branch Rickey," she laughs.

"Well, look at you, my little Irving Vaughan. I didn't know they taught you baseball in college. My, my, you're definitely your daddy's little girl," Isaac says. "By the way, you know who Irving Vaughan is?"

"Irving Vaughan, the Dean of American baseball writers? *Chicago Tribune*? I didn't learn about him in school. You and Daddy talk about him all the time."

"Okay, my little Zora Neale, please put your daddy on the phone, and any time you can get out here, your Uncle Isaac will show you the Lone Star State in style."

"I'd love that, Uncle Isaac. You know I would," Leola beams. She pulls the phone down and covers the receiver with one hand as she calls out, "Daddy, come to the phone! Uncle Isaac is calling from Texas!"

Columbus is sleeping in his favorite chair with an issue of *Ebony* magazine resting face down in his lap. As excited as she is, Leola wakes him up gently. He smiles and lets her help him up and over to the telephone.

"Isaac, my goodness, it's so good to hear from you. I guess I dozed off waiting for the call. How are you and the *Catfish* doing in our grand experiment?"

"I think we're ready, Boss," Isaac says excitedly into the receiver. "The team and our home field are whipped into shape and all we need is your seal of approval."

"You know you've already got that, old friend," Columbus tells him. Isaac hears the gratitude in his best friend's voice. The pride he felt earlier looking at the field swells again until it almost chokes him.

"Well, I got other reasons for wanting Mr. Mayor to come out. I'd like to introduce you to people who can help the *Catfish* along. You know you've always had a way with people."

"Now, cut it out," Columbus interrupts, a bit embarrassed by Isaac's compliment.

"Stop being so damned humble all the time, Mr. Mayor. It's the truth. I may have built a team using my passion for the game to help me scout the best players, but I still need a few players, mostly a good pitcher. That means making deals, and nobody is better at dealing than old Columbus."

"I'd love to but . . ."

Too excited to let Columbus finish, Isaac interrupts. "Mr. Mayor, you'll be impressed with your team, I can tell you that. We're scoring tons of runs and I've got a schedule that takes us over the whole eastern half of the state of Texas. But it's time for your magic touch, Mr. Mayor. We need pitching and I know where the best ones play. Those team owners don't know it yet, but they're just waiting for you to come over and pick their pockets while you hypnotize them with that old smile of yours." Isaac imagines Columbus doing just that and knows Columbus's touch would make the *Catfish* the team to beat in Texas.

"Well, Isaac, I can't imagine anything I'd rather do. I'm so proud of you and the boys. But as willing as the spirit is, this old body of mine is telling me to stay put and let Hoyt take care of me here in Eatonville."

"You still feeling green behind the gills, Mr. Mayor? What's the doc say?" Isaac asks. Columbus hears the concern behind his friend's words.

"Nothing serious," Columbus lies, "but for a little while, anyway, I can't come out there, at least not yet."

The doctor told Columbus the previous week that his diabetes and gout were signs that he had to lose weight fast, or else. He doesn't want to share that information, though, and hopes Isaac won't push the topic any further.

"Mr. Mayor, that doesn't sound like nothing serious," Isaac proceeds. "What exactly did the doc say?"

"Whose idea do you think it is that I stay put?" Columbus laughs. "Try as I might, I can't convince him otherwise. And the Lord knows, he's the one man I can't beat in a debate. Not that I haven't tried." Isaac lets the conversation about Columbus coming out to Texas die, even though he needs him.

"Well, I can always come to Eatonville and maybe we can scare up a battery over the telephone. Leola tells me Hoyt has a pork roast on and I sure ain't eatin' like I was back home."

Columbus pauses a moment. He knows this is the perfect time to bring up Leola's plan. "Isaac, what do you think about me sending my college girl in my place? She's smart and quick on her feet. You know she has my business sense. I think between you and her, the *Catfish* won't miss my sorry old self at all."

Isaac pauses for a moment. "Mr. Mayor, you know how much I love Leola and I agree she's the brightest young lady in all of Florida. But baseball is a man's game. Think of what the other owners will think when she shows up for a meeting. They'll try to take advantage of her, or worse, they'll think we don't take the game seriously. I don't see how it can happen."

Columbus's heart becomes heavy in his chest – he has the same reservations. "I hear you, old friend, but, if I can't go, I need someone you and I both trust to help you out. These matters can't be handled over the phone. The owner needs to be there. If I still had a son . . ."

Both Columbus and Isaac grow silent, thinking about the day the sheriff showed up on the Jones's doorstep and remembering why their sons are no longer here to step in.

"I trust you, Isaac. I know it's going to be hard at first, but believe me, this is going to work. You wait and see. Leola and I have talked about the possibility and you know her well enough to know she's rarin' to go. But she and I both agreed that it wouldn't happen without your blessing. I won't force you, but Lord knows I don't have a better answer right now and I know you need me there. At least until the doctor comes around to our way of thinking, Leola is the best answer I've got."

Isaac stays quiet as he mulls this over in his head. Can Leola handle herself in the tough world of baseball? He also thinks about his old friend Columbus, and how he shouldn't agitate him if he is really in poor health. He realizes there is only one answer.

"Okay, Mr. Mayor, you've convinced me. Leola and I will try to piece ourselves together and, between the two of us, make up the equivalent of one of you. It'll be tough, but I know we'll make it. One thing you need to promise me in return, though."

"What's that?" Columbus asks.

"Take care of yourself, Mr. Mayor."

With both her father and Isaac on board, Leola has to take a minute to digest what is happening. She was sure she would be able to talk them into letting her manage the business side of the team, but she hadn't quite slowed down enough to think about what came after that. She walked out to her favorite spot on the lake, next to a big open field where she and her childhood friend, Clarence, used to play baseball with the neighborhood kids. She was such a tomboy in so many ways – they had spent so much time playing ball, swimming in the water hole, and climbing trees. The boys would tease her all the time. Over the years, they learned to regret that teasing. Not only was Leola one of the best sportsmen among all the kids; she was also one of the toughest. She had no problem showing you just how hard she could be if she had to. She thought back to those days when they were young.

1928

"Clarence is it!" the children yell as they scatter in all directions. Clarence, who is a great sportsman and just as competitive as Leola, makes a dash for her. She makes a hard left and runs right past him as Clarence's arm goes sailing out to catch her.

"I tagged you, Leola!" he shouts as she darts away.

"You did not," she yells back as she keeps heading for the flag.

Clarence clenches his teeth and glares at the back of Leola as she runs. He doesn't take off after her. He just stands and glares. He's going to call Leola out. Leola stands at the base, flag in hand, jumping in celebration as Clarence marches toward her, determined to put her in her place.

"You'd better not, Clarence," one of the other boys whispers as Clarence passes.

"Just let it go, man," another boy advises. "This is not a smart idea."

But Clarence is an outspoken kid, which gets him into trouble a lot, and he has no problem saying what he has to say. Plus, Leola is his best friend, and everyone but Clarence and Leola know she is also his best girl. Because of this, Clarence doesn't think she would ever take a swing at him for calling her out. Even if she did, he knows he could beat her anyway.

"You cheated, Leola," Clarence says, drawing out her name. "I tagged you before you got the flag," he says with a full audience to witness the whole thing. Everyone is shocked. They wait to see what Leola will do.

"You did not, Clarence, and you know it. I won fair and square, so you need to stop whining about it."

"You're a liar!" he screeches.

Leola balks at the words and then pounces. That is enough; she is not about to put up with that!

Leola lunges at Clarence and takes him to the ground. The two begin to struggle, both with fists flying wildly. By the time they are separated, Clarence has a fat lip and a black eye, and Leola's hair is hardly out of place. She has proved him wrong: he cannot take Leola. Leola is tough in a fight; she's been trained by her brothers, and she has learned well.

When Clarence realizes that she has whipped him good, he runs off to tell Hoyt, who is like a mother to him.

"Mama Hoyt, Leola is cheating again, and she punched me in the face."

"Now, Clarence, haven't I told you before not to mess with her like that?" Hoyt says as she wets a towel.

"Well, I didn't do my hardest fighting, because I don't wanna hurt her. You know me, I would not want to hurt Leola."

Hoyt snickers. "I know you would not want to do that, Clarence. Now, how would that look if you had beat up a girl? You did the best thing by letting her get a few good hits in ya so she could look good in front of all the other kids," Hoyt says, knowing that Leola had whipped the pants off him. "Now, I am going to tell you this. You both need to stop with this fighting. Being the gentleman that you are, I mean not doing your hardest fighting and all, she is going to have you half senseless if you two keep up this foolishness, don't you agree?"

Hoyt gives him a kiss on the forehead and sends him on his way. As he runs off, Hoyt laughs and gets lunch ready.

"When those two grow up and have kids, they are going to be hellions. I can just see it now."

Leola knows that as ambitious and tough as she is, she will need back-up. She also knows only one person other than her daddy who has never let her down. Clarence. The problem is, Leola hasn't talked to him in a while. His parents sent him up north to Boston just after Leola's brothers were lynched. Clarence lived with family there, working day and night so he would be safe and get a good education. It was hard on Leola at first, losing her best friend, but he came back every summer when school was out. The day in late June or early July when he arrived home in Eatonville was always like a holiday. They would spend the whole summer together, playing baseball and swimming as they grew through their teenage years. When both of Clarence's parents passed away, Columbus and Hoyt made sure he stayed up north so he could be safe and continue his education. They wanted Clarence to have opportunities that their sons never had, so they made sure that his school bill was always paid. Clarence never forgets this. From Boston, Clarence went to Washington, D.C., where he attended Howard University and pledged Kappa Alpha Psi.

After graduating college, he got involved in the National Association for the Advancement of Colored People's anti-lynching programs and moved to Baltimore, where things seemed to be taking off. Now that he's in Maryland and a college graduate, he wants his life to make a difference and count for something. Columbus and Hoyt are in full support of him; they know he is smart and will make them proud.

Leola knows that she is going to need someone who is not intimidated by the South, someone who has a strong business sense and a lot of loyalty. No one else comes close, but she is not sure that Clarence will come back. He despises the way Negroes are treated in the South and has vowed never to live there again. In fact, as he grew older, his summer visits gradually became shorter. Eventually, he didn't come back at all. Somehow Leola has to get him to return and help her. She needs her Clarence by her side. However, there are some complications.

Since their childhood, everyone in Eatonville just knew that they would end up together. They always had an unbreakable bond. When they went their separate ways, they were heartbroken, but they knew they had different goals in life.

Still they knew that even with different passions, they'd always be family in one way or another. They also realized that because of their differences, they'd never be together in "that" way. The conflicting emotions created some distance between them, but they were still always there for one another. Even so, Leola hadn't asked Clarence for anything big since he went north so long ago. She isn't sure what he will say. They are both grown up now, with very separate lives. Most important, she knew she would be asking quite a lot from him.

Leola picks up the phone to call. She immediately notices Clarence still has a Southern accent when he answers. They spend some time catching up. Then Leola gets to the point.

"Clarence, I did not just call you out of the blue. Mama and Daddy tell me that you speak with them a lot, so you must know what kind of shape Daddy is in."

"Yes, I know he does not sound right. They lie to me and tell me not to come home – that everything is fine. But I know it isn't. I think they lie because they know how much I hate the South. What they don't realize is how much I love them. I would move home in a heartbeat to take care of them, just as they have taken care of me," Clarence says.

"Well, I want you to keep that frame of mind when I say what I have to say."

"Okay," Clarence says tentatively.

"Daddy has moved the team to Texas, but he is just not well enough to join them."

"How sick is he?" Clarence interrupts.

"He is fine, but doesn't have that kind of energy left in him. Uncle Isaac has gone with the team and I've talked them into letting me run the business end of things."

Leola hears nothing but silence on her end of the phone. "Hello?" Leola says into the phone, "Hello?"

Clarence explodes. "Have you lost your mind? Let me get this right. You plan to run a baseball team, as a woman, in Texas!? I know you have lost your mind and, apparently, so have Isaac and Daddy Columbus!"

After his outrage, Clarence hears nothing on the other end of the phone.

"Look, Leola, I know better than anyone how strong you are, how smart you are, how hardheaded you are, but do you realize what you are getting yourself into? Those crackers are racist people! Texas is ten years behind the rest of the country; colored people aren't even considered human down there!"

"Are you done yet?" Leola asks. She is clearly agitated, but keeps her cool. "Hear me out. I know all those things, but this is something I have to do, not only for myself, but for Daddy. He really wants this team to move on to bigger and better things, and I really want that for him. I will have Uncle Isaac with me, so it's not like I won't have family there. This is something I just have to do, and I am not going to be talked out of it."

Clarence paces his small apartment as he imagines Leola at the hands of those bigoted people – with only Isaac as backup. Isaac is a capable man, but he'll be busy running the team and this makes Clarence nervous.

"Look, Leola, I cannot talk to you right now. I'll call you back."

Leola is devastated that Clarence didn't even give her the opportunity to ask for his help, and shocked that the one person she thought would be there for her has just hung up the phone. Not five minutes later, Hoyt comes to her bedroom door and tells her that Clarence is on the phone and wants to talk with her.

"Look, Leola, I don't like this at all. When do you plan to head to Texas?"

"Well, a lot of plans need to be made," Leola tells him, still crushed after their first conversation.

"I have a few things that I have to take care of here, but there is no way that I am going to let you go to that godforsaken place without *me* watching your back. I want to talk to Daddy Columbus and figure out how I can help with this team and arrange to help you run it."

With a smirk on her face, Leola thanks him several times, but then gives him a warning. "Now look, Clarence, I know you are coming to help, but you forget that I am going to be the boss and what I say, goes!"

Clarence laughs and says, "When haven't you been the boss where I am concerned? All I want to do is make sure the fellas stay alive – and you along with them. Beyond that, your wish is my command – to a point, I mean. I am still who I am."

They both laugh.

"Well, it seems that the Clarence-and-Leola team is back together and we're gonna show Texas something they've never seen before," Leola says.

"But I want you to understand that Texas is gonna show us a thing or two as well. I just want us to be prepared for that," Clarence said.

"I know we are going to have to watch out for each other," Leola replies.

"I would have it no other way. I love you, Leola."

"I love you too, Clarence. Always. No matter what."

They hang up the phone. Leola realizes that she really never even had to ask him to come. Clarence is still the one person she can count on. She thanks God for him.

CHAPTER SIX

THE RECRUIT

In a dorm room in College Station, Texas, a farm kid from a small town named Crockett sits pounding a dirt-smeared baseball into a glove, over and over again. He's a sturdy kid, with hair the color of wheat just before it's harvested. His name is Peter Smithfield. His dream is to make it to the Majors, not just because baseball has been his passion since he was five, but because he knows the Majors might be his only ticket out of Texas.

"Mail, Pete!" a short, squat kid shouts in from the hallway as he tosses a letter on the small dormitory desk. The kid's name is Don. He is both the RA for the baseball dorms and Texas A&M's star catcher. Peter happens to be the pitcher for the team, so he and Don have a unique relationship.

"Thanks, Hands," Peter says as he gets up to retrieve the letter. Peter nicknamed Don "Hands" after he caught one of Peter's fast balls with an ungloved hand during a playoff game their sophomore year of college.

Don nods and walks away to deliver the other players' mail. Peter picks up the envelope and inspects it. He is surprised to see that it isn't from home. The only mail he generally receives is from his mother, letting him know how the crops are doing, or maybe that all the heifers are suffering from a pink eye outbreak. The return address has the name "Isaac Manns" on it, a name Peter has never seen or heard of in his life. He tears the envelope open and begins to read.

Dear Mr. Smithfield,

My name is Isaac Manns and I am the Manager of the Eatonville Catfish. I have been scouting you since last summer and, I must say, you have proven to be a very talented and promising player. I am writing to ask if you would be interested in trying out for the team. Tryouts will be held this coming summer in Houston, Texas. If you are interested, I will provide further details.

Sincerely,
Isaac Manns

Although Peter has never heard of the *Eatonville Catfish*, he is thrilled about the offer. He immediately scribbles a response to this Isaac Manns.

Dear Mr. Manns,

I am honored to have been contacted and will definitely be there on the day of tryouts. Just tell me when and where. I will be ready.

Yours,

Peter Smithfield

Peter stuffs the letter into an envelope with excitement. All he can think about is that he wouldn't have to work on his parents' dairy farm again if he makes the team. He smiles at the thought. The farm is doing well and his father has plenty of help. So this is the perfect time to strike out on his own. Peter has dreamed of this day his whole life.

As summer approaches and the tryouts near, Peter can feel a pride he's never felt before. The Texas air has never smelled sweeter. He wants nothing more than to announce to the world that he's going to try out for a team, but he is superstitious, as athletes tend to be. He doesn't want to jinx it. What if he doesn't make the cut? He decides to keep this tryout to himself until he sees what happens.

Back in Houston, Isaac rereads Peter's response with nervous excitement. He is anxious about this whole thing for several reasons. Nothing like this has ever been done before. But the National League is scouting Jackie Robinson and looking at several other Negro players. *If they can do it, why can't I?* Beyond asking a white man to join a Negro team, he knows that he has several hurdles to jump just to get this off the ground. He didn't mention in his letter that the *Catfish* are a Negro team. It isn't that Isaac is trying to deceive the young player. He knows that, if he can just get Peter out to see the team play, the pitcher will see for himself that this is an opportunity to play with the best there is.

What he doesn't know is how this white college student will react or how they will get around the Jim Crow laws that prohibit integration among Negroes and whites. Isaac tries to brush off that last worry. "Who's going be looking down here in the Negro Baseball League for white people?" he asks himself. "No one," he answers himself to ease his mind. Isaac's whole scheme relies on Peter seeing what the

Catfish can do, how good they really are. If Isaac knows nothing else, he knows how to scout and read players. He just has to get that white pitcher on board with his plan. If he can, he is sure the *Catfish* will blow every other team out of the water.

His second problem is how the team will react. Putting a white man on the mound with colored men who have been held down their whole lives by whites could be a recipe for trouble. But Isaac knows this team could use something big to wake them up and bring them over the top. He has searched everywhere for a Negro pitcher to join the *Catfish*, but could not find one. All the top pitchers are already signed with other teams. Isaac knows he cannot poach from another Negro team. You either make a trade or wait until that player leaves his old team. It's part of the unwritten code. Isaac is willing to throw a white man on a Negro team before he'd break the code.

Isaac knows that, if he gets Peter, for good or for bad, it will put the *Catfish* on the map. Everyone in Texas will know that the *Catfish* are the team with the white farm kid on the mound. But he also is well aware that it could all blow up in his face. To get big rewards, he has to take big risks, and this biggest risk of all just might work. Still, he is uncertain enough about his decision that he holds off telling Leola for a while. He figures there's no need going through all the hell she would give him if, in the end, this white boy wants nothing to do with the *Catfish*. Leola isn't one to make a judgment based on someone's race, but Isaac still doesn't know what she'll think about putting a white kid on their team as a pitcher. It isn't so much her own feelings, but the fact that she understands Jim Crow laws better than most – and what whites are capable of doing. After all, she has seen firsthand what an angry white mob can do and get away with. Isaac knows that Leola is not going to take this lightly and he knows she has good reason not to.

Isaac is convinced that if his plan does somehow work out, this could make magic. The *Catfish* could be even greater than they already are. The team traveled all the way from Florida for a better future and things are definitely improving. However, a serious run for a championship has been just out of reach – they can see it, but can't quite get their hands wrapped around it. The players have the skills; anyone can see that. Isaac believes in his gut that all they need is a little magic. He is willing to take whatever hits come his way to make it happen. He knows they could all end up in jail or even worse. But success could be huge, not only for the *Catfish*, but for baseball and America. It will all ride on that first moment when Peter meets the *Catfish* and they meet him.

As fate would have it, one bad game gave Isaac the perfect opportunity to convince the team to go along with his plan. Isaac, always the baseball man, decided to lay it out on the line for them after a disappointing loss against a team that the *Catfish* should have dominated. He knew he needed to be strong and bring some attitude if he was going to pull off his master plan with his players. After the *Catfish* lost 12-0, he stormed into the locker room in a rage and laid it all out for his team. The time had come; Isaac got the team ready for what is coming.

"Let me tell y'all something!" he bellows to the group of men, dusty from the game and discouraged by their loss. "We've worked too hard, and too many people have sacrificed everything to get this team to Texas for y'all to have played the way you played out there."

Isaac notices a few of his players looking shocked at his comment. This only adds fuel to his fire.

"We all know what I am talking about, so don't just sit there and look stupid!" He shouts, locking eyes with the shortstop who missed a pop fly in the bottom of the seventh.

"You know as well as I do that we need something special to get this team back on track. And right now it looks like it's all on my shoulders to make that happen." Looking each of them in the eye, he continues, "And when that happens, I do NOT want to hear a single moan or groan out of any of you. If I put the Easter Bunny on that mound, not a one of you better say one thing. Do I make myself clear?"

Isaac knows this little talk will give him more leverage when he brings a white kid in for a tryout. He's tilled the soil for the introduction. Now, on to the hardest part: how will he break the news to Leola? He's glad she's out of town; it buys him some time. Plus she doesn't attend practices or tryouts as her presence can be distracting for the players. This means the likelihood of her being there for Peter's tryout is slim to none. But Isaac is going to have to come clean at some point. If his plan actually works and Peter does decide to sign on with the *Catfish*, there is no way Isaac can keep Leola in the dark.

The night before Peter's tryout, Isaac can't sleep, tossing and turning, his brain working on overdrive as he imagines every possible negative thing that might happen when a white farm boy shows up on the field.

Back in Crockett, Texas, where he's gone back home for the summer, Peter also spends a sleepless night, staring at the homemade curtains with baseball bats and catcher's mitts on them. Peter is anxious, but for very different reasons than Isaac. He's worried about how he'll throw the next day and whether or not the scout will be as impressed with him as he has been in the past. When morning finally comes, he can barely sit still at breakfast. As he fidgets with his toast and shifts in his chair, his mother and father exchange glances. Both wonder what has gotten into their son, who generally eats more than both of them combined at every meal. Finally, his mother asks him, "Son, are you okay? You can't even sit still in that seat long enough to eat your breakfast."

Peter doesn't know how to tell them the truth – he can't, not yet anyway. So he makes something up on the spot.

"Me and some of the guys are going to get together for a big baseball game today, and I'm just a little excited about it, that's all," he replies. A knot forms in his stomach as he forces out the little white lie. He's not accustomed to fibbing to his parents. Luckily for him, that's reason enough for them, and they don't ask any follow-up questions.

"Now, don't you go and wear yourself out, because I am expecting you up bright and early *tomorrow* to help around here on the farm," his father says after a short pause. "We could use the extra hand. Besides that, it will keep you out of trouble over the summer," he says with a little wink.

His father's words send a hard jolt through Peter. He knows that, if he makes the team, he will have to tell them that he is going to play ball for the summer and not work on the farm. He can't be distracted by twinges of guilt though, and he knows it. He shakes off the feeling and focuses on what he's going to do on the mound today.

None of the other A&M players have been scouted – that he knows of. Peter is the first. He can't help but think of the bragging rights he would have if he landed this. He's a quiet guy, not much of a talker, and certainly not the sort to trumpet his own successes. But Peter still daydreams about what it would be like to tell Don and the guys that he would be heading for the big leagues. He doesn't even know how much the team would pay him if he makes it, but that's the least of his worries. He would do it for free in a heartbeat if he could play ball with a team as seriously talented as this scout described in his letter. Thinking about playing for a professional team gets Peter's heart pumping. He cannot get out of the house fast enough.

"Well, I'd better get going," he says as he pushes his plate away. "Thanks, Mama. I'll see you all this evenin' for supper."

With that, Peter grabs his bag and makes his way to his old Ford pickup. He tosses his equipment in the rusted bed of the truck and roars off down the dirt road. Houston is quite a drive from Crockett, a hundred and twenty miles south of the small farming community. Peter wants to be extra early. Isaac's letter said to be there an hour before tryouts began. Peter aims to arrive even earlier so he can warm up his arm. He wants to put on the show of a lifetime, and he has to be loose to do that.

Three hours later, Peter gets to the address the scout mentioned in his letter. He panics when he sees all the cars in the parking lot. He quickly digs through his bag and fishes out the letter. He scans it to find the time. It says to be there at three in the afternoon. It is only one o'clock. Peter sighs a breath of relief and parks his truck. There must be something else going on at the field, he thinks. He heads up to the grandstands and sees there is a game going on. He figures the home team must be the one he'll be trying out for. He goes to the top of the stands to get a glimpse of who he'll be pitching for if every-thing goes the way he hopes. When he gets there, all he sees is a sea of colored people in the stands and two Negro teams playing on the field. He is not surprised. It is a common occurrence for Negro teams to play their games before the white teams take the field. He decides to stick around and watch the end of the game as he waits for other white folks to show up. The game is in the eighth inning; the next game would start soon enough.

As Peter takes a seat on the aluminum bleachers, several of the fans throw him a look as if he has two heads. Peter is dressed in his A&M uniform and has a glove in his hand. He hardly notices the stares as he settles in to watch the end of the game. Because of his past, he's comfortable around black folks, although they don't know that about him yet. As always, he's friendly and respectful to everyone. The fans who are leery of him see that he is just excited to be there. They relax a little. Some even smile and nod.

As he watches the game, he is amazed at the power and skill on display. He had no idea there was so much talent in the Negro League, since his only experience with colored folk and baseball had come from his childhood. He hadn't played with anyone other than whites since his early teens. There weren't any colored players on the A&M team. He is so impressed that he starts cheering and yelling as batters prepare and the pitcher winds up. Now, the colored folk are getting a big kick out of this strange white kid. By the time the game has ended, Peter is on his feet, clapping and whistling. What he does not know is that from the side, Isaac is watching him to see how he is reacting to watching Negro baseball – teams that he might be pitching against one day soon. By the end of the game, Isaac knows Peter is the one he wants. This kid is perfect. He just hopes Peter will see it his way.

When players start to disappear from the green of the field, Peter gets up and goes to the back of the stands. He stands and waits. He figures the black fans will empty out so the white fans can fill the stadium to watch the team he is expecting to try out for. He knows the routine. There should be a cleanup crew coming in to clean the stands, and then the white people will start piling in as the white teams take the field. He knows that Negroes are not allowed to use the locker rooms and the black spectators have to use the "Blacks Only" bathrooms out in the parking lot. It should be a fairly quick transition. Concession stands aren't open for the Negro League games either, so there was little to do to prepare for the whites coming in.

As Peter is standing there, he sees the teams leaving the field, but no one seems to be moving into the stands. His eyes start to dart around, looking for signs of white fans coming in, but there aren't any. He starts to panic again. *Did I come to the wrong field?* Isaac can see Peter's confusion; it's painted on his face. When two new teams start taking the field, that look is intensified. The two new teams are also Negro teams. He clutches at his glove and squints down at the field trying to make sense of what is going on. He is convinced now that he is at the wrong field. His heart nearly breaks through his ribcage as he searches for the worn letter yet again, to make sure he has the right field. It's not in his bag. He left it in the truck when he checked it the first time to make sure he had the time right. He takes off like a shot to the parking lot to find that letter. He knows he is going to be late now, and being late is not a good way to start a tryout.

Still watching, Isaac knows he had better catch Peter before he makes it to his truck.

As Peter is rushing through the lot, he hears, in a very deep voice booming from behind him. "Mr. Smithfield, Mr. Smithfield!"

Peter doesn't turn around because he has no idea the man is calling for him; after all, who the hell would know him here? But, when the call persists, he spins around toward the person who seems to be calling after him. A large, imposing black man is running toward him, still calling his name. Searching for a proper explanation for what is happening, Peter thinks Isaac Manns has left a message for him, and that this black man must be the messenger. The man approaches him with a disarming smile and a sincere compliment.

"Son, you have some speed on you!"

Peter nods and smiles back a bashful smile. He replies, "Well, it seems I'm in the wrong place, so I got to haul ass and get to where I am supposed to be."

Realizing his response was a little blunt, he continues, "Sir, I am at a disadvantage here. You seem to know who I am, but I have no idea who you could be."

"Oh, I am sorry," Isaac retorts. "I would like to introduce myself. My name is Isaac Manns, Manager of the *Eatonville Catfish*."

Taken aback, Peter laughs and says, "What is this, some kind of joke? Is this part of the tryout hazing for the new guys?" He looks around as he talks to see where the real Isaac Manns is.

"No, sir. I assure you that is what my mama named me, sir. I am Isaac Manns. I am the one who sent you the letter."

The smile fades from Peter's face. His expression goes rigid, and his eyes narrow a bit as he tries to process what Isaac is saying to him.

"This can't be . . . this can't be happening to me right now," he says, talking to himself as much as to Isaac. He turns to Isaac and explodes. "Do you think you left something out of that letter? I finally get my chance to play some serious ball, and it's all just a big joke? I hate to be rude, Mr. Manns, but I'm here to tell ya that I don't find this funny at all, sir! Why would you do something like this to me? I mean, I don't even know you! What in the world is wrong with you?" Peter demands, his hand gripping the letter and shaking with anger.

"I assure you, this is no joke," Isaac replies, standing tall to show this guy that he is the real deal. "I have been scouting you for a while now, and that offer was 100 percent real."

"Not sure if you are blind as well as crazy, but you are colored, and those are Negro teams playing in there! What's wrong with you?" Peter spits back. His face turns a deep red as he speaks. He nearly chokes on his words as they come out.

Without waiting for a response, Peter walks toward his truck, kicking dirt and grumbling to himself as he goes. Isaac knows it is now or never. He has to hook this kid, or he'll be gone for good.

"Look, I've seen you play and I've heard you talk. You want to play with the best? Well, the best are playing right here on this field. I thought you were serious about playing ball. If you are serious, you'll have the guts to take the field with them. Now, if you want to run off to some white league not half as talented, that's up to you. But if you want to develop your skills, you'll have no chance of doing that in the weak, sad-assed, talentless group of white men they call a league."

Peter stops in his tracks, one, because he cannot believe that this stranger is talking to him like this, and, two, because he knows he is right.

Isaac continues, "I watched you in those stands today, and I know you know what I'm talking about. These are some of the greatest ball players alive today, no matter what your white sports columns tell you. These guys are blowing the records out of the water. The only reason they aren't in the record books is because we don't count for much in your world. Trust me, there is a reason they won't let us coloreds play with you, and it has very little to do with color." Isaac pauses a moment to gather himself, and then continues. "Look, just come play one game. If you don't feel in your bones that this is the kind of ball you should be playing, then all you have wasted is one day of your life."

Peter turns to him and asks, "What about all those black folks? Are you trying to get me killed? They have laws about this. We could all go to jail or get lynched."

Isaac wastes no time responding. "I didn't say it was going to be easy, but let me tell you something. These people are here to see good ball. They may be hard on you at first, but if you put on a good show, they'll come around. You stink, they'll run you off. I promise you that."

Peter's brow relaxes a bit and his jaw softens. Isaac can see that he's calming down. He waits for Peter's response, holding his breath, but trying hard not to show that he's about to fall over from the suspense.

"What about your team?" Peter finally asks. "Is this something they'll be okay with? I mean, this is their world. I'm sure they don't want some white boy coming in, trying to take over."

Isaac knows that once Peter has started asking about how the team would feel, he has him – at least for one game. The team will have to do their part next. He knows it's going be a hard sell. But he also knows that this boy has some serious talent and the team will respond to that. He just has to get them all on the same field first.

CHAPTER SEVEN

MILK MAN

"Alright, then," Peter finally says. Isaac lets go of the breath that he'd been holding the entire time he was waiting for Peter's answer. "I'll give you one game."

"Alright, then," Isaac repeats. "But let's not put the cart in front of the horse here. I'm giving you one game. Let's see what you got."

Peter lags behind a bit as the two walk toward the field. With every step that Peter takes, he feels the urge to dart off back to the truck, put the key in the ignition, and get back to Crockett where he belongs. But there's another force pulling him back to the field . . . deep down he knows he is impressed with what he has seen on the field today. He keeps moving forward, and he knows why; he needs to know how he measures up against major talent like this.

"It's time to do this," Isaac says as the two step on to the field. The team is warming up. "Why don't you go loosen up while I talk to them?"

"So they have no idea?" Peter asks. Isaac senses his resistance returning and scrambles.

"You get stretched out," he says. "I just need to tell them you're here." It was a half-truth. He had told the team they'd better not complain even if he decided to bring in the Easter Bunny. Technically, he had prepared them, but not completely. Not yet.

"Huddle up," Isaac calls out to the team. The last few players make it to the huddle. "Remember what I said, not a peep out of you! If any one gives this new pitcher any trouble, you will be heading back to Florida before the sun sets on your sorry ass."

"What new pitcher?" a center fielder named Raymond Lewis asks, looking around the field.

"He is stretching out and will be here in a minute," Isaac tells him.

Almost in unison, the entire team turns toward a bulky blonde kid with a farmer's tan walking toward them. The team pulls back into the huddle as soon as they see this country boy, freckles peppered across the bridge of his sunburned nose, coming their way.

"You have GOT to be kidding!" Freddy, an infielder exclaims into the huddle. "Have you lost your ever-loving mind? Are you trying to get us killed?"

Isaac looks right into his eyes and says, "Are you questioning me, boy?" Freddy doesn't respond. He is in shock. Between the white kid on the field with them and Isaac's outburst, he doesn't know how to respond.

"I asked you a question!" Isaac shouts, inches from Freddy's face.

Freddy is stunned into silence for a moment, trying to sort out what to say. He can see that Isaac is serious; the entire team can see that too. Finally Freddy's lips start to part, but before a single syllable can escape his mouth, Isaac, who is much larger than poor Freddy, grabs him by the back of the neck and drags him off the field. Freddy trips over his own feet trying to keep pace with Isaac because if he doesn't, he knows Isaac will drag him to the gates with the big paw he has clenched around his neck. When they make it to the gate, Isaac tosses a disheveled and disoriented Freddy on the other side of the fence.

"You just try to come back in here, you little shit!" Isaac barks. "You are done! I warned you – and you thought I was kidding. If I see your face anywhere near this team, you and I are going to have a show-down, you hear me? Now get your ass out of here!"

When Isaac turns to head back for the huddle, the team can see that he is not messing around – and they'd better not either. They are dazed and a bit taken back by what just happened. Isaac can see the fear and intimidation in their eyes as he approaches. That is exactly what he wants in the moment, because he knows he won't have any more problems getting the team to give the new pitcher a shot. Everyone else outside the *Catfish* players – now that could be a different story – but he's taking it one problem at a time. It's the only way he can handle things right now.

"Anyone else have a problem with the new guy?" Isaac asks in a stern voice as he reaches his team. Dead silence is their answer. "Good. I'm gonna go ahead and get this out of the way right now. If anyone gives this white boy a hard time, you are going to have to deal with me, and you don't want to have to deal with me, I promise you. Understood?" The team nods, each one looking like a fawn in the middle of a highway with a Mack Truck coming straight at them. "Now, I am going to call him over here and y'all remember what I said. I will tell you this. This kid has some serious talent. He is going to bring us just what we need to beat every other team in the state of Texas. Back him up no matter what, you hear me? Or so help me, God!"

"Yes, Coach," the team mumbles as one. Isaac nods and then turns toward the man responsible for all the chaos.

"Smithfield! You ready to meet the team?" he calls over to Peter, who is blushing and feeling more nervous than he has since he received the letter.

"Yes, sir," he calls back as he trots over.

"Everyone, this is Peter Smithfield from Crockett, Texas. He's a pitcher – and a damn fine one at that."

When Isaac finishes the introduction, no one seems to move. There are a few nods, except one guy, Jeremiah Gray, the *Catfish* catcher.

"Hey, I am Jeremiah. They call me Jazz, and I'll be catching for ya," Jazz says as he extends a hand to the frazzled pitcher. "Well, as long as y'all will have me"

"Jazz, nice to meet you," Peter says, relieved to have a friendly face to focus on. He shakes Jazz's hand. "Peter, Peter Smithfield. Nice to meet all y'all."

As the team starts to walk away, Jazz can see the fear on Peter's face.

"Don't worry about them; they will come around. This is all just a bit of a surprise, is all."

All Peter can muster is a short "You're telling me."

Jazz keeps up the chatter as they walk toward the field.

"Well, let's just get a few things out of the way."

"What's that?" Peter asks with some hesitation, afraid the next thing that comes out of Jazz isn't going to be as friendly as his introduction.

"I like to see those pitches fast, hard, and down the middle. I can catch anything that you can throw at me. Coach tells us that you have some game, so let's do some warming up and see what'cha got."

Peter is pleasantly surprised with Jazz's comment. He feels some of the nerves fall off as he heads for the mound. He takes a deep breath and shakes his arms. His hands are clammy. He waits for his pulse to return to normal. As Jazz walks toward home plate, he says, "Oh, and here's a little something about me since we are getting to know one another. I am partial to my rum dark and my women darker... just for the record." Jazz winks and lets out a little chuckle after he says this. Peter feels his mouth curl into a smile, too. He takes another deep breath.

"Now, before you head out to the mound, we need to get on the same page about what you're going to throw," Jazz says, showing Peter his signs.

As Peter walks up to the mound, it's as if the whole world has frozen around him. The people in the stands and the players on the away team all stop what they were doing and stare. It's like they've let a giraffe take the mound. No one has ever seen anything like this. They have no idea what to think. There is a white man on the field playing in a Negro league game. There was no obvious way to react.

The visiting team from Dallas burst out in complaints. Every single player grimaces, their eyes locked on the big white kid standing on the mound. The coach of the Dallas team trots over to an umpire who happens to be white, too. Only white men are allowed to officiate so they can keep an eye on what is going on with the Negroes. They are there to call balls and strikes, but they are also on the field to make sure things don't get out of hand.

"You gonna let this go?" the coach asks indignantly. The umpire says nothing at first; he is just as shocked as everyone else. "Well?" the coach prods the umpire to do something. "What the hell are you gonna do?"

"Get back to your dugout," the ump commands. He keeps an eye on the coach and then makes for Peter. Isaac sees this and knows it is going to be Peter's first real test. Most umpires are fine with black players, at least on the field, but this is something entirely different. Here's a white kid trying to play ball with the black players.

"Boy, what the hell are you doing here? Have you lost your mind?" the ump hisses as he approaches the mound.

"No, sir, just here to play some ball, is all," Peter replies, taking his cap off to speak, showing the umpire he means no disrespect.

"Then, why don't you do it with your own kind? Do you know what this mob could do to you?" the ump demands, waving his hands in the air as he talks. "I'm not going to be able to protect you. These people cannot be trusted. They can act like savages," he warns him with a deadpan expression on his face. Peter blinks in response. He knows this guy is like all the other white people he has known throughout his life when it comes to dealing with black people . . . closed-minded and stupid.

"I'll be just fine, and I am going to give these folks a great show," he tells the ump, as politely as he can.

The umpire surprises Peter with his next response. "Boy, these are some of the best ball players around, despite their color or what you think. We don't need you coming in here and making a fool of all of us, you hear me!?!"

Peter smiles again and says, "Sir, if I may say so, please give me a chance. I promise that I am going to do my job. I'm not trying to make a fool out of you or anybody else. I just want to play ball with the best."

"I ain't going to be able to help you, boy. So you better have the stuff, or these Negroes are going to eat you alive and put your bones in a pot of greens for flavor," the umpire snaps back, outraged that Peter isn't heeding his warning about the "savages."

"I hope you know what you are doing," he says, looking Peter straight in his eyes.

"Yes, sir, I think I do," Peter retorts, giving a nod to let the ump know that he is finished talking about the subject. The ump snorts, turns on his heels, and walks away. A few steps into his journey, he snaps his head back toward Peter and says, "I would love to know what your daddy thinks of all this. I know this can't be his proudest moment."

As the ump turns back around, the cordial smile Peter had been wearing melts from his face. As he waits for the "Play ball!" he thinks of his mama and daddy back in Crockett. Suddenly, he is seized with guilt and uncertainty. How in the world will he tell them about all of this? What if somebody else does first?

Before he takes his place behind Jazz, the disgruntled ump waddles over to the other team's coach and tells him, "This boy is playing, so let's go – or forfeit the game and get off the field."

Isaac sees the umpire walk to the plate and put on his mask. He lets out a quiet but deep breath of relief. He knows the umpire could have called the whole thing off, using Jim Crow laws to do it. But now, it's the crowd that's outraged. As soon as it's clear that the ump isn't throwing this insane white kid out of the park, shouts fill the air. Obscenities and threats are hurled at Peter and Isaac from all directions. Peter is rattled by the commotion, but he prides himself on being able to play under any condition. He is determined to show these people that he can hang with the best of the them. He knows this may be his only shot; he does not plan on wasting it. He pushes the insults and foul words from his mind and focuses on Jazz. The big farm boy from Crockett, Texas, grips the ball in his right hand, knuckles white and eyes shining. He hurls the ball toward the plate. The snap of the ball on Jazz's glove is the only sound he hears now. He throws another. And another. His pitches aren't bad, but they're also nothing great. He sprays a few, from sheer nerves, but then it's time to play ball.

The first batter comes to the plate, but something odd happens. The whole opposing team has turned their backs to Peter and so has the batter. And all the spectators – except for a handful of people who had gotten a kick out of watching the white boy cheering from the stands earlier that day – are facing away from Peter and the game. He stands there, looking around for some kind of help – anything. He doesn't know what to do. He looks at Jazz, who is ready for a pitch, and then looks over at Isaac. Isaac looks back at him and mouths the words, "Show them what you got, boy."

Peter's arms suddenly feel like they've got two tons of sand attached to them. His legs have gone to jelly, and he is certain they're about to give out. He can't move. Standing there on the mound, paralyzed like a possum, Peter has no idea what to do next. Jazz calls a time-out and runs to the mound to meet his dazed pitcher.

"What the hell is your problem, man? Don't you know how to pitch?" he asks, slapping Peter in the ribs with the back of his mitt.

"But his back is to me," Peter replies, nodding toward the batter. "How can I pitch to that?"

Jazz doesn't miss a beat. "The same way you pitch to everyone else, by putting it over the plate and in my glove, fool. You're making me look bad, white boy, so get to it or get off the field."

"But I—"

"Look, this has nothing to do with you being white; they do this to every new pitcher they come up against! So stop thinking you are so special, and let's play some ball. Because if you don't pitch that ball, you are going to be off this mound and off this field. I promise you that!"

Peter looks over to Isaac one more time. Isaac's eyes dart from Peter to the batter three or four times. Peter can almost hear his thoughts. *What are you waiting for?* He knows he has to do something, either pitch or walk away humiliated, and he is not about to do the latter. He has come too far and gone through too much to walk off the field now. By the time Jazz gets back to the plate, Peter is ready to pitch. He has never thrown to a batter facing backward before, but he knows that he has to now. He throws out his first pitch. Inside and low.

"Ball one!"

From his unusual perspective, the batter sees the pitch hit Jazz's glove.

This white boy is pitching to my back, he thinks, as he looks over to his team. The coach gestures for him to hold his ground. The batter stays planted where he is.

Peter throws his next pitch straight down the middle. The snap of the ball against the leather of Jazz's mitt fills the stadium like a thunderbolt, waking up both teams and some people in the stands. Still, everyone stands strong. They are interested in what is going on behind their backs, but they will not turn around. Meanwhile, Jazz has to take off his glove and rub his hand after he lobs the ball back to Peter. *That felt good*, Peter thinks as he spins the ball around his palm inside his glove. He gets ready to throw another. When he throws the next pitch, it sprays inside and slams right into the batter's back with a heavy thud. The *Catfish*, who are the only ones watching, wince as the ball nails the batter. The impact of the ball knocks him to his knees. When he recovers, he tries to complain to the umpire, but he doesn't get the response he's hoping for.

"Don't you dare," the ump stops him. "First of all, I will make sure you hang old style for going after a white man like that, and, second, you are the stupid one with your back to him, boy. Now, I am guessing you will turn around and play the game the way it should be played. No telling how many nervous throws this boy has in him."

The batter doesn't say anything in response. He winces in pain as he looks back over to his team. Not a single one of them meets his gaze. They are all looking down or away. No one saw the hit, but they can still tell by the thud it made that he must be hurt. Still, no one can help him. He's on his own out there now.

The batter returns to the plate. To the ump's surprise, he stands his ground one more time to prove his point. Squinting his eyes, waiting for the impact of another fastball in the small of his back, all he hears is the smack of the ball into Jazz's glove. The pain in his back flares at the sound of the ball hitting the glove.

"Strike two!" the umpire yells.

The players in the Dallas dugout gradually come around and turn, facing the field one by one. And with the second strike on record, the batter realizes it might be worse to be shown up by this white boy in his own league, just to prove a point. He remembers when he and some other players had talked about what they would do if they ever got the chance to play ball against white players.

"I'd show him up," he remembers saying then. "I'd let 'em see once and for all what they're missing in the white leagues."

It suddenly hits him that this is his chance to show up one of those star white players and he is blowing it by standing there with his back to the mound. So he turns around. When Peter sees the batter's eyes, he knows the game is on. There's a lot at stake now, for both sides.

Peter knows he needs to bring the heat so these boys will take him seriously. He may have gotten a couple of strikes with the batter's back turned, but now it's time to really pull out all the stops. Jazz gives him the sign for an overhead curve ball. Peter calls him off. Then, Jazz calls for a slider, but Peter calls him off again. Then, Jazz gets it. *This white boy is bringing it*, he thinks. He makes the sign his pitcher wants: fastball down the middle.

Peter takes the windup and sends a fastball. Jazz knows it is going to hurt like a son of a bitch when it reaches him. The player at the plate sees the fastball coming and takes a massive swing that nearly rips his shoulder right out of the socket. Too slow; his bat meets nothing but air. The sound of that ball hitting the glove echoes around that stadium. Now, the people in the stands are starting to turn around. They're coming to the same conclusion the team did:

they probably should not turn their backs on this white boy. The people who hadn't turned their backs in the stands, the ones who had seen Peter's enthusiasm earlier, burst into cheers. One yelled in a loud voice, "Strike three; you're out!" There are only a handful of *Catfish* fans in the crowd, but their voices are loud enough to reach the mound and make Peter feel like he has a hometown crowd.

By the third inning, bets are being made in the stands. Everyone is captivated by this white pitcher who won't give up. The *Catfish* know this is just what they need to get people talking about them; it is also what they were missing all along. Peter is the real deal. He allows only five runs that day. The *Catfish* win, 17-5. By the end of the game, it's hard to tell that there is a white kid tossing pitches in a Negro league. The crowd has turned – and in his favor. They can see this kid has some heart – maybe no brains, but he has heart.

Both Peter and the entire *Catfish* roster feel good about the win as they exit the field. Isaac just sits back, smiling. He has found his pitcher. Even with the excitement of a blow-out game and the high of a victory, not all the *Catfish* are convinced that Peter Smithfield is the answer to their problems. But, even if he isn't the best idea for the team, they can't deny the boy has game. They are sure to tell him as much.

"Great pitching, white boy," a twenty-one-year-old outfielder named Ralph from Jacksonville says as he ribs Peter. "That arm has some heat in it. I guess we'll see you next game."

Peter is surprised, but feels good to hear that from Ralph. He hasn't thought far enough ahead to consider the next game. His initial plan was to pitch this game just to prove to himself that he could play. Then, he'd walk away. But, now that he has pitched against the best and won, he thinks maybe he should give this team a shot.

Jazz walks up to him after everyone else has cleared and says, "I knew you could do it, Milk Man. And, now that you've proved yourself worthy, it is time to drink, *Catfish* style."

Peter does not know what drinking *Catfish* style means, but he trusts Jazz and goes along with it.

"Okay," he tells his catcher, "but I have to ask you a question. Does the crowd really do that to every new pitcher?"

"Oh, what, that back thing?" Jazz asks as they walk. Peter nods. "Hell no!" he blurts out with a laugh. "I have never seen them do that before in my life. I just knew you'd better pitch or get your ass outta there, so I tried to play it off. Worked like a charm, right?"

Peter explodes into a laughing fit when it hits him what has just happened. Jazz does the same. Just seeing the timid farm boy in such a state gets him worked up.

"You're a real son of a bitch, aren't you?" Peter finally said as he wipes a tear from his eye.

"Just follow me, Milk Man, because we are gonna celebrate!" Jazz replies with a grin.

Peter hasn't a clue what he is in for, but he's feeling adventurous. He has just pitched his first game in the Negro league, so he is ready for anything. He hops in his pickup and follows Jazz to . . . wherever they are heading.

Peter stays right behind Jazz as he leads him out to celebrate. They are on the highway for a while, but then Jazz turns off onto a washed-out dirt road that keeps going deeper into the woods. As Peter loses sight of telephone poles and all signs of civilization, he starts to get a little uneasy. He keeps reminding himself who is in front. It's Jazz, and he somehow knows he'll be safe with him. Jazz is no small guy. People seem to respect him a lot. *You'll be fine*, he tells himself as they drives deeper into the mesquite trees.

Finally Jazz pulls into a long drive. At the end of the drive is a massive, old shack. They are in the middle of nowhere. The only thing around is a river and even more mesquite trees. Still in their uniforms, all the *Catfish* players get out of their trucks and head for the shack. As Peter opens his door, he can hear music, black music.

"You ever been to a juke joint, Milk Man?" Jazz asks as the two walk up to the place.

"Nope, never," Peter answers. "But that music sure does sound good."

"Well, this here is called the Rainbow, and today is your lucky day because not many of your kind ever get to party with the other half," Jazz says in a mocking tone. They both laugh.

When they walk into the place, Peter sees another, bigger sea of colored folk, more than were there at the game. As they walk through, they pass by some of the *Catfish* players, who all give Peter a much warmer welcome than they had on the field earlier that day, many of them thumping him on the back. Peter walks past Isaac, who seems to be in deep conversation about something with another man. The guy Isaac is talking to has his eyes trained on Peter, looking like he is almost in shock. He stares Peter down and then goes back to talking with Isaac. He is almost yelling at him, but the place is so loud that Peter can't understand a word of what he's saying. Jazz pushes Peter along, away from the argument. He is not about to let that spoil the fun.

Jazz and Peter make their way to the bar. A beautiful black woman greets them with a loving smile. "What can I get for you, baby?"

When Peter heard that he thought to himself, *this is the friendliest bartender I have ever seen.* Jazz notices the amazement on Peter's face and laughs. "Peter, I would like to introduce you to the big boss, my mama. People call her Little Helen; I just call her Mama."

"Mama, this is Peter Smithfield; he is the –"

Little Helen interrupts, "I know who he is!" She lets out a laugh and gives a big smile. She continues, "News around here travels even faster than you, son. You should know that." She hands them two mason jars, one with dark rum, of course, and one with some kind of clear liquor.

Peter gives her a big smile back.

"We didn't pay for that," he says.

"Don't worry; my family built this place and they run it. So we drink free here, Milk Man," he tells him. Jazz holds up his glass toward Peter. Peter clanks his mason jar to Jazz's and smiles.

"To a great win and to our new pitcher," Jazz says.

Peter nods; he doesn't have the heart to tell him that this is a one-time deal. At the same time, he is not sure anymore whether it will be. He has not talked to Isaac or decided what he would do if Isaac were to ask him to play again. He decides to leave that until later and to just enjoy the rest of his day. They throw a few more back, and Peter realizes he is getting drunk.

"What the hell am I drinking?" he slurs.

"Corn liquor," Jazz responds, laughing.

"I need to ask you a question," Peter says.

"What?" Jazz asks.

Peter is feeling the effects of the corn liquor. "Do you call me 'Milk Man' because I'm a white boy?"

Jazz smiles. "No. It's not 'cause you're white. It's 'cause you always deliver – like the milk man!"

CHAPTER EIGHT

CROSSING THE COLOR LINE

As Jazz and Peter stand side-by-side, sipping from mason jars and enjoying the music, four players from the team that they just beat approach the two, calling out "white boy!" loud enough for some of Peter's teammates to hear. They stand up – they know something is going down. Peter is pretty drunk at this point. When he hears "white boy," he swings around toward the calls and asks, "What can I do for you, fellas?"

Jazz tries to get in between them, but Peter puts up his arm for Jazz to stay behind him.

"You made real fools out of us today," one of the bigger guys says to Peter.

Peter slurs, "Well I just did what I always do, which is pitch."

As they are going back and forth, the *Catfish* players slowly make their way over to Peter. Isaac stands in the background, watching and waiting to see how this is going to play out before he makes a move. Although Peter is a white boy, he is also a *Catfish,* and the *Catfish* never let one of their own get taken down without a fight. For tonight at least, Peter is one of them.

"Well, I will tell you what," the leader of the other team starts inching closer toward the somewhat bobbling Peter. As he moves in closer to Peter, so do the *Catfish.* They are wound tight now and ready to pounce. So are Isaac and the man he's been talking to since they got there.

"What? What do you have to tell me?" Peter responds, the liquid courage fueling him.

"Next time, we are going to have to get ready for you," the guy replies. He laughs. The guys with him do too. Then, he grabs Peter, messing up his perfectly combed hair. Everyone around starts to laugh, and the atmosphere seems suddenly more relaxed. The tension flows right out the door and down the river.

"Now, let's get this white boy another drink and see if he handles his liquor as good as his pitches!" the leader of the team says as he rests a hand on Peter's shoulder.

The bartender pours Peter a third drink. He takes it with a nod and a grin and gulps it down. As he slams his mason jar down, he looks over his shoulder to say something to Jazz, but Jazz is no longer there. Peter starts to feel a little nervous, even through the fuzziness of the alcohol. Then he hears someone up on a stage at the front of the bar making an announcement.

"And now, put your hands together for our main attraction, the one and only, Jazz," a woman's gravelly voice calls out over the noise of the place. The room erupts in applause. Peter looks up at Jazz in shock, watching while he hops up on the stage and grabs a saxophone. Jazz throws a strap around his neck and blows out a melody that Peter cannot believe. This man has some serious talent. Peter suddenly realizes where the nickname "Jazz" comes from. While Jazz croons out one tune after another, Isaac and his friend are still in a serious conversation. Peter notices and begins to wonder who the man is. He studies the man, who looks about his own age, but seems much more serious than most twenty-somethings. When the man looks over toward him, Peter looks back at Jazz.

"Clarence, can't you see that this is who we need to have for this team to really take off?" Isaac insists as Clarence glares at the only white man in the house. "This guy put a hurtin' on those guys today like you've never seen, and they are a damn good team that has beat us pretty good in the past. That Peter, he was the difference, I'm telling you. This is not only going to put our team over the top; it will keep the stands filled for sure, which means we get paid. And anyway, isn't that what you're here for?"

"What does that mean?" Clarence snaps back. Isaac doesn't bat an eye at his brusqueness. He's on a roll now, and he knows it.

"To help figure out ways to keep this thing going for Columbus, for this team, and, most important, for Leola. That is why we are all here, Clarence, and you know it."

"Now, I know you have lost your ever-lovin' mind, Isaac," Clarence scoffs. "You expect us to go to Leola and tell her that this is our solution? Putting this white boy out on the mound? We are not in Eatonville anymore. Your hare-brained schemes may have worked there because people knew you and we were the best. That allowed our team to get away with a lot, even with white folks. But this could get us all killed, including him," Clarence says as he points a finger at the white kid. "They have laws against this stuff down here. We're not in New York or Washington, D.C. These white people down here are something else, and they would just as soon string us all up on the largest tree to save themselves from looking like fools! You know what I am saying is true. Think about what you are doing."

Isaac doesn't respond immediately. He lets what Clarence is saying register. Most important, he keeps his cool with Clarence, like he always has. He knows exploding right now won't get him anywhere.

"Just meet him," Isaac says, his voice even and calm. "Get to know him a bit. See him play. And, if you don't feel the same way I do, we never go to Leola with this. We just forget the whole thing."

"Isaac, you don't know if this man is even willing to play for our team again," Clarence barks.

"Yes, I do. Look at him," Isaac says, nodding in the direction of their new pitcher.

Clarence looks over at Peter. The tall, white kid is standing in a black juke joint, talking to people, drinking, dancing (pretty badly), just having a good time. Clarence is a little taken aback at how comfortable the farm boy seems to be. Nothing about his demeanor makes him look like he is uncomfortable around black folks. Clarence does have to admit that Peter seems to be able to handle the situation, but Clarence isn't ready to concede that the kid would do this on a regular basis.

"Okay, I'll meet him." Clarence finally agrees.

With that, Isaac knows he has Clarence on board. And, if Clarence is on board, Isaac knows Leola will at least listen. Clarence has a way with her, as she does with him. They trust each other with their lives. They have a closeness that God himself would have trouble breaking up.

"Well, let's do this," Clarence says, moving toward the tipsy white pitcher. The two approach Peter. Isaac makes the introductions.

"Peter, this is Clarence. He is a long-time friend from Eatonville. He is like family to Mr. Jones, the owner of the *Catfish*."

"It is a pleasure to meet you, sir," Peter says, trying hard not to slur. "It was a real honor to play with the *Catfish* today."

Although drunk, Peter is respectful and friendly, which means something to Clarence. When it comes to Leola and her well-being, Clarence looks at everything with a critical eye.

"So, I hear you played some amazing ball today," Clarence says.

"Well, I think I did okay, but it wasn't just me," Peter responds, looking around at the other *Catfish* players. "These guys are some of the best players I have ever played with. No one player on a team wins a game alone. It takes a team, and this is a pretty good one. I mean, they scored what, sixteen, seventeen runs?"

Clarence gets right to the point. "You think you might be interested in playing a few more games with us and see where this thing goes? I know this is going to be complicated for everyone, so I think one game at a time would be a good approach, at least for the time being."

"Absolutely," Peter blurts, stumbling forward a little but catching himself before he slams into Clarence. "Now, I just have to figure out how I am going to tell my mama and daddy that I am playing on a Negro team," he adds, looking at Isaac now.

As he laughs nervously, some people drag him off to dance again. Isaac just looks at Clarence and Clarence at Isaac. Watching Peter dance, they both laugh long and hard. He might be the worst dancer they've ever seen.

"I hope he pitches better than he dances," Clarence says to Isaac over the music. Isaac leans in to respond but suddenly jumps back as the doors are broken open at the front of the place. Suddenly, there are white men pouring in from what seems like all directions. Isaac and Clarence freeze in place as people scatter around them. It's as if a baseball bat had hit a beehive. People scream as they scatter, dodging the billy clubs and boots of the police who are raiding the place.

As people run and shout, Jazz sprints from the stage to get to Peter who has no idea what is going on. Before Jazz can make it to Peter, a stout policeman in his early twenties takes Jazz to the ground and begins slamming his club into Jazz's ribs and back. Peter runs to knock the cop off of his friend, but he is tackled by another officer and taken to the ground. Peter covers his head and face and waits for the assault to end. His eyes search for Jazz in all the chaos but there are too many legs scurrying between them for him to see what is happening. Suddenly, Peter is yanked from the floor as cold, steel cuffs bite into the flesh on his wrists. He blinks in the light that filters in through busted doors and windows. He sees everyone is getting arrested now. They all end up in a big bus heading off to the town jail.

"What's going on?" Peter asks Jazz as they sit, hands tied behind their backs, in the large, white bus.

"My family didn't pay off the officials," he explains in a hushed voice. "This happens to blacks in this area all the time if they don't pay off the police."

"Pay them for what?"

"It's illegal for blacks to congregate without permission here in Texas," Jazz tells him, shaking his head. "I should have never brought you along. I'm sorry, man."

"You don't need to apologize for anything," Peter insists. "This is one of the most exciting days I've ever had!"

At the police station, a gruff, stubby officer with a red mustache takes Peter away from the others and leads him to the police chief's office. Meanwhile, all the others are beaten and battered and put into cells. In the chief's office, Peter is uncuffed. He sits in a chair as the chief reads him the riot act.

"What in the hell are you doing at a juke joint with a bunch of niggers?" the chief spits the last word so that Peter can hear the hate in it. "A clean-cut white boy like you listening to jungle music. It's a crying shame," the chief yells, slamming his pudgy fists on his desk to emphasize his point. The chief goes on to scold him for what seems like hours, until he is interrupted by a knock at the door. In walk Peter's parents, Willy May and Charlie Smithfield. They've driven all the way from Crockett. Peter's eyes drop to the ground, and his lips seem to go numb. He knows this is going to be hell.

The Smithfields are shocked when they see their son in blood-stained baseball clothes, his face bruised and smudged with dirt.

"What the . . . what has happened to his face?" his mother stutters.

"I think the better question here is how you could allow your son to be socializing with a bunch of savages," The chief explodes, "I mean, what kind of upbringing did he have for him to think it was okay to be where he was?"

Mortified, Peter starts to yell at the chief. "How dare you talk to . . ."

"Quiet!" his father cuts him off. "You've done enough, son."

Once the room is settled again, the chief tells the Smithfields that he's going to let Peter go home with them. He'll even provide an escort to get them back to Peter's truck. But before he lets him go, he turns to Peter and says, "You best go home and get cleaned up – and clean up your act as well."

The entire way back to retrieve Peter's truck, his parents keep fussing. They just cannot shut up about what Peter has done. Rather than explain himself, he decides to let them get it all out of their system. As he listens to them, he is shocked at some of the things his parents are saying. Even his mother, who is much more tolerant of races than his father, catches him off guard.

Charlie has no problem telling his son how he really feels. "A juke joint in the middle of nowhere with these people! They could have killed you, Peter, and no one would have ever found your body."

"I don't understand what would possess you to even be around those people to begin with," Charlie adds. His father is a true product of his environment. "I can't stand to think that my son was seen with niggers, never mind playing on the same team as them."

The disgust he feels toward his parents' words sobers Peter right up. After listening to it all, Peter is even more sure of his decision, which is not to work for a man who would say such hateful things, even if that man is his own father. He is surely going to play ball with the *Catfish* no matter what his parents say. He knows he will still have to talk it all through with his parents, just not tonight. He'll wait until everyone, including himself, has had time to cool off.

The Smithfields follow their police escort to the juke joint, where they drop their son off at his truck. Peter gets out of their car without a word. Before he leaves, his father says, "We'll talk about this at breakfast. You just be sure to head straight home."

Peter cannot get the *Catfish* out of his mind, especially after what has happened to them at Jazz's family's juke joint. He looks at all the cars there – Jazz's and all the other guys. He thinks about how they are sitting, bruised and battered, in jail cells right now. None of them are as lucky as he has been. Not only did he get out with only a slap on the wrist; he even got a police escort back to his car because he is white. Peter is sure that several of those people had been beaten pretty badly, men and women alike.

Peter saw the police attacking everyone. Not a person came out without a black eye or busted lip – and those were the lucky ones.

Peter drives back past the police station, where he sees Little Helen, Jazz's mother, being taken away in an ambulance. He knows he can't stick around there, in case any of the police recognize him. So he drives to the Negro hospital. He watches from afar as they take Little Helen in. Once the officers are gone, Peter rushes in and asks the person at the front desk if she is okay.

"We don't know yet," a sleepy-eyed nurse tells him. "You are welcome to stick around until we can tell you something, though," she adds with a tired smile.

After a while, the same nurse comes out and tells Peter that it doesn't look good.

"How bad is she?" Peter asks.

"They don't think she is going to make it," the nurse says. "Her beating was pretty severe. She has internal bleeding. We just didn't get to her in time; it is such a shame that someone did this to her." She walks away to tend to other things.

After the nurse disappears again, Peter asks the woman at the admittance desk if he can use the phone. He calls over to the white hospital to tell them that he is bringing her over.

After he tells them the situation, the woman on the phone tells him curtly, "We do not take Negroes here."

"But she'll die if you don't," Peter protests.

"We won't take a Negro, sir, not even to save her life," the woman says coolly, detached from her words. Peter is aghast at how inhumane the woman is being.

"What am I supposed to do then?" he asks. "Just let her die?" The woman hangs the phone up on him.

After he gets off the phone, the black nurse tells him that all they can do is make her comfortable at this point. Knowing that all she has is Jazz and that Jazz is in jail, Peter decides to stay there. He will not let her die alone. Peter sits with Little Helen most of the night, holding her hand until she slips away. He cries all the way home thinking about the life that was just lost – and for what? At home, Peter sneaks into his room through a window so his parents won't know that he wasn't there all night.

When Jazz and the rest of the team get out of jail the next morning, they rush over to the hospital to check on his mother. When Jazz gets there, they tell him that she has passed away. Jazz collapses into a chair, holding his face in his hands so the others won't see him cry. The nurse who was there the night before is still on duty. She hears Jazz say that his mother should never have died alone.

"Sweetheart, I know it may not help much, but she was not in pain," she consoles him. "And she didn't die alone."

"What do you mean?" Jazz asks. They don't have any family in these parts anymore, so this makes no sense to him.

"Some white man sat holding her hand the whole time, until she was gone," the nurse explains as her eyes got a little misty.

Jazz and the others know that could be only one person, Peter.

The next morning, hung over and livid from all that had happened to Little Helen the night before, Peter can't believe that anyone would treat a lady, or for that matter, anyone like that. While getting dressed, he hears a news story on the radio about a riot that had broken out at a Negro establishment.

"Action had to be taken," the radio announcer states, "and one Negro was killed in the scuffle, resisting arrest."

Peter bristles at the false report. His skin burns with anger. He tries to imagine how Jazz is feeling right now. Not only was his mother just murdered by white policeman, but now they are saying it was her fault for resisting. Peter cannot forgive this pack of lies, despite the fact that the police allowed him to go. He starts questioning all the stories he's heard in the news and on the radio about other incidents where the police said that the Negroes had gotten out of hand and people were hurt or killed. Realizing how deep the deceit runs, he gets more and more upset.

Peter wants to reach out to Jazz, but doesn't know how to get in touch with him, or if he is even out of jail yet. The only person he knows how to get in contact with is Isaac. He decides he'll track down Jazz as soon as he can, but for now he has bigger fish to fry. It's time to tell his parents he's playing for the *Catfish*.

Chapter Nine

Growing Up

Peter's parents wait for him at the kitchen table. They are on edge, Charlie especially, ready to tear into his son as soon as he joins them. Peter sits on his bed, trying to make sense of everything. He hasn't gotten a wink of sleep. Between thinking about Jazz's mother, Little Helen, and what he is going to do about signing up with the *Catfish*, his mind has been too busy to shut down. He knows he needs to come to some decisions before he walks into that kitchen – and he has. He is going to play with the *Catfish*. Nothing is going to stop him. There are several reasons he's come to this decision, but the things he heard his parents say the previous night, especially what his father said, have really opened his eyes. It would be easy to just join the *Catfish* and not tell his parents, but he now knows that isn't an option. His parents already know that he has played with the team. They would be looking out for that. Besides, he knows it is time to start making some adult decisions – some difficult ones.

As disgusted as he is, Peter knows that he does not want to get into a conversation about race with his parents. From what he saw last night, it would be a losing battle anyway. Peter loves and respects his father. He knows that he is a good man at heart. As good as he is, though, his father has a blind spot in his humanity; he believes in the separation of the races. After all, that is what his father before him believed. As he thinks about his father's views, Peter realizes that these views had been a part of his life since he was a kid. His mom did not want him around Negroes as long as Peter could recall; he wasn't even allowed to play with the Negro children. But that had never stopped Peter from doing just that, not even then.

"You can be a fool, Petey Smithfield, but you're my best friend, no doubt about it."

"Me, too," Peter replies. *"I don't care that people say that we can't be friends, Lummy. It's stupid. You are the only one I can really trust."*

"Really?" Lummy asks as he squats at the edge of the creek and peers in. "You don't care that you could get in big trouble?"

"No, I really mean it. We will be friends forever, and no one will ever change my mind about that."

"Makes no difference our skin don't look the same, Lummy. Some day other people'll see that."

"I sure hope so," Lummy says, standing up and wiping his hands on his tattered pants. Lummy wears well-worn hand-me-downs from his older cousins that are almost too small for him. His best friend, Peter, is dressed in pressed slacks and a button-down shirt.

"Brought this for ya," Peter says, pulling out a baseball glove out that had been tucked under his leather belt, hidden by his trousers.

"What for?" Lummy asks, taking the glove and admiring it. The name "Peter Smithsfield" is inscribed in the palm of the glove.

"Just because," Peter answers. "Because I want you to have it. We play so much baseball together, and I want you to have a good glove to play with. When you get home, put your name in here and it's yours forever."

"I would," Lummy says, looking down and digging a bare toe in the sand, "but I don't know how to write my name."

"The next time we play, I will write your name in it for you, and I will teach you how to write it yourself too."

A smile flashes across Lummy's face. "Thanks, Pete," he says. "Looks like it's getting dark now, so I better get back home."

"Guess so," Peter agrees.

The two boys begin walking in opposite directions. After rounding a bend, Peter stops dead in his tracks when he hears a bloodcurdling scream coming from the direction Lummy was walking. He stops and worries that it is his friend. He runs frantically back in the direction he had just been. As he gets closer, he sees a bunch of drunken white men beating up the small, black boy. They're asking him where he got the baseball glove.

"I got it from my friend," Lummy whimpers as a boot lands in his tiny ribcage.

"What friend does a nigger have that could give 'im somethin' like that?" one spits.

"You stole it, ya little thief," another man barks. "Stole it from a good, little white boy, I'm sure."

Peter continues to watch from his hiding spot. He is not supposed to be there and is afraid that he might get hurt as well if he speaks up. The white men continue to beat Lummy until his flesh is red and purple and his eyes and lips are swollen. When Lummy can no longer even whimper, the drunks hang the small boy. Peter sees it all, and his heart breaks as he watches the men hoist the small body from the ground. He does not know what to do. There's nothing he can do to the group of giant, drunken men. He just lies there crying, until the men leave – laughing, taking turns swigging from a moonshine jug as they go.

Young Peter cuts his friend down from the tree and drags him to the edge of the woods where his family lives, so that someone can find him. He remains hiding, crying all night and into the morning, waiting for someone to discover his friend's body. When he hears the shriek of a young woman, he knows that Lummy has been discovered. He lets out a quick howl himself, then claps his hands over his mouth and runs home.

On his way home, he works to devise a story to explain where he has been all night. He can't tell his parents the truth; he isn't allowed to associate with Negroes. He doesn't know how he could tell his parents that he has secretly been playing with a black boy who he just watched get lynched in a part of town he is not supposed to go to. He arrives home with a heart full of pain. His father beats him for not coming home all night. His entire family had been out the whole night looking for him.

Peter keeps his secret, but it would forever change him. He never again looks at the black race without feeling guilty that he did not help his friend that night.

Remembering that terrible day so long ago, Peter realizes who his father is. He just did not know how deep it went – until last night. His head swims a bit as he grapples with his parents' shortcomings. It's never easy facing that moment when you realize that your parents aren't infallible; it's even harder for Peter because his parents' flaws go against his beliefs. But he knows he needs to stand by his own convictions, even if it goes against the man who raised him. Even if this is the first time he's ever stood up to father. Peter knows that, if he isn't true to his beliefs now, then he never will be. Now is the time to stand up and be counted, no matter what the consequences.

When Peter walks into the kitchen, his mother, Willy May, is busy cooking. His father sits at the table, eating and reading the *Almanac*. Willy May smiles at him and asks, "What do you want for breakfast, son? You can have anything you want." She smiles at him again, an apologetic smile to be sure – her way of trying to put salve on the open wounds left by the previous night's events. Her support for Peter can only come in hidden smiles; she knows her husband would not approve.

"Just some eggs, toast and black coffee, Mama," Peter answers. "Thank you . . . but I can make it myself."

"Since when do you cook?" his father, still feeling ornery, finally acknowledges his son. "I have never known you to pick up a pan – and for good reason. No man in this house is going to do woman's work, I will tell you that. My father didn't, I didn't, and my son ain't gonna to do it either. And when did you start drinking coffee?"

Peter looks at his mother as he answers. "At school. I have a hot plate in my room, and I cook all kinds of things." Peter pauses to wait for a response. His father offers none. He goes on. "And I don't know when I started drinking coffee. I do a lot of things I did not do before."

His dad just scoffs in response, his eyes narrowing, his jaw set firm. Willy May looks at Peter with soft eyes. She knows her son has become a man.

"Yeah, boy, that is apparent from your behavior last night, with all those Negroes in the middle of a riot," Charlie growls. "What were you thinking? Have you gone completely crazy?"

Willy May turns back to the stove, uneasy about her husband's approach to the subject.

"Well, first of all Daddy, it was not a riot. It never was," Peter responds, his demeanor suddenly changed. He's not timid anymore.

"Well, the police chief said it was," Charlie bellows back.

"I don't care what he said. I was there and all that was going on was music and dancing. Now who are you going to believe – him or me?"

"You have never given us a reason not to believe you son," Willy May interjects. Charlie glares at her silently.

"With your behavior last night, I don't know who to believe anymore," he finally says, cutting his eyes toward his son.

Peter is taken back by his father's words. Charlie seems as shocked with himself as Peter is. His expression shifts from hard to embarrassed. His brow softens as he looks away from Peter. Still, he is not the kind of man to take words back once they have been said. Rather than admitting that he has gone too far, Charlie shovels eggs into his mouth. Willy May stares at her husband, her gaze hardening now. Feeling her eyes burrowing into him, Charlie shoots her a stern glance to let her know she's not to interfere. She returns to making biscuits.

"Well, whether you believe me or not, that is what was going on. The police just came in there and started beating on people." Peter points to the bruises on his face and body. "So do you think I was a rioter too? They were beating people just because they were Negroes and only because they were Negroes. I saw it with my own eyes." Peter turns to Willy May. Her eyes are moist, her hands clenched at her chest.

"Well, even so, they ought not provoke the police. They should've just given up – all of 'em," Charlie says.

"Given up from what?" Peter demands. "From having a good time? They were just protecting themselves is all – and me for that matter."

Peter's face burns red hot and his veins throb in his neck. He can feel his heart speeding up and taste the bitterness of his anger in his mouth.

"Did you know that a woman was killed last night?" he asks, outraged.

Charlie stops eating now and looks up at his son. Willy May freezes in place, motionless and listening intently.

"Yes, they beat her to death for just being there and because they could!"

A silence comes over the room. The hard tick of the grandfather clock is the only noise in the room. Charlie finally breaks the silence.

"Well, a proper Southern lady would never have been in a place like that, where something like that could happen."

Willy May's muscles thaw. She returns to her dough, pounding her fists into it, her lips pursed as she does. She bangs pots and pans, moving in quick, violent motions. In a low voice whispers, "God be with her, that poor woman! Her family must be devastated."

"What was that?" Charlie says. "Why are you even talking, anyway, Willy May?"

"No lady deserves to die like that for being anywhere, proper or not!" The words explode from her breast. Peter has never heard his mother state something so strongly to his father, to his face. She surely means it. Charlie instantly calms down and rushes to change the subject.

"You were still in your baseball clothes when we got you."

Peter knows that the time has come. He is going to have to lay all of his cards on the table.

"Were those Negroes you were with the ones you had been playing baseball with?" Charlie asks.

"Yes, those *Negroes* were who I was playing ball with all day," Peter answers without hesitation. "They took me to celebrate our win, and that is how I ended up there."

"You played with a Negro team?" Charlie scoffs and then turns to his wife. "Well, lucky the police chief did not know that."

Willy May refuses to return his glance or acknowledge what her husband has just said. Charlie knows he has lost all support from his wife. He looks at Peter now. He softens again. He knows he is on his own now.

"Son, with your skills you can play with the finest white team in the area. Hell, you already have all your school teammates. So what I want to know is why would you play with these, those niggers? Do you know what this could do to us? Do you know what this could do to you? You could lose any chance of playing any serious ball, boy."

"That's not true!" Peter retorts. "Things are changing out there! Isaac told me that the National League is working on recruiting a Negro this season."

"Isaac? Who the hell is Isaac?" Charlie demands. "One of those tar babies you were playing with? They will tell you anything to get whites to play with them. Don't you see, whites make them legitimate, and then they think they are somebody. Why can't you see that?"

Peter and Willy May both look at Charlie in disgust.

"Well, then, Daddy, I guess they are going to think they are somebody. These are some of the best players I have ever played with, and I am not going to stop playing with them."

Charlie looks at his son in shock. Willy May knows it is time to intervene. She is a bit surprised Peter has said this to his father because he has never gone against his father's wishes before. She knows now that Peter's journey to manhood is complete. Before she can say anything, Charlie says, "That fancy school has made you lose your mind. What the hell are they teaching you up there?"

"That the world is more than just two colors, I guess," Peter says. "I know it's not going to be easy. But this is what I am going to do, and you are either going to be my father or you are not. You decide."

Willy May turns away now as Charlie looks to her with searching eyes. He is at a loss with his son and looks to his wife to find some answer.

"Well, it seems you have made up your mind, son," Willy May says.

"I have, Mama. This is important to me," Peter replies adamantly.

Charlie finally breaks his silence, asking, "Do you know what can happen to you? Do you know what can happen to this farm if people find out? We could lose everything on account of you making up your mind. Not only can you get hurt or be put in jail – so can those people you're playing with. Do you want that?"

"If they are willing to take the risk on me, I can take the risk on them," Peter tells his father. "Look, Daddy, I know it's not going to be easy, and I may even miss some school. But they are the best and I want to experience that for myself. I will do everything in my power not to bring attention to the farm – and I will talk to them about how we can keep the whole thing quiet."

"I hope this is what you really want son, because it is going to be hard for everyone, including those colored folks," Willy May says.

Charlie starts to offer a rebuttal, but before a syllable can get past his lips, Willy May explodes. "I say that this matter has been settled and we will have no more talk about it!"

Willy May takes a step backward and braces herself, both hands on the stove behind her. She has surprised herself by her outburst. She is exhilarated by the feeling of having stood up for herself and her son – something she has done a thousand times before, but *never* against her husband. This time, it has never felt better.

Charlie stands up and, looking Peter in the eye, says, "You are my son and I love you, but as long as you play with those ni –" Charlie looks at Willy May and sees her eyes burning and her muscles taut. He stops himself from finishing the word. "Those people, I will never come see you play with them. I am going to let you learn on your own how untrustworthy those people really are. Trust me, they will never have your back like your own kind."

"You mean like those law men?" Peter snaps back.

"Just know I will not let you throw away your future and abandon your studies. I don't care what you do, but you are going to finish school," Charlie says.

"I have every intention of finishing, Daddy. I hope you change your mind about seeing me play."

Charlie's eyes drop to the floor as he says, "Don't hold your breath."

After Charlie walks out of the room, Willy May approaches Peter. Smoothing his hair into place, she says, "Don't you worry about him. His father was like that too. He will come around. And if he doesn't, well, you're a man now, and this was your first real man decision. You have to take the good with the bad. But let me say this to you. Don't be like him. If you feel you have made a mistake, you need to say so, because that makes you no less of a man, okay?"

"Okay," Peter replies, giving her a kiss.

As she goes back to her dough, he says, "I am proud of you, Mama. Today was a big day for you too."

Willy May does not look up. Smiling a bit, she says, "Yes, it was, son; it was for sure."

———————

Once released from jail, Isaac and Clarence make it to the Negro hospital to get checked over and to see Jazz. They are fine, except for some bruises and deep cuts. Jazz, on the other hand, has suffered an injury that no doctor or medicine can repair. Clarence is quiet as Isaac comforts Jazz. He silently seethes. All the reasons for his leaving the South in the first place bubble into his consciousness. It's as if Clarence had gone back a century in time coming back down here.

After some time with Jazz and the team, the two men leave the hospital. Outside, a pickup truck awaits them. Leola is behind the wheel. Her expression is stoic as the two climb in. Her eyes stay fixed on the road before her. As they drive away, everyone is silent. Leola finally breaks the silence.

"So, are you both okay?" she asks, her eyes quickly taking in their scrapes and bruises.

"Yes." They nod in unison. Then, Isaac goes on to tell her about Jazz's mother.

"I already know," Leola says. "I've already informed the undertaker. They will be over soon to the hospital to get her body and speak with Jazz. I want to make sure things are going to be taken care of right. The *Catfish* are going to make all the arrangements.

Clarence and Isaac nod solemnly but say nothing.

"I do have one question I would like to ask you," Leola says. "Who is the white man people keep talking about? He seems to be all over the place. I would like someone to share what is going on and how he got into our game yesterday."

"Who told you that?" Clarence responds, glaring back at Isaac.

"You should know that nothing happens on this team that I am not, in one way or another, going to find out about. Let me just ask this: do you think that the raid had anything to do with that white man?"

"I never thought of that," Isaac replies.

"Do you realize the danger you two put that boy in – and everyone else for that matter?" Leola demands. "Do you know what can happen to him and both of you for just being associated with each other? At best, you can be put in jail for it. I'm sure I really do not have to go into what the worst could be."

Clarence starts to speak, but Isaac interrupts him. "Look, Leola, if you heard that, then you also had to hear what that white boy did on the field today. He is what this team needs. His name is Peter Smithfield by the way. Now, I know this is taking a serious risk for everyone, but we are here to make the best team possible and make enough money to pay the bills. This white boy is going to help us do that."

Leola ignores most of what Isaac has said and goes back to talking about the dangers again – until Clarence interrupts her.

"Look, the National League is going to take Jackie Robinson, and that is a fact," he tells her, trying to gain some ground. "Once that happens, more Negroes will start playing in the majors. And, once they do, who is going to come looking at our team? Things are finally changing out there, and we cannot live in the past. Negroes and whites are going to start playing ball together. We have to move forward, Leola, toward the future. If there is one thing I have learned from spending so much time up north, it's that you are either leading or you are following. To stay out in front, we have to lead. We will take every precaution to make sure we keep him safe, maybe even having him use a fake name. But we are out of options. We need some pitching, and this boy is one of the best."

Leola looks at Isaac and says, "I see your hands all over this. I did hear that he blew that team out of the water. This is going to do one of two things. It is either going to put the *Catfish* on the map, or it is going to get us all killed."

"You asked me to come down here to help you make this team a success," Clarence says, shrugging his shoulders. "You know how much I never wanted to come back to the South, the land that time forgot. You are going to have to trust me that this will work. I am not saying it is going to be easy; we are going to have some setbacks. But from a business point of view, this is going to fill the stands. I can feel it in my bones."

As Clarence talks to Leola, he cuts his eyes toward Isaac to let him know that he had better make sure that he can deliver on the promises being made to Leola.

"Do you really think this white boy has what it takes to play on a Negro team, Isaac?" Leola asks.

"For sure, Peter, which is his name, is special," Isaac explains. "I have been watching him for a long time. I watched him in the stands watching Negroes play, and I also watched him on the field when he had every reason in the world to walk away. He stood his ground, and, on top of that, he pitched a hell of a game. He has it; trust me on that one."

"Well, if you both believe that we can do this and not get anyone killed, then let's do it," Leola says with a heavy sigh. "Do you even know if he wants to continue playing with us after last night?"

"Well, if he didn't, he never would have showed up at a Negro hospital and sat with Little Helen all night," Clarence says. "That in itself was a big risk. And another thing, he was fighting back when the law came in the juke joint: he wanted to protect Jazz. He could have just walked away when they let him go, but he didn't. That is how sure I am that this boy wants to play serious ball."

"Okay, then. Clarence, you confirm with Peter. I will fill Daddy in on what is going on and may the Lord help us all," Leola responds.

———————

Young Peter sits at the makeshift dinner table, made of left-over wood from a lumber yard and set with metal plates speckled with rust. From here, he can see the entire house, which is more of a shack than a house that Peter is used to. He is the only white person at the table. Neither Peter nor his hosts seem to notice that, though.

"Lummy is always so happy when you can eat with us, Peter," Lummy's mother, Delilah says.

"Me too, Mama Delilah," Peter says smiling. "Nobody in the state of Texas cooks like you do!"

Peter sits between Lummy and his sister, Winifred. As Delilah finishes up dinner, she asks the three children how their days were. They take turns answering with fairly general responses. Lummy's father asks Peter if he has picked up his grades from the last time he was there.

"I know you've been having a hard time with math, Peter, but you got to keep those marks high. Doing good in school is the way you learn to do good in life. Education is an opportunity and a gift that should not be passed up," he tells the young boy. Peter takes Willie's speech to heart. He admires Willie and thinks of him as one of the wisest people he knows.

After dinner, Delilah notices a rip in Peter's pants. He ripped them when he was playing baseball with Lummy earlier that evening. She wants to mend the rip. She knows he is not supposed to be there and will get into a lot of trouble if his parents find out. She gives Peter a pair of Lummy's britches to wear as she sews his.

Peter hands Delilah his torn pants and watches her intently as she sews. Delilah looks up to discover Peter is staring at her, and she smiles warmly.

"What's got your interest, sweetheart?" she asks.

He just smiles and says, "I love you so much, Mama Delilah."

She reaches up and opens her arms, gives him a hug and tells him that she loves him too. But then she looks at him and warns, "You need to be very careful about where you talk that kind of stuff. You can get into a lot of trouble for saying that, and, if you ever sees me out anywhere and white people are around, you need to go on and make believe that you don't know Mama Delilah. You hear me, little one?"

"I'd never do that!" Peter exclaims.

"Now, you listen, Peter," Delilah says, very seriously. "You have to or there could be trouble for us both."

"But I'd never wanna hurt you like that," Peter argues.

Delilah smiles again at the boy and says, "I know how special I am to you, child, as much as you are to me. We will always have times like these to share. But in public we both have to know what we can and can't do. And hugging me is something that you can never do in public."

Peter looks heartbroken at this, so Delilah tells him, "Here, you can have as many hugs as you want. And I will always love you no matter what. We just gotta keep it our secret when we're out around other white folks."

Peter agrees. Delilah wraps her arms around him until Lummy interrupts them. Lummy tells Peter he needs to get ready so he can walk him to the woods.

"It's almost dark, and you know we gotta get you home."

Chapter Ten

New Connections

The day after he told his parents that he was playing for the *Catfish*, Peter's father came to breakfast with a sort of Cheshire Cat grin on his face. "I have news from the sheriff, son. He called me last night. Not only was that juke joint raided, but it was burned to the ground with everything in it. That hellhole will never be an issue again."

Peter was infuriated but speechless about how much worse the tragedy he witnessed at the juke joint had gotten. "Daddy, I . . ."

Charlie cut him off. "I'm not finished, boy. So all this nonsense about you playing ball with these niggers is something we ain't gonna have to worry about anymore. Now that those niggers ain't a distraction, you can get back to being the proper God-fearing Christian that we raised you to be."

When Peter's mother heard this come out of her husband's mouth, she looked at her son with a hurt heart. Although she did not agree with Peter being around those people, she knew he was hurting. She did not know the specifics about exactly why, but she could see in Peter's eyes that he was in pain. And she also knew it was not the time for his father to be gloating over the news he had just delivered. She saw that Peter was about to explode while his father kept trying to light the wick.

"Now, that is enough!" Willy May blurted out. Her shout took both Peter and Charlie by surprise, because she hardly ever stood up to her husband, no matter what he did or said.

"I don't like my boy being in places like that either. But these are human beings we are talking about, and they deserve to live their lives the way they want to. As long as they keep to themselves, they should be able to do that. I don't think it is right that they burned that place down."

Charlie looked at her with shock and anger. "Who are you talking to woman!? Did anyone ask you?" He moved toward her. She instinctively moved back and dropped her eyes to the floor, bracing herself to be smacked. Peter, knowing what his mother just did for him, was not about to let her get hit for it. He was raised to obey his father, but he was a man now and a bit larger than his father. He was just not going to let his mother get hit anymore. Peter jumped up and stood in front of his mother, face-to-face with his father.

"I know you are the man of this house and my daddy, but I am not gonna let you hit my mama, not now or ever again." They stood there eye to eye for a few seconds that seemed like forever. While his father contemplated what he was going to do next, he looked into Peter's eyes and saw something different. He saw that his son no longer feared him. If he was going to discipline her, he was going to have to go through Peter to do it.

"What have these niggers done to you? You think you can beat me? This is my house and that is my wife and I will do what I please."

With very little change in his demeanor, Peter stood his ground and said, "They have done nothing to me. This isn't about them. That is my mama, and, to get to her, you are going to have to go through me. And, Daddy, I would think twice about trying to go through me, now or ever. If I ever see one mark on her, I swear to you, I will hurt you."

As his mother heard her son stand up to his father on her behalf, her eyes lifted. Although she wasn't happy he got in between them, she drew strength from what Peter had done, and she knew she needed to defuse the situation. She let her instincts as a mother in her own kitchen take over.

"Okay, okay, now. I just think we have had a lot going on in the last few days," she said as she gently moved Peter back over to his seat and then went over and kissed her husband on the cheek. "Let's just have some breakfast."

Peter sat back down as he realized what he had just done, but his father just stood there for another second and said, "I am not sure what is going on in this house. But I will tell you this: this is my house, and if you don't like what goes on in it, then I welcome you to leave it and go with your nigger pack and see how far you get."

Peter knew any reaction he had at that point was going to just make things worse. Plus, he was thinking mostly of his mama. At least she was safe for the most part, and he still had her around, which brought him right back to thinking about poor Jazz and his mother.

He just kept his head down and nodded as his father stormed out of the kitchen and out of the house. His mother went back to doing what she was doing at the stove. Peter looked at her. Willy May was moving around like nothing happened. He realized that this was her coping mechanism – she had been doing pretty much the same thing his whole life.

"You okay, Mama?" he asked. But she just kept her hands busy.

After a while, she answered, "Yes son, I am going to be fine." She quickly looked up from what she was doing and gave him a fake smile. "Your daddy will be fine too. He is the man of this house, and you have to remember that, okay?"

Peter just looked down and did not respond. She stopped what she was doing and walked over to him, kneeling down to where he was sitting, and lifted his chin. "Look, son, I know you are hurting. And I know you are not going to tell me why. You know you don't need to."

Peter tried to look away, but she held his face and kept looking into his eyes, which were starting to well up. "You are my baby, and I sometimes know you better than you know yourself. So I am going to say this to you, and I want you to hear me. If you can't talk to me, find someone you can trust and talk to them. I'm telling you, baby, because I know, you don't want to let this build up in you or it will eat away your soul. You are going to have to trust me on this. If your daddy, or even me for that matter, doesn't understand or like what is going on, you have to follow your heart. Go make it right – for you."

A tear fell from Peter's face. Willy May wiped it away with her dish cloth, like mamas do.

"But what about you, Mama?" Peter could barely speak even those few words.

"Baby, I am going to be okay; I can handle your daddy. I have all these years. Under all that anger is the good man I married and had a wonderful baby boy with, so don't you worry about your mama. I am going to be just fine."

Peter knew his mama had not been just talking about today and what Peter needed to do right now. She was talking about the rest of his life. She stood him up and gave him a kiss and a hug, but it felt different than the millions of other hugs that she had given him in his lifetime. This kiss was releasing him and sending him out into the world as a man, and he knew it.

"Now, you get on and do what you need to do today. Go wash your face and let your daddy see you walk out of this house strong. Don't let him think he got to you."

As Peter was walking out of the room, his mother called his name. "Peter, please just think about things, and be sure you know what you are doing, okay? These are dangerous times, and not everybody out there is going be your friend or have your best interest at heart. Just know who your true friends are and make sure they'll stand by you in the hard times, just like you stand by them. That is how you'll know who your real friends are." He just smiled and walked out of the room.

Peter did just what his mama said. He went and washed his face and headed to his pickup truck. As he was going, he passed his father fussing with the plow engine. "I am going out for a while. Daddy, do you need me to do anything before I leave?" He was trying to break the tension.

His father just looked at him. In a calm voice, he said, "No, son, I am fine."

They both knew that exchange about needing something had nothing to do with running errands. And they were both good with that.

Peter got in his truck and found himself driving back to the hospital and town where Jazz and his mother lived, as did a good number of *Catfish* players. He had no idea where any of them lived or how to find them, but it was not a very big town. There was one main dirt road and a few buildings scattered around, so he was hoping that he would see someone he knew. He got to the town and must have driven up and down that main road fifteen times, each time looking out for the sheriff who was surely not too far away, with all the commotion that had gone on just a few days earlier. The last thing he needed was for the sheriff to see him back in that area. But he just felt like he had to be there and he really wanted to find his friend Jazz. He thought that, if he saw one of the guys from the team, he would tell him how to find Jazz.

As Peter was driving around looking for someone to help, he was not sure that he should even try. His friend had just lost his mama, and they could not have even had the funeral yet. He did not know what kind of reception he was going to get, but he had to do it. He needed Jazz to know that his mama was at peace when she passed and that she was not alone, even if it was with some white man she barely knew.

It was still early in the day, before the sun was at its strongest – before people would be trying to find some cool shady spot to sit. Just when he was about to lose all hope, who did he see walking down the road with fishing poles over his shoulder? Jazz. He drove up and honked his horn as if he had just gotten there and was only passing through.

Jazz looked up and saw a white man in a pickup and moved to the side of the road, thinking he was somehow in the way. He certainly did not want any more trouble. Peter drove past him a bit, letting Jazz look into the truck to see it was him; then, he pulled over to the side of the road. Jazz walked up to the truck slowly, still a bit unsure. "Jazz, it's me. Milk Man," Peter said.

When Jazz walked up to the truck and looked in, Peter was shocked to see what they had done to his friend. His face was all beaten and bruised and still swollen. "Milk Man, what the hell are you doing here?" Jazz blurted out into the truck, "Are you crazy man? If that sheriff sees you here talking to us, you'll be in a whole heap of trouble."

"I was just driving through and saw you; hop on in. I will give you a ride to wherever you're going," Peter said.

Jazz tossed his fishing rods into the bed of the truck and hopped in quickly, telling Peter to get off the main road and out of sight because the sheriff might come by.

"So, where are we going? Point the way." Peter was trying not to stare at Jazz's face, but Jazz of course noticed the look on his face.

"Don't you worry; it's not as bad as it looks," Jazz told him to ease his tension a bit. "I'm headed to the river to do some fishing and get my mind off some things. Just take a right down the next road and go about four miles."

"Four miles?" Peter replied, "And you were going to walk that? Why don't you drive? I know you have a truck."

"They burned all our cars and the juke to the ground after the raid," Jazz answered.

Peter's stomach dropped. Although he already knew about the juke joint, it was still gut wrenching to hear it from Jazz. "I am so sorry, man, I wish I could have stopped it." Jazz just looked down and never responded. They drove in silence until they got to the river, not too far from the juke. You could still smell the charred wood on the air.

When Peter pulled up to the water's edge, they just sat there for a second. Peter hoped Jazz would ask him to stick around – and he did. Jazz always brought a few poles and would fish the river with all of them. He had a big can of night crawlers and was ready for the day, with a satchel of food and a big bottle of hooch. Jazz offered him some.

"Is this the same stuff I had the other night?" Peter asked. "Because if it is, I am going to have to take this real slow because it knocked me on my ass!"

Jazz started laughing. "Yeah, it does take some getting used to, but it really did get you to moving those feet, at least until all hell broke loose." Peter could see the pain that Jazz was in and had no idea what to do or say. In his heart, he did not really think he would run into Jazz, so he hadn't rehearsed or planned what to say to him if he did.

"Jazz, I am really sorry about everything that happened. I didn't know what to do. I tried to fight, but there was just so many of them and I..."

Jazz interrupted him. "Look, I know you did everything you could. I should be the one saying sorry. I should have never brought you there and got you mixed up in all this ..."

Peter interrupted him. "Jazz, I don't want you to feel that way. That was one of the best nights I think I've ever had. Well, at least before everything happened there and to your mama and all." Peter looked right at Jazz and saw his eyes and saw them welling up. He instantly had regrets about bringing up Jazz's mama. "Hey, I am sorry. I should not have brought that up, man. I should just go."

"No, please don't. I am glad you are here," replied Jazz. "I was going fishing by myself because no one knows what to say to me and I think people are trying to give me some space. But I don't want space. I need people around. My mama was the last of my family; it was just me and her in the world. Now, I'm all alone."

Peter started to think of his own mother. "I know it's a hard time for you, but you are not all alone. You have all those people from your team. I could see how much they care; you should just let them in. I know that's not easy to do, but they fought for you and your mama that night. That tells me something and it should tell you something too. Plus, now you have a crazy white boy who is really starting to like this hell water you keep giving me." As Peter took another gulp, they both laughed and the tension eased a bit.

"Look, I just want to say thank you," Jazz said, getting serious one more time.

"Thank me for what?" Peter asked.

"I know that you sat with my mama until her last breaths, and I just want to thank you," Jazz answered in a soft voice.

"What makes you think it was me?" Peter replied.

"Man, there is only one white boy I know who would do that and he's the same crazy-ass white boy who would come pitch for a Negro team. You." Jazz looked away to the river.

"Well, anyone would have done that, knowing you weren't able to be there," Peter said.

Jazz looked him right in the eyes. "No, they would not have, 'specially a white man."

Peter just looked at him and thought for a moment before his next statement, because he wanted to make sure it came out right. "I just want you to know that she was peaceful and I was holding her hand the whole time. She was not alone, and that is the important thing. She was quite a lady," Peter told him. "And I hope she taught you how to make this fire water, because I'm going to be needing a lot of it if we're going to be playing together."

Jazz looked up at him like he was crazy. "After all of that, the beating, the jail, the hospital, you're still going to come play with our raggedy team?"

Peter looked at him for a second, and then they both laughed again. Words were coming more easily for Peter now. "Look, your team may be raggedy, but it has more heart than any other team I have ever played on – and I have played on a few. Plus, the *Catfish* have some of the best players anywhere in the game, even in the National League. And that is saying something. If I'm gonna play, I want to play with the best, with people who know and love the game."

Jazz just shook his head and looked at Peter. "You know how dangerous what you're talking about doing is, right? You know they got laws sayin' we can't play together? I am used to all of this, the beatings, the whites only, the back-breaking work in the hot sun. But are you ready for all of that? Because, once you do this, whites are gonna see you just like they see me, and I just want to make sure you're ready and all. I suggest you take a closer look at those laws before you tell anyone you're going to play anything, okay? Promise me."

Peter could tell from his friend's voice how great Jazz's concern was. But he wasn't quite done. "I'm telling you, Peter, no one will look down on you for not wanting this life. Hell, I don't even want it, but this is what I am stuck with – and not by my choice. I work hard every day, harder than most white men will ever work and I get next to nothing for it and it gets me nowhere. For what you did for me and my mama, I will be your back-up whenever and however I can for the rest of my life. But I don't know if that will be enough to protect you from what may come your way if you make this decision. I need to know that you are going to be okay with what might happen."

Peter looked at Jazz for just a moment before talking. "You don't owe me a thing, Jazz. And, yes, I have thought a lot about it. I know those laws, and they are dumb as hell. I'm a big boy and can handle anything that comes my way. I know I have a choice, and I am sure I'm making a good one. I know we are going to have bad days, in fact very bad days. But, on that field, I know we are going to have good ones, hell great ones too, and we are gonna play some great ball and that is all that matters to me. The rest I will take as it comes – like you do. Just know I have your back too."

"I already do," Jazz said. They spent the rest of the day talking about life, loss and baseball – drinking that fire water 'til the sun was well below the trees and Peter had to go home. He dropped Jazz off with his whole heap of fish. He hoped Jazz had a little better feeling in his heart than when Peter found him.

CHAPTER ELEVEN

NEW NAME, BIG MEETING

It's a week after the riot and Little Helen's murder. The entire *Catfish* team is still in mourning. The raid was a shock to everyone at the Rainbow, but raids on black establishments were nothing new in Texas. Little Helen's death, however, rattled everyone on the team, right to the core. As Peter sits and thinks about Little Helen and Jazz, about the way those white cops treated all his friends and about his own father's ignorant take on the whole thing, he knows one thing for sure: he is going to play on this team, regardless of the serious hurdles he knows he will have to get over. Meanwhile, Clarence is already one step ahead of him.

At the very next practice, Clarence pulls Peter aside and says, "If we're all going to do this, I want everyone going into this to know what the risks are. I know you are a college-educated guy, and, since you are from the South, I'm sure you are well aware of the Jim Crow laws." At this, Peter nods without saying a word. Clarence goes on, "You know we can all get in a lot of trouble if the police want to bother us about this. Now, I don't think they will because they have much bigger fish to fry than us playing some ball together, but, just in case, I think you should go by a pseudonym when you are on the field."

Clarence pauses a moment to let Peter process his request and then continues before Peter can protest. "I know this seems like a lot, but it will keep you and your family safe."

"Change my name?" Peter mutters, thinking aloud. "I never thought of that." He hesitates a minute, remembering his parents back home and the way they reacted to his playing with the *Catfish*. Then, he considers other people in his hometown, who are even less tolerant than his father. He realizes he might need to protect his family from what might happen once people discover he is playing on a Negro League team.

"I think that's a good idea," he drawls, "but what about all y'all? The law may give me a hard time, but they are more than likely going to string y'all up in a tree."

"Don't worry about us," Clarence answers. "We've made a few deals with the local sheriffs in the area. We just have to give up a cut of whatever we take in on games, which is not much anyway. But they will look the other way as long as no whites make too much of a fuss about the whole thing."

"Now, all we need is someone to talk to my daddy," Peter says jokingly, "because he is having a serious problem with it."

"Peter, I want to really make sure that this is something you want to do," Clarence says with a grave expression. "No one here wants you to get hurt or to destroy your family relationships, in any way. Do you need time to think about this?"

Peter holds off a second and replies, "I have done all the thinking I need to do on this. This is where I want to be. I respect my daddy a lot and really hope someday he will understand why I want to do this. It's killin' me inside knowing that he'll never see me play with y'all. But that's his decision, not mine, and one day, maybe he'll come around." After a moment's pause to consider what he just said, Peter adds, "So, what do we need to do?"

"Well, we need to come up with a new name for you and I think I have it. What do you think of Deacon, Deacon Johnson?"

Peter studies him for a second and says, "I like it."

"Peter is very white," Clarence blurts, as if someone has pinched him to get him to say it.

Chuckling, Peter responds, "Clarence, I am white." Clarence laughs as well and clarifies, "What I mean is, we don't want people to think of you as a white boy when they read your name in the papers. Since most white folks are not going to come see us play, changing your name to something a little less conspicuous might save us a tremendous amount of trouble."

Clarence ribs Peter and adds, "Colored folks just aren't naming any of their babies 'Peter' down here. They're not. But 'Deacon' – when people see that name, the first thing that comes to mind is not a 'white fella'. I can assure you that."

Peter smiles and says, "Okay then, Deacon it is. So who'll tell the team?"

"Don't worry about that. I'll take care of everything," Clarence assures him. "You just worry about playing ball and leave the rest up to us. I'll handle that part of it with the owners."

With that, Clarence leaves 'Deacon' at the field and goes to find Leola and Isaac to tell them about the name change.

"I can't believe he's decided to stay," Isaac says, shaking his head in disbelief.

"You still think this is a good idea?" Leola asks, her eyes trained on Isaac.

"I do," Isaac tells her. "If the team is going to move to the next level, we need Peter, I mean Deacon, on board with us."

"If that's what you think, I trust it," Leola says.

"And so do I," Clarence agrees. "It's worth the risk. So I guess from now on, our new star pitcher is Deacon Johnson."

"Deacon Johnson it is," Isaac says with a sly grin.

The next day the team gathers at the old juke joint to pick up the pieces from the raid. Spirits weigh heavy among the heartbroken players as they sift through broken glass that once held moonshine and charred splinters of wood that were once tables and chairs. The Rainbow was a place where you could always find happy-go-lucky men and women out for a night of music and drinks. Maybe one day it would be again, but the day after the raid it was in ruins in so many ways. As the *Catfish* work to clean up Jazz's family's shattered lifelong accomplishment, Leola and Clarence make arrangements for Peter's name change. Noticing Leola's pensive expression, Clarence says, "We're past the worst of it; now, it's only a matter of filling out paperwork. Leola nods and forces a smile, quietly saying, "I hope so." The ring of the phone startles Leola. Clarence puts a hand on hers as he answers the telephone on his desk.

"Clarence Holloman speaking," he answers. The person on the other end of the line explains that he is a newspaper sports writer named Davis Sterling from the *Houston Star*. Clarence knows the *Star* is the top white newspaper in the city. Immediately, his heart is in his throat. Leola sees the color drain from her best friend's face, but remains silent. How could they have learned about Deacon so fast? Clarence wonders as Davis goes on. As Clarence's expression turns from concern to panic, Leola begins to signal him, shrugging her shoulders hard and mouthing the question, "What is going on?" but he is not paying attention to her. When she can't take it anymore, Leola grabs the phone from him.

"This is Leona Jones, owner of the *Catfish*," she snaps into the phone. "How can I help you?"

Davis realizes his call is stirring some uneasiness on the other end of the line, so he comes up with a lie as quickly as he can. "Um, yes, I'm doing a story on new Negro teams in the area. I heard that the *Catfish* are from Florida and are really good. I just wanted to know more about them."

"You did say you knew that we are a Negro team, right?" Leola asks, suspicious of a white newspaper writing about a team of colored baseball players barnstorming from game to game across eastern Texas.

"Yes, I know you are a Negro team. I'm sorry, but I didn't catch your name at first. With whom do I have the pleasure of speaking?" Davis inquires.

"Jones, Leola Jones. I am the acting owner of the *Catfish* and the person with whom you need to speak," she snaps curtly. "What would you like to know?"

"Well, I was hoping you would give me a chance to sit down with you and get all the background about your team since no one in these parts knows who y'all are," Davis explains.

Davis's calm tone relaxes Leola a bit. She lets her shoulders drop and the bite comes out of her voice. "Well, sir, our time here so far has been short," she tells him. "And I am still not really sure what you want to know about us. But I would be glad to sit down with you and tell you anything you want to know about our team's background – and our plans to take Houston by storm."

"Great!" Davis responds, "We can meet anywhere you would like."

"I will meet you at your office," Leola responds, waiting to see if she will get a reaction out of Davis.

"Wonderful!" Davis exclaims. Having Leola come to the office could not be more perfect for his plan to stir things up at the *Star*. "I will arrange for a driver to come pick you up."

Leola blinks at Davis's enthusiastic response. She doesn't know what to make of his offer. She anticipated resistance to her even going to his office; adding a car and driver was not something she expected. Scrambling to push her game, she replies, "Can I bring my business partner Clarence Holloman with me? He is my right hand man."

Clarence begins waving his hands frantically in front of Leola when he hears this. She puts up her hand to quiet him.

"Of course," Davis responds, "I will have someone contact you to arrange everything."

"Okay," Leola responds, "until then."

Leola hangs up the phone and Clarence lights into her. "Why are you mixing me up in this mess? You know I cannot hold my tongue, and now you want me to talk to a reporter of the biggest white newspaper in Houston? Woman, have you lost your mind?"

"Now, I know you would never let me go into the lion's den alone, Clarence," Leola retorts calmly. She knows Clarence wants to be in the center of any action, so she teases him a bit. With the smile she knows he can never resist, she keeps going. "Something about that conversation is telling me that he is not out to hurt us. I am sure he is not telling the full truth, and you know that I would rather know the devil I am dealing with than the devil I don't. And you, Mr. Holloman, are going to help me get to the bottom of this."

"You don't think it is about Deacon, do you?" Clarence asks.

"My gut is telling me this is about a lot of things," she answers. "Plus, we just might get what other Negro teams are not getting around here – some ink in the biggest newspaper in this region. That's an opportunity we just can't pass up."

"What if it's about Deacon?"

"Well, if it is, better to know sooner than later. People are going to find out sooner or later. Like you told me when you guys came up with this crazy scheme: it's going to fill the seats one way or another."

"Leola, I hate it when you call me on my bluffs, but you're right. We are going to make a stir just walking into those offices."

She smiles and says, "Why do you think I suggested it? If this guy wasn't serious, he would never have invited us to his ivory tower. We'll meet him on his home turf and see what he's up to. Don't worry. You know that between me and you, we'll get to the bottom of what he really wants before that meeting's over."

The next day Leola receives a call from Davis's office to set up the meeting. "See? I told you this reporter was serious," Leola couldn't help telling Clarence. When the day of the meeting arrived, both

Leola and Clarence both put on their best business suits and waited for the car that would take them to the offices of the *Houston Star*. Right on time, a sparkling onyx sedan pulls up to the sidewalk. Clarence and Leola exchange a furtive smile as the driver opens the door for them. When they arrive at the *Houston Star* building, however, their smiles fade. It's more intimidating than they could have imagined: a beautiful skyscraper with enormous revolving front doors that open onto a polished marble floor with a massive *Houston Star* logo embedded in the center. When they walk in, the receptionist hardly even acknowledges them. Leola and Clarence walk to her desk and stand looking at her, waiting for her to look up from her work. She seems to refuse to meet their gaze.

"All of our cleaning positions are full, and you should know better than to use the front entrance," she finally says, still looking down at her typewriter, not even stopping what she is doing to address them.

Outraged but forcing himself to remain outwardly collected, Clarence stands with his back as straight as it will go and says, "We have an appointment with Davis Sterling, and we don't use rear entrances. If you please, would you kindly let him know we are here? That would be greatly appreciated."

Finally, the receptionist's eyes break from her transcription work and fall on the two well-dressed people standing before her. She looks surprised as her fingers fly through her appointment book and asks, "Are you Leola Jones and Clarence Holloman?"

"Yes, we are," Clarence replies coolly. "So if you could see to it that he knows we have arrived, that would be very helpful." Leola just smiles at her, raising an eyebrow.

"Please take a seat to one side while I try to reach Mr. Davis," the receptionist replies, with the same haughty tone in her voice.

Clarence takes a step forward. Leola can see he is about to comment on the receptionist's attitude, so she speaks up before he can say anything. "Thank you, kindly," she says, gently pulling Clarence off to the side to let him calm down a bit.

Walking over to their seats, Leola whispers, "We do not want to build any walls here. Remember, we are here to find out if this guy is going to blow us out of the water on this Deacon thing, so let's not start off on the wrong foot."

Clarence takes a deep breath and says, "You're right. I need to remember that I am back in the South."

He returns the receptionist's glare with a smile. At that moment, the phone rings. The receptionist picks up the phone and mechanically repeats, "Yes, sir," several times, then hangs up the phone, gets up from her desk, and announces with a sweetness that catches both Clarence and Leola off guard, "Mr. Sterling is tied up on a call and will be right with you. Can I get you something to drink while you wait?" Although her tone is kind, Clarence sees her jaw tense up as she is forced to offer her service to them.

"I think we are fine for now, but we will let you know if we change our minds," he says, wearing a smug smile on his face.

As the receptionist turns to leave them, Leola and Clarence exchange confused but pleased glances. As they wait, they overhear the receptionist talking secretively into her telephone. She is clearly telling someone about their exchange. Leola notices this and nudges Clarence to make him aware, but Clarence has already noticed. Before either of them can react, the elevator doors open. Behind the shining copper doors stand four women, chattering away among themselves until they notice Leola and Clarence, professional and well-dressed, looking right at them. In stunned silence, the staring group stays fixed in their stares until they disappear again behind closing elevator doors.

"Well, we have not been here fifteen minutes and already we are a zoo exhibit," Leola says to Clarence, with a snicker.

Minutes later, the receptionist's phone rings. After she hangs up, she walks over to Clarence and Leola and says, "Mr. Sterling is ready to see you now. Just let the elevator man know." She catches herself and apologizes. Turning to the elevator man, she continues, "Jeffrey, please take our guests to see Mr. Sterling, Jr."

Turning back to Leola and Clarence, she continues, "You see, we have a Mr. Sterling Senior and a Mr. Sterling Junior here, as well. Jeffrey will take you to the proper floor."

Leola and Clarence are a bit surprised that the man they are there to meet happens to be the owner's son, but they don't want the receptionist to see anything but cool.

"Thank you," Clarence says smiling, "And thanks for your kind hospitality." The secretary offers an embarrassed half smile and turns and walks away in a bit of a huff.

Inside the elevator, Jeffrey awaits. "We're here to see Mr. Sterling, Jr.," Leola says to him.

"Seems you all have stirred up quite a fuss here at the office today," Jeffrey says with a grin. "Mr. Davis is a good man, and he will do you fair; this I can tell you. But keep your eyes wide open and your ears even wider. You're in the lion's den, nonetheless, ya hear?"

"I said that lion's den thing to you the other day, do you remember?" Leola says to Clarence with a nudge, smiling at Jeffrey.

"You bet we will, sir, and thank you for the information and advice," Clarence says.

Stepping off the elevator, the two see several offices and a secretary at a desk. The secretary sees the two and rushes over to them. Much kinder than the woman downstairs, she greets them with a friendly smile, saying, "Miss Jones and Mr. Holloman, I am Georgia Mae. Can I get you something to drink? Mr. Sterling is ready to see you."

"No, thank you, Georgia Mae. I think we are fine," Leola responds.

"Okay, then, you can go right on in. Please let me know if y'all need anything," Georgia Mae says, as she closes the door.

"Davis Sterling," the gentleman says as he stands up and walks over to introduce himself. "You must be Miss Jones." He steps toward Leola to shake her hand. Davis feels a bit flustered as their hands touch. He feels his breath catch a little as he makes eye contact with Leola.

"Yes, please call me Leola. And this is Clarence Holloman." Leola cannot help noticing that Davis is quite good looking, but she tries not to make her observation obvious to him or to Clarence.

"Very nice to meet you, Mr. Holloman," Davis announces, regaining his composure as he looks at Clarence, who has already figured out what just happened between the two of them. He eyes Davis. Leola in turn notices everything going on with both Davis and Clarence and decides to move the conversation along.

"So, Mr. Davis Sterling, Jr., of the *Houston Star*, are you THE Mr. Sterling, Jr.?" Leola asks, to let him know that they mean business.

"Yes, my family owns the paper, but I thought if I told you that, you wouldn't have come."

"Interesting," Clarence huffs. "So what else have you neglected to tell us, Mr. Sterling?" he asks, but Davis has turned his attention back to Leola.

"Please, call me Davis," he smiles at her.

"Okay, Davis, what else do we need to know before we continue with this conversation?" she asks.

Clarence is a bit confused at first by Leola's exchanges with Davis. She isn't usually so severe in business dealings, but then he realizes this is no simple business approach that she is taking.

"Look, I am going to be up front with you," Davis says.

"That would be nice," Leola replies batting her eyelashes a bit. Clarence nearly guffaws aloud at this.

"I did not plan on telling you this, but I am rather new here at the paper. That comes with its own set of problems that I won't go into right now. But as you know, the *Houston Star* has never written about Negro barnstorming teams. Hell, no white people in Texas ever have." Then Davis tells Clarence and Leola all about his plan to be the reporter who changes the face of sports journalism.

"I want to be the sports reporter who changes all of that and I am in just the position to do it," he continues. "Look, everyone in this room knows some of the best players in baseball are in the Negro and church leagues. Let's be honest. We have always had the philosophy that, if we don't talk about it, it doesn't exist because no one wants to make our white players look bad in comparison, right?"

"No arguments there," Leola agrees.

"Hear, hear," Clarence adds.

Davis smiles and continues. "I have traveled most of this country, and the world for that matter, and I know things are changing out there. The National League is pulling in Jackie Robinson, and that is going to forever change the face of baseball as we know it."

Davis nearly jumps from his office chair and starts pacing the room like a caged lion. Leola tracks his every move as he does, which is what Davis had hoped would happen. Clarence observes the whole situation with disbelief. As much as he respects Davis's passion, he can't help but resent feeling like he is just an ornament in the room; the conversation is all between Davis and Leola.

"Now, I happen to know from a reliable source that you are doing the same type of thing here in Houston," Davis says directly to Leola. Those words are enough to break the spell she had been under since she first set eyes on Davis. Leola's eyes suddenly dart anxiously toward Clarence. Davis notices this and quickly gives himself another silent congratulation on his observation skills. Clarence shoots up and goes into protection mode.

"Now, see here, sir, I don't know what you are trying to do, but I think this meeting is over!"

Leola gets up to walk out with Clarence, but Davis stops them. He has to think fast to win Leola and Clarence over, and he knows that.

"Please. Please hear me out. I am not trying to hurt you or your team. I want to do just the opposite. I want to help."

They stop and look at each other and then face Davis.

"How? How can you help us?" Clarence demands.

"I think I have found a way to write about your team in a round-about way by focusing on this one player. And to write about this player, I have to write about your team." Davis continues, "Look, I am not saying it is not going to be without its dangers for all of us, but you had to know the dangers when you decided to take this player on. What's his name, anyway?"

Clarence does not miss a beat. "Deacon Johnson is his name. He's new to the area."

After a minute of hesitation, Clarence and Leola go back to their seats, and the meeting continues.

"Well, this Deacon Johnson could change the face of this newspaper and the face of baseball in these parts," Davis exclaims. "We could change how Negro barnstorming is looked at throughout this country!"

Leola starts to get cold feet about the whole thing, thinking of the possibility of the team going national. "I . . . I'm not sure about all of this. It's all happening too fast," she says.

Davis gets very close to Leola, grabs her hand, and looks her right in the eye. "Please don't be nervous. I think everyone will get something out of this if we do it well. No matter what happens, it's the right thing to do and we all know that."

The two seem to freeze in one another's stares. Clarence knows it's up to him to bring everyone back to earth. He grabs Leola's other hand and asks Davis, "Bottom line, what do you want from us? Seems to me if you had wanted to, you could have done all of this without us."

Davis realizes what he has just done, holding Leola's hand like that. He also realizes that his secretary has been peering into his office.

"What I am looking for in this situation," Davis says after he has calmed down a bit, "is the exclusive on this story. I don't want you talking to any other papers about Deacon or the *Catfish*, and I promise you that I will do you, your team, and your white player justice. I am not going to hurt any of you."

"So why exactly are you doing this?" Leola asks.

"Well, I have my own reasons, and maybe I can share them with you another time. But, for now I am just hoping you agree to give me the exclusive on this story."

Leola and Clarence exchange a quick glance; then Clarence shrugs. "Why not? We said we were in it for good or bad."

Leola turns to Davis and says, "Well, I guess you have yourself an exclusive on our Negro team, Davis, whatever that means."

Davis slaps his hands together and rushes over to shake both Leola's and Clarence's hands.

"Look, Davis, my first and foremost responsibility is my team and its safety and reputation," Leola says, relying on professionalism to counter Davis's excitement, and also his unmistakable charm. "I want in writing what you are saying to me. The moment the situation gets too dangerous for my team, I want your word that you will stop your writing. That is the only way we are going to agree to do this."

"Absolutely," he agrees. "I'll give you whatever you want in writing ... in triplicate!"

Before they leave, Davis asks if he can sit down with Leola to go over the details in a few days. Clarence interjects to answer his question. "I'm unable to meet later this week."

"I can meet with Leola alone," Davis replies. Before Clarence can say anything, Leola tells him, "That will be fine," to which Davis replies that he will call her personally to set something up. Leola quickly agrees.

By this time, a number of people from the surrounding offices are peeking into Davis's office to see what all the talk is about. When the three emerge, office employees don't bother to act like they're not eavesdropping. The three pretend not to notice them either as they chat and make their way toward the elevator.

"Thank you for taking the time to come down and speak with me," Davis says loud enough for everyone to hear. "I look forward to meeting you both again."

"Do you have nothing better to do?" Davis finally asks, looking around at everyone in the office. With Davis's question still hanging in the air, the gawkers scatter like leaves in a stiff breeze.

Once they're in the car, Clarence looks at Leola and begins to say something. But Leola stops him, saying, "I don't want to hear it, Clarence. I know what I'm doing."

"Do you? Do you really, Leola? We are in the heart of Texas. What are you thinking?"

"I'm thinking what we both were thinking before we went into that office. Good or bad, this is going to fill those stands. I am thinking about the *Catfish,* and I know you are too. Let's see how this plays out for a while. Let's see if this is going to be positive or negative."

They both know that that is not what Clarence is hinting at, but Clarence also knows Leola is not going to discuss anything that she doesn't want to discuss. Leola is a master of moving conversations in whatever direction she sees fit. Clarence knows it would be a complete waste of time trying to talk to her about whatever it was he just witnessed back at Davis's office. Although he opts to stay quiet for the time being, Clarence knows that he will eventually call her on it. This just isn't the right time.

"Okay, Miss Jones, let's just see how this plays out. But the first sign of trouble, and I am pulling the plug, agreed?" Clarence says to her.

"Agreed," she responds.

Even as they make their pact, both Leola and Clarence know that her promise is an empty one. Leola will do whatever she wants to do, regardless of what she has told Clarence. She has always had a mind of her own, and she has no intentions of changing her behavior just because they are in Texas.

CHAPTER TWELVE

THE INTERVIEW

As Leola finishes getting ready for her meeting with Davis, Clarence enters the room. "Leola, are you sure you know what you are doing? This could be so dangerous on so many fronts. I know this Davis guy is charming, but we really don't know what his true motivation is. I just don't want you putting yourself in a situation that could backfire on all of us."

"Do you think I can't handle myself, Clarence?" Leola demands, inflamed by his comments. "Am I not smart enough, not savvy enough? Or is it just that I am not a man? What is it, Clarence?"

"Look, Leola," Clarence quips back, "don't pull that with me – that 'I am not a man' thing! Don't forget who you are talking to! You know damn well and good it has nothing to do with you being a woman. I know you think you are the best at covering up your emotions, and with most people you can. But I am not most people. You don't think I saw what was going on in that room?"

"Clarence, I don't have any idea what you are talking about! This was our plan all along," Leola reminds him, as her cheeks burn red.

"Leola, we were off that plan five minutes into the conversation with that white man! You came up with a whole new plan, and I was left to just sit back and watch it all unfold."

"Look, Clarence, you don't know what you are talking about, and I am offended that you are even saying this. Is this you being protective? Or is this you being jealous that he wanted to talk only to me?"

Clarence is taken back by her statement. He glares at Leola as he starts up again. "Look, Leola, the fact that you just said that to me backs up what I have been saying."

"And what is that, Clarence? What is the all-knowing Northerner thinking? You've been gone from the South for a long time, and it is clear that you just don't want to see that maybe Southerners aren't as savage and backward as you think they are! Things are changing here too."

Clarence takes a deep breath and straightens his tie before he starts again. "Wow, then maybe I need to go back to where I came from, since I am clearly not needed here. But I will tell you this; I will be right here waiting for an apology when you remember where you are – and who you are dealing with. And, if I am not here, then kindly send me your apologies in a letter because it is going to happen. Would you like to know why?" Clarence doesn't pause long enough to let Leola respond to his question. "Because these people cannot be trusted. You are not a part of their crowd and never will be. He has something up his sleeve, Leola. He has other motives, and if he can get there by shining his pretty white smile to get where he needs to go, I guarantee he is going to do it."

"Why do you hate these people so?" Leola demands. "I thought you were all about change and moving forward. Or is that only what you preach, Clarence?"

"I am about moving forward," Clarence hisses back defensively, "but that does not mean I will ever forget the day I had to help cut your brothers down from the tree that those white folks hung them from! That doesn't mean I will ever forget how those two boys weren't even put on trial for their crime! That doesn't mean that I have forgotten them telling me I was next!" Clarence is spitting his words more than saying them by now. His face is hot and his eyes ablaze. "God creates fear for a reason, Leola, and by God I am not going to ignore that! And trust me – neither should you. You're going to get hurt. And if you aren't going to let me protect you, then I'm not going to sit by and watch them do it to you, which means I have no reason to be here."

Leola stands silent, so stunned by Clarence's outburst that she has no response.

"Leola, I love you and always will. But I am not going to allow you or anyone else to say those things to me. I still can't believe you'd talk to me like this. You called me here to do just what I am doing. One pretty white man bats his blue eyes, and this is how you behave? I'll be looking for that apology, but for now, you have an interview to get ready for." Clarence walks out of the room so Leola can see only his back as he leaves.

She wants to call him back, but her pride won't let her. Alone in the room now, Leola feels as if the room is spinning around her. Clarence and she have never fought like this. She has never seen him so irate. What's worse is that Leola is convinced he's wrong. She has a feeling about Davis; she truly believes his intentions are good – about both her and the team. As Clarence walks away, Leola stares blankly at the door, then takes a deep breath to pull herself together. There isn't time to mull over their fight right now. She needs to prepare for her big meeting – to brush up on her team's statistics, schedule, players' strengths and weaknesses, and so on. She runs over all the information she can as she scans her dressing room for something to wear.

"What does one wear for a meeting with a powerful, rich, white man?" she asks herself as she eyes her wardrobe.

Meanwhile, at his office at the *Star*, Davis is as deep in thought as Leola. He doesn't quite know what he is going to ask. He doesn't even have an exact date or location in mind for the meeting that he'll arrange with her. But he does know that he has to do a better job of keeping his composure this time than he did during that first meeting. To make the setting less stuffy, he decides to take Leola someplace where she can relax and they can talk. Besides, he realizes that he's already in deep – too deep to back away or, even worse, scare away Leola. He's worked the office into a frenzy, and he has to be sure he gets enough information for a solid article to let them know this is serious newspaper business, not just office gossip. To take the next step with Leola, he'll need to take her someplace where she'll feel comfortable.

"Would you like me to make a reservation, Mr. Sterling?" Georgia Mae asks over a crackling intercom.

"Yes, thank you."

"Where to, sir?"

Davis thinks a moment, and then replies, "the Rolling Lawns Country Club."

"The Club?" Georgia Mae asked, a bit of shock in her voice.

"Yes," he replies firmly. "My family has been member since before I was born. It's the perfect place."

It was true. Davis's family had a membership with Rolling Lawns as long as it had been standing. As a child, he would run throughout the place like he owned it. His family was and is very respected there. It seems it would be both a comfortable and impressive place to take Leola. He hears Georgia Mae make the call to the county club to let them know that he would be bringing a very special guest.

"Tell them I want a private room because I'll be conducting an important interview," he tells her as she makes the reservation. Georgia Mae nods and relays the information.

"And be sure they know that we'll want to be served dinner as well."

The Club is more than happy to oblige him; they assure Georgia Mae that they will make sure everything is perfect for the well-respected Mr. Davis Sterling.

With his reservation made, Davis decides to pick Leola up himself, rather than send a car and driver, to give him a bit more time to talk with her. He also has always trusted a ride in his own car as the best way to break the ice with important new acquaintances. As he considers the things they may talk about, Davis realizes that his palms are sweating and his pulse is a bit quicker than usual. Strange, he thinks. Interviews don't usually ruffle me so. He has done countless interviews – so many that he has become accustomed to walking in unprepared and doing fine. He can't figure out why this one is setting him on edge. Because the story that comes from this interview is going to break all hell loose, he tells himself. That's what the nerves are about.

Davis pulls his new chocolate brown Buick Road Master convertible sedan up to the address Leola gave him. The wide whitewall tires are as bright as his tuxedo shirt, and the shining hubcaps are as brilliant as his silver cufflinks. Between the car and his attire, Davis is quite a spectacle on the poor black side of the tracks. When Leola looks out to see the car, she can hardly believe her eyes. And Davis is behind the wheel! Clarence races to the window after seeing Leola's reaction to what is outside. He is not nearly as surprised as she is by Davis's display.

"You are trying to get us all killed," he grumbles as Leola fumbles with the hem of her dress. "I hope this white man is worth it."

People start to gather to look at the fancy car, like a piece of gold stuck in the mud of a riverbank. When Leola sees how many folks are ogling them, she gets a bit embarrassed. She pauses on the porch, waiting for the color in her cheeks to fade. As she does, Davis gets out of the car. Leola is surprised to see him dressed so formally.

"Mr. Davis?" Leola asks, "is that you? When you said you were sending a car, I did not imagine it would be you driving it!"

"Well, since you have been generous enough to take the time to do this on such short notice, I thought I would try to make this as painless as possible for you," says Davis, trotting up to open Leola's door.

When Davis gets to her side of the car to open the door, Leola's image stops Davis in his tracks. His eyes are fixed on her, his limbs so immobile that he looks all but paralyzed.

"My," Davis says finally, forcing his hand to move toward the door handle, "you really look nice."

"As do you, sir," Leola responds and smiles.

The two stand there for a moment as neighbors chatter in the background.

"Who is this, in this fancy car?"

"What's a white man doing here?"

"What is she doing going with him?"

As Davis opens the door and waits for Leola to slide into the car, he never breaks his gaze, not even as he moves to his side of the car. When he is in the driver's seat, he looks at her again.

"I hope I haven't embarrassed you in front of all these folks out here." Leola laughs.

"What's so funny?" Davis asks.

"Mr. Davis, you have to remember that I am new here in town. I don't know these people, so to be honest, I really don't care what they think."

They both start laughing.

Leola notices as they drive that they are not on the same route the driver had used to take them to his office last week. She feels her heart quicken and her hair stand on end.

"Mr. Davis? This is not the way your driver took us to your office the other day. Where are you taking me?" she asks, looking nervously through her purse. Davis notices Leola's discomfort.

"Please don't be nervous. We are not going to my office," Davis responds. Leola looks at him in a bit of a panic. He continues, "I have arranged for a private room at Rolling Lawns so we can enjoy a dinner and I can interview you. It's a bit of a thank-you for doing this. And please call me Davis."

Leola's taut muscles relax, and the strain on her brow disappears. She has no idea what Rolling Lawns is, but she trusts him. She sits back and enjoys the rest of the ride.

As the Buick moves along, Leola can see that they are in the nice part of town – the white part of town. She tries to imagine where they are going, but her imagination is put to rest when the car pulls up to a massive gate with cursive letters on it that opens to a long road. Massive rolling green grass stretches out as far as the eye can see on either side of the small road. As they get close enough to read the sign, Rolling Lawns Country Club, her heart jumps into her throat.

Leola is not sure what to do. She wants to trust Davis that everything is fine, but she also knows that this is Texas and she is colored in a whites-only area. She is a bit uneasy. Davis sees the anxiety welling up in her again.

"This has been all set up in advance, just like my office," he tells her to ease her worries. Leola smiles and tries to let her shoulders drop.

"Of course," she replies, an attempt at playing off her fears.

Davis pulls the sedan to the entrance of the building, where two colored men run out to open the car doors. Leola startles at the attendant who opens her door. It is Jupiter Monroe, one of the newest players for the *Catfish*! Leola does not know how to react; neither does Jupiter. Although Jupiter hasn't been in Texas long, he knows that seeing a colored woman with a rich, white man is not something that happens often in the Lone Star State.

As Leola waits for Davis to come around the car, she notices that everyone is staring at her. She feels her head grow hot, and the bubble of anxiety that she has been fighting swells in her stomach. Davis also sees people staring.

"Don't worry about them," he tells her as he offers her his arm. As Leola walks past Jupiter, she tells him to keep the car very close.

"You got that right!" Jupiter responds under his breath.

Before they can get to the host stand, the director of the club, James Conlon, rushes over to them.

"Would you mind stepping into the side room, so I can speak with you?" he insists. Davis nods and follows him but is perplexed by the brusque request since he has prearranged everything already.

Once the director has them off to the side, he asks if he can speak with Davis in private, which Davis refuses.

"Anything you need to say can be said right here."

Leola is very cognizant of the goings on and is getting more and more embarrassed. She asks Davis if they can just go someplace else. Davis refuses.

"We are not going anywhere. This has all been arranged," Davis tells her. "We are members here, and my family has held a membership here since before I was even born," he says, turning to Conlon.

"Mr. Sterling, I do know that you had prearranged your reservation. We are happy to accommodate you as always, but we cannot have this," he tells Davis in a rather stern voice.

"Let's just go," Leola says again, almost pleading this time. She prefers to leave before they are kicked out. Once again, Davis refuses.

The director continues, "When you made these arrangements, you were very detailed with us, sir."

"Yes, I was so. I do not see what the problem is."

"The problem is, sir, that you did not tell us that your guest was colored, and this club will not stand for that. We will not serve any colored woman or man as long as I am director here at Rolling Lawns."

As he finished his sentence, Leola's head drops. She can see other people gathering in the hall area, peering in at her.

"This is not happening," Davis says as he starts to raise his voice. "I see colored folks around here all the time."

"Well, did you ever take notice that they were just your servants?" Leola blurts, trading her embarrassment for a moment with the rage she feels about the whole situation.

"No," Davis shouts back, almost in knee-jerk reaction, "I did not, ok?" He catches himself and lowers his voice to continue.

"I'm sorry, Leola. No, I really never did. Many of them are my friends. I never looked at them any other way."

"Really?" Leola bit back. "Have you ever invited any of them over for one of your fancy Sterling parties I have heard so much about? Have you ever sat down and had a drink with any of them or maybe played a bit of golf with them on these fancy lawns of yours?"

Davis stays mute as she goes on.

"These people are not your friends. They are just people who serve you hand over foot while they can hardly put food on the table for their children to eat. What is this? What are you trying to do here?" she demands. "Clarence was so right – and it did not even take you a day. What kind of game are you playing, sir? I do not know, but I would like to leave NOW, and I am not going to ask again. If I have to walk, so be it!"

Leola stalks off to the car, biting back tears as she tries to save some dignity. Jupiter is waiting with the door open, outraged that this is happening to Leola, but as one of the club's doormen, he knows he cannot do anything for her. Davis runs out after her. A crowd builds to watch the spectacle. Davis sees the gathering onlookers and stops to shout, "What are all you staring at? Go on about your business!"

He runs around to the driver's side of the car, gets in, and speeds off. As they drive, no words are spoken. Once the country club has disappeared behind them, Leola starts to wipe the tears from her face and regain her composure. Davis just stares straight ahead down the road. After about a mile, he pulls off the side of the road abruptly. Leola grabs her purse and stares at Davis, utterly confused now. He looks over to her. She waits for an explanation, an apology, something. Davis looks at her and starts, "You just think you have me all figured out, don't you?"

Startled by his outburst, Leola stays quiet. He continues, "That whole speech you gave me about those people not being people I consider friends? Well, you know nothing about me, so I will thank you not to come to conclusions that you know nothing about! I do consider those colored people my friends. Hell, I grew up with most of them! When I would fall down, they were the ones to pick me up! When I had no one to play with, they came out and played games with me!" he ranted. "No, I have not invited them to a 'fancy Sterling party', as you put it, but those are not my parties! Those are my family's parties. And, in case you have not noticed, this is Texas and the Deep South. And this is how it is done and has always been done! I don't make the rules here, Okay?"

"What is this all about?" Leola demands, trying to get to the bottom of all this.

"It is just not that simple," he replies.

Leola once again asks, "What is this all about?" But, as he starts to say something else, she interrupts him, and asks again, "*Davis*, what is this all about?"

"OK, OK, OK!" Davis shouts, rubbing his hands through his hair. "Please give me a chance to sit down with you and I will tell you everything," he says. When he sees Leola has calmed down and feels his own heart slow, he starts again. "But you have to know that this is not how I intended the evening to go. It never dawned on me that the club was restricted."

"What were you thinking?"

"Well, I was trying to impress you, to be honest, with a nice surprise," Davis tells her.

"Well," says Leola as she takes a deep breath and starts to fix her face, "that was a surprise, for sure."

She gives him a small smile, softly smacking him on the top of his hand.

"Well, it seems that you still owe me a dinner and explanation, and I owe you an interview about the *Catfish*. At this point, I think I would like to choose what and where we eat. Your surprises are going to get the both of us killed, and that's not the kind of surprise I need today."

She slaps his hand again, and Davis smiles in return.

"Just tell me where to go."

Leola leads him to a place that she, Clarence and Isaac go to all the time – a roadside smokehouse in the colored part of town. When they drive up, people immediately start gathering around the car. Davis, although a world traveler, is nervous in this situation, even though this is his hometown. It's in a place he has never been to, nor would ever think to go.

Leola gets out of the car and starts to walk to the counter. Davis sits in the car, not looking left or right. He tries not to make eye contact with anyone since he is not sure of his safety. Leola turns and sees that he has not even gotten out of the car, so she walks back. Opening the door, she asks, "Are you coming?"

"Do you think it is okay?"

"Are you kidding me?" she responds. "After what I just went through, you'd better follow me into the fires of hell if that is where I were to lead you! Besides, they have a lot more reason to be scared of you than you have to be scared of them. Now, be serious and come on in. I'm about to show you some real food."

Leola orders the rib special for the both of them – to go. They take their meals back to the Buick and head for the shore of a nearby lake.

"I didn't bring a blanket, so I hope you don't mind their raggedy wooden tables," Leola says. Taking in the view, Davis nods his approval.

Once they set a proper table, the interview finally begins. Davis starts from the beginning, telling her all about his father's challenge. He talks about his plan to bring the paper into the modern post-war world, kicking and screaming if need be, and how this is his opportunity to do just that, under the radar. In return Leola tells him all about the *Catfish* and her father and family. Davis sympathizes with her and talks about his family. Leola also tells him about the awful fight she had with Clarence. Davis is sympathetic, but he's also relieved to find out that she and Clarence are not romantically involved. They end up finding out that, although they are from very different backgrounds, they have had a lot of the same hurdles. Leola is pleased to discover a bit of what this man is all about. Davis is pleased to get his story. They sit there for hours until the sun is almost gone.

"Well, Davis, I think it is about time you got me home. It would not be proper for me to be out here by the lake at night with a man, interview or not," Leola smiles.

Davis smiles back and looks into her eyes. "I know. But I am not quite ready for it to end yet. I guess if I am going to be reporting on the team, I am going to have to see you frequently to interview you. I'll need to find out what's going on, won't I?" he says as he opens her door for her to get in.

"Well, yes, I suspect that is true," she responds, touching his hand. Davis slides across the hood on his way back to his side of the car, showing off a bit. Leola laughs. But, on the way home her smile begins to fade. Leola knows she has a big problem awaiting her. She said some nasty things to Clarence, and she knows he is not one to take that kind of talk lightly. After all, he was right; she was way out of line. She knows she cannot do all of this without her best friend and business partner.

CHAPTER THIRTEEN

AN EMERGENCY MEETING

"I am very busy, gentlemen," Hunter Davis says as he looks up from his work at a small group of local businessmen, motioning Alice to close the door to his office. "You know it isn't proper business etiquette to stop by unannounced and without an appointment. I have a paper to run. But since you are here, what I can I do for you?"

"Now, Hunter, I know we didn't make an appointment. But this is urgent, and we needed to speak with you immediately," says a tallish man, stepping in front of the others in his posse. He sports heavy jowls and a head that shines like polished oak.

So, what's on your mind, fellas?" Hunter asks with an exaggerated sigh.

"We're having an emergency committee meeting tonight," Robert Prichard answers. Robert is the owner of Prichard Motors, one of Houston's most prominent car dealerships. "We have been instructed to get some information from you so immediate action can be taken."

"Action?" Hunter repeats shuffling some papers. "In regard to what? Look, you are going to have to make yourself a bit more clear, gentlemen. I really don't have an inkling of what you're talking about, and I don't have time to play guessing games."

"Surely, you've heard about the goings-on last night at the country club with Davis?" says John Frost, a big-time farmer and rancher. Hunter helped him establish his minor agricultural empire with some favorable press coverage fifteen years ago.

Hunter suddenly stops thumbing through papers and stares at the group as if he were studying them like specimens in a mason jar. The mention of his son's name cuts through any previous distractions. "Well, gentlemen, you have my attention now. What about my son do you all need to discuss with me in an emergency meeting?"

Robert steps up and takes the floor. He recites the details from the country club debacle as he heard them. As Robert works through the details, Alice sits on the other side of the solid oak door with the intercom engaged, taking careful notes, something she does every time Hunter has a business meeting – planned or otherwise. A meticulous record keeper and innate journalist, Hunter insists on notes for all his meetings. He has an archive of meeting notes in an extensive filing system.

Hunter sits patiently and listens to the account unfold, showing no emotion one way or another. He hardly even blinks as he listens. His stillness has the effect he intended, which is to make the men uneasy. They know they are talking to the most powerful man in Houston and they are talking to him about what they believe are his son's indiscretions. Hunter allows them to finish before he utters a single sound. He has learned never to react before all information has been presented.

"So, what do you need from me in all this?"

Robert is baffled by Hunter's question. "Well . . . because this kind of behavior cannot be tolerated; something has to be done. All due respect, Hunter, we cannot allow Davis or anyone else to think that they can do these kinds of things and get away with them."

"Hunter, we know this is your boy," Frost interjects, "and that will be taken into consideration. But action must be taken; niggers need to be put in their place."

"We can't allow coloreds to think they can just walk in the front door of our country club!" a man who has been silent adds. "They're already getting too big for their britches."

"It's true," Robert says. "You know that these niggers around here are starting to think they have the right to go places they got no permission going to. They're out there conducting themselves, like they're in the right, and we ain't gonna have that in Houston. It has to stop, or we are gonna end up no better than the North, where all those nigger-lovers let that kind of stuff go on."

As his face reddens just above his nose, Hunter asks again, "What do you want from me?"

"We want permission to talk to Davis and let these things be known. We want to find out who this colored woman is and do what we would do to any other colored who thinks they should be treated like a white . . . like one of our own," Frost explains.

"You know how this works, Hunter," Robert says. "It has to be done to these niggers in order to keep them in their place, and it has to be done now."

With his eyes trained on Robert, Hunter collapses back in his chair. Behind his pursed lips, his teeth are grinding. "So let me get this straight, boys; you want me to let you rough up my son to get the name of this colored woman so you can dress in your little ghost suits and go burn a cross in front of her house to send her a message?"

"Hunter, you know how things are done here," Frost replies defensively. "I would hate for your lack of cooperation to make this an even bigger issue than your son has already made it."

Hunter reaches over and turns off the intercom before letting out his bellowing response. "Let me tell you a few things that I want you to take back to your group because I don't think you realize who you are messing with, gentlemen. Now, I do not know what is going on with my boy, and he and I will have a good talking-to. But he will have that talk with me, not with you or any of your other lackey clowns, you comprehend? I don't care if Davis set that damn country club on fire; he is a Sterling, and NO ONE threatens a Sterling in this town. Hell, not even in this state!"

"We did this out of respect for the fact that you are a Sterling," Frost snaps back. Hunter's eyes cut from Robert to him.

"Since you were so kind in coming to tell me this, I am going to return the favor. I don't know what Davis is up to, but, before I let any of this happen to him, I will set this town ablaze," he admonishes, his tone as hard as his glare. "I helped create every damned one of you, and believe me, I will destroy you just as fast. Do you know what happens when a business can't advertise, gentlemen? Or when people stop buying your goods?" Hunter pauses to let his threat sink in and then continues, "I have dirty details on all of you: every corrupt business deal and every settled lawsuit, not to mention the names of every half-breed child you have running around here." His eyes fall on Frost at his last statement.

"If Davis gets so much as a curt greeting from one of you cowards, I will report everything I have on you, including the name of each and every member of your little cross-burning group. You're too afraid to show your faces when you're doing your dirty work, tormenting people while you hide under your pointy hoods. But I'm not afraid to put your damn faces in print, I'll tell you that."

From outside, Alice can hear Hunter's raised voice and so can several others. She shoos the eavesdroppers along. "This is none of your business; get back to your work, or Mr. Sterling will hear about it."

"Now, Hunter, there is no reason to fly off the handle," Robert says, trying to regain control of the situation he came into with so much poise and control. "This is really more about the colored girl than Davis."

"Is that right?" Hunter responds. "This is about the colored girl now? Because that is not what it sounded like to me when you came in here spitting out your veiled threats. You pay real close attention to what I'm about to say, boys. I want you to bring this message back with you. If my family or anyone involved, including those coloreds, gets as much as a long stare, I will blow the lid off of every shady thing you have ever done in this city. Do you understand me, gentlemen? And I mean it. Now, get the hell out of my office!"

In consternation, the group turns to leave. Robert starts to make a reply, but Hunter stops him.

"Oh, and Frost, if you ever wear that logo to my office again," he says, pointing to the secret KKK logo embroidered on his shirt pocket, "your name will go on the top of the list, in bold and on the front page! I hope my point is well-taken, gentlemen." No one dares utter a word. Each man knows that Hunter is very serious and that he has the resources and information to make good on his threat. They have seen him do it to others – for different reasons.

With nothing left to say to the group, Hunter calls out to Alice.

"What can I do for you, sir?" she answers.

"These men are leaving," Hunter tells her.

"This way, gentlemen," Alice states firmly. Robert turns to say something again, and again he is thwarted.

"Now!" Hunter bellows.

Robert is the last man out of the office. Just before he crosses the threshold, Hunter says one last thing. "Oh, and Robert, don't think anyone has forgotten your affinity for colored girls. Keep that in mind as you toss around your threats about my boy. I'm sure the people who just love to buy your cars would be very interested in knowing a few behind-the-scene details."

After seeing the group out, Alice returns and shuts the door. "What do you want to do, sir?"

"I am going to need you to call my wife and tell her that I am going to be working late tonight. And I am going to need you to work late too."

"Sir?"

"We are going to their goddamn meeting tonight, and I am going to look all those people right in the face and dare them to take this any further."

"Do you think that is wise?" Alice asks.

"I have more information on these people than you could ever imagine. So much, that it would start a battle the likes of which hasn't been seen since the Civil War," Hunter tells her. "And that information goes all the way to the state house – hell, all the way to Washington. The last thing those people are going to want is this bunch of yokels blowing it all up in their faces."

"What about Davis?" Alice asks. "Would you like to speak to him?"

"No. He doesn't need to know about this meeting," he tells her. "Although I don't know what in hell he was thinking. He's growing some wings, you know, and I want to see if he is going to stick with it and become a real man."

"Okay, then."

"I will warn him in my own way," he tells Alice, as if he needs to explain. "I told him I would not interfere, and, beyond making sure he is safe, I am not going to."

"But don't you think that he stepped over his bounds a little, bringing a colored girl into Rolling Lawns as a guest? I mean really, he should know better than that."

"My boy has been away from Houston a long time, and he sees things a bit different these days."

"But he . . ."

"I know. I know," Hunter says shaking his head. "I don't know what he was thinking either, but he needs to become his own man, even if I don't like it. These are the first signs of his doing just that and everyone needs to stay out of the way, including me." He paused for a minute before telling her, "But set up a lunch with him, so I can feel out what in hell he is up to."

Hunter makes a few calls to find out that the 'special meeting' is being held in the whites-only public library. As Alice listens to him on the phone gathering information, she becomes more uncomfortable about attending the meeting with her boss. She fears that riling the Klan could put her in their crosshairs. Besides the danger, she is afraid that people might get the wrong idea about her own views of segregation. She voices her concerns to Hunter, but he quickly brushes them off.

"I need you there to take notes," he says. "I'll be clear that you are attending the meeting in a work capacity only." Alice considers a rebuttal, but she knows it is futile. Instead, she puts on her pea coat and grabs her notebook.

As they sit in the car outside the library waiting for everyone to go in, Alice asks, "Don't you think that we should get in there so we have seats? I mean, what if we can't find a seat, or we have to interrupt the meeting looking for one. I just don't want to . . ."

With a sinister smile, Hunter replies, "Don't worry. I have a few friends who will make sure to save a few seats in the very front row so the leadership will have no choice but to look me right in the eye."

"I heard them say that you have been to several of these meetings. Are you a member?" she asks.

"I have been to several meetings, but this group started off as a group committed to maintaining the integrity of our communities. It isn't that anymore. It's turned into something else."

Alice stays quiet, so Hunter continues, "I do believe that people should stay with their own kind, but I have to admit that I have become fond of several coloreds. And you really do have to look at each person as a separate situation and not lump them all together."

"Fond of coloreds?" Alice asks, staring inquisitively at Hunter. "What do you mean, fond of?"

"Well, I know for a fact that you are fond of several yourself," he replies.

"Mr. Sterling, I beg your pardon," Alice retorts. "Although I am under your employ, sir, please don't presume that you know that much about me, thank you kindly."

"It's true. I have seen it with my own eyes, Alice," he challenges her.

"Please give me two examples of such a thing," she demands.

"Jeffrey, for one," he responds.

"You mean Jeffrey Fields, our elevator man?"

"Yes," he replies.

"I have seen you give him food, clothing for his family, and gifts for his birthday. Now, it may or may not be what you would give a proper white person, but, nevertheless you've done it for Jeffrey, Alice. And

God help anyone who treats him wrongly: you are all over them. I have seen that with my own eyes," Hunter tells her.

"Well, Jeffrey is a special person," she replies, her eyes darting everywhere but Hunter's face. "He is always kind, he knows his place, and he is always respectful. Jeffrey is willing to help me with anything I need, even on his days off. He is one of the only colored men I trust."

"That is not true," Hunter argues, "You go on and on about the man who works in your garden, and you go on and on about your maid. During bad storms, you even let her stay at your house!"

"Well, those are all special situations too, Mr. Sterling," Alice insists.

"I am not saying these are bad things at all. In fact, I am saying just the opposite. I see the problem as the fact that we lump all these coloreds together and maybe we shouldn't. I don't lump every white person into the same category or go into every encounter I have with a white person expecting them to act a certain way, so why do we do it with colored folks? That's all I'm saying here, Alice. I'm not painting you with the same brush. I'm trying to tell you that I am also fond of many colored people myself.

"I adore all the colored children of my house staff and make sure all of them get to go to school because, like their mamas and daddies, they will most likely work for this family. And I want educated coloreds working my land, people who will understand when I give them instructions about something. I'm not saying I want them making decisions, but I do not want any ignorant coloreds on my staff. Plus, they are lovely children. They can't help how they were born."

"Well, I guess when you look at it that way, I can see your point," Alice admits. "I do have coloreds that I trust and am even fond of. But these people here tonight don't think that way, sir. They are dangerous and would just as soon string somebody up for getting uppity – even you for liking or helping them, if it weren't for your status here in Houston. And as much as I like some of those colored folks, I don't plan on dying for any of them."

"Neither do I," Hunter tells her.

"Look, Alice. This falls on my shoulders. Trust me. This goes much deeper than these local whites and they know that just as much as I do. I have laid down the law with them. My attending this meeting is just insurance that they understand that I do mean business. This is a man thing, so don't you worry your pretty little mind about this.

If someone even looks at you funny, you just let me know, and it will be taken care of."

Alice knows how powerful Hunter is in the Lone Star State, and she also trusts his word. Her anxiety finally wanes about attending the meeting. She trusts Hunter will keep her safe.

"But I will tell you one thing," Hunter says.

"What's that?" Alice asks.

"For Houston to be taken seriously and to be a major player in this country, this kind of foolishness has to stop. All this cross burning and lynching has to stop. Things are changing, whether we like it or not. And we are either on board, or we will get left behind – and that's a fact," he says, as he gets out of the car. Alice follows closely behind.

The meeting has already started when Hunter and Alice walk in. Someone at the podium is ranting about how certain behavior cannot be tolerated and something must be done. When Hunter and Alice start down the aisle to their seats in the front row, the person speaking stops in mid-sentence. Everyone in the room traces the path of the speaker's eyes and a vibrating mumble fills the place. The board members, who are running the meeting, begin shifting in their seats and exchanging worried glances. Hunter says nothing as he sits down. Alice sits down too, confident and prepared to take notes, her steno pad and pen at the ready to write down everything said. The room is filled with business owners, police, politicians, firemen, and even schoolteachers.

"Mr. Sterling, we happen to have a secretary," Robert says. "I am sure we can provide you with the notes from this meeting in the next day or two."

Hunter lights a cigar and replies, "I understand that your organization has someone to take notes, but likely no names or details will be provided to me. A good newsman always makes sure he has all the details for a good headlining front-page story."

A few people make for the door at Hunter's comment. Hunter watches them leave and winks at Robert. "Now, please continue with your meeting."

The board members, including the mayor of Houston and Texas Senator John Mitchell, look uneasy in their seats on stage. As more people begin leaving the meeting, Senator Mitchell, who has aspirations of heading to Washington, D.C., addresses the board.

"May I make a motion?" the senator inquires.

"The chair recognizes Senator Mitchell," Robert announces.

"I would like to make a motion to withdraw the Rolling Lawns Country Club's previous motion and close the matter entirely. I am sure that it was an isolated incident, and I, for one, would like to avoid any more discourse or misunderstandings that may be developing here." Hunter does not take his eyes off the senator as he speaks.

Robert Prichard immediately seconds the motion.

"Well, unless there are any objections," the board chair says. Hunter looks at the board and around the room. No one makes a sound. It's as if the air has been sucked from the lungs of everyone present. "Then, the motion is withdrawn and this matter is closed," the board chair declares.

Hunter stands up and announces, "Gentlemen, I trust that this matter will never be brought up again. And, if it is, all pleasantries will no longer apply. I trust we are all clear on this matter." Alice scurries to record every word, but Hunter stops her, saying, "Let's go, Alice."

As they stand up to exit the meeting, Alice feels goose bumps spread across her flesh. She has never realized the level of authority her boss has. She is overwhelmed by the scene she just witnessed. As they walk toward the door, several people follow them, in a show of support for Hunter Davis and the *Houston Star*.

Halfway down the aisle, Hunter matter-of-factly turns around and addresses the group one more time. "Oh, and by the way, my secretary is here because I made her come. This is part of her job, and I am 100% sure she would rather be any place but here – just for the record."

He turns and walks out; Alice just stands for a moment, mute and paralyzed. She suddenly feels embarrassed that he brought it up, but she smiles. It was, after all, just what she had asked him to do in the car. Chasing after him, she follows along with several other people. Outside, people shake hands with Hunter, and they go their separate ways. Hunter smiles at the group and announces that he appreciates their show of support, but he must be on his way; then, he slips into the car. Alice gets in the car after him and just stares.

"What is it?" Hunter asks with a slight grin.

"You never even addressed the group and they closed the matter."

"Alice, here is where you can learn something. I did address the group," Hunter tells her.

"When?"

"I addressed the group when I gave my message to the gentlemen who visited the office this afternoon. I knew that, right away, everyone would start talking about this matter. My message to them all would travel – and fast. Sometimes, the only way to win the game is to not play it at all. And when it comes to my family, the game is over before it starts. Now, let's get you home to your lovely family."

Alice smiles and nods. She looks out the window at the town that she now realizes is in the palm of her boss's hand.

CHAPTER FOURTEEN

A RETURN TO ROLLING LAWNS

"What can I do for you, son?" Hunter asks. His question is almost rhetorical in nature. He knows exactly why Davis is calling. He is calling because Alice has just informed him that he is to meet his father at Rolling Lawns for lunch that week. That is the last place in Houston where Davis would choose to have lunch, but Hunter was going to get to the bottom of whatever happened at the club. He thought returning to the scene of the crime, so to speak, was the best way to gather all the necessary details and to get more than one perspective on the whole event. He also knew, when he told Alice to make reservations, that his son would be confused and reluctant. As always, Hunter was right.

"Daddy, I can only imagine that this lunch is about my little run-in at the club, and that's fine. But do you mind if we have lunch somewhere else? I respect that you need me to tell you want happened, but I don't understand why we have to meet there. I really just don't want to deal with any of those people at the moment."

"Now that you mention it, son, I think I did hear something about some small happening that went on with you there. I can see why you'd rather not return, but this is an opportunity for you to learn something. You hear? You are a Sterling!"

"Yes, Daddy, I am well aware of my heritage, but what does that have to do with going to a bigoted country club that nearly ruined a professional relationship?"

"That club has been a Sterling stomping ground since it was established. You don't think some small episode is going to change that, do you?"

"No, but –"

"Look, son, if you fall off the horse, you don't wait six weeks before you get back on; you get right up and dust yourself off! You look that horse straight in the eye to let him know that you are not going to put up with that! You get back on immediately and ride him until he is too tired to fight back!"

"This isn't a horse, Dad, this is . . ."

"Of course it is, Davis. That is what you are going to do with these people, do you hear me? This is what we are going to do, and we are going to do it together! I know you have all kinds of scenarios worked up in that thick skull of yours, but I assure you that it will not be as bad as you imagine."

"I don't have any scenarios built up in my head, Daddy; I just don't want to go back there," Davis protests.

"What? Are you just never going to go there again? What kind of message does that send?"

"I don't think I was trying to send any message at all."

"Everything you do sends a message when you are a Sterling, son. So when we have lunch at the club, you walk in like you own the place. You look everyone in the eye and greet them like the Sterling you are. Watch their reaction; I think you will be surprised."

Hunter knows his own message from the 'emergency meeting' has been spreading like wildfire, so he knows that people will treat Davis with the respect that the family deserves. He only hopes that Davis doesn't catch wind of the secret meeting while they are out, since he told him that he wouldn't interfere. He trusts his son, but he knows that Davis still doesn't grasp how to wield the full power of the Sterling name and that, even if he did know how, Davis is not the kind of man who likes to use his name to get his way. Still, Hunter wants Davis to *know* how to get his way, if he should ever need to in the future. He may want his son to grow his own wings, but, at the end of the day, Davis is his only son and Hunter cannot help but protect him.

"Well, if you think this won't cause more of a commotion, I am fine with it," Davis tells his father.

"Good," Hunter says, "I will see you there at two o'clock on the nose."

The thought of walking into Rolling Lawns makes Davis's stomach turn, but he doesn't want to let his father down. He also knows that his father is right to a degree; the longer he stays away, the harder it will be to return. As imperfect as it is, Davis looks at this lunch as an opportunity to come clean and explain the whole episode to his father. He has no idea how much his father knows, so he will play it by ear.

Hunter arrives at Rolling Lawns at twenty before two. When he arrives, the same club director, the same squat man with the same strained expression, greets him. James Conlon's nasal voice is slightly shaky. He seems to plead more than speak when he talks to Hunter. As he suspected, Director Conlon's behavior confirms to Hunter that he has already received the message.

"Mr. Sterling, it is very good to see you."

Hunter is unaffected by the niceties. He responds brusquely and treats James like just another staff person. Once again, Hunter Sterling is acting with purpose; he has not yet finished delivering his message to all who need to receive it. He needs to be sure that all of Rolling Lawns knows how to treat his son by the time he leaves.

"I trust our regular table is set up and ready for my lunch with my son."

"Your son?" James almost recoils at the words.

"Yes, my son," Hunter repeats firmly. "Davis Sterling. You know him; he has been coming here since he was old enough to eat solid food."

Hunter inches himself into an uncomfortable closeness with James and says with some amount of disdain and impatience, "I trust this is not a problem? Otherwise, I would have to go to the board meeting and request some changes around here. Mr. Conlon, I would not care if my son was trying to burn this place to the ground; I encourage you to never forget that Davis is a Sterling and should be regarded as such at all times. And, for the record, if I find that he feels mistreated or uncomfortable in this club at any time, I am going to hold you personally responsible. I assure you, you do not want to be the bearer of that burden."

"This is not something that you are going to ever have to worry about here, sir," Conlon replies, cowering in Hunter's shadow. "I regret the situation ever happened at all and was not fully aware of what transpired. If I had been, I would have handled it very differently."

The two stood in tense silence. Hunter offered no sign of a response. He hardly acknowledged Conlon's words. Through nerves and a desire to clear his name, the frazzled director continued, "But please understand, sir, that I neither own nor create the rules of this club. I am just here to enforce them." The corners of Hunter's mouth drop a centimeter lower, letting Conlon know that his last comment had not settled well. Hunter's eyes narrowed.

Frantically fumbling for words of reconciliation, Conlon tries again at a peace offering. "But, I am sure that exceptions and special arrangements can be made."

Hunter's face softens, and his grimace slowly transforms to what almost looks like a smile. At this, Conlon's expression also loses its nervous intensity. Hunter steps back and lands a paw on Conlon's shoulder. The thud nearly knocks the man over, but he catches himself and smiles the way a child would for family photos – in an awkward and unnatural manner.

"GOOD, that is all I ask, sir, and thank you for understanding," Hunter says. "Now I would like to say hello to a few people before my son arrives, if you don't mind."

"Of course. Your table is always ready for you, Mr. Sterling. Have a wonderful lunch, sir," Director Conlon responds. He makes a quick exit, relieved to be away from the searing gaze of Hunter Sterling.

As Hunter walks through the dining room, people go out of their way to greet him. "Good to see you out of the office!" one man says as he stands to shake Hunter's hand. "So good to see you," another man says. "Well, Hunter Sterling! Taking a little time off to eat, are you?" a local businessman remarks as Hunter passes. Hunter is fully aware of the purpose behind their exaggerated greetings. He also knows they have not chosen his side; he has forced them to take it.

In his conversations, Hunter makes sure to mention Davis and how much he looks forward to their lunch together. Everyone reacts just the way Hunter has planned. With the assurance that Davis will not have any problems at the country club, Hunter heads for his usual table to have a scotch and water and wait for his son. He knows that this is an opportunity to teach Davis some valuable skills, and he wants to make sure that Davis gets the full benefit of his years of experience.

While Hunter sips his drink, pleased with his accomplishments, Davis sits in his office staring at the clock as he dreads the coming lunch. He does not look forward to encountering all the people at the club who were part of the episode with Leola just days before. But the driver his father has sent arrives and Davis knows it's time to prepare for all of it. Actually, more than fear of rejection by anyone at the club, Davis fears losing his temper and embarrassing his father yet again. As he sits in the backseat of the car and watches the city pass by, he begins to wish he had never returned to Houston.

He cannot believe that simply bringing a client to lunch has caused so much chaos. He could have done the same thing in a hundred different cities in the North with no consequence – a side-glance, maybe, but nothing like what happened at Rolling Lawns. Davis realizes that he had forgotten where he was when he invited Leola to the club. Now, he was paying for that forgetfulness. All he wanted to do was show off a bit and impress her. He thought his childhood haunt would be a great place to do that. But Davis received a serious lesson that day. The Sterling name was powerful indeed, but in this case, only after the fact. The traditions and bigotry of Houston and the "new" South would continue to act on their own momentum until far more powerful forces could lead them to change on their own.

As he thinks about the event that he will soon be explaining to his father, Davis also realizes that he did have some idea of how all those country club snobs would react. In fact, this was one of the reasons he took Leola there in the first place. He wasn't really some innocent bystander after all. He wanted to force people to overlook the fact that she was black because he was a Sterling. If club members had any reaction, he thought his family's reputation was strong enough for members to keep their thoughts private. He never expected the lesson he learned that day. He found out that racism is a stronger force than the nepotism that he thought would carry the day. He was learning about Rolling Lawns, about Houston, about his father, and about himself.

"Meeting with the big boss today?" his driver asks, breaking Davis away from his thoughts.

"Yes," Davis responds, forcing a smile.

"Must be nice to spend a little time away from the office with your old man."

"Sure," Davis replies with as much cordiality as he can muster. In fact, there was nothing nice about his meeting, as far as he could tell. He knows his father is going to light into him for embarrassing the family name and is sure his father has chosen this place just to teach him a lesson. As much as he would like to tell the driver to turn around and take him back to the office, or home, or anywhere his father wasn't waiting to browbeat him, he cannot do it. Davis knows he must take this day and the uncomfortable meeting like a man and move on from it. To get past the fire, he has to first walk through it. He knows his father is calculating and has most likely set something up to make him feel uncomfortable as a way to drive his lesson home. Thinking about what Hunter's lesson might be, Davis focuses on how his father always makes sure that all his ducks are in a row before coming into any situation. The more Davis thinks about it, the more he is convinced that this will be his father's lesson.

As his mind wanders, Davis realizes that the lesson he has to learn isn't coming from his father – not this time. He knows that it wasn't a smart move bringing Leola to Rolling Lawns. If he were to do it all over again, he would never have attempted to take her there, not for his own sake, but for hers. Davis suddenly feels less concern for his father or the family name than he does for Leola. He is embarrassed and ashamed that he put her through all of that just to make a point – that without her consent, he used Leola to make some sort of statement about right and wrong. Whatever he was trying to do, Davis should never have made such a decision without thinking of how it would affect her. He is thankful that she forgave him, and he realizes that he should have listened to her in the first place when she expressed her concerns about the club.

The sound of the cobblestones under the car wheels brings Davis back to where he is: at the front door of Rolling Lawns, once again. Jupiter, as pleasant as ever, greets him with a smile as he opens the car door. Davis feels too ashamed to meet Jupiter's gaze. But he doesn't want to seem rude, so he forces himself to exchange hellos. After this first painful encounter, he knows things will only get worse. He braces himself, vowing that, no matter what these people say or how they look at him, he has to maintain his composure and remember that he is representing his family. It may be too late to avoid the pain that he's already caused Leola, but, today, he wants to make sure that he doesn't embarrass his father.

As he walks into the club, the hostess greets him. She seems cordial as she asks if he wouldn't mind waiting a moment.

"Not at all," Davis forces out. "Can I ask why? My father should have a table reserved."

"The director of the club has asked to see you upon your arrival," she replies with an overstated smile that has a chilling effect on Davis.

Davis takes a deep breath as the hostess disappears. He knows this will be his first and greatest test of the day. As the director walks toward him, his heart beats faster, and his temper begins to stir. He takes a few deep breaths to keep his composure.

"Mr. Sterling," the director says, extending his hand, "I was hoping that I could take a second to speak with you about what happened the other evening."

"Mr. Conlon, I am not sure that now is the best time to do this. I am here to meet my father for lunch. This is not something I want to discuss with you right now."

"I understand, sir," Conlon replies, "but this will take just a minute. I would like to apologize for the incident. You had arranged a private area, and I should have asked about any 'special circumstances' you may have had. If I had done so, all of this could have been avoided. You and your family are founding members of the club, and I would hate it if you felt that I had offended you or your family in any way."

For a moment Davis is shocked, but then he is hit with a piercing lucidity. "Let me guess. My father has already arrived, am I right?"

"Yes, sir," James responds. "But that has nothing to do with this apology. I can assure you, sir, I truly do regret the incident and hope that you can forgive us for any embarrassment we may have caused you or your lovely guest."

"My lovely guest?" Davis asks. "You found her to be lovely, did you?"

"Yes, sir. She was very much so, and I hope that we can make arrangements in the future to correct the situation without causing another uproar here at the club. Perhaps a late night dinner or something along those lines?"

A thousand responses jump to the tip of Davis's tongue, but he bites them back and swallows so that they settle somewhere in the depths of his stomach – invisible to Director Conlon or anyone else. He takes a moment to prepare a response that will balance his own feelings with his responsibility of being a Sterling. The only thing that comes to mind is, "No, I do not think that will be necessary, Mr. Conlon. I have a strong feeling that particular young lady will want nothing to do with this place ever again. But I will relay the message that you find her 'lovely'."

"Very good, sir, and again, we do apologize," Conlon replies, pretending not to notice the hint of disdain and mockery in Davis's response. "Please come this way to your table."

On his way to the table, Davis receives the same reception as his father had. People all over the dining room extend hands and warm welcomes. Some ask if he'd like to play nine holes; others mention the newspaper and his position there. Davis knows that Hunter has done something to put this into motion, but he can't imagine what his father could have done to elicit this kind of mass acceptance. For these people, headstrong about the traditions of the South and Jim Crow, it must have taken a lot. Davis can't imagine an act of God having such an impact.

Davis looks across the room at his father, sitting at the table reading the paper. Hunter is not paying attention to what is going on. Smiling, Davis goes over to the table. His father looks up when he hears Davis approach.

"Just in time! I was getting hungry."

"I am too," Davis replies with a grin. "Let's order, shall we?"

As they eat their lunch, Davis occasionally glances around the room, expecting to see people staring at the two of them – pointing and whispering perhaps. But they are not; everyone is going about their business as usual. Davis looks at his father and says, "Okay, you have me here now. You have obviously said something to several people, which means you've heard what went on the other day. So what do you want to ask me?"

Hunter looks at him, fork in hand, still chewing his last bite. He swallows hard and says, "I heard a few things about what went on. My question is, what are you going to do? You know how the word spreads in cases like this."

Davis doesn't respond at first. He knows his father well enough to avoid answering a rhetorical question, so he keeps quiet, waiting for the onslaught. When it doesn't come, he asks, "And I assume this is why you have asked me here?"

"Partly," Hunter answers.

"So what is the other part?"

"The other part is I wanted to have lunch with my son and check in with him to make sure everything is alright. Nothing more to it. I know we don't see eye-to-eye on some things, but you are still my son, my only son."

Davis searches for words to respond to this unprecedented show of affection from his father, but he can find nothing to fit the occasion. Of all the conversations they've had over the years and all the emo-tions that have been part of them, sentimentality had never seeped in, not even once. To circumvent his loss of words about how he feels at the moment, Davis starts talking about the incident itself. Somehow this seems more comfortable territory than the one his father had just led them to, which is saying a lot since Davis had dreaded this topic more than any other in advance of lunch with his father.

"So what things did you hear?" Davis asks.

"That you tried to bring a colored girl here for dinner and people did not react very well," Hunter responds in a very calm and relaxed way. He pauses for a moment and then looks his son in the eye. "That's all I know."

Davis is surprised at how comfortable his father is with their conversation. "That's just a fragment of the incident. It is an accurate fragment, but it's really just the end of a longer story. I had actually made arrangements to have a private room that day for my guest and myself."

Hunter stops him. "I do not need to know the details of the whole thing. You are your own man."

That is the first time Davis has ever heard his father say anything like that. The sounds of the room suddenly recede into silence. And all Davis can hear is, "*You are your own man.*"

"You are going to make some mistakes, just like I did when I was your age," Hunter continues, "but you will learn from them as well. I am going to give you this advice, and then we will never have to speak about this again . . . if you don't want to, that is." Davis just nods and allows his father to continue.

"Now, I know you have traveled the world and seen a lot of things that most people in the South would never understand or even like, for that matter. I would include myself in that group to some degree. I'm no mindless oaf, like those hood-wearing buffoons lighting fires in innocent people's yards, but I recognize the parts of me that still cling to some of the traditions I've grown up with. My point is, I wanted you to take some time out of your life to travel and experience things I have not experienced. I wanted you to see the world past the borders of the South, past its traditions and mentalities. As hard as it is for me to admit that I am a product of my environment, I want you to know that I am glad that you see the world in a way that few people around here can. But, son, I also want you to be careful."

Although he is serious, Hunter is very relaxed. He's speaking with his son, not at him. Davis can feel the beginning of a new relationship with his father. But true to form, Hunter doesn't let his son continue musing about anything in private while the two of them are together.

His words become faster as he continues, "Now, son, I am not really sure what you are up to . . ."

Davis leans forward and opens his mouth to speak, but his father interrupts him. "And I am not asking to know. We made a deal, and I plan to stick by that deal, as much as I possibly can. But I want you to remember what I have to say right now . . . I want you to take it with you wherever you go. I want you to keep in mind that everything you write as a newsman will have an impact. One of the greatest responsibilities of a newsman is to understand that this is part of the job. When you write something, you start a chain reaction, and you never know how far that reaction will go or who it will touch. For every action, there is a reaction, which may not necessarily affect you, but could affect the people around you, as well as the people you are writing about. That is why it is so important that you think things through, son. Research and double-check your facts.

"I'm not sure what you were thinking when you brought the colored girl here, but you must understand, Davis, that your decision to bring her here can affect *her* – not just you or me or our family name – but *her*. Now, you are a Sterling and that means something in this town. But for her, she is just another colored woman, and, unfortunately, people are going to look at her like that."

Davis's face begins to burn at his father's last comment, not because he is angry with his father, but because he is angry that his father is right in diagnosing the disease of the South. He suddenly feels claustrophobic in the restaurant – hell, in the city, in Texas, in the entire region. He tries to focus on his father, but the walls seem to close in on him.

"Of course, I am not saying that it's right. I know you won't ever see her like these dumb yahoos see her, but they will – you understand? Just her being here and trying to come into the club, she could be beaten or worse. I mean this, Davis; these clowns are still stringing men and women up for no reason other than their skin color, and no one is exempt from their indiscriminate hate, regardless of who brings them to an all-white establishment. I know that you're aware of this, but I wanted to remind you. When you take actions that may not have any consequences for you, you must think about the other people with you and how what you do will affect them. Neither of us can be around to protect everyone all of the time. Do you hear what I'm saying to you, son?"

He had heard every word his father said, although Davis was only starting to consider the weight of his actions and what they could mean for other people. He had never thought about his father protecting more than his family and his business. And yet here was Hunter Sterling, the public figure and father, talking about himself as a private man and how he understands the world. Davis is beginning to realize that there is so much about his father that he never knew – and needed to learn.

"Are you saying that you once had to protect someone?" Davis asked his father.

"I am not saying that at all, son. Please don't miss the message here, okay?"

"Yes, right," Davis agrees, letting go of his inquiries and letting his father continue revealing himself in new and mysterious ways. "I understand what you are saying, and I will think long and hard about it," he promises.

"Good," Hunter says, placing his palms on the table to indicate he is pleased with the outcome of the conversation. "This subject is closed now, as far as I'm concerned. So let's finish this wonderful lunch and maybe even go for a few rounds of golf."

"Sounds good to me," Davis replies.

After lunch and nine holes, the two men leave in their separate cars to go their separate ways, like business partners are expected to do at Rolling Lawns. On his drive back to the office, however, Davis cannot stop wondering what his father had done in the past, what kinds of adventures he may have had as a young man, and what they taught him. As a journalist, Davis cannot stand having only a few pieces of the story. He wants to know the rest – the parts he knows Hunter would never tell him. But he is certain there is so much more. He knows the only way to get to the truth is to go to the ultimate source of gossip at work . . . the secretarial pool.

Davis gets back to his office and tells Georgia Mae that he needs to have a meeting with her as he passes her desk.

"Yes, sir?" she says as she closes the door.

"Davis, not sir, Georgia Mae," he reminds her. She nods sheepishly.

"Now, I know you know everything that is going on in this place, including the lunch that I just had with my father," he says.

Georgia Mae doesn't say anything right away. After a long, uncomfortable silence, she asks, "Do you have a question?"

"You know I have a question and I know you have the answer," Davis replies.

"Well, after you ask the question, I will know better if I have the right answer," Georgia Mae says, in a sassy but playful way – assertive, but kind, the qualities Davis has always loved about her.

"I want to know what you know about my visit to the country club the other evening and what transpired with my daddy after that."

Georgia Mae looks around the office as if someone might be hiding behind the curtains or under the wallpaper. She leans in toward Davis and whispers, "If I tell you this, Davis Sterling, you can never divulge where you got this information if you choose to use it." Davis agrees.

Georgia Mae tells him that she has heard this from Alice, who accompanied Hunter to a special meeting that was held at the library, a meeting to discuss the incident with Leola. She explained the entire meeting just as Alice had told her – about the nervous board members and the way Hunter didn't even have to talk to take care of everything and how people even followed him out in support.

"You mean they had a special town meeting about what happened?"

"I don't think it was necessarily a 'town' meeting, but a lot of the same people from town were there, so I am told," Georgia Mae explains.

She describes how his father put the whole town on notice that, if anything should happen to Davis or the colored girl involved, Hunter would publish the names of every Klan member in the area and name their half-breed children on the front page of his newspaper and that he dared anyone to test him on that. Davis sees now why everyone was acting toward him the way they were, treating him as if nothing had ever happened. Davis is shocked that his father would do something like that for him, but he is also touched and grateful that he did it, not only for him, but for Leola as well. This makes him second guess his selfish plan. He knows now that he is going to have to rethink the whole thing before moving forward. He sees that he has put something in motion that could get people hurt, even though that was never his goal. He has to come up with a new plan – one that doesn't have so much risk behind it for others, especially Leola.

CHAPTER FIFTEEN

THE UNDERSTANDING

On a sunny August afternoon, Deacon receives a note from Davis.

Dear Deacon,

It seems to me that I really have not gotten a chance to have any in-depth conversations with you and, since my story is really going to be about the who, what, where, when, and why of the Catfish, I need to get to know you. I think we should meet and talk, but I feel some resistance. I hope we can meet at Saint Peters Park, Sunday at noon.

Thanks,
Davis Sterling

P.S. I would kindly thank you not to share the fact that we are meeting with Clarence, Isaac, or Leola. We can inform them later.

Deacon instantly panics, and, although Davis asked him not to share the letter, he goes straight to Clarence. Deacon trusts Clarence's advice; he has learned that Clarence is not only smart, but he has an old soul and understands things beyond his years. Leola knows this all too well, and she never makes a move without him.

"Clarence, look at this note I just got from Davis Sterling. What do you think it means? I know you told me to let you handle him when it comes to my personal stuff, but this guy is getting ready to just dive into the deep about my real life. Both you and I know that can't happen. What are we going to do if this guy goes digging too deep? It could destroy my family's farm business. As much as I would like to have my father know how much I love doing what I'm doing, this is not the way I want it to happen."

Clarence's heart drops to his stomach for a second as he reads the note. He reads it a second time before speaking. "You have to go meet him."

"You are coming with me, right?" Deacon replies.

"No, you read the note. I can't go with you," Clarence says, which makes Deacon even more anxious.

"You said that you would have my back on this stuff. What game are you playing at here? This is my life, Clarence, and my family's livelihood!"

"Calm down," Clarence tells him. "I do have your back – always. But here's what needs to happen . . . you need to talk with him and tell him just what you told me. That's the only way he is going understand how delicate this situation is – and whether he should still write about you as Deacon and your life with the *Catfish*."

"I'm not sure that will work," Deacon replies, "but I guess if I don't talk to him, he is just going to keep digging until he gets what he wants." Clarence just shakes his head *yes*.

After many nights of not sleeping, the day finally comes for Deacon to have a "Come to Jesus" talk with Davis. He has no idea how he is going to explain to the reporter that what Davis is proposing (putting his real story in the newspaper) could bring down the whole house of cards for him and, to be perfectly honest, for the team. There are laws about these things in Texas, and having more light shed on his situation could seriously upset some people and destroy a lot of lives. That is when it came to him. He knew how he would approach Davis with his concerns in a way that the reporter would understand.

Now, that he is feeling a bit better and his stomach has calmed, he heads off to Saint Peters Park for the meeting. As he reaches the park, he can see Davis in the distance sitting on a bench. He cannot help but be nervous and tentative about their meeting.

"Deacon, I'm so glad you decided to come and talk with me. I feel like, in all of the excitement of things, we have not really gotten to talk about you much. I want to make sure that I do all my homework and have a well-rounded story to tell." Davis gestures for Deacon to sit and pulls a cold soda out of a small cooler and hands it to him.

"Look, Davis, before we really get into this, I have a few things to say. I know you are a smart guy and I am sure you have done some . . . done some investigating into my life. But I need to say this to you right away. I really like my life right now, playing ball with the guys and learning from Clarence and Isaac, but most of all watching how Leola keeps this team going against all odds. Hell, I didn't even know a woman could do what she does and, man, she has really taken the bull by the horns." Once Deacon brings up Leola's name, Davis starts to pay close attention, just as Deacon hoped he would.

"However, if you do a story on me in the biggest paper in Texas and put it all out there, you could bring it all tumbling down. I would hate to have something I did, besides just being who I am – a beef and corn fed white boy playing on a Negro baseball team – destroy what that woman has built." Davis had always tried to be careful about how he reported because he had made a promise to Clarence and Leola, a ways back, about how he would do his reporting, about the goings on of the *Catfish*. So what Deacon was saying made him stop and think about what he was about to do.

"Look, Mr. Sterling, I think you know my name is not Deacon, and I am not from where I said I was from. But, for the *Catfish*, Leola, Clarence, and Isaac, that is exactly who I am and what my life has become. I know you are an upstanding guy, and I am not asking you to lie to your readers or your daddy. But I am asking you to please write your story about Deacon, not who I used to be. Write about who I am now. That can keep a lot of people from getting hurt."

"What do you mean?" Davis responds.

"Look, Mr. Sterling, let's not try to fool ourselves . . . as much as we like these folks, we have to understand the risks we are taking here. I suggest you take another look at the Jim Crow laws and think about exactly who all reads your paper and then ask me that again. It's so easy for us to forget the danger my friends are putting themselves in to interact with us – and us with them. This could bring ruin to my family's farm and their livelihood, not to mention get me killed. But most important, this could get the entire team hung from trees all over town in the blink of an eye."

"Then, why? Why do this? Why put your family, your future, your life all on the line for this?" Davis quickly turns the tables on Deacon as a good journalist does. "You are clearly a college boy with a good education, although I think sometimes you don't like to show it. You seem to come from a solid hard-working Christian family. Why take the chance?"

Without hesitation, Deacon responds, "Because I want to play with the best there is in baseball. No matter what all the white folks say, your newspaper prints, or the National League tries to sell, the Negro Leagues are where the best players are, hands down. If you can't see that, then I suggest you get another job, Davis, because you just don't have an eye for the game."

Deacon realizes that the people who are walking into the park are starting to take notice of his outburst, so he calms himself a bit. "I'm sorry, I got worked up," Deacon says to Davis. "It is just that baseball is my passion and, to be honest, I have learned more from these guys in the little time I've been with them than I learned in all the time I was playing college ball."

Davis looks at the passion in Deacon's eyes and he knows what he has to do. "Look, you are right. I cannot make this story just about you; it would put everyone in jeopardy, including Leola and Clarence, and I promised not to do that. I can figure out how to get the story across without putting everyone on the line." Davis can see the relief on Deacon's face and he seems to relax a little too.

"So what questions do you have for me?" Deacon asks Davis.

"I don't have any more questions." As Davis gets his stuff together, he says, "I have everything I need," and starts to walk away. Deacon looks confused as Davis turns back and smiles.

"Oh, and by the way," Davis walks back to the bench where Deacon is standing, "I can see that the Negro League has some of the best players there has ever been. It sickens me that the world will never see or understand that until it's too late. Why do you think I am still here and doing what I am doing? I started off on one track and quickly changed it once I saw these people, these players, and their passion for what they do. Baseball is in my blood too, and that's something we have in common along with making sure these people do well and stay safe. So now you know a bit more about me."

They smile at each other and shake hands as they come to a quiet understanding of each of their missions with the *Catfish*. Deacon smiles a bit to himself. He knows that, although Davis has a passion for baseball, most of Davis's talk was about Leola. And that is okay with him.

The first thing Deacon does after meeting with Davis is to stop by and see Clarence, who was on pins and needles about the meeting. He had gone out to the back to chop wood, something that did not take a lot of thinking. Deacon tells him everything went well and thanks him for pushing him to confront this head on.

"That was just what I needed to do. Thank you. I feel so much lighter now," he tells Clarence.

"I knew you would; this was something both of you needed to do, face-to-face. I'm here to make sure Leola is okay and that the team does well, but I'm also here for you guys. This team means everything to us." Even though Deacon knows he is a part of the team, hearing Clarence include him in the "you guys" statement strikes a chord. He knows he is making the right choices.

CHAPTER SIXTEEN

A NEW TEAM IN TOWN

Sports section, *Houston Star*, Saturday, August 14, 1948

Last night might have been the luckiest Friday the 13th in recent memory for this sports writer. Here in Baghdad on the Bayou, we've seen many a fine sports tradition, maybe none finer than the years when high school football rivals Yates and Wheatley match up in the Turkey Day Classic.

Our city has a proud tradition of rooting for athletes both white and Negro, dating back more than a generation. And the sports pages of the Houston Star *have reported on these great games for as long as they've been played here. This year, we're officially welcoming a new team in the Negro Leagues, the Eatonville Catfish. This is the first, but no doubt not the last, article you'll find about them in our newspaper.*

The Catfish have no official address here in Houston; they're a barnstorming team from Central Florida that moved to Texas last year. They're a talented bunch, led by Manager Isaac Manns and Owner Leola Jones – that's right, a woman owner – and she's as fine a presence on the field as any owner you've ever seen. The Catfish play a catch-as-catch-can schedule with other teams in our area from April through September, as they travel by bus through most of the eastern half of Texas. But just because they don't stay in Houston all the time, doesn't mean we shouldn't make them feel at home. They play a rousing, fast-paced game that is sure to entertain. And, from this vantage point, they're a team that looks like it's heading toward a championship.

They took the field last night against the hometown Houston Greyhounds under the lights of newly renovated Buffalo Stadium, before a small but enthusiastic crowd of about 6,000, white and Negro. Those of us who were there witnessed what may be a bit of hardball history. Among the Catfish who ran out of the dugout at the top of the first inning was their star pitcher, Deacon Johnson, a 6'3" white boy from West Texas. That's right, a white boy is the star pitcher for this Negro League team. Major League baseball may have integrated last year in Brooklyn, New York, but the idea of a white player in the Negro Leagues is something different altogether. And we have it right here in Houston.

Once Johnson threw his third straight strike past the speeding bat of Tommy "Tornado" Taylor, the great Greyhounds' leadoff batter, thoughts of hardball history or anything other than the game itself were gone. The Catfish ace then proceeded to mow down the next five Greyhounds he faced before giving up a walk to left fielder Hector Beaumont on a fastball that just missed the outside corner. It was a close call that left the Catfish fans on hand groaning. But no matter. He got the rest of the side out one, two, three, stranding Beaumont at first where he never got to take more than a few steps toward second.

Through five full innings, the fans were treated to a classic pitchers' duel. Sammy Peterson, the Greyhound's ace, matched Johnson batter for batter, doing his share to keep the bats quiet in Buff Stadium. Then, in the top of the sixth, Catfish shortstop Coathanger Barnes, "the fastest shortstop in all of baseball," beat out a slow roller to third for an infield single. It didn't look like much at the time since Peterson caught catcher Jazz Gray looking at strike three. It looked like even less when Peterson teased third baseman Maximilian "Emperor" LaRue into popping out to shallow left for two outs. But, then, the Catfish's giant center fielder Battleship Morgan met a three-and-one fastball with the meat of his bat, sending it high into the right field bleachers for a 2-0 lead.

That would turn out to be all the Catfish needed, as Deacon Johnson found a way to tie the Greyhound lineup in knots, striking out eleven and limiting them to one run on four hits. Their only score came in the bottom of the ninth as pinch hitter Freddy Travis scorched an RBI double just past the glove of second baseman Pipsqueak Phillips, bringing rival hurler Peterson home from first. But that would be the end of it as Johnson struck out the final two batters for his seventh win of the season, lifting the Catfish to a win in their first game in Houston this year.

This reporter caught up with the Catfish star hurler after the game and asked him about how it feels to pitch in the Negro Leagues.

"It's a great honor to play with some of the best teammates a guy could ask for," Johnson said. "They're talented and dedicated, and they love the game. And what counts more than that is we take care of each other." For the record, when asked for her own comments, team owner Leola Jones simply smiled graciously and walked away. Guess she'll let her team do the talking for her. Not a bad idea.

Davis makes good on his promise of additional interviews with Leola to learn more about the team, although they both agree it's better to meet at his office. As he drives her home from downtown, Leola's mind begins to wander. Leola has enjoyed her time with Davis, despite the country club incident, but she cannot help but view him as spoiled – or worse, privileged. The very fact that he has taken on the *Catfish* project as a sort of family rite of passage seems bizarre to her. Regardless of its underpinnings, Leola does see that Davis's rebellious disruption of his father's business may just force the *Houston Star* into the 1940s, whether they like or not. And she knows that the *Catfish* will be the beneficiaries of that. Because this little stunt has the potential to help her team, she is willing to overlook Davis's quirks and machismo. She feels a strange twinge of emotion (is it guilt or something else?) as she learns that not everyone can be as thoughtful, considerate, and self-aware as Clarence.

With that thought, it hits Leola that she has to deal with the conflict that has arisen between Clarence and her, and she has no idea how to do it. As much as she hates to admit it to herself – and dreads thinking about admitting it to him – she knows she has crossed a line that ought not to have been crossed. She put their lifelong friendship on the line for another man she barely knows, which is something Clarence has never done to her with any of his relationships with women he has met along the way. She begins to worry about the near future and plays out a number of possible scenarios in her mind, completely forgetting to pay attention to what Davis is saying as he drives her home. Regardless of Clarence's state when she returns, she knows that she owes him a sincere apology. She sighs upon the realization that he was absolutely right and she should have listened to him. Her mind continues to wander about the conversation she is sure to have with Clarence until the car stops and Davis opens the door for her. Even though her mind is somewhere else, she musters a "goodbye" and "thank you", followed by a smile and a wave as Davis drives off.

When Leola opens the door and steps into the hallway, she stumbles over two bags. Regaining her footing, she stops and sees that Clarence's steamer trunk is there too. Her heart sinks and the muffled hum of the radio in the living room fills her ears. She follows the sounds, expecting Clarence to be in the living room, but, when she walks in, it is Isaac she finds there, not Clarence. When she opens her mouth to explain, her uncle holds up his hand and says, "Fix it."

Silent, Leola stands studying Isaac for a moment. She hopes he will have some advice for her, but Isaac has always been careful to remain neutral when it comes to the complicated relationship between Leola and Clarence. She tries to speak, but Isaac stops her again.

"Fix it tonight because tomorrow will be too late," he says, his back turned to her. He hears Leola begin to fidget, something he knows she does when she is anxious. Leola has no response.

Leola turns to go upstairs and get herself ready for bed. As she slips into her nightclothes, she tries to figure out what she is going to say to Clarence. Admitting that she is wrong is something that has always been difficult for her. Clarence has always indulged her with that, but this time she has gone too far and she knows it. Her pride be damned, Leola knows she has to make the next move, and fast. She has never been in such a predicament with Clarence. In their past squabbles, she would let him cool down for a few days. Eventually, he'd come around. There was never any apology needed, and the two of them would just move on. This time was different. Leola didn't have two days to wait. Clarence had packed his bags and would be leaving in the morning. She was going to have to shoulder things alone.

Dressed for bed, Leola walks slowly toward Clarence's room. She pauses at the door, fighting her instinct to go back to her room and let him do as he would. But instead of running away, she stands resolutely and knocks on his door. Her hand feels like lead at the end of her thin arm. Her heart thuds away. She has never been so scared to talk to Clarence in her life. It's a horrible feeling for her. The moment before Clarence opens the door, she realizes he feels ten times the pain she does.

Leola has always known and cherished the fact that she and Clarence share a unique and unbreakable bond. Even when Clarence was sent north, and Leola did not follow, their relationship remained strong. Something special would always bind them.

Still, Leola knows this argument could change their relationship forever. She has to face the fact that, if the tables were reversed, she would have been as protective of him, if not more so. She needs to figure out a way to convey this to Clarence before it is too late.

Clarence does not answer when she knocks, so she knocks again. Nothing. Leola walks in. The room is dark. Leola calls out his name.

"Clarence, are you awake?"

"No," Clarence responds.

"Well, can you be? Please?"

"No," he responds in the same abrupt monotone as before.

"Okay, well, just listen then," she sighs. "I wanted to come up here and tell you how sorry I am. I was entirely out of line and you have every right to be angry with me. It's just . . ."

"Leola, I cannot believe some of the things you said to me," Clarence interrupts, finally sitting up in his bed. "I cannot believe that you think that of me."

Leola takes a step toward Clarence and explains, "Clarence, I don't think that of you, not at all. I guess my competitive side came out, and I just could not let you win that argument right then and there. I am really sorry."

"Leola, this is not some kind of game we are playing at here. People can get hurt. And not just their feelings – people can die."

"I know, Clarence, and I am not sure what came over me. I guess I just wanted to think the best of him and that he had it all together. I mean he is the son of a newspaper tycoon, and he seemed so put together when we were at his office." Leola stops before another word leaves her lips. She waits for Clarence's reaction.

"Leola, he has something up his sleeve, I am telling you."

"I know," she says as she crawls into the bed next to him, "he showed his hand tonight."

"What happened?" Clarence demands, ready to spring into action to help Leola.

"Calm down. Everything is fine now," she says.

"What happened?" Clarence asks again, a little more softly this time.

Leola goes on to explain every detail of the evening's events – how Davis told her about his plan and why he is doing it.

"Well, I am glad you are okay," Clarence says after Leola finishes. "Now, I guess we just have to see what he writes. It's the only way to tell if things are going to really be okay for the *Catfish*."

Clarence is confused. How could Leola not be worried?

"What I am concerned about is if *we* are okay. Clarence, I cannot do this without you. If you are still hell bent on leaving, I will understand, but I hope that you will stay and see this thing through with me."

Clarence sits and stares off into the distance. After a long pause, he says, "Leola, I will stay, but, if I see things that I don't think are right or I have a concerns about anything, I am going to speak up whether it is to your liking or not."

"I know you will," Leola replies. "And I would have it no other way. Now, let's go get those bags unpacked."

"It's late," he tells her with a smile, "I will do that in the morning."

"Okay," she says as she gets up and kisses Clarence on his forehead.

Leola leaves the room to go to bed, but she can't ignore Clarence's bags as she goes downstairs. She decides to gather the bags and put them in Clarence's room, but, when she lifts the trunk she notices how light it is. She opens it up and finds there is nothing in the trunk. All the other bags are empty as well. Isaac walks past her, stops for a second to look at the empty luggage, and just shakes his head on his way to his room.

The old *Catfish* bus heaves and gasps as it carries the team across the state line into Louisiana. After four hours on the road, Jazz makes his way to the front of the bus, where a cooler keeps the ham sandwiches and fried chicken cold. He grabs two sandwiches and collapses beside Deacon.

"Hungry?" he says, holding out a sandwich.

"I'll just wait until we stop," Deacon answers. "I'm in the mood for something hot."

"You're a real riot, Milk Man. I mean Deacon," Jazz says as he shoves the sandwich at him. "Maybe you could sit on this a while, then you could get something hot."

Jazz walks away, leaving the sandwich with the confused young pitcher. Deacon leans over the back of the seat to talk to Isaac, who is dozing in the seat in front of him.

"Isaac," he whispers. Isaac doesn't stir. "Excuse me, Isaac," Deacon says again, louder this time.

Isaac opens an eye and stares at Deacon. "Yes?"

"Aren't we going to stop for lunch?" Deacon asks. Isaac closes his eye and settles back in to finish his nap.

"Isaac, I need to go to the bathroom. Plus, I'd like to get a hot meal before the game." He badgers the drowsy coach. After a bit of this, Isaac flies from his seat and shouts, "Fine, fine! Let's stop at the next diner. Mr. Deacon here wants a hot meal."

Deacon sits back in his seat and looks back at the rest of his team. He thinks they'll all appreciate a stop, but their faces show something different. Rather than grateful, they all look concerned and a bit confused. Isaac only looks irritated. Jazz makes his way up to Deacon and slides in beside him again.

"Doesn't anyone want to stop?" Deacon asks.

"Oh sure, we want to," Jazz says. "But we have no idea where we are or what kind of folks are around here, Milk Man."

"What kind of folks?" Deacon repeats.

"Yeah, what kind of folks, or, better yet, what kind of folks *aren't* welcome in this town."

The bus pulls into a gas station next to a diner to fill up and let Deacon get his roast beef. A sign on the diner door reads in big bold letters, "Whites Only!" Deacon sees the sign and then looks back at his team. They all sit quietly with their eyes cast down. Deacon looks at the sign again and then at a young couple leaving the diner. As they walk past the bus, they shoot a hard glance at every person in it. Deacon looks at his teammates again. They shift uneasily in their seats.

"Everybody not using the bathroom should probably stay on the bus," Isaac says as they wait for the gas tank to click off. "And

Deacon, try to keep your head down, okay? You're no safer here than we are."

Deacon does not understand, and Isaac offers no explanation. Heeding his warning, Deacon stays on the bus and stays down.

Just as the driver tops off the tank, a couple of drunks stumble by the bus, loud and boisterous. When they see the driver hanging up the fuel nozzle, they stumble toward him. With bloodshot eyes, the two men stare menacingly at the players coming back from the coloreds-only bathroom.

"What's a bunch a niggers doing in our town?" one calls out.

"You boys coming back from pickin' that cotton?" the other one bellows.

Deacon hears this and waits for his team to defend themselves. But everyone remains silent. Deacon sits, waiting, becoming increasingly agitated that no one is challenging the two drunks swaying outside the bus.

"You boys watch your p's and q's now, or your momma will have to cut ya down from that tree there yonder," one man calls. The other drunk blocks the players' path to the bus and smacks one of them on the back of his head.

At that, Deacon explodes from his seat on the bus in a fit of rage. He jumps between the drunks and his teammates, pushing them back to put some distance between them. The rest of the team sits in awe of what they are witnessing.

"What the hell are you doing, boy? You realize them boys you're travelin' with is niggers, don't ya?" one of the drunks demands.

"You must be a nigger lover," the other says. "That pretty much makes you a nigger too."

"I guess it does," he says. "And I'll tell you this, if being like you is being white, I don't think that's anything I want to be. One of these boys is worth a thousand of either of you sloppy drunks!"

"I'll show you sloppy drunk, nigger lover," the taller man says as he takes a swing at Deacon. His buddy joins in, holding Deacon's arms to keep him from fighting back. Afraid of what might happen if they hit a white man, the players outside the bus stand frozen. Alarmed at their teammates' lack of action, Jazz and a few others dart off the bus to pull the men off Deacon. Jupiter grabs a baseball bat on his way off the bus and comes out swinging. He hits the first drunk in the ribs and the second in the knees. They both collapse in a whimpering heap.

"We need to go in and call the sheriff!" Deacon shouts as he scrambles to his feet.

"We need to get the hell out of here," Jazz says, pulling Deacon to the bus. "Sheriff would take all of us right to jail and give those men a medal."

As the bus rolls along to Baton Rouge, Deacon realizes that he caused everything that just happened – that he put his teammates' lives on the line with his fit of rage. He also realizes that they defended him, regardless. As Deacon sits and ponders this, Jazz, in the seat behind him, comes to his own realization – that Deacon couldn't sit quietly in the face of such blatant disrespect for his teammates. From that moment on, a bond is made that will never be broken and everyone on the bus knows it.

Jazz takes the seat beside Deacon and says, "You are something else, Milk Man."

"Look, Jazz, I'm really sorry about that. I mean, I just didn't think and . . ."

"Cut that out, Deacon," Jazz interrupts. Then, he stands in the aisle and turns back to the rest of the team. "Anyone got a problem with what Deacon just did back there?"

The bus explodes with loud responses, all at once.

"No way, man!"

"I didn't know the farm boy had so much vinegar in him!"

Jazz sits back down and looks at his white friend. "See? Nothing to say sorry about. But I will tell you this; next time we're stopping at a Negro place. Black folks don't have the same strong reaction to a white boy."

"You got that right!" Jupiter chimes in.

––––––––––

Rose Sterling whisks around her large Houston home as she reviews six different sets of silverware and crystal serving dishes along her large mahogany table. "I don't know; the blue patterns are so classic, and the colorful Chinese design is festive. Do we want to go with whimsy and fun, or should we make our guests appreciate that they're part of an historic Houston event?" she says, as she scrutinizes the designs on the plates and the flatware.

"Oh, Mama, no one's going to notice the design on the serving tray," her daughter Abigail, the future bride, says.

"This is my oldest daughter's wedding, and it'll be the kind of wedding this town has never seen," she replies, her eyes trained on the butter knives before her. "Mark my words, dear, this is going to be the social event of the season, and ladies at social events of the season notice everything. I'm going to give them so much to see that they'll be talking about it for months."

Rose's two younger daughters, Olivia and Evangeline, giggle as they watch their mother and sister fuss over the coming wedding. "Mother, those Chinese plates will certainly get noticed, but is that the kind of attention you want?" Evangeline says, not wanting to miss the opportunity to keep the show going on a bit longer.

Rose turns to her with a look that might burn a hole in anything flammable, but, as she opens her mouth to speak, her servant Jane enters and interrupts the conversation.

"Mizz Davis, the florist, um, I mean, the florists are waiting to see you. Shall I send them in one at a time or all together?" Jane says, a bit flustered by the challenge Rose's wedding preparations have brought to her.

"Wonderful, thank you, Jane," Rose knows the names of the florists she has invited and doesn't skip a beat on the choreography of the day. "Send in Francois from 'Le Fleur de Paris' first – and tell Carlo from 'Fiore Classico' to wait in the foyer. Oh, and when Rhett from 'Beauregard's' arrives, don't let him see Carlo. They don't like each other."

"Mother, what are you doing?" Abigail protests.

"Darling, don't you worry about a thing," Rose drawls. "Everyone at the wedding will have the same place settings, but there's no reason why we can't mix it up when it comes to flowers. I'm going to hire all my florist friends to make sure every table's centerpiece is unique. It'll give our guests a reason to visit each other and mingle."

"But, Mother, that's . . ." Abigail starts.

"Now, now, dear, like I said, don't worry. You'll be the only one with roses," her mother answered. And with that, she turned to Jane.

"Please send Francois in; we'll see him now," Rose said. "We need to be quick; the string quartets are coming for their audition in two hours."

As his wife specifies the perfect centerpieces and attends auditions of several string quartets to find the perfect music for the reception's cocktail hour, Hunter Sterling is at lunch at the Houston Club, busily working his own very different side of town – campaigning and running all kinds of booster events in the hopes of making Houston the heart of the New South. He's planning a benefit auction to raise money for the campaign's public relations program, and Houston's most prominent business leaders are all present. As the lunch begins, a man by the name of Simon Reed asks him, "I hear your boy is writing about a Negro team. Is that true, Sterling?"

"That's what I hear," he replies, buttering a roll.

"Aren't you a little concerned?" Simon asks.

"You let me worry about that, Reed," Hunter replies. "I think Davis's talents will surprise a lot of people in this town."

Later that afternoon when he arrives home, Sterling tells his wife about his interaction with Mr. Reed. He suggests they go see this Negro team play and find out for themselves what the talk is all about.

"That's an interesting idea," Rose says. "But however will you know where those people play without asking Davis? And will it be safe for us?"

"Don't worry, dear, Jeffrey our elevator boy knows everything about Negro baseball. I'll ask him tomorrow."

As promised, Hunter arranges for their visit without telling Davis, until everything is all set. Father and son have a brief argument in Hunter's office, but, ultimately Davis agrees to Hunter's plan.

"It might do some good for you and Mother to see things for yourself. It's really a wonderful team," he says.

As they arrive at the game, Hunter and Rose unexpectedly meet Leola, who is talking with their son as the car pulls up to the field.

"How does a woman end up running a team?" Rose asks. Leola gives a vague response, so Davis fills in the gaps. As Davis tells his parents about Leola and the team, his mother notices something that has escaped his father. She sees the way Davis's eyes light up when he talks about Leola, and the way Leola blushes when Davis talks about her. She knows this will never do; she needs to put a stop to it immediately – before others notice. As the Sterlings are leaving at the end of the evening, Rose tells Hunter she has forgotten something. She rushes off to get her forgotten item and calls back to her son and husband, "I'll meet you at the car!"

She rushes back in, finding Leola. "Miss Jones, I'd like to invite you to tea at my house tomorrow. Can you make it?" Although a bit confused by the invitation, Leola accepts. She knows Rose is up to something, and her curiosity won't let her refuse.

––––––––––

The next day, Leola arrives at the Sterlings' sprawling estate. There, she meets a number of the servants who are all black and shocked to see that she has been invited to have tea with the mistress. Leola notices the servants' confused expressions.

"What are you all looking at me like that for?" she asks.

"In all my years, I've never seen a Negro woman use the front door," one woman tells her as she takes Leola's coat. Leola purses her lips and nods; that tells her all she needs to know about the Sterlings.

"Please, God, give me strength and composure no matter what comes my way," she whispers to herself as she walks into the Sterlings' home. Rose greets Leola, welcoming her in to the foyer of their large plantation-style home. Leola's skin crawls at the greeting. As she walks toward the sitting room, Rose stops her. "Oh no, this way, dear. The sitting room is for guests. We will be sitting in the garden, where no one will interrupt us."

Where no one can see us, you mean, Leola thinks.

Once in the garden, they sit and have tea. Rose barks orders at the servant with the teapot.

"Jane, this tea is just awful. Has no one taught you to make proper tea? Really," she says, turning her attention to Leola, "It is so hard to find a decent servant capable of anything bigger than sweeping the floor."

Leola looks at the young woman as Rose speaks. Leola wants to comfort her, to tell her that it isn't true, and that she is better than all this, but she knows she cannot. Rose notices Leola silently commiserating with her servant and turns it up a bit.

"Go on, Jane," Rose says. "You aren't needed here. Surely, there is a chore you have left undone that you can tend to."

Rose watches Leola as she says this. She wants to be sure Leola knows her place and where she is. She wants to keep Leola a bit off balance. In response, Leola makes sure to speak to the servants with respect and reverence, to demonstrate to Rose that she is not so easily rattled.

"I think the tea is wonderful, Jane," she says as Jane departs. "And you have a beautiful smile, by the way. I do hope you are able to use it more."

After small talk, Leola's curiosity still gets the best of her. She asks, "Ms. Sterling, so why am I really here?"

Rose isn't fazed in the least by Leola's question. "So you and Davis spend a lot of time together?" she asks.

"I wouldn't say so," Leola answers.

"And how did he come to find you again?"

"I'm not quite sure," Leola shrugs.

Rose continues with roundabout questions, but Leola offers little in response, as she herself is still foggy on the nature of her relationship with Davis. When Rose is unable to figure out what is going on with Leola and her son, she cuts to the chase.

"Look, I do not know what kind of savage behaviors go on in Florida, but things like this just do not happen in Texas. The community may be allowing you to run this team, but that does not give you free rein to do whatever you like, and that means manipulating your way into my family's good graces."

"Excuse me?" Leola blurts.

"I find your education level alone highly out of the ordinary. Not only are you are a Negro woman, but you're running a baseball team. This is a man's job, my dear, and you are no man."

"I'll respond to your first comment by letting you know that I have no interest in your family, Ms. Sterling. It was your son who came knocking on my door. Furthermore, my own family would be very surprised to know that I had even accepted your offer of tea. In fact, I believe I've overstayed my welcome." Leola rises from her seat and places her tea cup gently on the saucer. "Thank you so much for the tea," she says with a smile. "I can show myself out."

As she is leaving, she passes a line of servants who have just witnessed Leola's blunt conversation with Rose. Neither the servants nor Leola say a word. They quietly exchange smiles and nods of approval as Leola makes her way out.

A few days after the terrible tea party, Davis arrives at the *Catfish* baseball field to cover the day's practice which has become an excuse to be close to Leola. She is very cold to him, which confuses Davis.

"Is something wrong?" he asks.

"No, nothing," she replies and walks away.

Davis turns to Clarence to try to figure out why Leola is being so cool to him, but Clarence offers the same response. When Davis pushes it, Clarence loses his cool detachment.

"Listen, you need to go away and stay away and stop dabbling in the 'Negro experience' or whatever you think this is!"

Not willing to take Clarence's advice, Davis goes to Deacon, the only one who will talk to him. Davis is livid as he listens to the retelling of the story. He rushes home – still not sure what to do about his mother's antics. He finds her with all three of his sisters, preparing for the wedding. In his frustration, he launches into a tirade, insisting nothing is going on between him and Leola and that it is all about his love of baseball plus the unique story of Deacon, the white pitcher for the Negro League.

His speech is lost on the Sterling women. "If this is just about sex, why a Negro woman?" Evangeline asks.

"Yeah, Davis, we know plenty of loose white women if that is your goal – and so do you," Olivia pipes in.

Infuriated with their ignorance, Davis just gets up and leaves. He decides to get back at his family in any way he can, and in a big way. He is going to bring his very outspoken friend, confidante, and former journalism professor, Elvinia Kincade, to the wedding. He knows that his family thinks she is a strange combination of crass and uppity because she is British. Besides, they do not like the seeds she has planted in Davis's head, such as the progressive thinking he brought home from school. He knows bringing Elvinia to the wedding is the perfect way to turn up the heat on his family and the impression they want to make on Houston society. He chuckles to himself at the thought of Elvinia's debut.

In the meantime, Davis also knows he has work to do. He needs to make things right with Leola and the rest of the *Catfish*.

The only way he knows to do that is through his writing and trying to draw favorable attention to the team. His articles begin to get bolder in their praise of the *Catfish* style of play. He also gives less ink to Deacon and more to the Negro players on the team, which is unheard of – outside of local Negro papers. Not only does this impress Leola and the rest of the team, but Negro communities across Houston as well, who start buying the newspaper for the first time since it began publication.

This puts Hunter in a difficult position. On the one hand, his son's column and its popularity outside the white community is bound to ruffle the feathers of his conservative colleagues across the city. Many of them work on the Houston booster committees and believe this sort of attention will hurt their cause. He also knows that a backlash from these affluent white people could affect his daughter's wedding, which could jeopardize his agenda for Houston. If people decide to protest, they will undoubtedly boycott what Rose has planned to be the most memorable wedding in Houston's history.

But, on the other hand, Sterling cannot ignore the money he is making. The *Star* is selling like never before. There is still the looming question Hunter has to face: *are profit margins worth the risks that come with the newfound attention his son has brought to the paper?*

"Catfish a Hard Team to Catch"
Sports Section, *Houston Star,* Wednesday, September 8, 1948

Houston's newest and most exciting baseball team took the field at Buffalo Stadium the night after Labor Day with a game against the Homestead Grays. For a one-night switch, the barnstorming Catfish were our home team, hosting Negro League Baseball royalty from Washington, D.C., as the Grays continued their tour through the South. Much to the delight of local fans, the Catfish were rude to their guests, despite the Grays' reputation as one of the oldest and finest Negro teams in the nation. Enjoying their role as the home team, the Catfish scored early and often on their way to an 8-3 win that wasn't as close as the score.

Star pitcher Deacon Johnson watched from the dugout, flanked by the team's gutsy manager, Isaac Manns, on one side and their charming owner, Leola Jones, on the other. Instead, we were treated to the talents of Stormin' Nelson Whitman, the lefty Catfish phenom, who is as much a reason for the team's late-season surge as anyone else on the roster. He was nothing short of brilliant, considering he stymied a lineup including greats like Luis Marquez, Luke Easter, and the unstoppable lefty Bob Thurman, limiting the heart of the Grays' lineup to two singles in 11 total at-bats. When it was all said and done, Whitman scattered seven hits through a complete game. Two of them were home runs, but he still coasted through the late innings after the Catfish bats gave him a comfortable lead of six early runs.

With the Grays in town, Buffalo Stadium was full of out-of-towners who came to see the visiting team. At first, the energy in the old stadium made it feel like an away game for the Catfish. Negro fathers and even grandfathers brought young boys to see a team that had done them proud for more than 30 years. They cheered for pitcher William Bell, who is rumored to be in his early 50s but can still command the mound. The Catfish, though, showed determination to hold onto their home field advantage on a beautiful late-summer evening.

They struck quickly. Coathanger Barnes sent the third pitch over second base for a clean single, followed by Jazz Gray, who waited out a full count, fouling off four pitches before drawing a walk. As some fans were still settling into their seats, Emperor LaRue drilled a fastball over Luke Easter's glove at first base that kept going all the way to the wall, scoring the game's first two runs. That would be all for the Catfish in the first, but after Whitman made quick work of the Grays in the top of the second, the Catfish came back with two more runs in their half of the inning. Bo Jefferson doubled to left, and the next batter, Jupiter Monroe, hit a towering blast over everything in right field, into Buffalo Stadium's famous winds.

A four-run lead proved to be all Stormin' Nelson would need. The hometown nine entertained the fans with outstanding fielding, turning double plays in the fourth, sixth, and eighth innings. Solo home runs by Emperor LaRue and Jazz Gray, who continues to hit like a monster despite his thin frame, brought the score to 6-0 before the Grays got on the scoreboard in the top of the fifth. They scored on their first homer, a towering blast by Buck Leonard, still reliable as he pushes 40. Later, with Luis Marquez on first in the top of the seventh, young Dave Pope took a Whitman fastball over the fence to cut the lead to 6-3. But that's as close as they would get. Fans who came to see the long ball weren't disappointed when the Catfish came back with a two-run homer of their own in the eighth. After Coathanger Barnes drew a walk from the Grays' right-handed reliever Bill Pope, Battleship Morgan slammed a line drive to straightaway center that cleared the wall quickly. It was a good thing for Morgan and the Catfish since speedy outfielder Luis Marquez might have tracked down a slower ball. With the Catfish now 14-10 on the season and their pitching and hitting starting to come together, the future looks promising for our barnstorming heroes. It was a night when baseball royalty came to town and a big crowd was treated to five home runs by both teams. But, in the end, it was the Catfish who held court.

Chapter Seventeen

The Attitude Adjustment

During batting practice, Davis approaches Leola. "I know I don't have a great record with introducing you to people in my life, but I was hoping that you'd agree to having lunch with the professor I've told you about from back East. She'll be down for my sister's wedding, and I really think you'd like her. She isn't like the people around here, I promise." It's an odd conversation for Davis and Leola, given the crazy adventures Davis has created in the past.

In fact, Leola does know about Elvinia Kincade. Months ago, he told her the story about how his journalism professor at the University of Maryland 'saved his bacon' when he wrote a controversial paper for her American Issues course. It was a great story and one of the reasons Leola was first intrigued with the depth of character that seemed to lie beneath Davis's playboy façade. Professor Kincade had asked her students to pick an event in American history and write an editorial about it based on the sensibilities of the time, not using today's point of view. Davis chose John Brown's 1859 raid on Harper's Ferry as the event and decided that his editorial would be written in support of John Brown's plan to start a slave rebellion. He knew that, despite admirers in the North, including Ralph Waldo Emerson, John Brown's raid was a shocking event in the South and that College Park, Maryland (just twelve miles north of Washington, D.C.), was in many ways still a Southern town. He ended his editorial with a call for clemency for John Brown before he was scheduled to hang. His paper created a sensation in the Journalism Department – in no small part because Professor Robert Staniford, the department's chair, was the scion of an old money family from Montgomery, Alabama.

Professor Staniford called a meeting of the department to call out Professor Kincade, whom he saw as a renegade, to demand that she give Davis Sterling a failing grade for his impudent senior paper. Even worse, the chair took the unprecedented step of writing a note of personal reprimand directly to Davis.

"I don't care if Ralph Waldo Emerson, an abolitionist, or anyone else from the North had sympathies for John Brown," he railed, "the raid killed innocent people and it divided our nation. Your student needs to learn the cost of irresponsible journalism, and he needs to learn it here."

Elvinia Kincade was shocked at the response to her student's paper, and, since she had encouraged her students to stretch their points of view, to reach back into the past, she felt obligated to defend Davis.

"Professor Staniford, I'm surprised at your reaction," she said in a packed and tense department meeting. "This is not a case of crying 'Fire!' in a crowded theater, as you claim. It's really about the exercise of free speech. In my class I encourage students to practice that art in an environment that is safe and instructive. If this is, as you believe, an irresponsible act on my student's part, I think the proper way to deal with it is through a full-throated debate in class and not through disciplinary action that punishes my student for testing his writing skills. We are an institution of learning. What does giving my student a failing grade for a very well-crafted and carefully researched paper do to further that goal?"

"I disagree, Professor Kincade," the department chair stated in a dismissive tone. "I don't call department meetings like this for trivial reasons, and I believe we need to teach responsibility and restraint as well as 'freedom of the press' in our work with future journalists. In my opinion, responsible journalism is one of the most difficult things to find in today's newspapers. You're doing nothing to encourage it by allowing students to fly off the handle and think they're on some moral high ground. It's cheap sentiment and, ultimately, just noise that plays to popular opinion."

"Well, call it what you will, Professor Staniford, but I refuse to back down on this. I invite you to attend my next lecture and make your point to my entire class if you would like; that is up to you. But I will say, here and now, in front of the entire department, that if you insist on my giving Davis Sterling a failing grade for his paper, you'll have my resignation on your desk the same day." Elvinia's challenge startled the room. She was a popular member of the faculty, and her departure would certainly be a black eye for the Journalism Department.

Professor Staniford re-thought his strategy on the spot, deciding he would take the situation under advisement and would speak with Elvinia Kincade in private. It was his standard way of withdrawing without admitting defeat. Within days, Davis Sterling received his paper back from Professor Kincade with a B+ grade (she had some issues with his cavalier attitude about the loss of human life in John Brown's raid). Professor Staniford never did accept the invitation to attend Elvinia's lecture. Because one of the graduate students attending the department meeting was a friend of Davis, he heard the entire story before receiving his paper.

Leola's eyes sparkles as she answers, "I would love to meet the woman who taught you how to write so well. I'd like to thank her for all the things she instilled in you that your mother never did." And, then, she winks at him.

Davis flashes an uneasy smile in response to Leola's comment. While he agrees with her statement, it does create some amount of reservation in him about the meeting. It occurs to Davis that two strong women in the same place may be more of a force than he is able to handle, which is not something Davis is accustomed to. Reservations or not, it is too late for him to turn back. He swallows hard, takes a deep breath, remembering to trust his original instincts about the introduction.

"Great, then. I'll pick you up this evening and we'll go together to get Elvinia from the airport," Davis says. "I thought it would be nice for you to meet her when she lands."

"I will see you this evening, then," Leola says. "I think I'll head home for now; I have some things to do."

Davis arrives just as the sun is setting. Rather than park in the street as he has done in the past when picking up Leola, he pulls right up to her apartment, just as any guest would. Davis's subtle action breaks down a barrier that was once there – a barrier that most people from his kind and class would prefer to keep solidly in place.

"Hello, Davis," Leola says as she opens the door. Her cheeks are rose colored, and her eyes are as lively as Davis has ever seen them. Her dress is a deep aqua blue off-the-shoulder number, hugging her curves and stopping just below the knee. She looks as if she's walked right off a fashion magazine cover, and Davis isn't shy about saying so.

"You, Leola Jones, look…you look…absolutely stunning this evening."

"Why, thank you, Mr. Sterling," Leola replies in a very flirtatious way. "You seemed to have almost lost your words there. I didn't know that such a thing could happen to such an accomplished writer as Davis

Sterling. I wonder if your newspaper editor daddy would love or hate such a loss."

"Maybe a bit of both," Davis replies with a little boy's sheepishness. "Shall we?" he says, offering his arm and trying to regain his footing. The drive to Hobby Field is a chance for them to discuss his most recent columns.

"Reading your latest articles, I'd almost accuse you of becoming too much of a fan of the *Catfish*," Leola tells Davis as they drive. "Whatever happened to your journalistic objectivity? Aren't you concerned at all that your connections with the team will cloud your impartiality?"

Leola's comments and insights no longer catch Davis off guard, although they still make him a bit nervous. He expects Leola to pay close attention to everything he does.

"You know, I'm almost single-handedly responsible for your entire fan base," he replies. "The *Catfish* play some very good baseball to be sure, but who would know about them without these stories?"

"Well, Mr. Miracle Worker, if you want to quit your job at that teeny little family newspaper of yours and join my staff, I think there's a position in our publicity department you might be able to hold onto for a while," Leola teases. "Then, you could gush all you want about Jazz, Deacon, Uncle Isaac, and all the other *Catfish*. I might even grant you more exclusives with me. That is, of course, if you play your cards right."

Leola reaches out and puts a hand on Davis's shoulder as she finishes her statement. When her hand touches him, he jerks the steering wheel, but quickly corrects himself. Leola sees Davis blush and shift in his seat. She pulls her hand back and smiles a bit to herself at Davis's reaction.

"I'm sorry, did I startle you?" she says, making light of his embarrassment.

"I guess so," Davis replies, keeping his eyes on the road before them.

At the airport, Davis parks the car, and the two walk up to the gate. They watch Elvinia's plane touch down and ease its way to a stop on the tarmac. They watch as she makes her way down the stairs, luggage in hand. As always, Elvinia looks glamorous and stands out as a European among her fellow American passengers. From where they stand, Davis can see the way those around her are intrigued by the elegant Brit.

"Thank you for flying Eastern Air Lines," the stewardess says to Elvinia at the bottom of the stairs, "and thank you for telling me about that mysterious visitor to Edgar Allan Poe's grave. I'm going to watch my newspaper next January for sure!"

"Why, darling, aren't you sweet to remember!" Elvinia exclaims, "Yes, it is quite a story, I agree. Do enjoy the flight back, love." Davis isn't surprised to see that Elvinia has made friends with the stewardess. She sees every event in life as an opportunity to teach something to someone, even if it is only a bit of trivia.

Upon reaching the gate, Elvinia immediately spots Davis and Leola. She waves a gloved hand and hurries toward them.

"Did you see that delightful stewardess I was speaking to?" she asks even before saying hello. "I'll have you know she promises to buy your paper next January if you write about the mystery visitor to Edgar Allan Poe's grave." Davis ignores the tease and moves to introductions.

"Professor Elvinia Kincade, meet Leola Jones, Vice President of the *Eatonville Catfish* – the best baseball team in the Lone Star State."

Elvinia drops her luggage and extends her hand. Leola takes it and says, "Professor Kincade, Davis has told me so much about you. I can't believe we're finally meeting. Welcome to Houston."

Elvinia smiles warmly. "Call me Elvinia – and that goes for both of you," she laughs. "For heaven's sake, when you win the Pulitzer Prize and I'm with you to accept the award, I don't want anyone to know how old I am."

"Well, Elvinia, if you insist, I shall call you by your first name. Are you hungry?" Davis asks her, "They can't have fed you very well on that airplane. Why don't the three of us go to the diner near the office and get something to eat?"

A rollicking conversation follows from the airport exit to Davis's car to their table in the diner. Elvinia knows what Leola means to Davis, and she has come to Houston with something to say to both of them. After an hour of lighthearted storytelling and compliments on everyone's appearance and good nature, the two women excuse themselves to go to the ladies' room. Before they have made it into the restroom, Elvinia stops and faces Leola.

"You both must know how hard it will be on you every day," she says suddenly. Leola is surprised by the declaration that seems to come from thin air. "The legality alone poses a tangible threat to the whole thing, you know, and God forbid you should have children and subject them to the endless harassment and even alienation they'll encounter in this most backward region of your country. I suggest you think about moving somewhere far more civilized if you plan on staying together."

Leola is stunned silent. Davis tried to prepare her for Elvinia's candor, but it still felt like she had been hit in the head by a very British two-by-four. Leola is surprised that Elvinia knows about her feelings for Davis and is only slightly less offended by Elvinia's remarks than she had been by Rose's comments at tea. Mama was right. Maybe we should just keep to our kind after all, she thinks. Elvinia senses that she may have gone a bit too far and tries to recover.

"Of course, I'm only saying this because you've obviously come a long way, longer than anyone I know in your situation, and I want the best for you." Elvinia sees that Leola is not softening, so she tries once more to make it clear that she is no enemy. "Darling, you know that any good friend of Davis is certainly a good friend of mine."

Leola forces a smile and changes the direction of their conversation. "Of course. Have you been able to read any of Davis's articles on the *Catfish*? I'm interested in what you think about all of this."

Back at the table, Elvinia directs her conversation elsewhere. She and Leola talk about Leola's past and the creation of the *Catfish*. Davis takes their cordial conversation as a sign that the two are getting along well.

"Well, ladies, it's time I take each of you to your respective homes for the evening. Tomorrow is the big wedding, and I want my date fresh for the occasion."

"Have you ever known me to be any other way, dear?" Elvinia asks with a quick wink.

Davis drops Elvinia at her hotel and continues to Leola's house.

"So, what did you think of her? Do you like her?"

Leola smiles back and replies, "Of course, I do, Davis. And I see who taught you to ask tough journalistic questions on the spot."

Davis wants to ask her what she means, but they are already at Leola's front door. She laughs a bit and leaves his car.

"Have a great time at the wedding with your date!" she calls from her front porch. "Goodnight, Davis."

The next day Davis and Elvinia arrive at the wedding. Inside the massive chapel people are dressed in their finest flowing gowns, gorgeous hats with fresh-cut flowers pinned to them, top hats, and tails. The choir and organ are playing at full volume throughout the short service, the music reverberating in everyone's ears as they leave for the reception at Rolling Lawns Country Club.

Servants, dressed in tuxedos, are seating people, fanning them to keep everyone cool, and handing out programs. The last florists are just leaving in their delivery vans as the first guests arrive. Davis and Elvinia bypass the gathering guests and immediately head for Rose, who hasn't seen them yet.

"I just don't know why Trevor and Abigail aren't coming," Rose is saying to Barbara Shope, the owner of the most exclusive men's boutique in Houston, as Davis and Elvinia approach. "They just sent a note saying she doesn't feel well. I saw her last night at the beauty parlor, and she looked healthy to me. And they're not the only last-minute cancelations."

"I think I know what – or rather who – is at the bottom of this, and it's . . ." Barbara stops and fastens her eyes on Davis, who has just planted himself beside his mother. Rose follows her gaze.

"Why, Davis, when did you arrive?" Barbara says, further emphasizing who she believes the culprit is.

"Davis, I want to talk with you about those . . ." Rose stops midsentence when she notices her son's guest. She is shocked when he introduces her as Elvinia Kincade, the professor he has quoted for so many years, back when he became so willful and disrespectful.

"How do you do," Rose says, coldly, turning immediately to Davis so that her back is to Elvinia. In a stage whisper meant for Elvinia to hear, she continues, "I hope your professor remembers that she is in America now and needs to keep her place."

"No need to worry, my dear," Elvinia replies, "I assure you, I am fully aware of proper etiquette. Keeping our place is something we British consider an art form. You know, it's a talent we've tried to teach our American friends for centuries. I'm happy to say that many of you seem to have learned it, although not always very well."

Rose's eyes flash, and the skin on her neck reddens, peeking above her high-collared dress. She bites her lip as she smiles in response.

She has no choice but to remain civil and ladylike given the role she must play as mother of the bride. She has already let her manners lapse once because of this English woman, and she will not let her presence cause any further disturbance on her daughter's wedding day.

"I do hope you enjoy the wedding," Rose says with cool detachment and an even cooler smile. Then, she turns and walks away.

"I will indeed," Elvinia retorts, a wicked grin on her face.

———

"How was the wedding?" Leola asks as Davis approaches her. Even perched on a chilled stadium seat and wrapped in a big overcoat, she is as beautiful to Davis as she was the first time he saw her.

"Less eventful than I imagined," Davis replies. "My mother was as visibly perturbed by Elvinia as Southern manners would allow, but her pride and sense of social grace kept things tamped down."

"Clarence would like to speak with you," she tells him. The thought of Rose dampens Leola's mood, even if it would be fun to hear more about how Elvinia might have caused a bit of mischief. In any case, Leola isn't really interested in the wedding or the people in attendance.

"Do you know about what?"

"I'm sure the best way to find out is to ask him," Leola replies.

Clarence is indeed awaiting Davis's arrival. Both he and the *Catfish* are skeptical, if not cynical, of the white playboy journalist's sudden interest in their team. Clarence, in particular, views Davis as an immature brat in the throes of an extended and dangerous temper tantrum of sorts, using both Deacon and the team to work out his daddy issues. More important, he sees what Rose Sterling sees when Davis is in Leola's presence. Each flirtation and each furtive glance rattles Clarence to his core and acts as yet another example of the privilege someone like Davis enjoys – a privilege that makes him oblivious, if not apathetic, to the effects his actions have on the people around him. Regardless of his feelings about Davis, or perhaps because of them, Clarence has decided to invite him to go on the road with the team. The invitation is less of an olive branch than it is Clarence's way of feeling out the shifty journalist. He wants Davis to get a sense of how the team interacts with Deacon.He also wants to show Davis that having a white pitcher is not just some kind of publicity stunt to get people to come to the games.

———

"Time to gas up and get grub," the driver calls back as the bus pulls into a truck stop; this time they pull into a Negro establishment to avoid the same kind of confrontation they had come across on the last trip.

The team and Davis make their way into the small diner to grab a quick bite to eat. Inside, both Deacon and Davis are met with blatant hostility. Once they sit down to order, the animosity of the other patrons is evidenced by their icy stares toward not just the white men in the room but the team as well.

"I think your white boys would do best to keep movin'," the diner owner tells Clarence and Isaac.

"I beg your pardon?" Clarence retorts.

"This is a Negro establishment. They have plenty of other places they can eat. Just not in here. If they want my food, they can eat it out in the back alley."

As luck would have it, a local sheriff pulls up to do his periodic checking in on the Negroes to get free food. When he sees what is happening, he walks up to the owner and says to him, "These men here are white; you see that boy? Even though I don't know why they would want to eat with a bunch of niggers, you had better be treating them with respect. Ya hear me? Now, get these men whatever they want, and the rest y'all get back to whatever you were doing," he says, addressing the black folks.

After the sheriff makes sure they order their food, he drives away. Deacon does the right thing to keep things calm and gets up from the table to walk out the back door. Davis, realizing what is going on, follows suit. Clarence watches them disappear to the alley where the owner has said he would serve them, looks at the rest of the team, and follows. Outside, Deacon sits down on the ground, and Davis sits next to him. Deacon nods as his eyes meet Davis's, but not a word is exchanged. Clarence keeps walking until he's next to Davis, and sits on the ground next to him. One by one, the rest of the *Catfish* players file out the door and join the others. The rest of the clientele watch in shock and confusion.

"We'll all have the fried chicken," Jazz says, the last to exit.

In silence, the team eats a meal together in the alley. And for the first time, Clarence sees something different in Davis. Clarence and Davis's relationship changes that day. It is never spoken about, but they have a new level of respect for each other that never wavers.

The event also has another consequence: the stress leaves Leola's face on that day, because she realizes the profound way this small gesture has changed the way Clarence and Davis see each other.

As the season wears on, Davis and Leola spend more and more time together. Late in the summer, Leola, an alumna of Bethune-Cookman College, agreed to help plan the 1949 Bethune-Cookman College Cotillion, also known as the "Black Ball." The theme she has chosen this year is "Breaking Down Barriers." She has finessed her way into convincing Deacon to speak after the dinner.

"I know it won't be easy or comfortable to speak at a Negro female college, but I was hoping you'd consider it."

"Oh, it's no problem at all, Miss Leola," Deacon insists, although his heart jumps to his throat and barely allows the words to pass by.

"You don't even need time to consider?" Leola asks, a bit surprised by his immediate response to such a complex request.

"After all you've done for us, it's the least I can do," he tells her.

When Clarence catches wind of Deacon's first public speaking engagement, he is not pleased with Leola.

"Are you sure you're not just showing your white boy baseball player off?" he asks accusingly. "I think you're just flaunting your accomplishment of getting this white boy to play for the *Catfish*."

"That's ridiculous, Clarence," she protests.

"I hope it is," he replies, "Because you're playing with fire here – and the kind of fire that isn't worth some silly bragging rights back home around college friends."

"You're worrying too much," Leola says, sidestepping the gravity in Clarence's warning. "Why don't you come home with me? You can keep an eye out to settle your mind, and I'll show you how it's also a great place to meet a nice Southern girl so you can settle down."

The seriousness fades from Clarence's expression. He grins and replies, "Don't you go getting any fancy ideas."

Leola isn't the only one with big plans for the trip home to Florida. Davis sees this as an opportunity to travel with Leola under the cloak of covering the story for his series about Deacon. Elvinia also decides to meet the gang in Florida to see "how the other half lives", as she puts it, although she declines the opportunity to drive there with the rest of the group. Since her experience at the wedding, Elvinia has been gripped by the urge to see for herself how everything plays out. She is certain something will happen. Exactly what, she does not know.

When Columbus finds out that Deacon and Davis are going to be in Florida, he requests that they stop in Eatonville so he can meet the two white men who have been causing such a commotion in Texas. Leola has been sending her father all of Davis's articles, as well as essays and write-ups by others around Texas. The two quickly agree to meet with Columbus.

"I think it'd be nice to see where you come from, Miss Leola," Deacon says. "I am looking forward to meeting the people who have raised a fireball like yourself."

"Well, meet them you shall, Mr. Johnson," Leola replies. "And they are as intrigued to meet you!"

Crammed into Davis's fancy town car, Leola, Isaac, Deacon, Clarence, and Davis make their way along the Gulf, following U.S. Route 90 from Texas through Louisiana, Mississippi, Alabama, and into Florida. They are on the "Deep South Tour," as Clarence calls it. As they pull into Eatonville after a three-day trip, everyone in the car is charged with excitement – each for different reasons. Leola, Clarence, and Isaac are eager to see family after such a long time away. Deacon anxiously awaits meeting the man who started the *Catfish*. He is also anxious about his own speaking engagement at the ball. Although nervous, he feels important and still cannot believe that anyone, black or white, would want to hear what he has to say.

Davis is most interested in meeting Columbus and seeing where Leola was raised. Even though Leola has described the ambivalence she feels for her hometown, he knows she loves the town where she was born, and he wants to be a part of her visit, even if it's just in a small way.

The small tribe stops at the Jones's general store and walks into a tidy, well-stocked space in which black and white people shop side by side. Leola enters first and just takes it all in: the look, the smell, the sounds of home. As Leola stands reveling in nostalgia, her mother comes out from the back room, wet and sudsy from making her famous blossom soap. A large group of people are waiting to buy the newest batch. When Hoyt sees Leola and Clarence across the room, she drops the soap on the floor and rushes over to them.

"My babies," she exclaims as she wraps her damp arms around her daughter. "My babies are home."

When she finally lets loose of her daughter, Hoyt's eyes fall on Clarence. "Well, get over here, right now, baby boy!" she orders as she opens her arms again. She embraces him just as tightly, as tears dampen her cheeks. "Look at you! You have grown up into a fine-looking man. When you left here, you were just a nappy-headed boy looking to see what the world had to offer, and now look at ya, a strong strapping handsome black man – and I see you are still under foot. I knew Leola was not going to let you get away for too long."

Hoyt shoots a glance back at Leola and continues, "Now, this is the way it should be, you and Clarence." She takes Clarence's hand and puts it in Leola's. Neither corrects her or attempts to move. They stand holding hands as feelings from a lifetime of shared experiences well up in both of them. Davis interrupts the soft exchange by stepping between the two and introduces himself.

"It's so nice to meet the journalist I've heard so much about," she says shaking his hand. "I've heard all about you and Deacon from Leola's letters." She wipes her hand before shaking his. Then, she turns to Deacon and states, "And you must be the famous Deacon Johnson. I feel like I already know you."

Hoyt raises her arms to hug Deacon but stops herself. Remembering her place, she steps back and offers her hand, recovering quickly with a smile. "Sir, you sure do know how to make a splash. Yes, you do, sir." She laughs and walks away to gather her soaps from the wooden slat floor. As she does this, Isaac enters with the bags. Hoyt stops again and nearly throws herself into Isaac's arms.

"My family is home, my family's home! Thank the Lord! I knew you would lift me up . . . I knew you would!" she exclaims.

Leola turns from the homecoming activity to Davis and says in a quick breath, "Let me show you around the place."

Davis agrees so enthusiastically that Hoyt takes notice. Hoyt watches the two of them as they wander the store and sees what others have already noticed. She looks at Clarence with raised eyebrows. Clarence returns her gaze with a look of hurt that he forces away with a half smile. Hoyt feels an immediate urgency to break the two away from one another. Isaac notices the silent exchanges and tries to refocus everyone's attention.

"Where's Columbus?" he asks.

Hoyt's face saddens at the question. "He is lying down," she says. "He's in a bad way right now. I pray every day that the Lord sees fit to heal him. He has so much to live for." She then looks to Clarence. "He has so much more he wants to do, you know?" she says in a near whisper.

Hoyt sees the change in everyone's faces and tries to recover the lightness of the moment. "But the Lord has brought you home, and this is the best medicine he could ever get, ever. The Lord has really blessed us today, yes, we surely are blessed. Now, let's bring you to see him because, if he knew you were all here and hadn't poked in to say hello, he would be sure to raise some Cain." She laughs a little and adds, "And no one wants to hear that mess." She laughs again.

Hoyt leads the group to the back of the store and out the back door. They pass the chicken coops and the livestock. Everything is in perfect working order, just as it was when Leola left. A blossom field stretches off to the west of the homestead where Hoyt keeps several large man-made beehives to make her famous wild blossom honey. As they walk, Hoyt grabs Clarence by the hand and says playfully, "I hopes you haven't forgotten everything you learned growing up while you were at that big fancy school. There are things that need fixin' around here, and I plan to put those college hands to work." Deacon hears Hoyt and lights up, saying, "I can help you with that, Clarence." Surprised by the offer, Hoyt turns to him and asks, "You would do that?"

Deacon begins to answer Hoyt and is suddenly struck mute. There is an aura that hangs around Hoyt and reaches out to Deacon that resonates in his heart and somewhere deep within his subconscious. Hoyt's voice and her demeanor evoke a warm but sorrowful nostalgia in Deacon that he cannot put his finger on. As Hoyt smiles and asks, "Are you okay, sweetheart?" the origin of the strange yet familiar sensation occurs to Deacon. Hoyt is a strong reminder of Mama Delilah.

In her eyes, Deacon finds the same sad hopefulness – the same love singed at the edges with a history of hurt.

"Yes, ma'am," he finally says, trying to push back the rush of emotions that the memory of both Delilah and Lummy brings. "I grew up on a farm back home and love keeping my hands busy. Makes me feel like I'm in the right place doing that kind of work. I would love to help get things in order if you don't mind me doing it."

"Mind? Young man, I have been waiting for someone to come along and help ease the burden," Hoyt exclaims. A shadow falls over her face as she stops to correct herself. "I shouldn't say burden. I count myself fortunate to have so much to do, you know. It's just that with Columbus . . ."

Hoyt doesn't finish her sentence, and Deacon can see that she struggles against the words caught in the back of her throat. "Well, I am glad to be of assistance, ma'am," he says, allowing Hoyt time to recover. "Plus, it will be a great way for me to see the other side of Clarence here. I want to see some of the South in this new Northerner," he says, ribbing Clarence and grinning a mischievous grin. Everyone standing there laughs, including Clarence.

The group walks past the chickens and livestock until they come to a cluster of large orange and grapefruit trees that look to be reaching their fruit-covered arms to the heavens, as if trying to touch God himself. On the other side of the trees lies a clearing on which a house sits. In front of the simple but strong two-story white-shingled home is a massive garden filled with beautiful flowers. Bright blues, reds, purples, and yellows pop against the white background of the house. Deacon notices how well maintained the garden is – not a weed can be found and the arrangement of the flowers is as coordinated as one of the carefully designed and knitted Afghans his grandmother used to make.

"It is so nice to be home, Mama," Leola says as they walk through the garden.

Leola and Hoyt are the first to step onto the porch that stretches across the length of the front of the house. Like the garden, the porch is pristine and inviting. Hoyt has planters of all shapes and colors bursting with natural flower bouquets lining the steps to the porch. There's a swing on one side and a wood bench with small tables on the other. At the top of the three stairs, Hoyt calls out to Columbus.

"Give me just a moment to make sure he is ready for visitors," she says to the group before she turns to go into the house. She disappears into the house for a moment, and then calls out to tell them to come in. With Leola as leader, the group files into the Jones's home. In the living room, they find Columbus sitting in an easy chair listening to the radio. His posture is slouched, almost crumpled. Leola can see the effects of the illness from where she stands. Columbus, who has always been strong in character and stature, looks frail and weatherworn. It's a strange realization for Leola as she wraps her arms around him, blinking back tears and forcing a smile to mask the sorrow she feels. Isaac notices both Columbus's weakened state and Leola's reaction and attempts a bit of levity.

"Just like you, old man," he says with a chuckle. "Sitting around while everyone does all the hard work and you just supervise."

"Well, you know me, Isaac, always thinking about my next big idea," Columbus says, as he struggles to lift himself out of the chair.

Isaac sees that Columbus is so weak that he can hardly pull himself up. Before Columbus can collapse, he says, "Don't get up on our account. We're no company." Columbus is thankful for the words that come just before his arms give way and send him back into a sitting position.

"I suppose I might as well stay put anyhow," he says, as he falls back into the chair.

Leola collapses down to her knees at her father's feet and rests her head in her father's lap as she reaches up with both arms to embrace him in a hug so firm and meaningful that Columbus nearly loses his breath.

"How good it is to have my baby girl back home," he says as Leola loosens her grip. "I've read all your letters. I'm just so, so proud of the . . ."

Hoyt sees the emotion welling up in both her husband and daughter. Knowing that both are too prideful to break into tears in front of a group, she steps in and says, "You two can visit later when we're all not dying of thirst waiting on you," as she shoos Leola along playfully. "Can I get y'all something cold to drink?"

Hoyt's question is rhetorical, as she exits to grab a pitcher of lemonade before anyone can answer. As she steps into the kitchen, Isaac introduces Deacon to Columbus.

"And here is your latest *Catfish*, Deacon Johnson, who is taking the bull by the horns," he says, putting a paw on Deacon's shoulder. The introduction startles the young pitcher, who has lost himself in the family pictures on the wall. He jerks his eyes from a picture he has been studying, one of a young Leola and Clarence standing with two boys who look to be in their teens. Deacon wonders who the two boys are, but redirects his attention to Columbus as Isaac nudges him forward.

Columbus makes a second attempt at getting up. Isaac makes a move to interfere again, but Columbus shoots him a warning to stay away.

Once he has found solid footing, Columbus extends his hand to Deacon.

"I have heard so much about you that I feel like I know you, young man. I know you have been through hell, and I know you are going to go through some more hell. But I would like to thank you for being a part of my *Catfish*. And I hope that, even with all the hell, you feel it's all worth it," he says as he takes Deacon's hand in his and shakes it.

A knot forms in Deacon's throat, and his eyes begin to sting as he replies, "No, sir, it is really my great honor. And I would like to thank you and your family for allowing me to play with the best. I will gladly take a short trip through hell any day to continue to play with the best team in the barnstorming league. The *Catfish* are the best players I have ever played with."

In the back of the room, Davis writes everything he sees. His hand moves wildly as he captures the moment as best he can on paper. The scribbling catches Columbus's attention. He looks past Isaac and Deacon to the strange man writing in a frenzy. Isaac follows his friend's eyes and takes his cue to introduce Davis.

"This is the man who has been writing all the articles I have been sending you about the *Catfish*."

"Davis Sterling?" Columbus asks.

"None other," Isaac confirms.

Davis is suddenly tongue-tied. He has lost the comfort of his objective journalistic position and is thrust into a new one that he is less equipped to deal with. Without his professional list of questions about the *Catfish* and baseball, he is thrust into a less safe place. Columbus has moved from the position of the man Davis is interviewing for an extensive story for the *Star's* sports pages to the father of a woman he is smitten with. His mouth dries, and his lips stick to one another as he searches for the right words – the first words he will say to Leola's father.

"It's always nice to put a face and voice to a name, sir. I would like to thank you for all that you have done for this team and my players. It is an honor to have you in my home," says Columbus.

"The honor is mine, sir," Davis squeaks as he bows awkwardly. He blushes at the delivery of the words. He has never felt so unsure of himself – so self-conscious about his every move.

"Sterling. I seem to remember seeing that name somewhere," says Columbus.

"The paper he writes for out in Houston that you've been reading is owned by Davis's father, Hunter Sterling," Isaac explains.

Columbus laughs. "Oh boy! Your father must be fit to put a whipping on you like no one's done before."

Davis feels his muscles relax a bit at the joviality in Columbus's response. He chuckles and tells him, "You don't know the half of it, sir. But I'll tell you, the worst of it has come from my mother. I won't subject you to that, though. Everyone here can thank me later," he adds with a wink, falling back into Davis Sterling form.

"But, in all fairness, sir, and please excuse me if it seems I am slipping into a bit of bragging, but it seems that some people think that what I am doing constitutes some of the best sports writing in Texas. And I would agree, not because I am a phenomenal sports writer, but because I'm writing about some of the best baseball in the United States. It is a true shame that others will not write about Negro barnstorming and the amazing players who play in the Negro League. The skill of these players rivals that of the best players in the country."

Columbus lets out a small laugh and says, "You're not telling us anything we haven't known for years, son, but times they are changing, whether people are ready or not. It's people like you who are helping to do that, and I want to thank you, because I know this can't be easy for you."

"I should be the one to thank you, Mr. Jones," Davis insists. "It has been an absolute pleasure working with Leola. She is…an incredible woman." Again Davis blushes. Everyone in the room, including Leola, takes notice of his flushed cheeks. Everyone falls silent for a moment, trying to make sense of Davis's statement and his blushing at the mention of Leola.

"And you must have been working with Isaac too," Columbus finally says, pointing at Isaac.

"Of course!" Davis says nervously. "Of course, Isaac too. He is … Isaac has been a pleasure to work with too. He's …"

The gaze of all the eyes in the room fall on Isaac who is amused by the man of so many words suddenly being at a loss for them.

"Interesting," Isaac says grinning at Davis as he struggles to spit out his words. "I won't take it personally, son. I know Leola leaves a strong impression on everyone she meets."

Hoyt and Leola enter and break the awkward tension with a pitcher of cold lemonade. Leola senses the discomfort in the room; she also sees the strained expression on Davis's face.

"I'd like to spend some time with Daddy," she announces. "Would you take these gentlemen and show them what all needs to get done?" she asks her mother.

"Wait a minute, Boss," Columbus interrupts. "I'd like Clarence to stick around, if that pleases you," he teases his daughter. "I want to see you both. Isaac can go and see what can be done with the chores."

As the others leave the house, Columbus asks in a rather direct tone, "So what is going on?"

Neither Leola or Clarence offers an answer. Instead, they both drop their eyes to the floor. They know what he is referring to, but neither wants to address it. It is the elephant in the room that they'd rather ignore. Leola changes the subject and starts talking about the team and team business.

"Since my daughter is going to act like her father is stupid," Columbus interrupts, "I am going to ask you, Clarence, and don't you lie to me. What is going on?"

Clarence is paralyzed by the question, but he knows he has to produce some kind of response; Leola's approach obviously wasn't going to cut it. He starts to speak, to explain the situation as far as he sees it.

"It's complicated, I think," he starts. "A lot is going on, so these things can be misinterpreted. As far as I can tell . . ."

"No, this should come from me," Leola blurts. She sees that Clarence has been put in an impossible situation. "Davis and I have been spending quite a lot of time together, and I think I am developing some unexpected strong feelings for him."

Leola lets out an exaggerated breath after her statement. Her conscience is clear. Like a Catholic in the confession booth, she has cleansed herself of a secret so that she can be absolved. It's the first time that she has said it out loud. The words have a physical effect on Columbus. His shoulders cave and his head drops. Leola can see the impact that her admission has on her father. She turns to Clarence for some moral support, and, as she does, she finally recognizes the look on his face. It is the same look that he had at his mother's funeral. In that moment, she realizes the depths of hurt that her relationship with Davis causes him. She reaches out to hold his hand, but Clarence pulls away.

"Not this time," he says, coolly.

Clarence has been very aware of Leola and Davis's blossoming relationship, but he has never had to face it in such a direct way. Leola's words bring it into reality; they confirm what Clarence had hoped might have been some sort of illusion he had created. And it is painful, very painful for him.

Columbus looks at Clarence and tells him, "I love my daughter." He keeps his eyes locked on Leola as he speaks, "But she is a fool and this is your family, regardless. I never want you to forget that, do you hear me?"

"Yes, sir, I hear you."

Looking at Clarence, Leola says, "I may very well be a fool," she admits, "but I never meant to hurt anyone's feelings." Once again, she reaches out to grab Clarence's hand. Clarence accepts her this time, grabbing her hand back. He looks at Columbus.

"I'm going to be just fine; you can count on that." Then, he looks to Leola and tells her, "I am always going to be here for you no matter what. But are you sure this is the road you want to go down? I mean, this can go wrong in so many ways. People get killed for things like this."

"It just feels right," she tells him, squeezing his hand in hers.

Columbus interrupts her. "This may feel right, Leola Jones, but you and me are going to have to have a long talk about this before anything else goes on."

As Hoyt, Davis, Isaac, and Deacon's footsteps echo through the house to signal their return, Leola quickly says, "Yes, Daddy, I agree. Right after the Black Ball, I plan to spend loads of time with you and Mama. We can talk all about it – all you want."

"Talk about what?" Hoyt asks as she enters the room. She looks at Leola. Leola just smiles and kisses her on the forehead.

"I love you, Mama," she says softly. "We will all talk after the ball, but right now, I have so much to do. We still have to get to downtown Daytona."

Puzzled, but compliant, Hoyt replies, "Alright, you know where we will be, baby." She then turns to Davis and Deacon. "You are in for a treat – a Black Ball is something to see," she says as her chest puffs out with pride.

Davis looks at Leola and, then, a bit nervously at Columbus. "I am looking forward to it," he says, giving a half smile to Columbus, who gives him a half smile back.

CHAPTER EIGHTEEN

BROWN TOWN

"I'd like to speak to my daughter alone, if you all don't mind," Columbus says to the small group gathered in the house. Hoyt and Clarence hear the seriousness in his voice and quickly lead Deacon and Davis out of the room.

"Well, Deacon, you did it now!" Clarence jokes as he ushers the men out of the room to leave Columbus and Leola alone. "Mama Hoyt is going to put you to some hard labor around here. You are going to regret offering because she will work you to the bone." The two men laugh.

"Let's go get you some work clothes and see what we can do to shape this place up," Clarence tells him.

"You got that right," Hoyt responds, following behind. "Now, that chicken coop needs some fixin'. And then I am going to need some help over at the store movin' some stuff around."

"Before you put us all to work, I was hoping I could get some background and history on this town. I mean, is it the original home of the *Catfish*?" Davis interjects in the midst of all the shuffling around.

"You mean of Leola and her family, don't ya?" Hoyt responds with a raised eyebrow.

"No, I really want to know about Eatonville and Columbus's connection with this town, and about the town itself," Davis responds.

"Well, to learn about this town, you can't help but learn about all of us – me, Columbus, and Leola. This town runs through our blood. Let Clarence and Deacon handle that chicken coop and you sit down and let me tell you about Brown Town," Hoyt says.

"What is Brown Town?" Davis asks.

"Well, Brown Town is what our neighboring blonde sister town calls us. Maitland is the white town that is next door to Eatonville, and they are the people that helped us become the very first incorporated all-black, free-voting town in this here United States of America."

Hoyt stops walking and sets her eyes on Davis as she reaches her hand out to touch his arm. When Davis feels her hand, he immediately stops and pivots on a heel to meet her gaze. "I want you to listen close, because this is important, and I want to you get this right."

Davis nods, but says nothing. He knows it isn't time for him to talk; it's time for him to listen – that's all. Keep quiet and listen to what this small, but sturdy woman has to say to him. They start to walk toward Hoyt's beehives. She grabs a head net hanging on a post and hands it to Davis.

"You gonna help me with Hoyt's famous honey as we talk," she tells him as she slips her own head net on.

"I am going to start from the beginning," Hoyt says. She motions Davis to follow her and mimic her action. "I have been told that there are 22 all-Negro towns in America with about 25,000 Negroes in them all. We are the smallest, but we are – and always will be – the first. Yes, the first all-black free town in America, right here, Eatonville, Florida. About 60 years ago now, Eatonville had around 350 people in it. We are not much bigger today."

Hoyt moves from hive to hive, collecting her honeycombs as she speaks. Davis can see that this is something that she loves to speak about and is good at telling. He loves listening – as much as she does telling – the story of her hometown and family. He knows he is being treated to something special and hearing Hoyt tell this amazing history makes him feel a connection to Leola.

"Now how we came to be was that the Negroes from Eatonville used to live in Maitland, the place we call Eatonville's blonde sister. And the white people of Maitland were instrumental in helping the Negroes of Maitland found the town of Eatonville out of good will and mutual respect. Some say it was to get all the Negroes out of their town, but that just is not true. A man named Captain Lawrence, one of the three white sponsors, donated three buildings. And Captain Eaton, who the town is named after, made a tract of land on a 22-acre site available." Hoyt continues to move methodically throughout her beehives as she tells the history – her history. Davis sees that both the beehives and the history are truly a part of Hoyt. He tries to collect honey, to keep pace with her as she tells her story, but he is lost in her narrative and can focus on nothing else. Hoyt doesn't seem to mind.

"This tract was bought by Judge Lewis Lawrence from Captain Eaton on May 24, 1881, and was added to land previously purchased by Joe Clark from Eaton. The town was incorporated in August of 1887 by a unanimous colored vote of the 27 qualified voters as the first incorporated all-black town in the United States of America. The name of Eatonville was proposed by Judge Lawrence, after the man who had sold him the land that the town of Eatonville was built on." Hoyt stops her work and suddenly says, "Now, this is important, and you have to get this right."

"Absolutely," he says quickly.

"Eatonville and Maitland always got along. Maybe it was because Maitland never imposed on it. Eatonville never did anything special, but always did what it pleased.

"Eatonville is like any other place. It has its big folks and its small, and, although we are not a big place, this town has always had what it needed. In the past 60 years, this town here has produced a doctor, a dentist, two pharmacists, two nurses, and a few successful businessmen, along with some preachers, some more successful than others . . ." Hoyt stops and lets out a quick burst of laughter and then goes on, "several school teachers, and one author named Zora Neale Hurston, whose father, John Hurston, was the very first mayor of this town. But our blood, the Jones's blood, has always been flowing through the veins of this town, and always will."

Davis starts to work on his own honeycomb, following Hoyt's lead.

"Can I ask you a question?"

"Of course you can, baby boy."

Hoyt knows she would never want her daughter to be with a white man, but she finds herself a bit taken with this man who is so intent on learning everything he can about the town. It warms her heart to think that this Eatonville history will be passed on, not just to this handsome young reporter, but to everyone who will read what he writes. She hopes that his pen and paper will keep the history alive.

"Who was that grand regal old woman sitting in the front of the store on the porch?" he asks.

"Oh, her name is Laura Henderson and she is the reigning belle of Eatonville. She's its oldest woman since Grand Ma Biddy passed away at 104. Miss Laura is 90 years old. When her great, great grandbaby named Jacqueline was born, that gave our family five living generations, all in this town. Now, that is something to be proud of," Hoyt exclaims, flashing Davis a quick smile as she works at the honeycombs. "That Laura Henderson in her day, boy, she was a looker. She turned the heads of many a man – and she has outlived both of her husbands. I am not sure she is done yet, to be honest." Both laugh at this.

"Now, where does Columbus come in as mayor?" Davis asks.

"He is the tenth mayor of Eatonville and has big plans for this town. Work has already begun on building our own firehouse and putting in the water pipes. We are even going to have street lights! Can you imagine? Our little old town having fancy street lights!" she exclaims.

Hoyt is so proud of Columbus's accomplishments. Davis memorizes every word as he listens to this woman talk about her husband and her town. Neither of them is working the hives at this point; Hoyt is sitting on an old tree stump in a meadow, slightly away from the beehives. Davis sits on the ground taking notes, writing like a crazy man, trying to get it all down while she talks.

"I am so sorry. Once you get me going on this town and our family history, I can just go on for hours. The stories I could tell you," she says, laughing.

"Miss Jones, I am enjoying every second of it. You just talk as long as you want."

"We have work to do, though," Hoyt says lifting herself from the tree stump, brushing the wrinkles from her britches. "It is not often I have these kinds of treats in the way of all this help, and I am going to take advantage of it and get some things in order." Hoyt's expression darkens, and her brow furrows. "Columbus is not strong right now, and I don't like to push him hard these days. I believe God sent you to hear me at this time, to help me get things in order and take some of the burden off Columbus. I know he worries so. And you call me Hoyt, you hear? Everyone does." Davis nods.

"I think that is enough for now. But now you know what this town is and who we are. You know Leola. Her father has always told her that you have to work twice as hard, being black in this world, to be considered half as good. And without an education, your life is limited. She took that to heart, and now she has a fine education and is doing some things that no woman in this family could ever even imagine. I want her to do well. Not that I don't want lots of grand babies and to see her settle down with a nice educated black man, like Clarence," Hoyt watches to see Davis's reaction as she says this. Davis flinches, trying to hide the pang of jealousy that ran through him from those words. "When they were children, we all just knew that they would end up together, but, with so much going on in the South, Clarence was just too much of a free thinker for these parts. His parents sent him north where he would be safe and not end up like my boys," Hoyt says, tearing up, ". . . strung up on a tree by the neck just for being who they were."

Hoyt stops and fights back tears, straightening her back to regain composure as she says, "No, we could not see that happen to Clarence. Now, look at him! He's tall, strong, educated, and as handsome as the devil. We are still holding out that Leola will smarten up, marry Clarence, and make us some grandchildren."

Davis feels the family history working against him personally. This new information about Leola's brothers and her long past with Clarence explains a lot about the loyalty Clarence has for Leola – and she for him. Davis could always see that they were close, but he had no idea how deep that friendship has always been.

Davis changes the subject with "We'd better get to those chores you need done and put me to work, then. I want to make sure we get everything you need done finished before we have to go."

Hoyt agrees. They leave the meadow to find Clarence and Deacon, who are sure to be knee-deep in work by now.

———————

The Bethune-Cookman College Band has transformed themselves into a symphony orchestra for the Black Ball; their version of "The Blue Danube" fills the dance hall with just the right amount of music to guide gentle conversation.

"Leola, I can't believe you arranged for live music. I swear it makes the evening," her friend Susanna Fields gushes.

"Why, Susanna, that's so kind of you to say," Leola says as she smiles back. "Yes, they're really rising to the occasion."

As has been done every year by the women of the Cotillion Committee, the hall is impeccably set for a proper Southern gala. The gentlemen are dressed in their finest tuxedos, and all the ladies are in white gowns with long white gloves. Standing at the edge of the dance floor, Deacon takes deep breaths and rocks from one foot to the other as he watches several couples glide across the floor. His palms are clammy and his mouth dry. His eyes are glued to the people on the floor.

"My God, Clarence, they're all dancing in unison," he says at last. "It looks like one of those damn Fred Astaire and Ginger Rogers movies. They're so good. I can't get out there and keep up. I can't."

Clarence smiles, relieved that Deacon isn't worried about the speech he is going to deliver after dinner.

"You'll do fine, Milk Man," Clarence says, slipping into using Deacon's nickname as he coaches him on how to dance. "Remember all those lessons Leola made us take before this trip. Just relax . . . one, two, three, bow . . . one, two, three, bow," he says, swaying to his own lesson. "And besides, if you feel like you're losing the beat, just let your partner lead. You can't go wrong with that one, trust me."

Elvinia, who has met them at the ball after arriving at her Maitland hotel room earlier that evening, marvels at the entire spectacle. She leans over to Davis, who sits beside her at a table near the stage, and whispers, "Davis, remember your sister's wedding and how everything had to be perfect for your mother that night? This is real perfection, believe me."

Elvinia looks like a foreign dignitary in her gown; her hair is swept up in a mass of elegant gray curls. She can't help but stress the British accent as she speaks to the other ball-goers.

"Most impressive." she continues, "It really is. And I can't wait to hear Deacon's speech. He showed his notes to me this afternoon, and I must say that there are some special words in there. He's a brave boy to be talking to a room full of black people about his time with the *Catfish*."

Davis, who has not taken his eyes off of Leola since they arrived, snaps his face toward Elvinia. "He asked you to read his speech, too?"

Elvinia bursts out laughing.

"You didn't have to tell me that, Davis. I saw some of your handiwork in what he gave me, believe me. And when are you going to learn that 'hopefully' just isn't a word? My goodness, all those years of education, and you still find yourself doing harm to the world's most descriptive language. You just had to inflict your sins onto that dear, innocent farm boy?"

"Actually, Elvinia, it wasn't my idea at all. Deacon told me that Clarence came up with the idea that you and I should look at his speech," Davis retorts, flashing a sly grin.

"Yes, I know that too," says Elvinia. "Clarence told Deacon he'd be a fool not to, with Houston's best sports writer, and the woman who taught him everything he knew along on the ride."

Leola, Davis, Clarence, and Deacon are the stars of the evening. Everyone wants to meet Deacon, the only white player in the barnstorming leagues. As the evening wears on, rumors fly about the looks Leola and Davis share with each other during conversations with the other guests. It doesn't take long for a pattern to develop. All the women want to dance with Davis, a veteran of formal balls who knows what he is doing. And all the men take their turns twirling Elvinia across the floor as she makes it her own, gracefully presiding over and enjoying every moment. Meanwhile, Clarence, Leola, and Deacon make their way from table to table, exchanging greetings and smiles, barely giving themselves time to sit down for dinner.

The time grows near for the Black Ball's formal program. There will be introductions by Leola Jones and her court, followed by welcoming remarks from the president of Bethune-Cookman College, and – what everyone is waiting for – the speech Deacon will deliver about his experience as the unique *Catfish* star pitcher. But just before dessert, Susanna Fields rushes over to Leola and asks her to step out into the hall. When she explains why, the hall is filled with Leola's wailing.

"No, no, not Daddy . . . not Daddy . . . not Daddy!"

Clarence gathers Davis, Elvinia and Deacon, excusing themselves to be with Leola in the hall as the rest of the guests sit in stunned silence, listening to the cries of their maid of honor.

"He had a heart attack," Leola sobs as the four rush to her side. "Daddy's gone," she bawls as she buries her face in Clarence's chest. Davis steps up to comfort her, but Elvinia stops him.

"Go get the car, dear. It is time for all of you to go back to be with Hoyt. Someone else will manage the situation here," she assures him. "Poor Hoyt is all alone. She and Leola need you all right now. I'll bring them out to the door to meet you, Davis. Please go and get the car."

Davis hugs Elvinia, impressed and grateful for her cool instincts, and then takes off for the car.

"Come with me, child." Elvinia says to Leola, "We're going home. All of us. Davis is getting the car now."

With Deacon on one side and Clarence the other, Leola is escorted out of the ball and into Davis's car.

Everyone stays in Eatonville three extra days to be with Hoyt and to attend Columbus's funeral. They all agree that Deacon's speech, which he had written for the Black Ball, will be delivered at the service instead. He is even more nervous to speak at Columbus's memorial than he was at the ball. Deacon leans heavily on Clarence, Davis, and Elvinia for support as he prepares to speak at this great man's funeral, a man he had just met in the past week.

"I worshiped the guy, based on what everyone told me about him. But, Good Lord, I only met him for a day, and now I'm speaking at his funeral?"

"Deacon," Elvinia replies, "you wrote a speech thanking him for the opportunity he gave you to play baseball with the best group of teammates you could imagine. And you also wrote how he made you feel like a part of the family, first with Leola, Clarence, and Isaac, and then with himself and Hoyt. I think you should deliver the same speech. It's okay to make people smile when you eulogize a great man."

Elvinia's candor is a comfort to Deacon. He glances down at his speech and takes a deep breath. *She is right*, he thinks. *This speech is perfect to remember a great man. Whether I knew him a day or a lifetime, he touched my life in a big way.* But he does decide to change it, just a bit. This time, he will ask no one to look it over. He will write from the heart and deliver a eulogy worthy of the man he just met, a man he owes so much to.

The church is overflowing the day of the funeral, and the service lasts twice as long as most funerals. People have come from all over Florida, and Isaac Manns brought a few *Catfish* players from Texas to be there for his old friend. Hoyt is strong as usual, comforting everyone else and thanking them for their kindness. But, even as she smiles, there is a sad loneliness in her eyes. Leola sees this better than anyone and won't leave her mother's side.

"Friends, I am here to honor a great man," Deacon says from behind the pulpit as hundreds of eyes are trained on him. "Someone who gave so many of us here so many opportunities to get the most out of life. In the very short time I knew him, it was easy to see that he was a strong man, a family man, and a wise man. For Leola, he was Daddy. For Hoyt, he was the love of her life. For Isaac Manns, he was a lifelong best friend. These are the ways in which he will always be remembered, and justly so. But there are others here – many of us – who will remember Columbus Jones in another way.

"He was a great teammate. His team is the *Eatonville Catfish*, the best barnstorming baseball team in both Texas and Florida, and we will always be his team. All of *our* accomplishments would not be possible without *his* dream of giving men a chance to succeed on the baseball diamond. While he wasn't able to get to Texas to run the team himself, he did the next best thing and sent Leola Jones, Isaac Manns, and Clarence Holloman. Together, the three of them come pretty darn close to doing what he would have done – on his own."

There is a soft laughter that breaks the reverent silence in the church. Deacon's muscles relax a little, hearing the chuckles. He feels more comfortable and finds his rhythm up in front of a church full of strangers.

"I came here to Eatonville to thank Columbus Jones for giving me the chance to play for his team and to represent his tradition of success and achievement. I thank God that I had the opportunity to do that earlier this week in person. It may seem remarkable that someone who looks like me can be a *Catfish* and can take the field with my teammates – to win baseball games together. Some people don't even like the idea that I do it, but when it comes right down to it, I'm just a lucky pitcher who found his way onto a great team. That's all. I found my way like this: I was invited. The *Catfish* brought me in. I got the chance to play ball instead of having to work on my family's farm – only because these people gave me that chance." He gestures toward Isaac, Leola and Clarence.

"The real achievement of the *Eatonville Catfish* is not the fact that there's a white pitcher on a Negro League team. It's not even how many home runs Battleship Morgan hits or bases that Coathanger Barnes steals, or even the way Jazz Gray calls a game from behind the plate. What the *Catfish* mean, and always will mean, is teamwork, above all else. It's giving an opportunity to folks who just need a chance and then helping them turn that opportunity into success.

It's happened for me, and it will happen for many others as long as there is a team called the *Eatonville Catfish*. Columbus Jones will always be the leader of our team. Thank you, Mr. Jones, for giving me the chance to be on your team."

CHAPTER NINETEEN

A NEW SEASON

The 1950 season comes too soon for Leola and the *Catfish*, which Columbus left to Leola in his will, making her the first female owner of a baseball team in American history. All of this is recorded and delivered to the front steps of homes and businesses across Houston, thanks to one Davis Sterling. As momentous as the occasion should be for Leola, it is eclipsed by the grief of losing her father and concern for her mother being alone out in Eatonville. For weeks, she has moped around wherever she goes. Leola is a powerful presence, so the gloom she carries with her is contagious. It seems to have replaced the brightness she once brought to any room she entered. She is a different person than she was when she inspired Uncle Isaac and Clarence to do great things. She is lost in her grief and, as a result, the *Catfish* are adrift.

"Clarence, we've got a season to play here," Isaac announces one April afternoon in the living room of the house that he, Clarence, and Leola are renting in Houston. "It's been a hard winter in a lot of ways, but the mayor would want us to come back fightin'. I'm ready to do just that, but I'll need your help. We've got to pull the *Catfish* together – now more than ever. I'm sure you know that our best players are being watched by scouts from the major leagues, just like they're watching all the other teams we play. We've got to get the team rolling before we get picked clean."

"You're right, Coach. We're in a bad way right now and need to get our heads back on right. But Leola is . . ."

Clarence stops midsentence when Leola walks into the room.

"Good afternoon, gentlemen," she announces. "I've been doing a lot of thinking, trying to decide if I need to go back to Eatonville to take care of Mama during the busy season – or stay here and run the team."

Isaac begins to say something, but Leola doesn't let him. "It's a tough choice, as I'm sure you both appreciate. I'm sorry it's taken so much time for me to make up my mind, but I think I finally have."

"And?" Clarence says.

"And my father didn't leave me the *Catfish* so I could go home to Eatonville and help Mama with her chores. Shoot, Mama wouldn't like me doing that if you asked her, I can promise you that. So let's get going, boys; we've got a season to play!"

Clarence's eyes flash as Leola says this; he almost glows with excitement, not just for the team, but also because Leola is back.

"Leola, I cannot tell you how happy this makes me. It's going to be hard, with your heart tugging you back to Florida and the Major Leagues tugging at our players, but you're right. Your daddy would want you to get the *Catfish* out on the field to defend their title. We are as sure of that as we know Galveston has a dirty brown beach. I'm with you."

"Well, look at you, a regular couple of Harry and Bess Trumans, you are, givin' 'em hell," Isaac breaks in. "And you know I love a good bull session as much as any other guy. I'd love to stay here and have one with you two, but, if we've got a season to play, there's a lot of work to do. Starting today. Clarence, how are we set up for our schedule? Leola, how much money do we have in the bank? When was the last time we checked up on that bucket of bolts we call a team bus? You don't think I've been sitting around moping, do you?"

Leola laughs. "No, Uncle Isaac, I never thought you were sitting around moping. And we've got $2,500 in the bank from Daddy's will, just waiting to be spent to take the *Catfish* all over this giant, godforsaken state. I'll call Fester's Garage and see what they think the bus needs to take us from point A to point B. Clarence, how long do you think it will take to work up a schedule for the year?"

"I've got twenty games lined up from Mother's Day through the Fourth of July. All we need to do is sign on the bottom line," Clarence answers.

"The *Huntsville Hangmen* on Opening Day, then the *Galveston Flyaways*, a Memorial Day doubleheader with the *Austin Black Senators*, the *San Antonio Black Indians* in June, and a big game at Buff Stadium against the *Houston Eagles*. You don't think I've been sitting around moping either, do you?" Clarence winks at Isaac with his last statement.

"Well, I'd love to stay and shoot the breeze with you both, but I've got some phone calls to make," Isaac replies, ignoring the jab. "Jazz wants to start practicing on Saturday."

Isaac plants himself by the phone and gets right to it. For the next two hours, he remains planted as he calls each of the *Catfish* players, one by one, back for the new season.

He starts with Jupiter Monroe (first baseman), then Battleship Morgan (the hulking outfielder), and Coathanger Barnes (their spunky short-stop). They are all ready to go. Next, there's Stormin' Norman Whitman on the mound. Jazz Gray is the team's catcher and a hell of a sax player and, of course, there's Deacon Johnson. Maximilian "Emperor" LaRue declines the offer to rejoin the 1950 *Catfish* season; he has left third base vacant for a minor league tryout with the *St. Louis Cardinals*. Outfielder Bo Jefferson is in jail for passing bad checks, and nobody has seen Pipsqueak Phillips, their rookie second basemen, since he drove out West with his girlfriend in February.

"I'll just replace them all with new players," Isaac says when his phone calls are complete.

Saturday, May 13, twenty players, Isaac, Clarence, and Leola board the team bus for the drive to Old Alamo Stadium in Huntsville. It will be the Sunday game against their biggest rival, the *Hangmen*. The bus rolls away, its brand-new official *Catfish* sky blue and gold paint sparkling in the spring sunshine. A big Florida state flag has also been painted on the driver's side.

"Do you like the new paint job?" Leola asks Clarence and Isaac. "Jazz did the painting last week behind Fester's Garage with his friends."

"He's a regular Picasso, I'd say," Isaac answers. "Let's just hope it drives as good as it looks," he adds as the bus lurches forward.

The game is a typical *Catfish* vs. *Hangmen* grinder. Waterbug Nelson, the *Hangmen's* firecracker pitcher, holds the *Catfish* scoreless through six innings, while the *Hangmen's* big bats score two early runs on a double, and a home run in the third. Jupiter Monroe scores the first *Catfish* run of the season with a towering bomb over the clay outfield walls in the seventh. The score stays 2-1 until the top of the ninth.

Deacon Johnson leads off, staring down Waterbug Nelson as he walks to the plate. He never stops staring and draws a walk. Everyone in the *Catfish* dugout and fans wearing *Catfish* blue in the stands knows Deacon isn't as quick with his feet as he is with his fastball. The crowd, including several players' mothers dressed in their Sunday best, wait for Coach Manns to pull him for a pinch runner. But Isaac plays a hunch and keeps him in the game.

"You sure about this, Coach?" Clarence asks, sitting beside Isaac in the dugout.

"I figure we might need some solid pitching at the end of the game," Isaac tells him.

The hunch doesn't work. On the first pitch, Barnes hits a screaming grounder to second base. The double play goes from first back to second base, beating Deacon to the bag.

"Damn!" Isaac murmurs.

"We got one more out. We can do this," Clarence encourages him.

The *Hangmen's* manager calls for a pitching change when he sees that Battleship Morgan is on deck. Battleship is nursing a sore knee he got diving for a fly ball earlier in the game, but he still has power. While the new pitcher throws a few in the bullpen and Morgan stretches out his knee, a minor commotion breaks out behind the stands.

"Hey, Coach Manns, can you put me in the game?" a voice calls.

Isaac stops and squints at a figure approaching the dugout. It is Pipsqueak Phillips, with his girlfriend, Mona Lee, on his arm.

"Me and Mona went to San Antonio to visit her family and wound up getting married. They had the reception at the Gunter Hotel. It was something, I can tell you that. Wasn't it, Mona?" He is mobbed by the *Catfish* before the new Mrs. Phillips can answer.

"I'd like to make a substitution as well," Isaac calls out to the ump.

"Whaddaya say? Phillips for Morgan? I know he's not in the lineup, but y'all know he's a big part of our team."

In fact, Pipsqueak did make a couple of big plays in last season's game with the *Hangmen*, including catching a vicious line drive to end the sixth inning with two men in scoring position. The teams are friendly rivals, so they agree. Pipsqueak goes right in to bat for the *Catfish* in seven minutes flat. Unfortunately, Pipsqueak could have used a little warming up. He swings at three bad pitches in a row and strikes out, ending the game. The *Catfish* may have lost their opening game. But the season is on, and that is reason enough to celebrate.

The 1950 season continues with much of the energy and fun of the previous year. In a week's time. Morgan's knee heals, and he returns to launch a home run out of the park. Deacon is a master on the mound, pitching back-to-back shutouts in Austin and San Antonio.

Their game against the *Eagles* in Houston's Buffalo Stadium draws a large Fourth of July crowd, and the *Catfish* romp, ending the game at 8-2. Back on the bus, Coach Manns delivers his usual colorful congratulatory message to the team, "I'm so glad we won that game, particularly in that god-forsaken stadium," he says. When Jazz asks him why, Isaac continues, "It's been haunted ever since that poor laundry worker shot himself in the press box during that game last month."

"Thank God we didn't know that before the game," Jazz replied. "Some of us would never have gone out onto that field." The rest of the *Catfish* burst out laughing; they all knew Jazz was right.

"Johnson Spins a Gem, Catfish Beat Eagles 8-2" Sports Section, *Houston Star*, Wednesday, July 5, 1950

For the second year, Houston's two Negro baseball teams played on Independence Day in hallowed Buffalo Stadium. This year's affair was a sellout as the newcomers from New Jersey and the barnstorming Catfish combined their fan bases to celebrate liberty, freedom, and pride in the growing movement to integrate America's pastime. They stood in unison for a rousing rendition of the national anthem, led by the combined marching bands of Jack Yates and Phillis Wheatley High Schools, which hail from Houston's Third and Fifth Wards, respectively. There were real rockets' red glare on cue, as fireworks were launched during the anthem from behind the bleachers. The fans gave the bands, and themselves, a five-minute standing ovation when the anthem was over. And, then, the teams played some baseball.

The Houston Eagles were this year's home team, and they ran out onto the field before the star-spangled cheering ended. Lefty pitcher Max Manning, one of the team's stars from its years in Newark, New Jersey, took the mound and proceeded to strike out the side, mowing down Coathanger Barnes, Pipsqueak Phillips, and Bo Jefferson on just 13 pitches. Then, under the lights on a hot summer night, the Catfish trotted out of the dugout to their respective bases, led by pitcher Deacon Johnson, pounding his mitt with his throwing hand.

The team's star hurler has the look of a man possessed this season. Going into last night's game, his record was already something special. So far, he's pitched in eight games, and the Catfish have won seven of them. Their only loss was on opening day, to their archrival Huntsville Hangmen, when pinch hitter Pipsqueak

Phillips struck out swinging on three pitches to end a 2-1 heart-breaker. Johnson was as hot as a firecracker himself, retiring the first nine batters he faced, striking out five.

For three innings, the two pitchers went toe-to-toe. Manning held the Catfish scoreless, allowing only a single and two walks. Nobody on either team saw second base. It all changed in the top of the fourth when Jazz Gray lined a double to left center, beating the throw with his legendary speed, sliding in just under the tag. Jupiter Monroe was up next. Half of the crowd was already rooting for a home run. Instead, he hit a lazy seeing-eye single right between second and the Eagles' shortstop, with Gray holding his base. That brought up the pitcher himself, and, true to form, Johnson grounded into a fielder's choice, with Gray thrown out at third. The next Catfish batter, Coathanger Barnes, stole some of the magic fans expected from slugger Jupiter Monroe and hit his first long ball of the season. It was a screamer down the right field line, a hit that often turns into a triple given the dimensions of Buffalo Stadium. Last night was no exception, and, just like that, the score was 2-0, Catfish.

It held that way for two more innings as the pitchers matched each other in frustrating their opposing batsmen, until the Eagles got to Johnson in the bottom of the sixth. Matching his teammates for doing the unexpected last night, he walked Bob Harvey, the lead-off man, on four pitches. He gave everyone, including himself, an even worse surprise when he allowed center fielder Willie Williams to take his first pitch over the wall to tie the game, 2-2. Johnson stalked the mound between pitches for the rest of the inning in obvious frustration, but he was good enough to get the next three batters out in order. The game went on to the seventh inning.

It took nearly 20 minutes to get to the stretch, and, by that time, the Catfish had exploded for six runs to take a commanding lead. They were led by another double from Jazz Gray, then a walk by Jupiter Monroe, bringing up Deacon Johnson himself with two men on and no one out. He helped his own cause and brought Catfish fans to their feet with a stroke that torqued every bit of his 6'3" frame into a human rocket launcher. With a loud crack of his bat, Johnson hit a hanging curveball out to deep left field and over everything. It was 5-2, Catfish, but, with no outs, they weren't done. Coathanger Barnes, who got his nickname from his wiry physique, somehow managed to continue hitting for power, following his earlier triple with a stand-up double that one hopped the right field wall. Then DeSoto Olivera, the Catfish's new third baseman this season, smashed another double off Manning, making it 6-2. Jupiter Monroe struck out on eight pitches after that for the inning's first out.

The Catfish's smallest player, Pipsqueak Phillips, was up next and, if there was ever going to be a surprise to top them all on a magical Fourth of July, it would be a two-run homer from their spark-plug leadoff hitter. That's exactly what he gave his fans, streaking a low line drive just inside the right field foul pole. It brought the crowd to their feet. Everyone in the Catfish dugout, to a man (and a woman, for that matter) ran out onto the field to congratulate him. Owner Leola Jones was standing there as he crossed home plate, greeting him with a big smile and a warm handshake before she wisely got out of the way, as he was mobbed by his teammates and Coach Isaac Manns.

The rest of the game was anticlimactic, with no more scoring and a return to the pitching clinic given by Catfish ace Deacon Johnson. He retired the side in order in the bottom of the seventh, walked and stranded a batter in the eighth, and ended the game with a double-play ball to second base with one out in the bottom of the ninth. It was a night that began with music and fireworks commemorating our nation's birthday and Houston's civic pride. And the fireworks continued with a display of power that left Catfish fans hoping they'll have more to celebrate. Maybe, like Leola Jones standing at home plate in the top of the seventh inning, we'll all have something to smile about come September.

The Fourth of July game is a monstrous victory for the *Catfish*, but it is also the beginning of a disturbing trend. The *Eagles* have lost several key players and are well on their way to having the worst record in the history of barnstorming. At the end of the 1950 season, the *Eagles* fold. When Isaac hears about the team breaking up and dissolving, he takes the news hard.

"This is not just bad news for the *Eagles*," he tells Clarence. "This could be a warning for all of us about what lies ahead. This could mean tough times are comin' for the *Catfish*."

As shaken as he is, he doesn't let his fear stop him from going on to develop the *Catfish* into the best barnstorming team in the country.

He takes the dissolution of the *Eagles* as an opportunity to recruit third baseman Bob Harvey to fill the hole left by Emperor LaRue earlier in the season. The *Catfish* finish the season with a winning record, but the Texas Negro League Championship goes to the *Hangmen*. Still, there is some good news; except for the *Eagles*, no other team disbanded that season.

The 1951 season is another good year for the *Catfish* in terms of their play on the field and growing crowds, but the absence of the *Houston Eagles* takes its toll. There are rumors of other teams dissolving as well. Some of these rumors come to pass.

"We have to keep driving farther and farther to play our games," Leola tells Clarence and Isaac. "I don't know how much longer the old bus can take it. The folks at Fester's Garage are miracle workers, but y'all can hear that engine struggling. It sounds like we're climbing when we're on a road as flat as a pancake. I'm no mechanic, but that's not a good sign."

Even with the struggling bus and the loss of a rival team, Isaac is able to hold his players together and keep spirits up. The *Catfish* ride on another great pitching season from Deacon Johnson. The team ends the season with only one loss, and they go on to win their first championship. The *Catfish* beat their old rivals the *Hangmen* in Houston's Buff Stadium in front of a sold-out crowd.

The *Catfish* aren't the only ones making waves that year. Davis has his best sports writing season to date covering every game and traveling on the team bus so he doesn't miss a play. Without the *Eagles*, Houston's Negro League fans need a new team, and Davis is only too happy to oblige with flattering articles about the *Catfish*, Coach Manns, its star pitcher Deacon Johnson, and, most of all, its owner, Leola Jones. More than a few readers take notice of the obvious infatuation the journalist has with his subject matter. One is Jeffrey Fields, elevator operator at the *Star*.

"Good morning, Mr. Sterling," he greets Davis one morning. "You sure are writing some fine stories about the *Catfish* these days. And I especially enjoy reading about that beautiful woman who owns the team. She is a credit to our city; I can tell you that." Then he adds, with a chuckle, "As if you need me to tell you." Instead of trying to deny the subtle accusation, Davis breaks into nervous laughter, which makes Jeffrey chuckle even louder.

"Well, thank you, Jeffrey," Davis says when he regains his composure.

"You know, you were the one who pointed them out to me in the first place."

"I might have pointed out the team, Mr. Davis, but nobody had to tell you anything about Miss Leola. You found her all by yourself. Yes, you did."

The elevator doors open before Davis can respond to Jeffrey. He gives him a wink and a pat on the shoulder and heads to his office to work on his next article.

Their 1951 championship is the first and only *Catfish* title. The next year, competing in a still-smaller Texas Negro League, the *Catfish* lose Barnes to the *Baltimore Orioles* farm team, the *Norfolk Tides*, in Virginia. Shortly after that, Morgan's knee finally gives out. His retirement dinner at Jazz's family's rebuilt juke joint is a bright spot in the season. Battleship leaves the team with one last speech that no one will forget.

"Now, all y'all who aren't on the *Catfish* team are probably wondering how we all get along in the locker room with our white pitcher," he starts, looking over at Deacon with an ear-to-ear grin. "I'm here to tell you it was an educational experience. Until old Deacon came along, we didn't know anything about the kind of things white folks deal with. For starters, there are tan lines. Until we had to suit up with the Milk Man, not a one of us knew the same person could be two different colors."

The entire room, Deacon included, burst out into laughter; then, he stands to offer some proof, rolling up his sleeve to show his tan line. The laughter escalates into roars as Deacon shows off a lighter shade of pale beneath his shirt sleeve. When the room settles down, Morgan continues with his improper roast.

"Then, there's the tragedy of pimples. All of us have them, but people like Deacon really show them off. I mean, those suckers are red now! Poor Deacon just can't hide them! They just have to run their colorful course, which we've all learned from observation takes about a week. And, of course, there are freckles, which some of us have too, particularly Jupiter, who has more of them than anyone I know, except Deacon, of course. The difference is, Deacon's freckles become super-charged in the sun. If you have never seen a pale white boy come in from out of the sun, you are missing out. The first time I saw this, I thought my eyes were playing tricks on me.

"I am telling you now, you can learn a lot from having a white team-mate. But, at the end of the day, we all share freckles. They're one of God's great equalizers.

"Finally, there is the greatest scourge of all for people like Deacon – hickeys! I mean, the poor man would come back after a hot date, and we could all tell exactly what that woman did to our star pitcher. We could see it, all of it! Man, Deacon, I just don't know how you're able to survive the shame."

Battleship went out in a blaze of laughter, but the laughter faded soon thereafter for the *Catfish*. The *Catfish* entered the 1952 season on a somber note – with fewer teams to play, fewer players on the *Catfish*, and even fewer stories about the team coming out in the *Star*. As the *Catfish* flail, Davis is experiencing a fair amount of acknowledgment and accolades from his colleagues, who encourage him to write "bigger" stories as barnstorming baseball teams fade. Even so, Davis still breaks the news about George Kirksey's ultimately unsuccessful efforts to buy the *St. Louis Cardinals* and bring them to Houston, a story that brings him national attention. As a result, he begins to get assignments writing about Houston politics and statewide stories. Once a regular on the *Catfish* team bus, Davis often misses games and trips because he is off in Austin, or Dallas, or even Washington, D.C., covering stories about the upcoming presidential election. He is even sent to London to cover the death of King George VI and the coronation of Queen Elizabeth. He makes the trip with Elvinia, who is thrilled at the opportunity to guide his reporting. Leola, Clarence, and Isaac all take note of Davis's absence, and its timing.

"He sure was here when it was bringing him a hot new story to put out in that paper," Clarence says to Leola one day after reading a piece Davis has written in a national newspaper. "I guess we don't have enough to offer him anymore," he adds, cutting his eyes toward Leola.

"I guess we don't," she replies brusquely and leaves the room.

"It was only a matter of time," Clarence says to Isaac when Leola is gone. "I was starting to warm up to him, but I think I always knew this was coming. She should have, too."

"It's easy to be blind to some things," Isaac replies.

"It's only easy for a little while though," Clarence says. "Once your eyes are open, then it gets hard."

CHAPTER TWENTY

OBITUARY FOR THE CATFISH (1955)

The glow of the fading evening sun spreads over the kitchen table as Isaac, Clarence and Leola look over the coming schedule. "I need a shortstop, a left fielder, and a first baseman," says Isaac. It's early in the season and things are off to a rough start. The barnstorming leagues are dwindling as more players move over to Major League teams. "No matter what I promise them, they just won't stay," Isaac continues. "But you know, can't blame them. Blame or no blame, though, I don't know what we are going to do."

Clarence knows that the end is near, but he won't be the one to say it aloud. He searches for something to say to Isaac that doesn't belie what he feels is the inevitable.

"Isaac, you're the only person I know who can find talent anywhere. I've seen you pick up all-stars from places no one would think to look – Lake Killarney, Kissimmee, Titusville. My father himself said you could look at a man and tell where he belonged on the field and how good he'd be. I've seen it, too. You can also do that anywhere across Texas. Talent is talent, and I will never meet anyone who knows how to spot it better than you."

"I thank you for your confidence, and I hope that I live up to it. But even if I can and do find the talent, there's no money to offer once I find them. We can offer travel on our old team bus and maybe a championship, but what we can pay won't keep a roof over a man's head, let alone take care of a family if that's what he needs," Isaac says. As he paces around the kitchen table, Leola and Clarence sit. "The major leagues have discovered our players and they got the money to get them. Even with minor league contracts, they can offer security and potential that we never could, even on our best days. You've seen it yourself. How many of our stars have thanked us for the chance to get a start, but left us the second the *Dodgers*, the *Milwaukee Braves*, or even the *Baltimore Orioles* came sniffing around? And why wouldn't they? These men want to play ball for a living. It'd be insane to think they'd stay in a league that can't feed them. I just don't know how we'll convince anybody to come here, let alone stay here. There are teams out there we never thought would give them the time of day that are now offering them things we just can't."

"So when's the last time any of you took a look at the team bus?" Leola asks, changing the subject. She wants to help Isaac figure out some way to get players to come to the *Catfish*, but she is a businesswoman and she knows that they have other problems to take care of if the team that they do have is going to keep going. "It's on its last legs. We either have to buy a new one or forget about traveling around Texas. We've already had to forfeit one game because the bus didn't make it past the Woodlands. We need money for fixing the bus or getting a new one. And with all our players going to the Big Leagues, we're losing more money all the time. We may not pay much now, but if we don't play games, we can't pay anything."

Clarence knows it's up to him to speak the truth, no matter how difficult it will be on everyone in the room. Isaac will keep looking for talent anywhere and everywhere, and Leola will hope against hope that she can keep Columbus's dream alive. The two have more invested than time and money, they have invested their hearts. Clarence knows the heart has a way of clouding the mind.

"Well, Leola, how much money do we have in the bank?"

"You know the answer better than anybody, Clarence. Enough to make payroll for the next two months. Unless we buy a new bus, in which case we can't pay anybody until September, and that's only if we're able to book the same games we scheduled last year. At this rate, I wouldn't promise anybody we can do that. The teams in Desoto and Abilene have already folded. We may be able to play everybody up by Wichita Falls, but only if we buy a new bus." Leola stops a moment and bites at her lip. She taps her finger restlessly on the kitchen table and then says, "I just don't see how we're doing anything but stalling for time, and I can't look at our players' families without letting them know what's coming. They need to know we can't give them what they deserve for staying with us." She looks directly at Isaac and says, "It kills me, but that's the truth, and we all know it. My daddy would never want us to take advantage of the players, knowing what we know."

"You know, you remind me too much of your daddy," Isaac replies; as much as he wants to rebut, he knows Leola is right. "It breaks my heart, but I have to agree with you. It's been a great run, but we don't have much of a choice. I think we have to fold the *Catfish*."

The room goes silent when Isaac says this. It's as if a doctor has called a time of death on a patient after pounding on his chest trying to save him. They all know that they are at the end of an era. After a championship, steady crowds, and great press, the *Catfish*'s heyday is over. They are done.

"Who do we need to tell?" Leola says, breaking the silence. To keep her emotions at bay she jumps into the business end of things. If she can just focus on those, she won't have to focus on the fact that her father's team is about to go under. "I can cancel our games and can tell the people at the dealership that we won't be buying that new bus, but who else needs to hear from us?"

Neither Isaac nor Clarence says anything. Both sit, studying their hands, mulling over everything that is happening. They try to process this the way a family member tries to process the news of a loved one's passing. It's not easy to think – or to speak.

Finally Isaac says, "Well, Leola, you've led us on an incredible journey and we've all enjoyed every minute. If it's time to take the *Catfish* and ride them into the sunset, then I'm all for it – reluctantly, believe me," he says as his eyes turn glossy with tears. "But I don't want to do it without remembering what all of us came here to accomplish, and we need to give my friend Columbus his due. The *Catfish* will always be the best barnstorming team anyone could ever have managed, and we are the three people who managed it. I don't use the term much, but I love the both of you for all you've done."

Leola feels the lump in her throat swell. She fights even harder to keep the well of tears from bursting out of her. She doesn't know if she can respond to her Uncle Isaac's speech, but she knows that it's her turn to talk, so she does.

"I can give the players and staff the bad news, but how do we tell the rest of the world? Do I just pick up the phone and call Davis? Is there something else we should do, given how important this is?"

"Yes, let's call Davis," Clarence replied quickly. "He's been covering the *Catfish* for years and has done a solid job of it. I think he deserves the chance to break this story. I expect he'll do it justice. But Leola, I think you should be the one to call him. He's always written his best stories when he talks to you. It just –" Clarence stops midsentence. He knows his emotions are about to get the best of him and he decides to quit while he is ahead.

"You're right, I'll call Davis," she says. "I'll tell him the news. I'm sure he has seen this coming."

Leola goes into her bedroom and shuts the door.

"I'm sorry, but Mr. Sterling is in California this week covering a story," Davis's secretary, Bridget, tells Leola. "He's due back on Wednesday the 20th. I can leave a message for him at his hotel in Anaheim if you'd like."

Leola's heart sinks as Bridget speaks. All she wants in this moment is to be able to speak to him – to tell him what has happened and hear some words of condolence or comfort, or anything. But he isn't there; he's off covering another story – probably a bigger one that will get him more fame, Leola thinks. An appropriate ending to all this. Davis isn't there at a crucial moment because he has more important things to tend to.

"Yes, Bridget, I'd like that. And please tell him it's urgent."

Leola hangs up the phone and pushes the sudden anger she feels aside. She has another important call to make, to her mother. She calls Hoyt. Finally she doesn't try to keep the knot down that she's been fighting. They both have a long cry over the phone.

Disneyland! It's every kid's dream come true . . . like being there when a television show comes to life and you can just walk and walk and walk and forget everything about the real world outside the gates, Davis scribbles on a piece of paper before he approaches a family outside the entrance to the new amusement park. He begins interviewing random people on Opening Day at Walt Disney's crowning achievement. After talking to a couple of families, he returns to his notepad. *Sunday, July 17, 1955, a hundred degrees, and thousands of people wandering around a strange and wonderful world.*

The story will run in Monday's *Star*, and Davis already has more than enough to write a front page article. Celebrities are everywhere: Frank Sinatra, Art Linkletter, Danny Thomas. Apparently, someone counterfeited the invitation-only tickets, so there are 28,000 people onhand; 11,000 were expected. The asphalt melts underfoot in the heat; several women actually lose their heels in the tarmac. The chaos is everything a reporter could hope for. Davis is in his element. He positions himself up front for Walt Disney's dedication speech which is being broadcast nationwide. Camera crews curse the soft asphalt as they try to roll into position.

"To all who come to this happy place, welcome. Disneyland is **your** land. Here age relives fond memories of the past and here youth may savor the challenge and promise of the future. Disneyland is dedicated to the ideals, the dreams, and the hard facts that have created America with the hope that it will be a source of joy and inspiration to all the world," Disney says to a sunburned crowd.

Old Walt is mercifully brief in the Southern California heat. As he exits the small stage, he turns and heads for the Sleeping Beauty Castle. He takes his own picture of the occasion, even though the Disney publicity people have given him more pictures than he could possibly use.

Davis mixes pleasure with work this trip. He rides Mr. Toad's Wild Ride with some of the children, and "interviews" Fess Parker as Davy Crockett. He makes his way through Kaiser Aluminum's "Hall of Aluminum Fame", posing for a picture below the TWA Rocket to the Moon in Tomorrow Land – just before a gas leak closes this section of the park for the afternoon. By evening, Davis is ready to call it a day; he has more than enough material for his story. He needs to hit the teletype machine at the *Los Angeles Times* which he has reserved for 8 p.m.

On his way to the *Times*, Davis stops by his hotel to check his messages. The desk clerk hand him a single piece of paper, a message from Bridget at the *Star*.

"Call Leola Jones. It's important."

Davis stuffs the note in his pocket and heads for his room. Inside, he sits down on the bed and dials her number. Leola answers on the second ring. She speaks as if she has a cold. She is still recovering from her conversation with Hoyt.

"Leola? What's going on?" Davis asks.

"We're closing down the *Catfish*," she says in a single breath. "We've considered it from all angles, but any time we get a good player, or every time Uncle Isaac makes a good player great, we lose him to some major league team's farm system."

Leola pauses moment and says, "It's funny to be a casualty of something as great as the integration of baseball, but we just can't hack it any more. I wanted you to know as soon as we decided."

"Leola, I'm so sorry," Davis replies. "That's terrible to hear. I wish I were in Houston right now. How are you holding up?" Davis is certainly not in the land of childhood dreams anymore.

"I'm doing all right," Leola answers. "Uncle Isaac and Clarence helped me make the decision. We all know it's best for everyone. Still, I can't believe it. And there are so many people to tell, so many loose ends to tie up. We're shutting down immediately. No final game, no going-away party, no nothing. Any money we can scrape up, we're going to distribute to the players to make things just a bit easier for them." Leola started the call feeling disappointment, even anger toward Davis for not being there, but that has vanished now. She feels comforted by his voice. It's as if they've not been apart the last several months – since he's been out chasing bigger stories.

"What are you going to do?" Davis realizes that with the *Catfish* gone, there might not be anything in Houston to keep Leola around. And the thought of her leaving terrifies him.

"Oh, I don't know. I'll probably go north where a woman like me can build a career in business," she tells him. "Clarence and Deacon have always talked about going to New York City to start a sports equipment business once they were done with the *Catfish*. I guess none of us thought it would come quite this soon."

Davis is crushed. He is in a hotel in California and all he wants is to be back home in Houston, with Leola, who needs him.

"Leola, I'm so sorry, I'm so sorry," is all he can muster.

"Davis, thank you for your kind words," Leola replies softly. "I wish you were here. I will see you when you get back. You've been very kind to the *Catfish*, and to me, and for that I will always be grateful."

Davis feels a sudden shift in the world and it jars him. Leola's news turns things upside down for him. He'd taken so much for granted for a while now, focusing less on the *Catfish*, spending more time on the road, and seeing Leola every once in a while because he's been chasing bigger and better stories. But he had never really thought of their relationship as being over. He was just "away." Now he realized how much might be really gone for good.

"I miss you, Leola."

The line goes dead.

Davis rips up his notes from his visit to Disneyland. He knows what he has to do. Any time he has faced a big crisis in his life – and the possibility of losing Leola is one of the biggest – he has always turned to his writing. This time is no different. He pulls out his typewriter, puts in a piece of paper, and begins typing.

Eatonville Catfish, 1934 -1955
Integration of Major League Baseball Claims a Local Treasure

(Anaheim, California, July 17, 1955). Progress is at the heart of the American dream. Every day is better than yesterday, and tomorrow will surely be even greater. For baseball, better tomorrows began on April 15, 1947, when Jackie Robinson took the field for the Brooklyn Dodgers and ended the Major League's color barrier. It was progress, far more important than the accomplishments of the New York Yankees and Brooklyn Dodgers in that year's World Series, or the winner of any World Series since. And it's progress that still continues. Today, thirteen Major League baseball teams are integrated on the field of play, leaving only three – the Detroit Tigers, the Philadelphia Phillies, and the Boston Red Sox – to come around and join the modern age.

But this is not the story of baseball integration. It is, instead, the obituary for a local team that has given Houston and all of Texas something special since 1947, ironically, the same year Jackie Robinson played his first game for the Dodgers. The Eatonville Catfish, a barnstorming Negro baseball team, a very special team that came to the Lone Star State from Florida and literally rose to the top in just four years, are no more. Today their owner, Leola Jones, the first and only female owner of an American sports team, announced that they are ceasing operations, effective immediately.

The same progress that has brought integrated play to baseball diamonds across America has put the Catfish out of business. No longer able to keep players talented enough to be recruited by Major League farm teams, the Catfish, once a beacon of opportunity for great Negro players, has outlived its reason for being, like the March of Dimes might one day if the new Salk polio vaccine works as well as we all hope.

The March of Dimes can go away proudly, victorious, if the scourge of polio has truly been conquered. The Catfish's end ought to have that same feel-good quality, since it's surely a good thing that young Negro baseball players can now dream of playing at the highest level of the sport, free from the prejudice that kept them down as second-class citizens for too many years. It ought to be good news when Negro League teams are no longer needed as a consolation prize for players skilled enough to beat anyone, anywhere, but unable to prove it without fear of ignorance, prejudice and hate.

But for me, and for thousands of fans of the 1951 Texas Negro Leagues Champion Catfish, their demise is a tragedy. It is a loss that we will never again see Jazz Gray call for a fastball, low and inside, so Stormin' Nelson Whitman can strike out an opponent's best batter with the bases loaded and the game on the line. It's a loss that we have seen the last inside-the-park home run from Coathanger Barnes, the fastest shortstop in all of baseball. And it's a loss that the Catfish's own grand experiment in integration – the sterling career of Deacon Johnson, their white pitching phenom – is also over. It has truly been a pleasure to report on the Catfish, not just in their 1951 Miracle Season, but every year since 1947. It is with a heavy heart that I write this one last story about them.

In addition to all the great players (and they are legion), the Catfish also had one of the finest coaches ever in Isaac Manns. His eye for talent, and his ability to make talent great, are beyond description. The Major Leagues will showcase many of his star players for years to come. They've also had the most singular owner in all of professional sports, Miss Leola Jones, who brought grace and class to baseball like no one else ever has, and maybe ever will.

The team may be gone. But for me, it will always be September 18, 1951, bottom of the ninth in Old Alamo Field, the Catfish down by two against the Huntsville Hangmen, with Deacon Johnson on third, Jupiter Monroe on first, and Battleship Morgan at the plate. With the Championship on the line, Morgan works the count against the Hangmen's great Waterbug Nelson, all five-foot-six of him, until it is 3 and 2. With a swing that might still be swaying sycamore branches across Sam Houston National Forest, Morgan sends a vicious curveball over the centerfield fence to win the game. The Catfish erupt from their bench and, because they can't lift Battleship off the ground, they choose instead to carry Coach Isaac Manns and Leola Jones around the field on their shoulders, perhaps the most beautiful victory lap ever run. Thank you, Battleship. Thank you, Deacon. Thank you, Eatonville Catfish. Thank you, Coach Manns. Thank you, Leola Jones. You've done us all proud.

CHAPTER TWENTY-ONE

GOING NORTH

The phone rings in the living room just as Leola is leaving to clean up the now-empty *Catfish* offices.

"Leola, it's Davis. I'm in St. Louis changing planes for my flight back to Hobby later this afternoon. I miss you and want you to know how sorry I am that I was in Disneyland when the *Catfish* folded. I haven't felt this way since your father died."

"Well, thank you for calling; I understand your feelings," she says, not quite sure of what he means by that. "We should have seen this coming months ago. I can't believe we waited until the old bus broke down to make our decision so abruptly. I hope our players will forgive us. They're the ones I'm most worried about. I've never seen Jazz cry, even when his mama got killed, but he bawled like a baby when Clarence and I told him the news."

"Is there anything I can do when I get back?" Davis asks, hoping for an encouraging answer.

"No, Davis, I do believe Clarence, Uncle Isaac, and I have done all that can be done at this point. Everyone is still just in shock."

Leola knows that her relationship with Davis has also changed forever with the demise of the *Catfish*. With the team gone, they can no longer rely on business concerns to explain the time they spend together.

She sees his absence in her time of need as somehow prophetic. She could rely on Clarence and Uncle Isaac when the going got tough, just like her mother could always rely on Columbus. Davis is different. He is great in the good times, but the Jones family learned long ago that life isn't always about the good times. Leola knows that she is always going to have to rely on herself in any kind of life she might choose that would involve Davis Sterling. And, if that is the case, she decides that she might as well rely on herself completely.

She had fallen in love with Davis and was willing for some time to make things work, even in Houston with Jim Crow laws. And she knows she will be the rock in any relationship she has with any man. She just doesn't want to be Davis's rock. Not any more. Davis's absence when the *Catfish* folded was just the top of a mountain he'd been climbing without her and away from her – away from them. Although her love never completely faded, she had learned to turn off her feelings for Davis once he started traveling more and was around the *Catfish* less and less. Leola always knew that Davis was just following his dreams, and the fact that chasing his dreams meant seeing her less seemed like a bad omen to her, even from the beginning. Now, she was finally allowing herself to feel her heartbreak. And, even though it really hurts, she also realizes that she has experienced far more painful heartbreaks in her life. She couldn't bring herself to put these feelings into words until now, because she still loved Davis enough not to hurt him.

It didn't matter. Davis felt every one of her thoughts in every second of the silence that went by while Leola sorted through her feelings. He knows her well enough, and loves her truly enough, to imagine what she is thinking.

"Did you read my article in yesterday's *Star*?" he asks.

"Yes, Davis, I did, and so did Uncle Isaac and Clarence. Thank you so much for writing it. We thought it was beautiful, a great tribute to all we've done together. I'm making copies today to mail to all the players with a thank-you note. You've really become quite a writer. I'm sure your father is very proud of you."

Davis loses himself in Leola's voice; he feels the warmth of her emotions over the phone. He can't wait to see her, despite a sense of foreboding that he can't shake from his gut.

"Leola, I meant every word in that story and could have written much more, particularly about you. Whatever you do next, I hope I'm around to write about it and tell the world."

"Davis, writing about things is your special talent, but sometimes just being around is more important," Leola says. She hasn't thought the words through. They just escape her lips. She is more surprised than Davis when she hears them in her own ears and is glad Davis can't see her blush. She almost apologizes for what she is sure will hurt Davis deeply. Now Davis is silent.

"I, I … I understand, Leola, and that is why I am so sorry my work took me away. But I'll be home tonight and will call as soon as I get in."

Davis has hurt her, but she knows he never had that intention; he's just a man driven by what he wants to do. He's never been one to think of others. Even if he did hurt her unintentionally, Leola doesn't want to hurt Davis any more.

"You're a good man, Davis Sterling, and I'm proud to call you a friend. It'll be good to see you when you're back in town."

Her emotions start to get the best of her, losing her team *and* the hope of a life together with the man she wants to love, all within a couple of days.

"Have a safe trip back," she says.

"Thanks, Leola, I will," Davis responds and hangs up the receiver.

Davis realizes that he may indeed be a good man. He just isn't quite good enough.

During the entire flight home Davis hardly notices the world going by from his window seat. Bridget had booked him on his favorite airplane, a TWA Lockheed Constellation, and his favorite seat, just behind the left wing. But he is lost in thought for the entire flight; he knows what he has to do when he gets back to Houston. He is going to rededicate himself to the two things he loves in life above all others: Leola and his writing. His father has trusted him with writing features for the paper, and he has been able to take advantage of that trust and write some amazing stories. But, in the midst of these giant strides in his career, he realizes he has neglected something more important than front-page articles. He has neglected Leola.

From 25,000 feet in the air, Davis vows to himself that, from that day forward, he will never again write another sports story. He will turn his attention to real news and on stories about social justice. Leola and the *Catfish* taught him that there are bigger things in life than baseball. He hopes this shift in focus will prove to Leola that he is capable of being a mature man with a real purpose in life. He wants to show her that he is done with his party-boy ways and is ready to do something important with his life. He wants her to be there with him as he does it. He also wants to know that she will love him still, even without the *Catfish* to keep them together.

"Ladies and gentlemen," the captain announces over the intercom, "we have been informed that Houston Hobby Airport has been closed to inbound flights due to thunderstorms in the area. We will be landing shortly in Little Rock, Arkansas, where we will wait out the weather on the ground before proceeding on to Houston. All of us at TWA apologize for the inconvenience."

Davis's heart sinks. He will have to wait yet another night to see Leola.

Over the coming months, it seems that the universe is working against Davis. One accident of circumstance after the next keeps Leola and him apart. Many of these are the work of Clarence, who is going into business with Deacon in New York City. He and Deacon begin traveling to New York to start their sports equipment company. The entire time that Clarence is away, he is adamant in his opinion that Leola's best chances for success are in the Northeast.

While Davis takes a more subtle approach to win Leola's heart through his thoughtful newspaper articles, Clarence is much bolder with his persuasive efforts. He enlists the help of none other than Elvinia Kincade to convince Leola to move to New York City.

"Why, Clarence Holloman, what a pleasant surprise to hear your voice!" Elvinia chirps into the phone.

"Professor Kincade, it's great to speak with you also. I hope you're doing well."

"I am most certainly doing nothing but fine," she replies playfully. "I've heard the news about the *Catfish*. Terrible blow to us all. How are Davis and Leola handling it?" she asks.

"We're all fine, but it's time for some of us to move on. I'm calling to ask you for your help."

"Well, I will do my best."

"Deacon and I are going to start a business, Hoyt Sporting Equipment, in New York early next year. It's named after Leola's mother, who made all the *Catfish* uniforms in the early days. We've got some solid commitments from all sorts of potential business partners."

"It all sounds splendid," Elvinia says.

"Yes, I'm looking forward to working with Deacon. You know he's the salt of the earth, and together we're going to do some seriously good business."

Hearing himself talk about his new business with Elvinia, Clarence realizes how sincere his excitement truly is, and he quickly forgets the misgivings he had when he thought of the idea in the first place.

"Well, I, for one, think you and Deacon are two of the finest young men I've ever met, and I wish you every success. When you're in New York next time, you must call me so I can arrange for a dinner. But I am still not quite sure where my help is needed in all this." Elvinia is pleased to hear from Clarence but is also a bit surprised that it is Clarence and not Davis calling her for advice from Houston.

"Professor Kincade, it would be an honor to have dinner with you whenever that may be. But I do have another reason for calling you," Clarence announces, relieved that Elvinia has broached the subject. "I think New York would also be a great city for Leola to call home in the future. You know how talented she is in business, and I just don't see opportunities for her in Houston, or anywhere in the South, that will compare with the doors that will open for her in New York. I'd like to ask you for your help in getting her there."

"That is some truly insightful thinking on your part," Elvinia replies, "not to mention proof of a big heart. And I must confess that, as much as I'm looking forward to seeing you and Deacon, having Leola and Davis up here in the Northeast would be a wonderful treat! I'd love to make sure that happens."

Clarence is surprised that Elvinia thinks Davis will be coming to New York. He quickly gathers himself and breaks the news to Elvinia.

"Yes, well, I believe Leola will be coming north by herself," Clarence says, stumbling over his words. "Davis is staying in Houston to continue his writing career, which I'm sure you know is going very well. With much thanks to you, of course."

"Oh?" Elvinia retorts. Clarence can hear that she is shocked. "Davis will be staying home with Hunter, Rose, and all those other Southern savages?"

"If that's how you'd like to phrase it," Clarence replies with a grin.

"I suppose that's the responsible thing for him to do, but I do wish I had taught that young man to take more risks in life, instead of simply focusing on his outstanding literary skills." Elvinia continues with a bit of personal reflection. "But that's my lesson to learn. Even an old professor can take away the positives from tutelage long gone by and apply them to the current crop of students. You can be sure no one in my current class would ever choose Cowtown by the Gulf over the Greatest City in the World, although I'm not sure they would start out with all the creature comforts of home that Davis took for granted from birth."

Elvinia stops to allow Clarence the time to interject if he'd like. When he doesn't, she adds, "And, of course, you know that I'm going to give this same piece of my mind to our overqualified sports writer the next time we talk."

Elvinia nearly forgets what Clarence has asked her in the first place, but finally moves past the subject of Davis Sterling and remembers Clarence's main purpose for calling her.

"But you can also rest assured that I will do everything I can to help Leola Jones find the fame and fortune she deserves. I've always thought she could shine anywhere she chooses to call home."

"Thank you, Professor Kincade. I can't tell you how happy I am to have spoken with you. And we'll have dinner in New York soon, I promise you that," Clarence says, thrilled with Elvinia's response.

"Call me Elvinia, please, Clarence. We've known each other long enough for that," she says. "And I'm holding you to that dinner date in New York. Good luck with your new business; tell everyone I said hello."

Clarence obliges, "Of course, I will, Elvinia. I'll ask Leola to call you, and we'll all get together soon."

Clarence can hardly wait to tell Leola about his conversation with Elvinia. He hopes she is as thrilled as he is and that it will be the start of great new things for his old friend. Back in New York, Elvinia hangs up the phone, grabs her lesson plan, and races to the lecture hall to teach Journalism 301. As she makes her way to the classroom, she thinks of what a fine young man Clarence Holloman is. And her mind briefly wanders to a journalism class many years before, when a young Davis Sterling stunned her with his writing. Davis stayed within himself even then, and it seems he is still doing that. It took Elvinia time to reach out to him and convince him he ought to take his talent more seriously. If only he had more of Clarence's gumption!

"Good morning, class. Today, we are going to discuss the fine art of journalism from a different perspective. I'm going to ask you to assume the persona of one of several sides in a battle played out in print in a major U.S. city. It seems that a steel mill in Pittsburgh, Pennsylvania, has accidentally released dangerous chemicals into the Monongahela River and, needless to say, the city fathers are not happy about it. Because these chemicals are, shall we say, odiferous, they have made it into the news media as a major story for the evening papers. I'm going to pass out an article from one of the papers for all of you to read, along with a copy of the report submitted by the local police who responded to neighbors' complaints about the smell. Please read them both. Then, we will divide into four groups, each of which will caucus to come up with a strategy for handling this most unfortunate but newsworthy incident.

"Some of you will be the editorial staff of the *Pittsburgh Gazette*, the morning paper that will cover the story in tomorrow's edition. Others in the second group will work for Monongahela Steel Corporation in their public relations department. Your job will be to minimize the damage to your company's reputation in your hometown. The third group will work for Mayor Hugh Steinway, a reformers' darling. He is about to run for a second term by pushing for workers' rights against the establishment and its traditional bias toward the city's major industries. And, yes, of course, even an old English woman like me knows that the steel industry is king in Western Pennsylvania.

"The final group will work for WSTL Radio, which has recently begun broadcasting a fifteen-minute local news program at 6:30 p.m. every evening on its television station. You must compete with another establishment in American society – the press, which thinks of you as an uncouth upstart, unworthy of a place at the press conferences the city and Monongahela Steel will be holding. Please take five minutes to read the two papers I'm now distributing, and, after that, we will count from one to four, left to right, in each row of seats, to determine which group will be your home base for this modern American media drama. One will be the *Gazette* editorial staff. Two will be Monongahela Steel. Three will be Mayor Steinway's dedicated staff. And four will be our young upstarts on television.

"I want you all to ham it up as much as possible. This is big news, ladies and gentlemen! People are breathing air that has been fouled by the Captains of Capitalism, and fish are dying in the rivers that define our fair city. Someone must pay!"

———————

Leola and Clarence are still packing away the *Catfish* office into boxes when Clarence decides it's a good time to tell her about his talk with Elvinia and ask Leola to call her. "Clarence, you didn't call Elvinia Kincade on my behalf!" Leola gasps when Clarence tells her the news.

"I did," Clarence says, realizing a bit too late that his timing might have been wrong.

"Why, that is such an imposition. She's a busy woman, and I would never ask such a thing," Leola snaps back, with a flash of anger in her eyes.

"I know you wouldn't, Leola. That's exactly why I did," Clarence answers. "You know the North is the place of opportunity – real opportunity – for me and for you. I can't see you working as some secretary or retail saleswoman here in Houston after all you've accomplished. Your daddy wouldn't let me in his front door if he were still alive and I hadn't done everything in my power to make sure you use your Jones family smarts to their full potential. I know it'll be tough on you and Davis. But do you really want to be dependent on him, and indirectly on that wilting magnolia of a mother of his, for your future? I won't abide it, Leola, I just won't."

Leola can't help thinking about old Rose drooping in the hot southern sun, getting a little brown around the edges. "Clarence, you've always been my best friend, and, as smart as you say I am, you always seem to be one step ahead of me."

"It's not that I'm . . ." Clarence starts, but Leola stops him.

"No. You're right about Davis and Rose, I have to admit. But I am so fond of him. I wish there were some way to take him north too. Do you think Elvinia could find him a job at a Northern newspaper? She does know everybody in the business."

Clarence balks at Leola's question but quickly regains himself and hopes Leola didn't notice his instinctive reaction to her words.

"Leola, blood is thicker than water. Look at you and the *Catfish*. You are your father's daughter, and your mother's too. Remember how you did your best for the players even when the team had to fold? You have your father's head and your mother's heart. It's the same with Davis. He's working for his daddy's newspaper. When you go to the *Star* building, even just as a friend of Davis, you get, well, the star treatment. He'll never give that up, never. And he does have some of old Rose in him as well. He's stubborn as a mule, even if it's mostly in a good way. And his sisters? Can you imagine how they'd receive the news that their only brother is moving up north with a colored woman? You mark my words. I didn't come back to help you manage the *Catfish* only to wind up writing sad songs about the life you could have had. No way, no how."

"But, Clarence, Davis travels all over the country now that he's been promoted to writing feature stories. He's not in Houston enough to be tied down by old Rose and even his daddy's friends these days," Leola retorts, standing her ground. But she knows that, as soon as she says those words, she has lost the argument.

"Yes, Leola, he's going to Seattle, Washington, tomorrow to write a story about how someday soon there'll be new jet airplanes that can fly people from coast to coast in four hours nonstop. Later in the month, he's going to both Philadelphia and Kansas City to cover the move of the *Athletics* baseball team out west – not as a sports story this time, but as a story about how cities feel when they gain or lose a professional team. If it weren't for old Lyndon Johnson's power in Washington, God knows where he'd be going to write all those stories about the space race. At least Senator Johnson spends enough time in Texas for Davis to talk with him when he's here. Otherwise, you'd hardly ever see him," he snaps.

Leola crumples a bit in the face of Clarence's outburst, and the brightness in her eyes turns to sadness. Clarence sees this, and he feels that same sense of loss too.

"Look, Leola, when the *Catfish* were the big story in town, you and Davis had a wonderful thing going. He could come over all the time for interviews. There was always an excuse for him to be around then. But remember, he was selling newspapers!"

Leola's eyes shoot a hard glare at Clarence when she hears these words. He sees her reaction and backs down.

"It's not that he doesn't love you to death. I believe he does, but he will never give up his writing, or his birthright at the *Star*, for anything. He'll keep you here and do his best to keep you happy, but I don't believe that will turn out to be enough for you. His idea of a wife is someone who stands by his side and raises his children. And, if he has any ideas to the contrary, well then, he's right there in the damned Alamo with you. Only he eventually figures out that he's got more in common with the people storming the walls than he has with you. And, then, where are you? Like I said, I ain't come this far to write that sad song about you holding out 'til the bitter end in a coonskin cap."

"Damn it, Clarence!" Leola shouts and then catches herself. When her eyes meet Clarence's, they are full of tears, and so are his. She thinks for a minute, and, in that single minute, everything becomes clear.

She speaks softly now. "Oh, Clarence, I do think about what my daddy would want. And I even believe Mama would want the same. I remember when you went north, and I cried because you weren't there in Eatonville any more. But my mama and daddy told me it was for the best, that you were going to come back someday as a fine young man, smarter and stronger than anyone else in town. I hear them both talking through you right now."

"Leola, I . . ."

"You're right, Clarence, I can't stay here in Houston and ever be truly happy. And, God bless him, Davis will never go north with me." Leola drops her head in her hands. "Oh, what am I going to do? How can I lose the *Catfish* and Davis all in the same month?" she asks as she buries her face in her palms. Clarence slides beside her on the sofa. Leola falls into his arms and sobs.

"Leola, you keep strong and true to yourself, and everything else will work out for more than the best," Clarence tells her. "I'll always be there for you – and so will a lot of people. You may have lost the *Catfish*, but you'll never be without a team."

For months after the brutally honest exchange with Clarence, Leola tries to engage Davis in a heart-to-heart talk about what their future holds. Every attempt she makes ends in a near miss. Either Davis has a flight to catch, or there's a deadline to make. Before they resolve anything, their conversations always end in the same way: Davis says he is sorry and promises that he will have time to talk soon. Leola can almost hear Clarence telling her that this is just Davis telling her he'll get back to her when there is nothing else to distract him, nothing else beckoning him or vying for his attention. "Soon," Leola begins to learn, is just Davis's term for putting things off. It isn't a promise; it's more of a diversion. When she finally does catch Davis for more than a few moments between big stories, he insists they not waste their time talking about "depressing" subjects.

"Listen, Davis, life can be depressing sometimes, whether we want it to be or not." Leola says, bristling at Davis's inability to face the facts like an adult. "These 'depressing' things aren't going anywhere. Not talking about them isn't stopping them from rearing their heads and interfering in our lives again and again until we resolve them."

"I know," Davis returns. "I know that we can't run from them forever. But I want to enjoy the time we have together, Leola. It's special to me, you know? And I don't want anything to ruin it." Davis may have settled on one woman, but he is still able to conjure his playboy charm when he needs to.

Leola softens. Her sternness fades. Davis, in a way only he can, helps her forget that there are pressing discussions to be had. He makes her feel that they can live in the moment; that they *should* live in the moment, and worry about nothing else. In the back of her mind, the future and all it will bring still hovers, but Leola lets it all slide away to savor the time she has left with the only man she has ever been this close to loving.

As Davis puts off making future plans, Elvinia is in New York doing just the opposite, as are Clarence and Deacon. They're all throwing themselves into what lies ahead, making contacts and preparing for Clarence and Deacon's new venture. On a few occasions, Leola joins the two men on their trips to New York. And, every time she does, Elvinia has already prepared for her arrival. Leola can hardly grab her luggage before Elvinia has given her an itinerary for the coming days.

"I've arranged for you to meet Tom Smithson tomorrow at eleven for a brunch. Tom's a savvy business man who's really made a name for himself in the city. And, this evening, you and I will be going to a gala. Everyone you need to meet to get yourself started in this concrete jungle will be there. Be prepared, my Leola. This isn't Houston, and it surely isn't Eatonville," Elvinia tells her. "And I want you to remember, you have options here."

"What kind of options?" Leola asks.

"I'd like you to consider business school," Elvinia announces. "Women in university need women to look up to as business leaders. You can share that business mind of yours with others and inspire future Leola Joneses along the way."

Both Elvinia and Leola know that it is a lofty dream, but Leola throws herself into the challenge. She agrees not only to move to New York and begin a new life, but also to pursue yet another degree in business. With Elvinia's help, Leola enrolls at NYU Business School on a full scholarship. She will begin January 1956, the same time Clarence and Deacon officially start their business. But, rather than taking a part-time teaching job at a city college as Elvinia had hoped, Leola will work part-time at Hoyt Sporting Equipment as an adviser and co-developer of the company. Leola can't pass up the opportunity to work with Clarence and Deacon, nor can she pass up the experience it will give her in beginning a new business. And, besides that, she is thrilled that they have named their business after her mother.

As October comes to a close and the holidays approach, Leola knows she has to tell Davis about her plans. Everything is in motion now; there is no going back. She wants to wait until after Thanksgiving, however, so they can both enjoy their time with family, although they will not be spending the holiday together. She is going home to Eatonville for a turkey dinner with the two people whose blessings mean more to her than anyone else's – her mother and Uncle Isaac. Both Isaac and Hoyt know about Leola's plans, but while she and Uncle Isaac have been able to talk a little about them, Leola has not yet discussed her upcoming move to New York City with Hoyt at any length. Leola is both excited and nervous to ask what her mother thinks of her plans.

Uncle Isaac has his own announcement to make over the Thanksgiving turkey. Davis's constant reports of the manager of the *Catfish* had caught the eye of Hunter Sterling and his Houston booster friends. This small group of Houston's elite, many of whom would have preferred to die than to do business with a colored man in the past, have now been wooing Isaac to help with a task they see as central to their mission of bringing Major League Baseball to their city. Their prejudices are eclipsed by their desire to make Houston the capital of the New South. They know one sure way to do that is to get an expansion baseball team into their city. They also know that no one in Houston knows baseball talent like Isaac Manns. Because he wants to continue his career, Isaac agrees to join in the effort to bring a team to their city.

As busy as he has become working to get a professional team in Houston, Uncle Isaac would not miss the chance to spend a holiday with the apple of his eye. He and Leola fly out of Houston together to enjoy Thanksgiving with Hoyt. They take the flight as an opportunity to catch up with each other's eventful lives.

"Uncle Isaac, I know you're going to find fame and fortune on your own working with Hunter Sterling and all those rich white men in Houston. I don't know any Negro man, not Clarence, not Jazz, not even my own daddy, who could charm them the way you do," Leola tells Isaac as they float through the clouds on a bright November day. "I'm going to miss you when we all move north. But we'll stay in touch as much as we can. More than anyone else on this earth, you will always be the closest thing to what my daddy was for me. Rest assured I'll need you more than ever while I'm making a name for myself in New York."

"Don't you worry, my soon-to-be Lena Horne, you're going to be a star of your own, and I will never ever be far when you need me. Remember that before Clarence, you, and I built the *Catfish*, I promised your daddy to make sure you were safe and happy. You've never really needed help from anyone, but any time you do, you just say the word and I'll be wherever you ask me to be."

The plane lands in Orlando. Hoyt is there in the terminal, waving and smiling. She is about to burst out of her own skin as she sees the pair stroll off the plane. The only family she has left is finally home. After their short drive to Eatonville, they see that Hoyt has the entire spread ready to go, warming in the oven and on the stove. Even though it is just the three of them, she's made a meal to feed an army, just like she did when Leola was a girl and there was a house full of Joneses to feed.

After dinner, Uncle Isaac clears dishes and Leola serves coffee. She knows it's time to tell her mother the news. "Mama, Uncle Isaac, I know you both will support me no matter what. But moving to New York with Clarence and Deacon is a big step, and one I don't take lightly. Each of you has talked to me before about it, but this is the first time we'll be able to discuss it together. Please tell me honestly how you really feel." Leola wants confirmation that she is doing the right thing. And she gets it.

"Leola, darling, you know how much I wish your brothers had gone north so many years ago, even though I didn't foresee what would happen to them when they stayed here. I don't fear for your safety if you stay in Houston, but I do believe you will be happier and more successful in New York. Plus, you'll be there with Clarence and Deacon. I think they are both fine young men who will watch out for you and take care of you if you need them. I know there's no real difference in you coming here for a visit from New York or from Houston. So go, my love, and don't you ever look back."

Hoyt doesn't mention Davis's name, which is a statement in its own right. Her silence about him speaks volumes to Leola. She realizes Hoyt feels that leaving Davis is best.

"My little Queen Elizabeth, I agree," says Uncle Isaac. "You have done great things in Texas. I know; I saw them. And there are many people there who admire you and would support you in whatever you do. I just see you eventually hitting barriers there, even with the fact that you are the only woman who has ever owned and operated a sports team. We still have a long way to go in this country, especially in the South. Many folks are fighting the change and holding onto prejudice, calling it a tradition. Now, there's a part of me that wants to see them take their best shot at you because I know you'll whup them upside their tiny little heads. But I want a life for you that's full of love, not fights. If I could go north with you, I would. But, really, the day is not far off when it'll be time for you to help your old Uncle Isaac, not depend on my help or anyone else's." He leans closer to Leola and adds, "And that even goes for Clarence Holloman, who I know would give his right arm for you anytime, anywhere. He may be the strongest man I know, but you know what? You're still stronger than him and all the rest of the men in your life put together."

Leola blushes at her uncle's words but remains silent.

"I can't wait to see how you use that strength in a city where talent and dedication count more than race, or who you know, or what people say about you when you're not around. Go, Leola. Go north. And I promise you this: I'll fly from Houston to Florida, pick up your mother, and we'll both come for a visit. Hell, I can't wait to walk into the Cotton Club with the two most beautiful women in the world on either side of me. We'll have some good times up there; I can tell you that," Isaac says, winking at his niece.

"Mama, Uncle Isaac, I can't tell you what it means to me to hear these things from you. It isn't that I expected anything different, but to hear you say them tells me I'm making the right decision. You've been in my heart every day we ran the *Catfish*, and you'll surely be there as well when I go to New York City. And, yes, Uncle Isaac, I'll be there with bells on when you and Mama come up for a visit. I can't say that I won't be sad to leave Texas and so many wonderful people behind, particularly you, Uncle Isaac. But what's done is done, and the *Catfish* were the real reason we went to Texas in the first place. I don't think I can ever find another opportunity like running the team out there. But I can see new and wonderful opportunities for me in New York. I can't wait to give it my best. With your blessing, I will do that, starting in a couple of weeks."

"Well, you certainly have our support and blessing, sweetheart," Hoyt says with tears in her eyes.

Lightening the mood a bit, Leola announces, "Let's have some of that pumpkin pie that Uncle Isaac and I traveled a thousand miles to taste." Hoyt goes into the kitchen to take the pie out of the oven.

As Hoyt tends to the pie in the kitchen, Leola looks at her uncle and says, "I really am so happy with my decision now that you and Mama and I talked about it. I hope you're serious about taking her to New York for a visit. More than one, to be honest."

"My little Gwendolyn Brooks, you are going to take New York by storm, and we both know it. Clarence and Deacon are going to build a great business, but you . . . you are always going to shine brighter than any of the other millions of people who live there. I've always believed it since you were a little girl, but I never thought I'd get to see first-hand how great you are as a businesswoman and as a leader. Don't you worry. You're going to be so happy!"

"Oh, Uncle Isaac, I love you, I really do. You are the best man any woman could ever want in her life, although I do think you may be a little biased," Leola laughs. "But, now, I have to go and tell Davis Sterling about my decision. That's the toughest part of it all, honestly. I couldn't bring it up in front of Mama, but you know what he's meant to me. He has his flaws. But he's a good man, and I've enjoyed his company for a long time. Promise me one last thing, Uncle Isaac. Will you please look after him while you're both in Houston and I'm up north with Clarence and Deacon? I'll sleep more soundly knowing he has you to confide in while he's trying to keep up his career and stay sane in that crazy family of his."

Isaac puts his hand on Leola's shoulder and tells her, "I'll make sure your Romeo doesn't do anything stupid. God knows the real one could have used that help, and, if he would have had any, Shakespeare could have written a much happier play."

Leola sneaks off into the bedroom to make the call.

"Davis, hi! It's Leola. I'm back from Florida. How was your Thanksgiving?" Leola is happy to hear Davis's voice.

"Leola, my family never ceases to produce more holiday entertainment than any other family in America, with the possible exception of Lucy and Ricky Ricardo. There's always something."

"I don't doubt that," Leola replies with a chuckle.

"This year my Great Aunt Maisie flushed her false teeth down the toilet after the French onion soup, and my sisters had a great debate about whether to chop her serving of turkey and stuffing into tiny pieces or blend them into a puree. It was a truly spirited argument, I can tell you that."

Leola laughs long and hard with Davis, even though she isn't sure the story is true.

"Davis, I have something to tell you, and I'd like to do it over dinner next week. Do you have any time?"

"Why, any day this week works for me. But I could use a day or two to digest my mother's cooking. Why not make an evening of it next Saturday, December 3rd? I'll come and get you, say around six?"

"That's great, Davis, see you then. And take care of yourself."

Leola is relieved that she has the whole week to figure out how she is going to tell Davis about her decision to leave Houston for New York.

A few days later, on Thursday, December 1, in Montgomery, Alabama, Rosa Parks refuses to give up her seat after the driver of the bus moves the "Colored Only" sign back behind her row to make room for more white passengers. For that, Rosa Parks is arrested. On Friday, December 2, the Montgomery Bus Boycott is conceived by Rosa Parks's lawyers and Professor Jo Ann Gibson Robinson, an English professor at Alabama State University.

Professor Robinson calls her friend Elvinia Kincade to tell her the news. Elvinia immediately calls Davis.

"Davis, get yourself to Montgomery, Alabama, right away. One of the great civil rights stories of the year is unfolding, and if you go tomorrow, you can be the first out-of-town reporter to break the story. My friend Jo Ann Robinson is organizing a citywide bus boycott that will continue until they seat people on a first-come, first-serve basis – and hire black bus drivers. The boycott is scheduled to start on Monday and will be organized all over the city on the weekend. Go there, Davis. It's going to be big."

"I'm already there!" Davis replies and slams down the phone.

The next day, he packs and flies to Montgomery, so excited he forgets to call Leola to tell her that they need to reschedule.

The Montgomery Bus Boycott takes days to organize. Once it begins on Monday, December 5, it continues for over a year. Davis covers the story from Alabama nonstop for two weeks, sending reports back to the *Star*, based on his unprecedented access to Jo Ann Robinson and other boycott leaders. He is thrilled to be part of such an important story and can't wait to tell Leola about it when he gets back. But, when he calls her later that week to apologize for missing dinner and to talk about his eyewitness view of history in the making, she doesn't answer. She, Clarence, and Deacon have already left Houston for New York.

CHAPTER TWENTY-TWO

BRING US A TEAM (1956)

"Hunter, you can't possibly still be on that kick of bringing a baseball team to Houston, can you?" Rose says to Hunter as their servants bring them breakfast in their stately dining room.

"Yes, Rose, I am on 'that kick' again," Hunter snaps, spilling a bit of coffee on the white linen tablecloth as he places the cup down a bit harder than he should to make his point.

"Don't get riled, dear," Rose says coolly. "I would just think that, after all the aggravation baseball has caused our family, you'd be on to something else." After their previous discussions about Davis's "affair with the *Catfish* in the sports pages of the *Star*," as she calls it, Rose doesn't need to spell things out for her husband. He is well aware of his wife's growing intolerance for sports in general, especially baseball.

"Your personal feelings aside, Rose, your brother's friend George Kirksey has been 'on that kick' since he first came to town after the War. He even tried to buy the *St. Louis Cardinals* and bring them here in 1952. I don't recall hearing you raise any kind of ruckus about bringing a baseball team to town then."

George Kirksey is a squat, balding man who looks perpetually sunburned due to dual afflictions of rosacea and a bad temperament. He and Hunter have the kind of relationship that calls for civility, but there is an underlying acknowledgment that neither man puts much stock in what the other believes.

"Yes, well, my son wasn't making a public spectacle of himself then," Rose retorts.

"Rose, this is my chance to take this city in a new direction. Kirksey's gotten some bad press lately with his Civil War Round Table meetings, and I see that as my chance to come in and give a new perspective. I want to bring in a baseball team *and* a new set of beliefs, Rose. How are we supposed to make people believe Houston is a forward-thinking city when we've got a bunch of old Confederates re-fighting 'Our Great National Tragedy'?"

"Surely, this isn't your attempt at holding me responsible for George Kirksey simply because he is an acquaintance of my brother? I'm no more responsible for his prominence in our social circle than you are, my dear. And George's Civil War Round Table is quite popular with many of my friends' husbands. I hear they had over fifty people at their last meeting. And they're not just Southern sympathizers . . . they're planning a series on the Battle of Gettysburg this year that will cover both the South and those *Yankees*."

"Those *Yankees* are the very people I'm counting on to help us make Houston the capital of the New South. Think of it, Rose! This is an opportunity for everyone if we could just move out of the damned 1800s. This country is growing by leaps and bounds, and I want our hometown to get as much of a slice of the pie as we can."

"How's that?"

"There's plenty of New York money looking for a place to settle south of the Mason-Dixon Line. Atlanta and New Orleans have caught on to this fact, and they're ready to take it. Dallas is already out of the running because they're so damned hateful. I will tell you this now, Rose. If we don't want to be left behind, we cannot have people up north thinking that we're woven from the same bigoted cloth. Hell, we're already part of the same damn state. Half of those *Yankees* probably don't know the difference."

"And you plan on showing them the difference?" Rose asks coyly.

"We need a baseball team, Rose. We need to be the first southern city to get one. It'll automatically bring people in from all the other cities with teams, all summer long."

"And how do you plan on doing that, dear? Baseball teams don't just fall out of the sky."

"Craig Cullinan has already put together quite a team to make sure we'll be first."

"It would be Craig," Rose replies. Craig Cullinan and Rose attended high school together. Craig was the class president every single year. He went on to preside over his fraternity and the University of Texas in Austin and settled back in Houston to build up his father's already thriving development company. Rose finds Craig's zeal and success both admirable and slightly off-putting. Hunter is aware of her ambivalent feelings about him and glides right by her aside.

"Now, we need to convince people that we're not itching to re-fight the Battle of Bull Run when they come to town and to make damn certain that we don't just get a team, but a good team. We want a winner here in Houston, that's for sure."

"Hmmm," Rose sips her coffee.

"That's where old George Kirksey comes in," Hunter continues, oblivious to his wife's growing disengagement with the conversation. "If he would only stop insisting on finishing what Robert E. Lee started! If he'd step out of the past, then Craig, Judge Hofeinz, and the rest of us would have an easier time working with Major League Baseball. If we can just get old Kirksey to let go of his Civil War sentiment, we'd be able to focus attention on baseball, instead of our fair city's opinions on desegregation. George is a great sports writer, and we need him to get with the program. If we can't get him on board, even if we do get a team, we'll end up with another version of the *Kansas City Athletics*. They're terrible. Everybody knows they're a *New York Yankees* farm team. Anybody good on their team automatically goes to New York the next season. Can you imagine a *Yankee* farm team here in Houston?" Hunter puts emphasis on the word 'Yankee' to regain his wife's attention. He hopes to get his Rose to bristle at the idea of losing players to a New York team.

"Hunter, this all must be terribly interesting to you and your friends in the Houston Sports Association, but whatever do you want me to do about it? I don't know much about baseball or Wall Street money. You know my daddy was in oil. And I've tried to stay away from the Civil War in any of my discussions with the ladies on the Houston Arts Council. We find the topic disturbing. It distracts us from our work in bringing culture to town. Why, the last time the subject came up, old Abigail Boudreau burst into tears about how her grandmother died of the consumption she caught while visiting her poor first husband's grave at the Civil War Cemetery in the winter of 1910."

She wants Hunter to remember that she too has long roots in the city's history and that she also is responsible for bringing Houston into the twentieth century.

"Well, Rose, there is something I'd like you to do to help. When I said we want to make our team a success on the field, I was being dead serious. And Judge Hofeinz, Bill Kirkland, Craig Cullinan, and I have a plan. We're going to hire Isaac Manns to help us scout talent," Hunter announces.

"You mean the uncle of that horrible young woman who got her claws into our Davis?" Rose exclaims as she throws her napkin on the table.

"Yes, Rose. He's a great baseball man. He can help us bring in the right ball players to make our team a real major league contender. Hunter can see Rose's adverse reaction to the very idea. "Listen, Rose, I want him to feel welcome here in town. And I want you to do everything you can to make that happen. Find out if he has a wife. If he does, take her to lunch. Hell, maybe even invite her to be a member of the Arts Council. Anything! Including, Rose," Hunter says, becoming very serious, "treating him and Leola Jones with courtesy and respect at all times."

"Well, then, thank God that woman is away in the North already, so I don't have to deny you your wish," Rose shoots back. "Because mark my words, Hunter Sterling, I would not likely be able to grant you that, not for anything in the world."

"Rose, you know what I mean. I want you to help me and help our city find success. It's 1956. Baseball is integrated. Rosa Parks can ride a bus and sit anywhere she damn well pleases. In Montgomery, Alabama! Those people in Montgomery tried to fight and preserve what they call tradition, but everyone up north saw it as prejudice, pure and simple. Do you want them to think that we're just like Montgomery? Do you think anyone is going to put a shoe factory, let alone a Major League Baseball team, there? Do you get what I'm saying?"

As resistant as Rose has been, she starts to see her husband's point. There are bigger things at play than her pride. She takes a deep breath and listens to what Hunter has to say.

"Let's start with Isaac Manns. He's a real gentleman, well respected throughout the country by anyone who knows anything about scouting baseball talent. Hell, he's working right now for Rice University. Now, if I could send old George Kirksey away on a six-month re-enactment of the siege of Atlanta, we'd be all set, but I can't. So I need you to help me."

"Darling, you know I'll do anything I can to help. When have I not?" They both know that is true of Rose. She might have problems letting go of tradition, but she is fiercely loyal to the love of her life. "I'm not saying I'm going to invite Leola Jones to tea next week if she suddenly pops back into Houston, but anything else I am willing to do."

"That'll be fine, Rose. That'll be just fine," Hunter practically purrs back. "Let's just start with treating Isaac and his family with respect, and I'm also going to talk with Davis about my plans so he can take the lead in breaking stories about how we're going to build our major league franchise. I don't want George Kirksey getting the byline on this one."

Rose decides that, if she is going to help her husband, she is going to do it her way – by holding onto as many traditions as possible.

"I know, Hunter! How's this for starters? Why don't we invite Mr. Manns and his wife or lady friend to the Emerald Room at the Shamrock Hotel? You know, they've made a movie out of old Glenn McCarthy's life. It has Elizabeth Taylor and Rock Hudson and that poor young actor who died in a car crash in it. Since they opened in 1949, having people for dinner at Glenn's hotel has always been a good luck charm for us. Remember, that's where we found out we were going to have our first grandchild. Why, we might even invite Mr. Manns and his guest to go to dinner and then to the movie right afterward. Make an evening of it. How about it?"

Hunter is stunned at how quickly Rose has come around. He's somewhat skeptical of his iron-willed wife's sudden change of heart, but opts not to look this gift horse in the mouth.

"Great idea, darling. I'll run it by Craig and the boys, and we'll start on it tomorrow. By the way, what's the name of the movie?"

"Giant," Rose answers.

"So, gentlemen, Rose and I are going to invite Isaac Manns to dinner at the Emerald Room next week. I agree he'd be a perfect addition to our team, and we want him to feel as welcome as can be here in Houston," Hunter announces at an early meeting of the Houston Sports Association. "We are going to get a Major League baseball team come hell or high water, and we're going to be the first city in the South to have one!"

"Here, here!" Craig blurts, letting the group know that he is behind Hunter completely. "Hunter, I admire the way you're starting off with a focus on quality baseball. That's very important, and I say full speed ahead," Craig adds.

"Isn't he currently on the coaching staff at Rice?" Judge Hofeinz asks.

"Yes, he is," answers George Kirksey, a bit subdued. "But do we really want him? I can think of a half-dozen baseball men who would serve us equally as well, if not better."

"Now, George," answers Craig, "you remember we covered this topic last meeting. We need to convince Commissioner Frick that we're a big-league city, with highly evolved social values and open minds. I know Atlanta is ready to pounce on the opportunity, so we have to go all out. Money, architecture, modern thinking, baseball talent, political connections – you name it, we have to have it. Isaac Manns may not be your first choice, but he's well-respected and knows our town. I'm asking for you to support the rest of us on this. There'll be plenty for everyone in Houston, including your sports columns, once we get a major league team."

Grudgingly, George Kirksey nods in agreement. He has no rebuttal, although he is still not sold on the idea.

"Well, gentlemen, we all know that Houston has the money angle covered," Craig says. "We have a long history of spending when we need to, so there will be no doubt in the commissioner's mind, or anyone else's in baseball, that we will match dollar for dollar with any team," Craig pauses for a moment and makes eye contact with every man in the room, then adds, "Even the *New York Yankees!*"

The room explodes with cheers. Everyone, even George Kirksey, joins in with loud support.

"Now, what are we missing?" Craig says to quiet the room down again. "I say two things: politics and architecture."

"I'll take on the architecture," Judge Hofeinz says. "Trust me, gentlemen, we will light a fire under the commissioner that's so hot, he won't be able to sit down during our entire presentation!" Hunter smiles at the judge's enthusiasm.

William Kirkland, another member of the group, chimes in, "I think we need Senator Johnson on this one, and I believe I know just the guy to get to him. Leon Jaworski is a good friend of the senator's, and we all know he's managing partner over at Fulbright and Jaworski. Heck, they added his name to the firm a couple of years ago because of his work as a war crimes prosecutor. I know Leon well and would be glad to approach him on this one. I don't think we can go wrong with Colonel Jaworski on our side."

The meeting adjourns with high hopes that Houston will indeed get a Major League team.

"Why, Hunter Sterling," Isaac says, answering the phone as he puts aside a scouting sheet, "it's great to hear from you. To what do I owe this pleasure?"

"Well, Rose and I were wondering if you'd like to go to dinner at the Emerald Room this week. We'd love to meet Mrs. Manns, if there is a lucky woman who holds the title."

"Well, the only woman that holds the title now is my mother, but I am involved with a beautiful young woman who I'd love to join us. Her name is Cassandra."

"Fantastic!" Hunter says. "Rose and I cannot wait to meet her. And I thought we'd see a show after dinner if you are up to it. 'Giant' is playing, and Rose is dying to see it."

"Absolutely," Isaac says. "It all sounds just fine."

"Now, Isaac, you know my friends at the Houston Sports Association and I are very interested in establishing a professional relationship with you in our efforts to bring a Major League baseball team to Houston," Hunter says, his tone changing from jovial to business. "I hope our evening together next week is the start of a long and mutually beneficial friendship that will be even stronger than the bonds we already have based on your fine work with the *Catfish*. My son Davis sings your praises, and I'm glad to tell you that he's not the only one in town, or in the country, for that matter, to do so. I hope someday soon to convince you to join us as a scout. We want to build our team quickly and not spend years waiting for a championship season. My instincts tell me you're just the man to help us make that happen."

"I'm flattered by your confidence in me," Isaac replies. "And I'd be honored to work with anyone who wants to bring Major League baseball to Houston."

"So glad to hear it, Isaac," Hunter says.

"Cassandra and I will be at the Emerald Room on Friday at 7 p.m., if that's not too late for us to take in the movie with you and Rose afterwards."

"No, that'll be fine," Hunter answers. "We're looking forward to it, as well."

_____

When Rose and Hunter arrive at the Emerald Room the following Friday, Rose scans the crowd to see if any of her friends from the Arts Association are there or, even worse, friends from her childhood.

Although she has assured Hunter she is fine with the dinner, it has taken all she can muster to walk through the restaurant doors. She breathes a sigh of relief when she doesn't recognize anyone, although she is sure she can feel the disapproving glances from around the room as Isaac and Cassandra join them at their table.

"Mr. Manns," she speaks in a perfectly measured tone, "it's so good to see you again. How is your lovely niece, Leola?"

"Well, first of all, Mrs. Sterling, you can call me Isaac, and Leola is fine, thank you. She's moved to New York, as you may know. I'd like to introduce you and Mr. Sterling to Cassandra Williams, who is an assistant professor of history at Rice University."

"So nice to meet you both," Cassandra says, perfectly charming in her own right and much more natural than Rose at pleasantries.

Hunter adds his own greetings, and the four of them proceed to have a time so enjoyable that Rose forgets her discomfort with the situation.

"Cassandra, what brings you to Houston?" Rose asks.

"Well, I grew up in Crockett, a few towns up north of here, before my family moved to Lacompte, Louisiana, when I was in high school. After graduating, I went to Spellman College in Atlanta, where I majored in American history and literature."

"Yep, Hunter, same hometown as our star pitcher Deacon Johnson – I mean Peter Smithfield," Isaac smiled as he interrupted Cassandra's story. "Sorry, my dear, I apologize for the interruption," he drawled to Cassandra. "Please continue ..."

Cassandra never minds Isaac's interruptions, and she carries on, "I then pursued my graduate studies at Rice here in Houston, and, well, here I am. They offered me the chance to teach and I took it. It's a wonderful city, I must say, and I'm happy to call it home."

"Well," blurts out Rose, "that's a refreshing change from what some of our other recent visitors have said about us."

Hunter gives Rose a wary glance, touching her leg with his right hand under the table. He hopes no one else has noticed her comment, but it is too late.

Isaac interjects to change the subject as quickly as he can. "Cassandra is being modest. She is one of the smartest members of Rice's faculty. Students literally line up to sign up for her classes. Plus, she is one of the most beautiful women on campus."

"I do not doubt that at all," Rose says, thankful for Isaac's intervention.

The dinner continues without incident, although Rose does become self-conscious midway through the meal and begins glancing around the room again to see who might be looking at them. Hunter eventually mentions that it is time to leave for the movie theater, but Rose demurs.

"Why, Hunter, we're having the best time here with Isaac and Cassandra. What's the rush? We'll get to the theater on time." She wants to prove that she is not uncomfortable, although her over-compensation is obvious to everyone present. She calls the waiter to the table, asking for another cup of coffee for everyone, even though everyone else is clearly ready to go.

The four finally adjourn to the theater to see 'Giant', a story about Houston businessman Glenn McCarthy, who built the Shamrock Hotel. Because of the movie's theme, there are frequent pre-show receptions attended by some of Houston's leading citizens. By the time Rose, Hunter, Isaac, and Cassandra arrive, however, the reception is over and people are filing into their seats.

"Hunter, darling, you know I like to sit in the back of the theater. Can you find us four seats in the last few rows?" Rose asks.

Hunter complies, although he is surprised, since Rose usually wants to sit near the center of the theater in every other movie they have seen together.

After the movie, the Sterlings say goodnight to Isaac and Cassandra. Rose promises to invite Cassandra to lunch with the Houston Arts Council sometime soon.

After Rose and Hunter begin walking to their car, Cassandra remarks, "Isaac, I'm sorry, but that woman would no sooner be seen with us than she would want to be found sleeping on the beach in Galveston in her prom dress. Can you believe how late we arrived at the theater and how she wouldn't even go inside until the lights dimmed?"

"Cassandra, there may have been a few strange moments this evening, but think about it," Isaac replies without pause. "Five years ago, the only way you and I would have even gotten inside the Emerald Room would have been if we were serving people their food or bussing tables."

In spite of the few outbursts from Rose, which he dismisses as involuntary, the evening worked for Hunter Sterling on virtually all counts.

Rose is committed to helping him court Isaac Manns for the Houston Sports Association. She has also done her best to move on from her intolerant past to a new era of equal rights, or at least to as many of those rights as she could champion while none of her friends are watching. And Isaac Manns is on board to help Hunter recruit the baseball talent his future team will need.

Before he and Rose retire, Hunter calls his son. It's late enough for Davis to think that someone has died.

"Daddy, are you all right? It's one o'clock in the morning."

"Son, I am not only all right; I am great," Hunter tells him. "Tomorrow, I'd like you to get yourself over to my office so we can talk about the stories you're going to write about how we're bringing baseball – professional, Major League baseball – to Houston. And I want a Sterling to write the stories, not someone inferior named Kirksey, or any other name for that matter."

"You know I'll be there. That's fantastic news. And for starters, even though I'll never print it, I want to hear how you got Mama to be part of this effort."

"Son, there are some things I can never tell you, and suffice it to say that the details of this achievement are among those things. Still, we can celebrate our good fortune in the morning. Good night, Davis."

"Goodnight, Daddy."

Four years later, in 1960, the Houston Sports Association makes its presentation to Major League baseball for a franchise. All the money, political influence, baseball talent, and archi- tectural plans are in place, especially the architecture. Many people still credit Judge Hofeinz's scale model of the future Astrodome as the reason why they are awarded a National League franchise on October 17, 1960, along with the New York Mets. The team will be called the Houston Colt 45s, named after the famous pistol. Davis Sterling gets yet another unforgettable story in the Star, this one, of course, in banner headlines on page one.

Davis walks into his office in the early evening, whistling to himself as he prepares to sit and hammer out his latest story. He looks around his office for just a moment and thinks about how far he has come. He could've spent his life as the boss's kid, doing whatever Hunter asked of him. But he opted to stray off the beaten path, and it has worked out beautifully. He smiles as his fingers rest on the keys of the typewriter. But, before he starts, a letter on his desk catches his eye. He picks up the envelope, slides his letter opener under the crease, and takes out the letter. Davis has a feeling that this letter is something he should not put off reading.

February 10, 1959

Mr. Davis Sterling
12 Hamilton Way
Houston, TX 77007

Dear Mr. Sterling:

We are contacting you in regard to an application submitted to us by one Elvinia Kincade. We have reviewed the application as well as your body of work. The committee was particularly moved by an article that you wrote named "Obituary for the Catfish."

We would like to invite you to the Ebony Excellence Awards, taking place May 16, 1959, in New York City. There you will be honored for your contributions to the struggle for the equality of the Negro in America.

We hope that you will accept this honor. Please contact us at Knickerbocker 6-3222 for more information and to have all your travel arrangements made. We look forward to hearing from you soon.

Sincerely,
Jean Alexander
Ebony Excellence Awards, Committee Chair

Davis rereads the letter three times to be sure he has not misunderstood it. "Elvinia?" he whispers as he reads the letter a third time, "how in the world?" He and Elvinia had not been terribly close as of late. Rather than calling her for life advice on a regular basis, he has talked with her only on holidays or the occasion of births and deaths in their circle of friends. Davis suddenly realizes the void in their relationship that has been somewhat invisible to him since it started, buried beneath deadlines and new stories. He picks up the phone to call her.

"Elvinia?"

"Well, hello stranger. It's been a while, hasn't it?"

"I can't believe you did this!"

"I can't believe half of what I do, dear. You'll have to be more specific," Elvinia quips.

"I just received a letter in the mail telling me that I am going to be honored at the Ebony Excellence Awards. I am not even sure I know what that is, but it sounds intriguing. What made you think of me for this?"

"Yes, well, I have been spending a lot of time working with inner-city black people on a volunteer basis and I learned about this award. It's very much a prestigious honor. They have never given it to a white person. You will be the first. How's that for groundbreaking journalism?"

Davis sits silent on the other end of the line, so Elvinia goes on. "I think back to when you were just doing the sports column at your father's paper. You took some big risks writing about that black team; you could have been put in jail for doing it. But you found your passion, and you were not going to let anyone turn you away."

"That's very romantic, but in truth we both know I'm not all that noble. I started doing this to get back at my father and all his racist partners. I was thinking less of social change and more of being a pain in the ass to a group of bigoted good ol' boys. It was not with the purest of intentions."

"I'm being anything but romantic, Davis Sterling," Elvinia replies. "I told you to find your passion and do what you love, and you did. Sometimes, it doesn't matter *how* we get somewhere. What matters is what we do once we are there. You could have stopped writing those pieces anytime you wanted, and, yes, you had some personal reasons for doing so. But you never gave up on them even in the end, and this is what this award is about."

"I don't know. I feel a bit like a fraud."

"No fraud ever feels like a fraud, Davis. You deserve this. Quit second guessing it. I have already talked to Clarence anyway. He is going to make sure that Deacon and Leola will be there."

"You have spoken to Clarence?" Davis responds.

"Oh, they all check up on me all the time. We try to have dinner at least once a month, although with that sports foolishness they are running they are always busy these days."

"So the business is doing well?"

"Oh, yes. I don't even think they know how well they are doing for an infant company," Elvinia says. After a pause she adds, "So you are just not going to ask, are you?"

"Ask what?"

"About Leola, you dunce. You have not asked about her once this whole conversation."

"Of course, I want to know how she is doing."

"Well, you are just going to have to find out for yourself because she will be there. After all, it was her team you were writing about."

"So you are going to tell me nothing? Why even bring it up then? I forget how wicked you can be."

"Ask her when you get here."

"She doesn't want to talk to me. I had so much growing up to do when she left, and I just feel like I let her down."

"You did have growing up to do; she had growing of her own to do. But you will find all of that out when you get here," Elvinia says, "Now, I want you to pick up a new suit and tie. Don't wear that rubbish you wore when they took photos of us together last time. This is a 'dress to impress' event, and I don't want you making me look bad! I have a gown that is going to stop traffic, and I do not want to make you look like a country bumpkin."

When they hang up the phone, Davis realizes his palms are sweating and his heart is beating faster than usual. He's anxious, but not about the award. It's Leola he is anxious about – seeing her again after all this time. He wonders if she knows what he is doing now and if she is happy where she is. He also wonders if she feels the same way he does about thinking that a great opportunity was lost back then. But he knows he can't break away from Texas, and that his family's grip on him is strong. He and Leola could never have worked out as a couple, and that thought makes him even more nervous. Davis pushes all those thoughts aside. *No use in dredging up things I can't control*, he thinks. He has plans to make, and apparently some clothes to buy, even though he thinks the ones he has are just fine.

As the day approaches, Davis can feel anxiety building inside his body; it flutters in his stomach and rattles his bones. The people he sees most often can tell that something has Davis on edge, although no one really knows what it is that has the usually cool and calm newspaper man flustered. Davis himself is not quite sure what has caused him so much unease. He has been a champion for civil rights for some time and, with the kind of work he has done with the *Catfish*, he obviously has no issue turning white worlds a bit upside down. He is outspoken about how he feels about racism and prejudice, and his very life reflects his feelings. But because of his family, he doesn't want to rock the boat too much – not if he doesn't have to. *Maybe it's Leola after all*, he thinks. Luckily for him, 95 percent of the people in Houston have never heard of the *Ebony* Excellence Awards and never will. He won't have to explain the award to anyone, or so he thinks.

"Do you think you can set up an appointment with your tailor for me, Dad?" Davis asks his father, hoping Hunter won't have too many questions. As a newspaper man, Davis should have known his journalist father would let nothing go without a little interrogation.

"You going to a ball, Cinderella?" he asks with a wink.

"Not quite," Davis replies. "I'm getting a little award. I just thought it'd be nice to show up in a proper suit, not my usual crumpled button-up."

Davis hopes his father will ask no more about the nature of the award. Their relationship has been difficult at times over the years, but Davis feels that the gap between them is slowly being bridged. They have a new understanding and appreciation for each other. Although Davis is coming to understand his father as more nuanced than he had ever believed (a product of his environment but, nevertheless, trying to break the shackles of Houston's small-minded traditions), he still doesn't want to go into detail about the award. He is relieved when his father glides past asking any questions without a blink.

"Well, it is about time you took some interest in your appearance, son. I've wanted you to get a new suit for a very long time. But you've always insisted on looking like a hack reporter in those old rags of yours," Sterling laughs.

"Why does everyone keep saying that? Does everyone think my clothes are so awful?"

"Look at you," Hunter says, turning his son toward a large mirror hanging on his office wall. "What successful newsman do you know that looks like this?"

"I'm a writer, Dad. I don't see –"

"You have to learn to dress," Hunter interrupts, "not only for the career you have, but for the one you want. Still, I have learned, much to my chagrin, that one cannot make Davis Sterling do anything he doesn't want to do. And I have had to learn to pick my battles."

"Funny, I have learned to do the same thing with you," Davis tells his father. This time Davis wears the grin.

The two men have come to an undeclared cease-fire about who they are to each other, and it seems to be working out well.

"So you have not talked much about this award, son. Who is honoring you?" Hunter brings the elephant back into the room.

Davis's heart stops and pounds so hard he can feel it in his throat. He almost escaped with a story that danced around the headline. He should have known that an editor like Hunter Sterling would never allow such a thing.

"Just a small group in New York that is recognizing some of my work." Please let that be enough, Davis thinks as he tries to act interested in a pen on Hunter's desk so his father won't see his pupils dilate or his face flush.

"What work is that? I mean, I do happen to keep up on these things, even if you think I don't."

"Do you remember Elvinia Kincade?" Davis blurts. He knows that mentioning Elvinia will immediately turn his father's interest. "Well, she submitted some of my work for the early years of my writing, and some of it is getting recognized. It's not that big of a deal."

"Elvinia. Is she that English spitfire who had that run in with Mother?"

"One and the same," Davis responds. He feels his muscles relax. His father is distracted now. Davis waits for a new topic to surface or for a good place to exit, but his father keeps his focus.

"I have to tell you what, son. I have seen very few women that could stand toe-to-toe with Mother. And man, could that woman do just that! And mother hated it. She had no idea what to do with her when she could not put her in her place."

As Hunter leans back in his chair and lets out a reflective chuckle, Davis can only stare at him in consternation.

"I thought you hated Elvinia," Davis states.

"No, I never have, but I can't let your mama know that. Like I have told you many times: when your mama is unhappy, I am unhappy. So better to keep your mama happy, I say."

Davis agrees, and they both laugh. Davis lifts himself from his seat and begins to excuse himself, but Hunter is not quite satisfied.

"So this award, what piece are you getting it for?"

Davis drops back into the chair he had almost escaped from. He feels trapped by his father's question, even though he thinks his father might actually be proud of him. *He's gotten so many inquiries and never blinked an eye. So why the intense interest in this one award?* Davis thinks.

"Oh, just some of my early sports writing. Why so much interest in my awards, all of a sudden?" he asks with a nervous grin.

Hunter can see the shift in his son's attitude. He is defensive now; he's on his guard. If Hunter knows anything, it's when someone is on their guard. A good journalist can always see when they've hit a nerve.

"I guess I should tell you, the paper was contacted weeks ago about your work. Davis. I know exactly what you are being honored for in New York, and by whom."

Davis sits dumbfounded and blinking. He can't find any words to respond to his father. He just sits and prepares for all hell to break loose. He did not come prepared for this battle.

"Why would they contact you?" Davis asks.

"The publication is always contacted before a piece can be used for something like that. You should know that, son. I have known about every award you have ever been given. In fact, there are copies of every one of them in the paper's archives."

"But you. . ."

"I know you don't think I knew or cared, but that is the way I was taught, and that is just who I am. This paper is about excellence, and that should be the norm, not the exception. So why would I make a big deal out of something that should be and, has become, your standard of excellence?"

"Look, Daddy, I am not going to fight with you about this." Hunter says.

"Did I say it was your turn to talk yet?" Hunter retorts, stopping his son before he can go any further. "Let me finish. I do not like what you write sometimes or who you write it about, but I am always impressed with how you write it. You once told me as long as you could stand behind what you wrote, that I would have to stay out of it."

Davis is shocked that his father remembers what he said that day, and he is still confused by what his father is telling him now.

"I have always tried to honor that, even when it seemed that the world wanted me to step in. But you have always stood by your work, and for that I have had to stand by my word. Nothing has changed."

"So about the award?" Davis says, ready to face whatever his father has to tell him now that everyone's cards are on the table.

"Although I do not like the topic or the people you wrote about and I am not very fond of the people who are giving you this award, I can tell you this, son: it was a good piece. Hell, it was a great piece! And that I can admit. Those people are doing the right thing by honoring you."

Davis sits speechless, trying to mull over what his father has just said to him. Davis knows he still has a long way to go as a journalist, but at the same time he may be further along than he thought. Before he can come up with some kind of response, his father begins again. "Hell, Davis, thank the Lord that this is all happening in Harlem, where no self-respecting Southerner would be caught dead! Nor will they see or hear of it!" Hunter lets out a roar of laughter, and Davis just shakes his head, happy to be finished with the conversation.

"Now, let's get you some new suits, although I'm not sure why this award is what motivated you to get some new clothes. In any case, it's gotten you to think about dressing like a respectable journalist."

Davis can only sigh. He wants to say something, to point out to his father what a bigot he sounds like, but he knows that now is not the time. He swallows his words, takes a deep breath, and the two of them head over to the tailor's shop.

CHAPTER TWENTY-FOUR

A BIG NIGHT IN HARLEM

The night before he leaves for New York, Davis checks and rechecks his suitcase to make sure he has everything he'll need for his stay. He feels a nervous excitement building. Although he has been all around the world and to New York a dozen times, there is something different about this trip. He looks forward to seeing all of his old friends, especially Leola. When he thinks of her, he feels his head go a little light. He doesn't know how excited Leola is about his visit, but he hopes she will be happy to see him after their time apart.

After checking his luggage a third time, Davis calls Clarence just to make sure that everything is all set for his arrival the following day and to make sure that everyone is coming. Clarence is thrilled to hear from Davis and can tell that Davis needs reassurance.

"I have arranged quite an evening when you get here," Clarence says. "Everyone is looking forward to seeing you, and we're all looking forward to seeing you get this award."

"Everyone is looking forward to seeing me?" Davis asks nervously.

"Yes, everyone," Clarence assures him. "Leola especially, since I know you were never going to ask me."

"I am really looking forward to seeing you all as well," Davis replies, sidestepping Clarence's comment about Leola. "I can't say what it means to me to have all of you there to support me. This is the first award I've ever gotten from a black organization. I have to tell you that I am scared as hell. But there's also a part of me that knows that was some of the best work I've ever done, and I am really glad that it helped."

"Me too, Davis," Clarence says. "You earned this."

"Clarence, I have to tell you …" Davis stammers.

"Tell me what?"

"I can't help but think that I really let Leola down, those last years of the *Catfish*. She needed something, well, someone solid to support her, and I let her down."

"Look, a lot of things were going on in everyone's lives. We all had to make choices. You both made some, and you both did what was best for you at the time. That's just how life goes."

"I just hate to think I let her down," Davis says.

"Look, just get here and you'll see that everything has worked out like it should've, okay? I assure you, we all followed the paths we were supposed to. You'll see."

"I hope."

"You will," Clarence insists. "Oh, and one more thing. Did you get a new suit? Because if you did not, the first thing we need to do is go shopping."

Davis laughs and tells him that it has all been taken care of, that he was already warned. They say their goodbyes, and Davis calls it a night.

The next day is a whirlwind of activity for Davis. He drives himself to the airport. Throughout the entire flight, he imagines and reimagines what he'll say when he sees Leola. He should be reviewing his speech, but all he can think about is Leola.

By the time Davis checks into his hotel, it is late afternoon. He rushes to his room and gets ready for the ceremony. Elvinia has given him direct orders to meet her in the lobby of the hotel, instead of picking her up. They are just down the street from the Savoy, where the event is taking place. He is in the lobby by half past five waiting for the professor. Davis looks as dapper as he possibly can in a pressed tuxedo with shining silver cufflinks and polished Italian leather shoes.

"Welcome to New York, young man," a woman's voice says to Davis. The minute he hears that British accent, he knows it is Elvinia. He turns from the bar and sees her. The two embrace. Davis realizes when he takes a step back how beautiful she is. She wasn't kidding when she told him she would 'dress to impress.'"

"I am so excited you are here!" Elvinia says as she takes Davis in. "This is going to be a night to remember! How dashing you look! You have really stepped up your game on the fashion front, thank goodness."

"Why, thank you," Davis replies. "You know I always enjoy your candor, which makes your praise that much more valuable." Davis is pleased to have the stamp of approval from a critic as demanding as Elvinia Kincade. If he can impress her, he hopes he will also impress others – or one other, anyway.

"We can catch up on the way. We cannot have the man of the hour being late, can we?" Elvinia says.

"Where are we going?" Davis asks.

"What do you say I explain to you where you are, first?" Elvinia replies. "We are in Harlem, the heartbeat of the black community in New York City. And we are going to a place called the Savoy, a very special place. Tonight is a very special night."

"Is that right?" Davis asks.

"Indeed," Elvinia replies. "The Savoy was closed a year ago and is scheduled to be torn down. This is a place where some of the most famous black performers got their start. If those walls could talk, the things they would say! *Ebony* magazine thought it would only be fitting to open up the Savoy one last time for such a special occasion. And you happen to be the man of the hour."

"It sounds like the kind of place I would love to write about."

"Not tonight, my friend. Tonight, others are going to write about you and how you have honored them. Sometimes, a good journalist has to be able to take off his writing hat and just be a man – and this is one of those times for you. So, let's go! Your chariot awaits."

Outside the hotel, two vintage Rolls Royces are waiting. In front of one of the cars stand Clarence, Deacon, and Leola. A knot forms in Davis's throat when he sees them. He has to gather himself before he can return Deacon's and Clarence's greetings. Once they have exchanged hellos, he looks over to Leola. She has never looked so beautiful. Her gown sparkles in the light of the setting sun; the dress glides along the contours of her body until it touches the ground. She looks fresh and vibrant: her eyes are as stunning as the gown. Davis is smitten.

"Leola. Wow. I have no words."

They can all feel the electricity in the air. Davis and Leola embrace. The two do not let go of one another for some time. Finally, Clarence breaks their reunion.

"Look, do that on your own time," Clarence tells them. Leola and Davis let go of one another and both take a step back. Both are flushed and smiling.

"So, where are your dates?" Davis asks as he straightens his tie and slips back into his ever-confident persona.

"This is all about us tonight, my friend!" Deacon exclaims. "No distractions! We're all here for you. Now we have a party to get to, so let's go!"

Clarence, Leola, and Davis climb into one car, and Deacon and Elvinia into the other. As they head for the ball, Clarence explains that the Savoy was one of the only integrated ballrooms in the area in its heyday and that Harlem has been buzzing about this "one last swing at the Savoy" event for weeks.

As the Rolls Royce pulls up in front of the Savoy, flashbulbs go off from all around as other party-goers step onto a red carpet. A massive Hollywood searchlight in the front of the building circles the evening sky and lights up the entire event. Clarence directs every-one to stay in the car until he can see if things are all ready for Davis. Left alone in the car, Davis turns to Leola. "Leola, I just want to tell you that I am really sorry." Leola takes her finger and puts it on his lips, telling him that there is nothing to be sorry for and that tonight is not a night to be sorry about anything. She leans over, and, giving him a soft kiss on the lips, she smiles.

"Not now, Davis. Let's let this be your night," she says.

"Alright, all. Everything is ready," Clarence announces as he leans in the window of the backseat of the car where Leola and Davis sit. Clarence notices the startled look on both Davis's and Leola's faces. He looks at both of them for a moment and then walks away to meet Elvinia, who is waiting for him to join her. Leola smiles quickly at Davis and then motions for him to get out of the car.

Together, the group strolls down the carpet. The crowd that has gathered on either side claps and cheers as Davis and Leola make their way to the entrance. Cameras flash, capturing forever the moment when two white men walk down a red carpet in Harlem. Davis cannot believe that the applause and flashing lights are for him.

Davis leans over to Leola, whispering in her ear, "I want this to be the Black Ball that you never got to have. I want this to be a special night for all of us."

In response, Leola just looks at him, amazed and a bit flustered by the surge of emotion within her. The crowd, the red carpet, the flashing bulbs of cameras, all fade into the background. All she can concentrate on is Davis, the fact that he still remembers her ball after all this time and that he remembers that night and all she lost.

Elvinia turns to Davis to comment on the moment and sees Davis and Leola sharing something more distant. She is very pleased to see them reconnecting and simply looks back toward the crowd, reflecting on the guilt she has always felt convincing Leola to leave Houston ... and Davis.

Suddenly, Elvinia remembers the conversation she had with Leola when they first met. She also remembers what she saw between the two of them that night and also the warning, the unsolicited advice, she offered that night. Now that they are all in another place and, in some ways, another time, she hopes against hope that she will see that same spark once again. This time she knows she won't interfere. The rest is up to Davis and Leola.

Davis is overwhelmed with the spectacle as he enters the ballroom. His senses are heightened. It all seems glossed with something special and sweet. The colors, textures, and even the smells that surround him are intoxicating. In all his experiences around the globe, he has never felt anything like this.

As the group makes their way to the head table, Davis sees familiar faces all around him. Louis Armstrong stands to the side of the stage, preparing to perform his famous "Stompin' at the Savoy", a show he has performed countless times before on that very stage. Davis's eyes also fall on Sidney Poitier, Harry Belafonte, Diahann Carroll, Ossie Davis, Ruby Dee, and Sammy Davis, Jr. They are famous people he has only seen only on record labels or television shows, some of the biggest names in American music. The realization of who is there makes the fact that they are all there to honor him, a Texas newspaper writer who happened to stumble onto an interesting story, even more remarkable. As unreal as it all feels, he decides he is going to enjoy every second of the experience. He knows his time in the limelight will be short lived – reality will pound down on him in no time. But not right now.

For this special moment, the people with him are the only people who are important, the only ones who could ever understand the significance of the evening. This makes him happy – and sad.

When the time comes, Davis accepts his award, and his speech leaves everyone at the head table in tears. Holding the crystal trophy with his name etched into it, he tells everyone in the crowd what the honor means to him. Just before he leaves the stage, Davis takes a deep breath, looks at Leola, and says, "I accept this award on behalf of a man more amazing than I could ever be – on behalf of a man who made all the writing I have done possible. This award is for Columbus Jones, who was braver and more dedicated than any man I have met. I am lucky enough to have gotten to know the most amazing legacy that this incredible man left behind. I am honored and humbled to have been invited into such an amazing community, to which I owe this award and so much more."

Once the tears dry, everyone hits the dance floor. Clarence and Leola share the first dance – a quick number that makes them both feel like kids again. The next song is slower and Elvinia asks to cut in. Clarence takes her hand. Leola turns to leave the dance floor just as Davis slides his hand into hers and pulls her back to the middle of the floor. For the rest of the night, the two are inseparable. As midnight approaches, Elvinia decides to call it a night and asks Clarence and Deacon to take her home. When Davis offers to leave with them, Elvinia quickly stops him.

"You are the guest of honor, and it is your obligation to stay. I am sure Leola will keep you company, and later, when you are ready to go, the car will take you wherever you need to go. And I am not asking here, Davis Sterling."

With that Elvinia, Deacon, and Clarence say their farewells to Leola and Davis and to so many others there for the event. Leola and Davis return to the dance floor. Sometimes, they talk; other times they stay quiet, their bodies close to one another with Leola's head resting on Davis's shoulder. When the lights finally come on to let all the party-goers know the time has come to say goodnight, Leola and Davis gather their things and go to find the car. Outside, the driver is nowhere to be found.

"I suppose we could walk," Leola suggests as the last car pulls away into the Harlem night. "My place isn't far. You could call a cab from there."

"I would be honored to walk you home, Leola Jones," Davis says.

CHAPTER TWENTY-FIVE

ASTRODOME OPENING NIGHT

Hunter and Davis look out on the sold-out crowd from team owner Judge Roy Hofeinz's private 'apartment' that hovers above the right field grandstands. Hunter glances across the crowd of 48,000, which he knows is well beyond the stadium's official capacity of 42,217. He isn't worried about the fire marshal today, however. All of Houston is thrilled to watch their own professional team in the first exhibition game of the season against the great *New York Yankees*. Hunter knows no one is going to shut down the chance for Houston to watch their own boys take on Mickey Mantle, Roger Maris, Whitey Ford, Elston Howard, Tony Kubek, and Mel Stottlemyre.

"Here we are, boys; everybody's going to remember today, April 9, 1965," Hunter says to George Kirksey, Bill Kirkland, and Craig Cullinan, as they all look out at the amazing scene they feel responsible for creating.

They are feeling the satisfaction of bringing Major League baseball to their city. Hunter Davis, whose *Houston Star* has championed their every move, is there to celebrate from Judge Hofeinz's tilted bar, complete with its trick magnets to keep their drinks from sliding away from them.

"We've come a long way," Craig says, giving Hunter a hearty pat on the back.

"I'd say," George says. "Did you see President Johnson is here? The President! Who'd have imagined it?"

"I would," Hunter says with a satisfied grin.

After the last high note of the "Star-Spangled Banner," the *Houston Astros* hit the field, named in honor of NASA's Manned Space Program. The team, originally called the *Colt 45*s, changed its name in homage to Houston's space program. To parallel the new team name, they also re-named the stadium, changing it from Harris County Domed Stadium to the Astrodome, the "Eighth Wonder of the World."

"The Astrodome will set the pattern for the 21st century. It will antiquate every other structure of this type in the world. It will be the Eiffel Tower of baseball stadiums," Hofeinz boasts as the men sip their drinks.

Mickey Mantle hits the first home run in the new stadium, but the *Astros* prevail in the twelfth inning, when manager Luman Harris calls on coach Nellie Fox – the biggest name in a Houston uniform and former American League MVP – to face *Yankee* reliever Pete Mikkelsen. Fox slices a pitch over the outstretched glove of shortstop Tony Kubek into left center as Wynn speeds home to win the game, 2-1. After the game, Mickey Mantle says the Astrodome "reminds me of what I imagine my first ride would be like in a flying saucer."

While Hunter and his friends bask in the glory of Houston's moment on the national stage, Davis works on his front-page column for the morning edition of the *Houston Star*. No longer a beat reporter or even just a sports writer, Davis is the *Star's* general features writer, happy to be with his father and the city's leading citizens for a while, but eager for his moment to get a quote from President Johnson when he makes his way to Judge Hofeinz's penthouse booth. He's also invited his friend, Isaac Manns, a scout for the *Astros* since their earliest days as the *Colt 45s*, to join them in Judge Hofeinz's tilted bar for a reunion and hometown prediction on how the *Astros* will fare in their inaugural season. Isaac is a tad late, caught in a chat with Clarence and Deacon, who are also attending the game as guests of the *Astros*. Rather than watching from Judge Hofeinz's apartment, Clarence and Deacon are out with the crowd selling uniforms and souvenirs, which they've been doing since 1962 in Colt Stadium, where the team played its first three seasons. The two have kept in contact with Isaac but rarely see Davis. Leola's desire to keep their relationship in the past has made a friendship with the *Star* feature reporter tricky.

"So did you know I'm a married man?" Isaac announces to his old friends. "That's right. Cassandra and I tied the knot two years ago. Never been happier, I can tell you that. Should have done it years ago, but then again, it was hard to find a proper woman driving all over creation in that rickety old *Catfish* bus," he chuckles.

"Well, congratulations, Coach! She's a lucky woman to have you," Clarence exclaims. "And so are you, I might add, so are you." After some more catching up and story swapping about the *Catfish*, Isaac says goodbye to Clarence and Deacon to meet the others in the VIP apartment. He turns to Deacon and says, with his trademark laugh,

"Enjoy yourself in the cheap seats, son. Lord knows we taught you how to do that!"

When Isaac enters the apartment, it is buzzing with excitement. Hunter, Davis, and Isaac haven't been together since the 1962 ground-breaking ceremony for the Astrodome, when Hofeinz and his friends shot actual Colt 45s into the ground instead of using shovels. Isaac still thinks that was one of the most comical events he has ever witnessed.

"So, Davis, how long do you think it would have taken them to build this damn place if they had stuck to using those little pistols, instead of real shovels?" Isaac asks, stifling his laugh from the gun-firing groundbreakers in the apartment with him on opening night. The *Astros* get a hit, and the eruption from the crowd drowns out his muffled laughter.

The three men share stories about the *Catfish* and their classic games, now ten years in the past. Hunter congratulates Isaac on getting what he deserves – a job with a major league team. When Mickey Mantle comes to bat, Hunter remarks that he reminds him of Deacon. The mention of Deacon quiets the lively apartment for a moment. Everyone in the room is attuned to the silence; they're all remembering the good old days. And they all wonder the same thing, but no one wants to ask. What is going on between Davis and Leola? Isaac finally breaks the silence.

"Davis, I know you don't want me to tell you anything about Leola other than the fact that she's doing fine there up north. And that she is, son, that she is."

Davis hesitates a moment and shifts the subject to the *Astros'* upcoming season.

"So, Coach, how do you see the team doing this season?"

Isaac, with a gleam in his eye, smiles and begins a long, position-by-position analysis. He is decidedly optimistic but rooted in true baseball knowledge. Davis listens intently as he stares out the apartment window, over the field and into the spectacle of opening night in the Astrodome.

CHAPTER TWENTY-SIX

THE FUNERAL (1971)

Time has moved on. The *Eatonville Catfish* are now nothing but pictures in a photo album along with some very fond, and some not-so-fond, distant memories.

Yes, time has moved on. Women are getting better jobs. Black people (still faced with obstacles brought about by latent racism in a country that only 100 years before counted their people as only three-fifths human) are no longer excluded from dominant discourses and society-shaping conversations. And all of professional baseball teams are now fully integrated; the *Boston Red Sox* being the final team to slam the door on segregation in the major leagues by drafting Elijah 'Pumpsie' Green, a strong and talented black player, in 1959.

Outside of a beautiful suburban home, children play together, tossing a baseball in the front yard. The Irish American boy with fiery red hair and freckles across his nose laughs with the same satisfied squeal as the little girl with caramel skin and braids in her hair. A silver-haired mailman walks up to the yard to deliver the mail. A boy, with deep brown eyes and a decent sized bandage on his knee, tosses the ball to the mailman. The mailman doesn't miss a beat. He holds his mailbag up to catch the ball.

"Nice throw, Columbus!" the mailman says as he digs the ball from the bag.

"Nice catch!" the boy replies, smiling. "If the *Senators* had an out-fielder like you, they might win some more."

"I don't know about that," the mailman laughs. "Is your mama home?"

"Yup," the boy answers as he returns to his game.

The mailman makes his way to the front door. Leola answers before he can ring the doorbell. She's been watching from the kitchen window.

"Got something for you, Miss Leola," the mailman says as he hands her a letter, clipboard, and pen. "Mind signing for me?"

"Not at all, Curtis," Leola says as she takes the pen and begins to scribble her name.

"You have a good one," Curtis says with a nod.

"And you do the same," Leola replies. She takes the letter and settles on the front porch swing to watch the children play.

"Hi, Mama!" her seven-year old daughter, Alicia, calls out.

"Hi, Sunshine," she says. Leola watches for a moment, and then looks down at the envelope in her hand. When Leola sees the *Houston Astros* seal on the face of the envelope, her heart begins to race. It's a letter from her Uncle Isaac about his new scouting discoveries. She looks forward to every one of his letters, not only because she loves her uncle, but because they keep her up to date on the goings on in the baseball world – one she has only seen through her uncle's eyes for some time now. She rips open the letter and starts to read. Suddenly, Leola drops the letter to the porch floor; her hand shoots to her mouth and tears form in her eyes.

"No," she whispers. "Oh, God, no."

———————

Leola sits clutching a tissue in one hand and Clarence's hand in the other in the pews of the Tabernacle of Prayer Episcopal Church. Pastor Helen Rose Freeman stands at the pulpit, preaching to the mourners that fill the pews.

Pastor Freeman gives a beautiful eulogy and sermon. Countless others follow her, telling stories about the man who rests in the casket before them. After everyone has said their piece and the choir has finished singing "Amazing Grace", the hundreds of people there file by to say their last goodbye. Nobody can believe old Coach Isaac Manns is gone. Everyone gives their condolences to Cassandra, his "bride" as Isaac used to say, and the rest of his "family", Leola, Clarence, and Deacon. One by one, Leola shakes hands, hugs, and cries with the people of her past – Jazz, Jupiter Monroe, and others who once wore *Catfish* jerseys. Leola is overwhelmed to see so many of her old team in one place. She is also happy to see so many there to bid farewell to someone she loved so dearly. Every face she sees brings back a specific memory. And then, a face that brings back countless memories appears before her. It's Davis.

"I'm so sorry, Leola," he says.

Leola smiles and thanks him, offering him her hand to shake.

"He died doing what he loved," she says. "Uncle Isaac worked until the day he died. He was out scouting when it happened."

"I think that is just what he would've wanted," Davis says.

"Me too. Thanks so much for coming to pay respects," she says and then moves on to the next person in line.

Once everyone has gone, it is the family's turn. Hand-in-hand, Leola and Clarence approach Uncle Isaac. Leola puts a hand on Uncle Isaac's and leans down to whisper to him.

"I will never let you down, Uncle Isaac," she says. "You always believed in me. Because of that, I am the woman I am today." Then, she turns to Cassandra, the woman who won her Uncle Isaac's heart. "You made him so very, very happy," she starts, before losing her composure for a moment. Recovering, she makes sure to say what she really feels. "Uncle Isaac was family to my mama and daddy and me, and just as surely, so are you, Cassandra. I hope you know how much I mean that."

Outside the church, Leola stands and chats with Clarence and Deacon and their wives when Davis approaches. The men all hug each other. Then, Clarence and Deacon excuse themselves, leaving Davis and Leola alone.

"I didn't get to say much in church," Davis says. "So how have you been?"

"I've been doing very well, living in New York now. I'm a teacher. What about you? How have you been? I read your column when I get a chance. Between motherhood and a career, though, it can be tough to keep up with everything. Uncle Isaac had always kept me up-to-date on all the goings-on out there."

"Oh, really? How many kids do you have?" Davis asks.

"I have four: Norman, Jonathan, Alicia, and Columbus."

"That's so great. I am sure they are as amazing as their mother."

"As ornery, anyway," Leola laughs. "Norman is going to be a hell-raiser; I can tell already. Jonathan wants to be a sports writer. He wanted to come to the funeral just to get interviews for a story about his Uncle Isaac, the baseball scout." The two laugh.

"Well, I will have to see if I can get some tips from him," Davis says, and the two laugh again.

"He'd be happy to share with you," Leola replies.

"I would love to meet him," Davis says.

"So, do you have children?" Leola asks.

"I do. I have two girls, Rose-Elvinia and Gabrielle. And I'm still here in Texas."

"Uncle Isaac mentioned that you married a Miss Texas. Is that true?"

"Yep, that's true. I guess I'm a Texan through and through. Her name is Tiffany."

"I am sure your mother is loving it," Leola says with a wink.

"Mama has changed a lot, but that is one thing that will never change. She is a Southerner and a true Texan to the bone. What about you, what does your husband do?"

Leola begins to answer but is interrupted when a man and two children approach. "Honey, I am sorry to bother you, but have you seen Junior?"

Davis tries not to show his shock at the man he sees, who is white.

"Davis, this is my husband Jonathan Thornton. He's a professor of economics at Columbia University," Leola announces.

Davis, Leola, and Jonathan continue talking, but they can't compete with the noise coming from a baseball field nearby, full of children of all ages and colors, both boys and girls, playing baseball, and laughing and cheering each other on. All that is, except one: Jonathan Thornton, Jr., who is sitting on the bench to the side, notebook open, watching the game and writing about it.

Leola whispers softly to Davis as her husband Jonathan walks away, "Look familiar?"

"Miss Thornton," a soft-spoken man in a black suit says. He is the funeral director and has come to ask everyone to move on to the cemetery.

"The service was just beautiful, Alfred," Leola says to the man.

"I'm so glad you think so. It's an honor to help fine folk like Coach Mann's family and friends," Alfred replies. "Mrs. Manns has asked me to let you know we're ready to go to the cemetery now if you are."

"Of course," Leola says.

The children are rounded up and escorted to their respective vehicles. Once everyone is accounted for, the procession leaves for the cemetery. Cassandra had made arrangements for her husband to be buried in the family plot in Crockett, a place he visited so many times during his barnstorming days and where he spent quiet times with her during his breaks from scouting for the *Astros*.

After a slow ride through Isaac's adopted hometown, they arrive at the cemetery. There are so many cars in the procession that they stretch nearly to the cemetery entrance. The sight of all the cars filled with people who loved Isaac touches Leola.

As the graveside service begins, Deacon is distracted. Leola can see from across the gravesite that Deacon's mind is somewhere else, but she cannot imagine what could be distracting him at a time like this. Deacon's mind is in a different place – or better, yet, a different time. She is sure he is thinking of the man they are there to honor.

But Deacon is really thinking back to 1937 when he was a young boy and still Peter Smithfield. He is thinking back to that horrible day when he saw his best friend beaten and hanged from a tree for nothing more than being a black boy holding a baseball glove. Deacon remembers how he tried to sneak away long ago to get to his friend's funeral that was held just a stone's throw away from where he is right now. But that day, Deacon's daddy caught him and beat him bloody for trying to attend a Negro's funeral. His father was terrified that decent white folks would see him there.

"We'll all get pegged as some kind of nigger lovers, and that is just not going to happen as long as I am breathing," he bellowed as he snapped his leather belt across Deacon's bared flesh.

Deacon never got to say goodbye to his childhood friend, and he always felt like he failed him, not once, but twice – once in life, being unable to save him from that lynching and again in death, when he couldn't go to his friend's funeral.

Deacon had tried in so many ways to honor his friend. Over the years, he visited his grave whenever he could and tried to keep it clean and decorated with flowers. He replaced his friend's wooden grave marker, which was all his family could afford, with a beautiful stone marker that he paid for with his very first paycheck from the *Catfish*; that was something he never told a soul about. But none of this released him from the turmoil he felt when he remembered why his friend was there in the first place.

Deacon struggles to be in the moment and pray for the soul of his friend Isaac, but the thoughts of his childhood friend pull him deeper and deeper into despair. He suddenly looks up into Leola's eyes with tears streaming down his face. Somehow, Leola knows the pain on his face comes from some place other than his heartache of losing Isaac. She looks over to Clarence. He too is looking at Deacon.

Clarence starts to walk over to Deacon, who shakes his head to let Clarence know that he cannot help him right now.

"Amen," the preacher says after a final prayer.

Clarence looks back at Isaac's grave to say his final goodbye and sees Deacon already walking away. Clarence starts to go after him, but Leola stops him.

"No, Clarence. Whatever demon he is fighting right now, only he and God can defeat. Give him some time."

"But …" Clarence starts. Leola keeps his arm in her hand and shakes her head, stopping him from finishing his thought.

"Just give him some time; we won't let him get too far."

Deacon walks to the old part of the cemetery; he walks faster and faster as he gets closer to his friend's grave. He has no plan, but he knows he needs to visit the grave. When the grave is in sight, he stops dead in his tracks and just stares. Someone is there, cleaning the grave. Who the hell is that? Deacon wonders.

He can think of only a handful of people who would know where Lummy is buried, and he always assumed anyone who would know, had passed away. He finally summons the nerve to get closer to the stranger at the grave. As he moves forward, he hears footsteps behind him; it's Clarence, and Leola is not far behind him.

"Deacon, what's wrong?" Clarence's asks.

"I am not sure how to say this, but I know who is laid to rest over there and that person over there should not be messing with anything."

"Okay, calm down sweetie," Leola tells Deacon as she catches up to the two. "We are going to do this together. We will walk on over and just see who it is. Maybe they are just at the wrong grave, baby, or maybe you are mistaken. It has been a very long time since you've been here. I'm sure it's been a long while since almost anyone has been here."

"No, no, no," Deacon says, almost shouting as he violently shakes his head. "I can never forget this place or that spot. Never."

Leola sees she needs to get control of the situation. "Okay then baby, if you say so. We can get to the bottom of this real fast," she says as she starts for the grave.

"Wait!" Deacon tries to shout, but the words creak out of his mouth in a whisper.

Leola doesn't stop. She is going to take care of whatever this is – and quickly. Clarence is one step behind her, to make sure she will be okay.

Leola and Clarence approach the woman who is diligently pulling weeds from around the grave. She looks to be in her 70s. A part of Deacon wants to go with them, but his feet are planted to the ground. He is as still as the giant sycamore growing in the middle of that neglected cemetery as he watches Leola and Clarence talk to the woman. He squints hard at the Texas sun, trying to see the expressions on their faces as they talk to one another. He can't tell by their exchange what is happening. When Clarence and Leola turn to walk back to him, the woman stays beside the grave. Deacon feels his pulse race as he watches the woman stand her ground. If Leola can't get her to leave, he knows he won't be able to.

"What? What did she say?" Deacon asks when the two are close enough to him to hear his words. "Who is she? Why is she there?" Deacon barrages them with questions.

"My friend, this is one you are going to have to field on your own," Clarence replies. "But we are going to be right here when you need us."

Clarence's response raises more questions than it does answers for Deacon. He begins to speak – to ask for some clarification, but Leola stops him.

"You need to just go on over," she says.

Deacon stands and mulls everything over and decides that Leola is right. Without saying a word, he picks up a heavy foot and starts for the woman by the grave. As he walks, he continues going over who this woman could be. Suddenly, things come into focus.

"It can't be . . ." Deacon says to himself. "It just cannot be; I haven't been able to find her in years. It can't be her."

"We went away and hid on purpose, Peter," the woman says, with her back to him. "We heard you were looking for us, but we weren't ready. We just weren't ready." Tears start running down his face. "Now, come here boy, and give an old woman a hug like you still have some love for her," she says as she turns to face Deacon. Her face is older, but so familiar.

Deacon walks up to the small, but still strong, woman and melts into her arms. His body heaves with sobs.

"I'm so sorry, so sorry, I never did anything when I could have," he cries.

"Shhhhhh . . ." she soothes him and then, holding his face, looks him straight in the eyes. "You did all you could do, baby. I just thank God two of you didn't end up dead that night."

Deacon shakes his head and she hushes him up again.

"Look now," she says, her voice is now stern instead of soothing, "Hear what I say to you, boy; you did what you could do. We all knew that then, and I still know that now. I am his mama, and I am telling you, if you had done any more than what you did, I would have two graves to clean off, and I don't like going to no white cemeteries. They are creepy."

For a moment, Deacon breaks his sobs with laughter.

"But how? How can you ever forgive me? It was my fault Lummy was killed that night."

Mama Delilah shakes her head and tightens her grip on him.

"It was my fault," he says again.

"Now, listen here, those mens that hung my boy was gonna to do that no matter what. It had nothin' to do with what he was holdin'; don't you understand that baby? Smart man like you has to know, that was about hate and nothing else. And, if you had done anything, aaannnnyyyy-thing that night back in '37, two of you would have hung that night from that tree."

Deacon struggles for words. "Where did you go? I never stopped looking for you. I've looked all over Texas for you. I wanted to help take care of you and do what I could."

"After that night, something died in us too. It came time for us to go. I just couldn't go on livin' in our old house," she explains. "We went to live with family down in the city, and I tried to forget everything that happened. But I couldn't. And neither could his daddy," she goes on, affectionately fixing his hair and pointing down to another grave where her husband is. "Lummy's father died of a broken heart; he really did. But, at least our family is together here."

Turning back to her son's grave, she smiles. "Look at this fine stone you got my boy."

"How did you know I did that?"

"I knows only one person in the world would do something like that for my baby, and I just knew in my heart it was you. As soon as I saw your face in the Negro paper, I knew it was you all grow'd up," she laughs. "But, who picked that name Deacon?"

He looks over to Clarence and Leola and points to them. "They did, and that great man laying just over there did too," he says as he points over to Isaac's casket.

"Well, then, Deacon," she says as she straightens up and smiles, "why don't you officially introduce me to your friends?"

Deacon offers Delilah his arm and together they walk over to Leola and Clarence. Just before they get in earshot, she turns to Deacon and whispers, "Well, I will tell you this much. That girl there, your friend, she's reeeaaal pushy."

Deacon sees Leola watching Delilah point at her, and he just laughs.

"You know it comes from pure love, don't ya? I hope you knows that," Delilah tells him as they walk.

"I do know that, better than anyone. And I will never forget it."

Delilah looks Deacon in the eye. "I know you won't, baby boy, I know you won't."

A FEW NOTES FROM THE AUTHOR

Barnstorming is a novel, it is historic fiction. It is about race – blacks and whites growing up and living in the South during a time of change. The story is also about love, honor, perseverance, and understanding with a backdrop of a violent era in United States history, often ending in tragedy. This was a time of lynching, of unspeakable hatred. And yet, there were many who stood up to the "wrongs" and worked hard to make them "right".

I hope "Barnstorming" lives up to the challenge of showing the good and the bad, the complexities of bias, and the triumph of so many Americans. People of many colors and backgrounds have worked to make our country, and the world, a better place for all.

The sport (and the business) of baseball for people of color started in 1885 when the first professional black baseball team, the *Cuban Giants*, was formed. Professional leagues came soon after, but failed due to poor attendance. Barnstorming, (traveling around to small towns with weekend games) brought the leagues to the people. Talented young men had a chance to "show their stuff". But finances were always a problem as games were not played in big forums where large audiences could support the teams' expenses.

The First Negro Southern League ran from 1920 to 1936 and was the only league that was able to complete its scheduled full season. The Negro National League was formed in 1933. They played in larger cities and were able to attract the best players.

The leagues experienced success and failure in the mid-1940s when the white baseball leagues started to recruit black players. But in 1950 the black leagues lost their "major" status as integration had begun.

Jackie Robinson was the first man of color to play in Major League baseball. He walked onto Ebbetts Field as first baseman of the *Brooklyn Dodgers* on April 15, 1947. He had started his baseball career two years earlier with the *Kansas City Monarchs*. His skills and values, on and off the field, are legendary. His commitment to non-violence influenced the Civil Rights Movement's approach during its fight for change. Robinson was inducted into the Baseball Hall of Fame in 1962.

There were still race-biased inequities, when Ted Williams was voted into the Baseball Hall of Fame in 1966. He spoke with passion for more Negro league stars to be included in the Hall in his induction speech.

"Barnstorming" is a novel with fictional characters. But so much of this book is based on truth.

Eatonville is a town in Florida, just north of Orlando. It was incorporated on August 15, 1887 and is the oldest self-governing black municipality in the United States. The town was home to Club Eaton which featured musicians such as Duke Ellington, Ella Fitzgerald, Ray Charles, B. B. King, and Aretha Franklin.

The town hosts the "Zora! Festival" every January, bringing together artists and writers who are still inspired by the author and folklorist, Zora Neale Hurston. Hurston's father, John, was Eatonville's first mayor.

Zora Neale Hurston at home in Eatonville
Photo: Ebony, 1946

Yes, Eatonville is a real town, but it did not have a baseball team. I chose Eatonville as the backdrop of this story as it is where my family has lived for many generations. A tenth generation lives in Eatonville today. I know and love this town.

This family photo was taken in 1925. Many of the names of my aunts, uncles, and cousins were used as characters in this book. Their names have inspired me and have been a way to honor my family, a family that has given me great pride and deep roots.

 My great, great granddaddy, Columbus H. Crooms (above on the left and at left) served as mayor from 1938 to 1963. During his term, the first fire station opened. The 1955 photo (above) was taken on the day of the fire station dedication. A city water system had been established and street lights were installed in the town for the very first time.

My mother, Jacqueline Leola Carroll, is the inspiration and driving force, not only behind the character Leola, but for this entire book. She had all the strength, tenacity and drive that my character Leola possesses.

I am so thankful that she was able to read an early draft of this book before her passing.

The second issue of *Ebony* magazine featured the town of Eatonville. The children pictured on the first page of the article are my cousins. We had five generations living there at that time in 1946.

ONLY PAVED STREET in Eatonville is called "The Hard Road." It runs right through the middle of town and connects with U. S. Highway 17. Eatonville doesn't even have a sign identifying itself for passing autoists.

BROWN TOWN

Eatonville, Florida, is oldest Negro village in United States

THERE ARE 22 all-Negro towns in the United States with a total population of 25,000. Oldest and still one of the smallest is Eatonville, Florida, the first attempt of Negro self-government in the country.

Incorporated 60 years, Eatonville has not grown much, still has only 350 dwellers. But today the tiny, picturesque town with its two square miles of land is a sign and symbol to the United States as it was when founded.

Eatonville has no wealth or industry to boast of but it has one uncommon thing for America—racial peace. Maitland, blonde sister of deep brunette Eatonville, is a good neighbor. It is one mile from the Post Office in Maitland to the main corner of Eatonville and in the 60 years of their co-existence, there has never been an instance of ill feeling between the two towns.

In the Ocoee race riot of 1920, only 12 miles from Eatonville, the white people of Maitland came over to Eatonville and apportioned every man, woman and child to some white home in Maitland in the event that the rioters invaded the Negro town. At the first threat, everyone was to go to Maitland to stay until things quieted down.

In the beginning Eatonville was founded on good will and mutual help. The Negroes were from Maitland and they got the help of the whites. Captain Lawrence, one of the three white sponsors, donated three buildings. Captain Eaton, for whom the town was named, gave the tract of land. Eatonville and Maitland have always been friends perhaps because Eatonville has not had the will of Maitland imposed it. Eatonville has not performed any civic wonders but it has done as it pleased.

FIRST BUILDING erected was the St. Lawrence A.M.E. Church, donated by Captain Lawrence, one of three white sponsors of the town. This building replaced the original, once turned into a library and now occupied by a family.

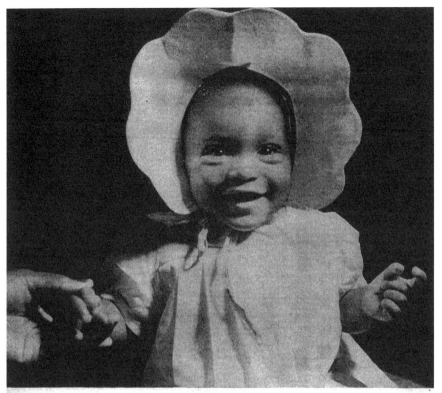

GREAT-GREAT-GRANDDAUGHTER OF LAURA HENDERSON.

The photograph (above) of the baby in the *Ebony* article is my mother, Jacqueline Leola Carroll. It occupies the same page as the photo (at left) of my great, great, great grandmother, Laura Henderson, at 90.

OLDEST WOMAN is Laura Henderson, now 90 years old. She is many times a grandmother and great grandmother and twice a great-great. She became the oldest person after death of Grandma Biddy at 104.

Eatonville was a special place. It still is. The Hungerford Normal and Industrial School was founded in Eatonville in 1889 by Robert Hungerford. The school was named in honor of the son of Hungerford's physician who had given his life to save the lives of African-Americans during a scarlet fever epidemic. The school

was considered the premier Negro school in Central Florida in the mid-1930s. It was the school my grandmother attended as a teen.

In 1950 the school was given to Orange County and renamed the Wymore Career Education Center, a public high school. The school gave a nod to its history with the Hungerford name.

In subsequent years, the school closed entirely. The buildings have been demolished.

My grandmother, Hoyt

My grandmother and her sisters
Left to right: Mimi, Helen, Hoyt, Malinda

SPECIAL THANKS

Tom Martorelli not only worked on the historic context, but was invaluable in character development and editing. He was an amazing storyline consultant. Tom was a driving force in the creation of this book.

I need to say a very special thank you to my friend and legal consultant John O'Brien. When I told him that I was going to attempt to create this book, he was 100% full steam ahead. He supported me not only on legal matters, but also as a story consultant, editor, and all around support system. Thank you so much, John.

A special thank you goes to Gail Honeystein who, from the very beginning, fully believed in my vision. She supported and encouraged me to push myself and was willing to take this long journey with me.

Susan Ferris / Bohemia Group, without hesitation, was willing to support and represent my interest regarding this book from very early on. Her support has touched me in ways that are very hard to express. Thank you for having my back, Susan.

Thank you to *Ebony* magazine for allowing me to reproduce their pages on Eatonville, Florida, and for assisting me in bringing the "Brown Town" of 1946 back to life.

Nancy Viall Shoemaker, my publisher, was an invaluable member of the editing team.

I give thanks to my father, Alfred Carroll, Jr., my sister, Alicia Carroll, and my brother, Norman Carroll, for their continued support and encouragement to create the book that was in my heart.

Of course, I thank my mother, Jacqueline Leola Carroll, for her inspiration, wisdom, love, life and guidance. But, most of all for instilling in me the belief that I only need to march to the beat of my own drum and stay true to myself, despite all the negative outside influences that try to convince me otherwise. I am a very thankful and lucky man to have been given such precious gifts.

A big thank you also to:

Jennifer Bingham
Traci Bingham
Jim Conlon
Keith David
Geri Denterlein
Artisha (Dottin) Herd
Richard Engelman
Elizabeth (Bit) Engelman
Brian & Patty Fitzpatrick
John Forcier
Robert Goldman
Ryan Jehangir
Lynn Martin Kerr
Cameron Kirkpatrick
Lowell Partridge
Janis Peterson *(posthumously)*

Jacqueline Leola Carroll

And to:

Alberto Ranck

Mary Richard

Julie & Mark Robarts

Kim Roderiques

Chrissy & Brian Rossini

Peter Schlessel

Barbara Shope

The Society of Arts and Crafts of Boston

Peter Stacey

John & Susanne Stadtler

Yusaku Takase

Christo Tsiaras

Cassandra Woody

Susan Yule

The entire team at Inman Oasis, Cambridge, Massachusetts

My mother with her parents

Although the Eatonville Catfish team
exists only in this book of fiction,
the dedication and sacrifices of those
who pioneered in the Negro League
are anything but fictitious.
We appreciate all their courage and efforts,
blazing the trail for future generations.

This book was designed and typeset
by Nancy Viall Shoemaker of West Barnstable Press.
www.westbarnstablepress.com

The bold font used for the title and chapter heads in *Barnstorming* is **Rockwell**. Designed by the Monotype Corporation in 1934, it offers a visual cue to the setting of the novel. The uppercase "A" is unusual with a serif at its apex.

Utopia, the text typeface, was designed by Adobe's Robert Slimbach in 1989. Its serif design and wide range of styles makes it a good choice on paper and on the web. Utopia is timeless, based on classical designs dating back to the 1700s.

Optima, a sans-serif typeface, was used in *Barnstorming* for the photo captions. Designed in 1950 by a legend in the world of typography, Hermann Zapf, its subtle swellings at the terminals of each letter hints at serifs. Zapf was inspired to produce this font by the stone carvings he studied on a trip to Florence, Italy.

The cover boasts an additional font, Frutiger, designed by Adrian Frutiger in 1975 and praised for its legibility.